THE
FACE

ALSO BY DEAN KOONTZ

THE

FACE

DEAN KOONTZ

HarperCollins*Publishers*

This novel is entirely a work of fiction.
The names, characters and incidents portrayed in it are
the work of the author's imagination. Any resemblance to
actual persons, living or dead, events or localities is
entirely coincidental.

HarperCollins*Publishers*
77–85 Fulham Palace Road,
Hammersmith, London w6 8jb

www.**fire**and**water**.com

Published by HarperCollins*Publishers* 2003
1 3 5 7 9 8 6 4 2

A catalogue record for this book
is available from the British Library

ISBN 0 00 713069 4

Set in Trump Mediaeval and Aquinas

Printed and bound in Great Britain by
Clays Ltd, St Ives plc

This book is dedicated to three exceptional men—
and to their wives, who have worked so very hard to
sculpt them from such rough clay. From the ground
up: To Leason and Marlene Pomeroy, to Mike and
Edie Martin, and to Jose and Rachel Perez. After The
Project, I will not be able to get up in the morning,
spend a moment at home during the day, or go to bed
at night without thinking of you. I guess I'll just have
to live with that.

The civilized human spirit . . . cannot get rid of a feeling of the uncanny.

—*Doctor Faustus*, THOMAS MANN

THE
FACE

CHAPTER 1

AFTER THE APPLE HAD BEEN CUT IN HALF, the halves had been sewn together with coarse black thread.

Ten bold stitches were uniformly spaced. Each knot had been tied with a surgeon's precision.

The variety of apple, a red delicious, might have significance. Considering that these messages had been delivered in the form of objects and images, never in words, every detail might refine the sender's meaning, as adjectives and punctuation refined prose.

More likely, however, this apple had been selected because it wasn't ripe. Softer flesh would have crumbled even if the needle had been used with care and if each stitch had been gently cinched.

Awaiting further examination, the apple stood on the desk in Ethan Truman's study. The black box in which the apple had been packed also stood on the desk, bristling with shredded black tissue paper. The box had already yielded what clues it contained: none.

Here in the west wing of the mansion, Ethan's ground-floor apartment was comprised of this study, a bedroom, a bathroom, and a kitchen. Tall French windows provided a clear view of nothing real.

The previous occupant would have called the study a living room and would have furnished the space accordingly. Ethan did too little living to devote an entire room to it.

With a digital camera, he had photographed the black box before opening it. He had also taken shots of the red delicious from three angles.

He assumed that the apple had been sliced open in order to allow for the insertion of an object into the core. He was reluctant to snip the stitches and to take a look at what might lie within.

Years as a homicide detective had hardened him in some respects. In other ways, too much experience of extreme violence had made him vulnerable.

He was only thirty-seven, but his police career was over. His instincts remained sharp, however, and his darkest expectations were undiminished.

A sough of wind insisted at the French panes. A soft tapping of blown rain.

The languid storm gave him excuse enough to leave the apple waiting and to step to the nearest window.

Frames, jambs, rails, muntins—every feature of every window in the great house had been crafted in bronze. Exposure to the elements promoted a handsome mottled-green patina on exterior surfaces. Inside, diligent maintenance kept the bronze a dark ruby-brown.

The glass in each pane was beveled at every edge. Even in the humblest of service rooms—the scullery, the ground-floor laundry—beveling had been specified.

Although the residence had been built for a film mogul during the last years of the Great Depression, no evidence of a construction budget could be seen anywhere from the entrance foyer to the farthest corner of the last back hall.

When steel sagged, when clothes grew moth-eaten on haberdashery racks, when cars rusted on showroom floors for want of customers, the film industry nevertheless flourished. In bad times as in good, the only two absolute necessities were food and illusions.

From the tall study windows, the view appeared to be a painting of the kind employed in motion-picture matte shots: an exquisitely rendered dimensional scene that, through the deceiving eye of the camera, could serve convincingly as a landscape on an alien planet or as a place on this world perfected as reality never allowed.

Greener than Eden's fields, acres of lawn rolled away from the house, without one weed or blade of blight. The majestic crowns of immense California live oaks and the drooping boughs of melancholy deodar cedars, each a classic specimen, were silvered and diamonded by the December drizzle.

Through skeins of rain as fine as angel hair, Ethan could see, in the distance, the final curve of the driveway. The gray-green quartzite cobblestones, polished to a sterling standard by the rain, led to the ornamental bronze gate in the estate wall.

During the night, the unwanted visitor had approached the gate on foot. Perhaps suspecting that this barrier had been retrofitted with modern security equipment and that the weight of a climber would trigger an alarm in a monitoring station, he'd slung the package over the high scrolled crest of the gate, onto the driveway.

The box containing the apple had been cushioned by bubble wrap and then sealed in a white plastic bag to protect it further from foul weather. A red gift bow, stapled to the bag, ensured that the contents would not be mistaken for garbage.

Dave Ladman, one of two guards on the graveyard shift, retrieved the delivery at 3:56 A.M. Handling the bag with care, he had carried it to the security office in the groundskeeper's building at the back of the estate.

Dave and his shift partner, Tom Mack, x-rayed the package with a fluoroscope. They were looking for wires and other metal components of an explosive device or a spring-loaded killing machine.

These days, some bombs could be constructed with no metal parts. Consequently, following fluoroscopy, Dave and Tom employed a trace-scent analyzer capable of recognizing thirty-two explosive compounds from as few as three signature molecules per cubic centimeter of air.

When the package proved clean, the guards unwrapped it. Upon discovering the black gift box, they had left a message on Ethan's voice mail and had set the delivery aside for his attention.

At 8:35 this morning, one of the two guards on the early shift, Benny Nguyen, had brought the box to Ethan's apartment in the main house. Benny also arrived with a videocassette containing pertinent segments of tape from perimeter cameras that captured the delivery.

In addition, he offered a traditional Vietnamese clay cooking pot full of his mother's *com tay cam*, a chicken-and-rice dish of which Ethan was fond.

"Mom's been reading candle drippings again," Benny said. "She lit a candle in your name, read it, says you need to be fortified."

"For what? The most strenuous thing I do these days is get up in the morning."

"She didn't say for what. But not just for Christmas shopping. She had that temple-dragon look when she talked about it."

"The one that makes pit bulls bare their bellies?"

"That one. She said you need to eat well, say prayers without fail each morning and night, and avoid drinking strong spirits."

"One problem. Drinking strong spirits is how I pray."

"I'll just tell Mom you poured your whiskey down the drain, and when I left, you were on your knees thanking God for making chickens so she could cook *com tay cam*."

"Never knew your mom to take no for an answer," Ethan said.

Benny smiled. "She won't take yes for an answer, either. She doesn't expect an answer at all. Only dutiful obedience."

Now, an hour later, Ethan stood at a window, gazing at the thin rain, like threads of seed pearls, accessorizing the hills of Bel Air.

Watching weather clarified his thinking.

Sometimes only nature felt real, while all human monuments and actions seemed to be the settings and the plots of dreams.

From his uniform days through his plainclothes career, friends on the force had said that he did *too much* thinking. Some of them were dead.

The apple had come in the sixth black box received in ten days. The contents of the previous five had been disturbing.

Courses in criminal psychology, combined with years of street experience, made Ethan hard to impress in matters regarding the human capacity for evil. Yet these gifts provoked his deep concern.

In recent years, influenced by the operatically flamboyant villains in films, every common gangbanger and every would-be serial killer, starring in his own mind movie, could not simply do his dirty work and move along. Most seemed to be obsessed with developing a dramatic persona, colorful crime-scene signatures, and ingenious taunts either to torment their victims beforehand or, after a murder, to scoff at the claimed competence of law-enforcement agencies.

Their sources of inspiration, however, were all hackneyed. They succeeded only in making fearsome acts of cruelty seem as tiresome as the antics of an unfunny clown.

The sender of the black boxes succeeded where others failed. For one thing, his wordless threats were inventive.

When his intentions were at last known and the threats could be better understood in light of whatever actions he took, they might also prove to be clever. Even fiendishly so.

In addition, he conferred on himself no silly or clumsy name to delight the tabloid press when eventually they became aware of his game. He signed no name at all, which indicated self-assurance and no desperate desire for celebrity.

For another thing, his target was the biggest movie star in the world, perhaps the most guarded man in the nation after the President of the United States. Yet instead of stalking in secret, he revealed his intentions in wordless riddles full of menace, ensuring that his quarry would be made even more difficult to reach than usual.

Having turned the apple over and over in his mind, examining the details of its packaging and presentation, Ethan fetched a pair of cuticle scissors from the bathroom. At last he returned to the desk.

He pulled the chair from the knee space. He sat, pushed aside the empty gift box, and placed the repaired apple at the center of the blotter.

The first five black boxes, each a different size, and their contents had been examined for fingerprints. He had dusted three of the deliveries himself, without success.

Because the black boxes came without a word of explanation, the authorities would not consider them to be death threats. As long as the sender's intention remained open to debate, this failed to be a matter for the police.

Deliveries 4 and 5 had been trusted to an old friend in the print lab of the Scientific Investigation Division of the Los Angeles Police Department, who processed them off the record. They were placed in a glass tank and subjected to a cloud of cyanoacrylate fumes, which readily condensed as a resin on the oils that formed latent prints.

In fluorescent light, no friction-ridge patterns of white resin had been visible. Likewise, in a darkened lab, with a cone-shaded halogen lamp focused at oblique angles, the boxes and their contents continued to appear clean.

Black magnetic powder, applied with a Magna-Brush, had revealed nothing. Even bathed in a methanol solution of rhodamine 6G, scanned in a dark lab with the eerie beam from a water-cooled argon ion laser generator, the objects had revealed no telltale luminous whorls.

The nameless stalker was too careful to leave such evidence.

Nevertheless, Ethan handled this sixth delivery with the care he'd exhibited while examining the five previous items. Surely no prints existed to be spoiled, but he might want to check later.

With the cuticle scissors, he snipped seven stitches, leaving the final three to serve as hinges.

The sender must have treated the apple with lemon juice or with another common culinary preservative to ensure a proper presentation. The meat was mostly white, with only minor browning near the peel.

The core remained. The seed pocket had been scooped clean of pits, however, to provide a setting for the inserted item.

Ethan had expected a worm: earthworm, corn earworm, cutworm, leech, caterpillar, trematode, one type of worm or another.

Instead, nestled in the apple flesh, he found an eye.

For an ugly instant, he thought the eye might be real. Then he saw that it was only a plastic orb with convincing details.

Not an orb, actually, but a hemisphere. The back of the eye proved to be flat, with a button loop.

Somewhere a half-blinded doll still smiled.

When the stalker looked at the doll, perhaps he saw the famous object of his obsession likewise mutilated.

Ethan was nearly as disturbed by this discovery as he might have been if he'd found a real eye in the red delicious.

Under the eye, in the hollowed-out seed pocket, was a tightly folded slip of paper, slightly damp with absorbed juice. When he unfolded it, he saw typing, the first direct message in the six packages:

THE EYE IN THE APPLE? THE WATCHFUL WORM? THE WORM OF ORIGINAL SIN? DO WORDS HAVE ANY PURPOSE OTHER THAN CONFUSION?

Ethan was confused, all right. Whatever it meant, this threat—the eye in the apple—struck him as particularly vicious. Here the sender had made an angry if enigmatic statement, the symbolism of which must be correctly interpreted, and urgently.

CHAPTER 2

B EYOND THE BEVELED GLASS, THE IRON-BLACK clouds that had masked the sky now hid themselves behind gray veils of trailing mist. The wind went elsewhere with its lamentations, and the sodden trees stood as still and solemn as witnesses to a funeral cortege.

The gray day drifted into the eye of the storm, and from each of his three study windows, Ethan observed the mourning weather while meditating on the meaning of the apple in the context of the five bizarre items that had preceded it. Nature peered back at him through a milky cataract and, in sympathy with his inner vision, remained clouded.

He supposed the shiny apple might represent fame and wealth, the enviable life of his employer. Then the doll's eye might be a worm of sorts, a symbol of a particular corruption at the core of fame, and therefore an accusation, indictment, and condemnation of the Face.

For twelve years, the actor had been the biggest box-office draw in the world. Since his first hit, the celebrity-mad media referred to him as the Face.

This flattering sobriquet supposedly had arisen simultaneously from the pens of numerous entertainment reporters in a shared swoon of admiration for his charismatic good looks. In truth, no doubt a clever and perpetually sleepless publicist had called in favors and paid out cold cash to engineer this spontaneous acclamation and then to sustain it for more than a decade.

In a black-and-white Hollywood so distant in time and quality that contemporary moviegoers had only a little more knowledge of it than they had of the Spanish-American War, a fine actress named Greta Garbo had in her day been known as the Face. That flattery had been the work of a studio flack, but Garbo had proved to be more than mere flackery.

For ten months, Ethan had been chief of security for Channing Manheim, the Face of the new millennium. As yet he hadn't glimpsed even the suggestion of Garboesque depths. The face of the Face seemed to be nearly all there was of Channing.

Ethan didn't despise the actor. The Face was affable, as relaxed as might be a genuine demigod living with the sureness that life and youth were for him eternal.

The star's indifference to any circumstances other than his own arose neither from self-absorption nor from a willful lack of compassion. Intellectual limitations denied him an awareness that other people had more than a single script page of backstory, and that their character arcs were too complex to be portrayed in ninety-eight minutes.

His occasional cruelties were never conscious.

If he hadn't been who he was, however, and if he hadn't been so striking in appearance, nothing that Channing said or did would have left an impression. In a Hollywood deli that named sandwiches after stars, Clark Gable might have been roast beef and Liederkranz on rye with horseradish; Cary Grant might have been peppered chicken breast with Swiss cheese on whole wheat with mustard; and Channing Manheim would have been watercress on lightly buttered toast.

Ethan didn't actively dislike his employer, and he didn't need to like him in order to want to protect him and keep him alive.

If the eye in the apple was a symbol of corruption, it might represent the star's ego inside the beautiful fruit.

Perhaps the doll's eye didn't stand for corruption, but for the downside of fame. A celebrity of Channing's magnitude enjoyed little privacy and was always under scrutiny. The eye in the apple might be symbolic of the stalker's eye—always watching, judging.

Crap. Cheap analysis. For all his somber brooding, in weather conducive to contemplation and to dark speculation, Ethan's every observation seemed obvious and useless.

He ruminated on the apple-damp words: THE EYE IN THE APPLE? THE WATCHFUL WORM? THE WORM OF ORIGINAL SIN? DO WORDS HAVE ANY PURPOSE OTHER THAN CONFUSION?

Stumped, he was grateful when the phone rang at a few minutes past ten o'clock, drawing him away from the windows and to the desk.

Laura Moonves, an old friend from the LAPD, had been tracking down a license-plate number for him. She worked out of the Detective Support Division. Only once before in the past year had he presumed upon their friendship in this way.

"Got your pervert," Laura said.

"Suspected pervert," he corrected.

"The three-year-old Honda is registered to Rolf Herman Reynerd in West Hollywood." She spelled each name and gave him an address.

"What kind of parents *Rolf* a kid?"

Laura knew all about names. "It's not so bad. Nicely masculine, in fact. In Old German, it means 'famous wolf.' Ethan, of course, means 'permanent, assured.' "

Two years ago, they'd dated. For Laura, Ethan had been anything but permanent, assured. She'd have liked permanence, some assurance. He had been too wounded to provide what she wanted. Or too stupid.

"Looked him up for a rap sheet," Laura said, "but he's clean. DMV says 'hair brown, eyes blue.' Says 'sex male.' I like sex male. I don't get enough sex male. Height six-one, weight one-eighty. DOB—June sixth, nineteen seventy-two, which makes him thirty-one."

Ethan had it all on a notepad. "Thanks, Laura. I owe you one."

"So then tell me—how big's his charlie?"

"Isn't that in the DMV file?"

"I don't mean Rolf's charlie. I mean Manheim's. Does it hang to his ankles or just to his knees?"

"I've never seen his charlie, but he doesn't seem to have any trouble walking."

"Cookie, maybe you can introduce us sometime."

Ethan had never known why she called him Cookie. "The man would bore your ass off, Laura, and that's the truth."

"Pretty as he is, I wouldn't need conversation. I'd just shove a rag in his mouth, tape his lips shut, and off we'd go to paradise."

"Basically it's my job to keep people like you away from him."

"Truman derives from two Old English words," she said. "It means 'steadfast, loyal, trustworthy, constant.' "

"You can't get a date with the Face by making me feel guilty. Besides, when wasn't I loyal and trustworthy?"

"Cookie, two out of four doesn't mean you deserve your name."

"You were too good for me anyway, Laura. You've got more to give than a shlump like me can appreciate."

"I'd like to see your old Ten Card," she said, referring to his record of service on the force. "Must be more brown stars for ass kissing on that baby than any hundred other cards in the history of the job."

"If you're done dissing me, I've been wondering. . . . Rolf. Famous wolf. Does that make sense? What's a wolf have to do to get famous?"

"Kill a lot of sheep, I guess."

By the time Ethan said good-bye to Laura, a thin rain had begun to fall again. Without the ardor of a wind, the droplets barely kissed the study windows.

Using the remote control, he switched on the TV and then the VCR. The tape was already loaded. He'd watched it six times before.

Exterior security cameras throughout the estate numbered eighty-six. Every house door and window and all the approaches across the grounds were monitored.

Only the north wall of the estate abutted public property. This long rampart, including the gate, was under surveillance by cameras mounted in the trees on the land directly across the street, a parcel also owned by Channing Manheim.

Anyone reconnoitering the front-wall security, the operation of the gate, and the protocols of visitor identification would detect no cameras on the public side or in the estate trees that overhung the wall. They would assume that surveillance could be conducted solely from within the property.

Meanwhile, they would be watched by the cameras on the farther side of the narrow Bel Air byway, barely two lanes wide, which lacked sidewalks and streetlamps. A zoom shot would provide a clear ID to help ensure a conviction if the subject proceeded from reconnoitering to any act of criminal intent.

The cameras operated 24/7. From the security office in the groundskeeper's building and from several points in the house, any videocam in the system could be accessed if you knew the command.

Several televisions in the house and a bank of six in the security office could receive the video feed from any camera. One TV could display as many as four views simultaneously in quarter-screen format. Therefore, the security team was able to study images from as many as twenty-four cameras at any one time.

Mostly, the guards drank coffee and bullshitted each other. If an alarm was triggered, however, they could have an immediate, close look at whatever corner of the estate had been violated. Camera by camera, they would be able to track an intruder as he moved from one field of view into another.

From the security-office keyboard, a guard could direct the video

feed from any of the eighty-six sources to a VCR. The system included twelve VCRs capable of simultaneously recording forty-eight
feeds in quarter-screen format.

Even if a guard were not paying attention, motion detectors associated with each camera would instigate automatic recording of that
field of vision when any living thing larger than a dog passed through
its area of responsibility.

At 3:32 A.M. the previous night, motion detectors related to
Camera 01, which ceaselessly panned the western end of the north
perimeter, picked up a three-year-old Honda. Instead of passing by as
the infrequent other traffic had done throughout the night, the car
pulled off the pavement and parked a hundred yards short of the entrance gate.

The previous five black boxes had come by Federal Express with
fake return addresses. Here Ethan had been presented with the first
opportunity to identify the sender.

Now, less than seven hours later, he stood in his study and
watched the Honda in full-screen format. The narrow shoulder of the
road prevented the driver from parking the car entirely out of the
eastbound lane.

In daylight, the exclusive streets of Bel Air didn't carry a heavy
load of traffic. At that late hour, they were hardly traveled.

Nevertheless concerned about safety, the driver of the Honda
didn't kill his headlights when he parked. He left the engine running
and switched on his emergency blinkers.

The camera, featuring advanced night-vision technology, provided
a high-resolution picture in spite of the darkness and foul weather.

For a moment, Camera 01 continued panning away from the
Honda—then halted its programmed sweep and returned to the car.
Dave Ladman had been on a routine foot patrol of the estate grounds
at that time. Tom Mack, manning the security office, had recognized
the presence of a suspicious vehicle and had overridden 01's automatic function.

Rain had been falling heavily. Ceaseless barrages of raindrops shattered against the blacktop with force, creating such a froth and dancing spray that the street appeared to be aboil.

The driver's door opened, and Camera 01 zoomed in for a close-up as a tall, solidly built man got out of the car. He wore a black waterproof windbreaker. His face was hidden in the shadow of a hood.

Unless Rolf Reynerd had loaned his car to a friend, this was the famous wolf. He fit the physical profile on Reynerd's license.

He closed the driver's door, opened the rear door, and took a large white ball from the backseat. This appeared to be the garbage bag containing the gift of the sutured apple.

Reynerd closed the door and started toward the front of the car, toward the driveway gate a hundred yards away. Abruptly he halted and turned to peer along the dark rain-swept lane, poised for flight.

Perhaps he thought that he'd heard an approaching engine above the rushing rustle of the rain racing down through the trees. The security tape provided no sound.

At that lonely hour, if another vehicle *had* arrived on the scene, chances were good that it would have been a cruiser belonging to the Bel Air Patrol, the private-security force that assisted in the policing of this extremely wealthy community.

When neither a cruiser nor a less-official vehicle appeared, the hooded man regained his confidence. He hurried eastward to the gate.

Camera 02 followed him as he stepped beyond the panning arc of Camera 01. As he neared the gate, Camera 03 watched him from across the street, zooming in for an intimate appraisal.

Immediately upon arrival at the entrance gate, Reynerd threw the white bag toward the top of that bronze barrier. Failing to clear the highest scrollwork, the package bounced back at him.

On his second attempt, he succeeded. When he turned away from the gate, his hood slipped half off, and Camera 03 captured a clear image of his face in the glow of the flanking gate lamps.

He had the chiseled features needed to be a successful waiter in the trendiest of L.A. restaurants, where both the service staff and the customers enjoyed the fantasy that any guy or gal ferrying plates of over-priced swordfish from kitchen to table during the Tuesday dinner shift might be offered, on Wednesday, a coveted role in Tom Cruise's next hundred-fifty-million-dollar picture.

Turning from the gate, having delivered the apple, Rolf Reynerd was grinning.

Perhaps if Ethan hadn't known the meaning of the man's first name, the grin wouldn't have seemed wolfish. Then he might have been reminded instead of a crocodile or a hyena.

In any case, this was not the merry expression of a prankster. Captured on videotape, this curve of lips and bared teeth suggested a lunatic glee that required a full moon and medication.

Splashing through black puddles filigreed with silver by the head-lights, Reynerd returned to the car.

As the Honda pulled off the shoulder and onto the eastbound lane once more, Camera 01 executed a swivel and zoom, then Camera 02. Both delivered readable shots of the rear license plate.

Dwindling into the night, the car conjured briefly lingering ghosts from its tailpipe.

Then the narrow street lay deserted, in wet gloom except for the lamps at the Manheim gate. Black rain, as if from a dissolving night sky, poured down, poured down, driving the darkness of the universe into the universally coveted Bel Air real estate.

Before leaving his quarters in the west wing, Ethan called the housekeeper, Mrs. McBee, to report that he'd be out most of the day.

More efficient than any machine, more dependable than the laws of physics, as trustworthy as any archangel, Mrs. McBee would within minutes dispatch one of the six maids under her command to Ethan's apartment. Seven days a week, a maid collected the trash and provided fresh towels. Twice weekly, his rooms were dusted, vacuumed, and left immaculate. Windows were washed twice a month.

There were advantages to living in a mansion attended by a staff of twenty-five.

As the chief of security overseeing both the Face's personal protection and the safeguarding of the estate, Ethan enjoyed many benefits, including free meals prepared by either Mr. Hachette, the household chef, or by Mr. Baptiste, the household cook. Mr. Baptiste lacked his boss's training in the finest culinary schools; but no one with taste buds ever complained about any dish he put on the table.

Meals could be taken in the large and comfortably furnished dayroom, where the staff not only ate but also did their household planning, spent their coffee breaks, and strategized all arrangements for the elaborate parties often held when the Face was in residence. Chef or cook would also prepare a plate of sandwiches or any other requested treat that Ethan might want to take back to his quarters.

Of course, he could prepare meals in his apartment kitchen if he preferred. Mrs. McBee kept his fridge and pantry stocked according to shopping lists he presented to her, at no expense to him.

Except for Monday and Thursday, when one of the maids changed the bedclothes—Mr. Manheim's linens were cycled daily when he was in residence—Ethan had to make his own bed each morning.

Life was hard.

Now, after shrugging into a soft leather jacket, Ethan stepped out of his apartment into the ground-floor hallway of the west wing. He left his door unlocked as he would have done if he'd owned the entire house.

He took with him a file that he'd made on the black-box case, an umbrella, and a leather-bound copy of *Lord Jim* by Joseph Conrad. He had finished reading the novel the previous evening and intended to return it to the library.

More than twelve feet wide, paved with limestone tiles featured through most of the main floor of the house, this hall was graced by softly colored contemporary Persian carpets. High-quality French antiques—all from the Empire period, and including the late-Empire style called Biedermeier—furnished the long space: chairs, chests, a desk, a sideboard.

Even with furniture to both sides, Ethan could have driven a car through the hall without grazing a single antique.

He might have enjoyed driving a car through the hall if he would not have had to explain himself to Mrs. McBee afterward.

During the invigorating hike to the library, he encountered two uniformed maids and a porter with whom he exchanged greetings. Because he occupied what Mrs. McBee defined as an executive position on the staff, he referred to these fellow workers by their first names, but they called him Mr. Truman.

Prior to each new employee's first day on the job, Mrs. McBee provided a ring-bound notebook titled *Standards and Practices,* which she herself had composed and assembled. Woe be to the benighted soul who did not memorize its contents and perform always according to its directions.

The library floor was walnut, stained a dark warm reddish-brown. Here the Persian carpets were antiques that appreciated in value far faster than the blue-chip stocks of the country's finest companies.

Club chairs in comfortable seating arrangements alternated with mazes of mahogany shelves that held over thirty-six thousand volumes. Some of the books were shelved on a second level served by a six-foot-wide catwalk that could be reached by an open staircase with an elaborate gilded-iron railing.

If you didn't look up at the ceiling to help you define the true size of the enormous chamber, you might succumb to the illusion that it went on forever. Maybe it did. Anything seemed possible here.

The center of the ceiling featured a stained-glass dome thirty-two feet in diameter. The deep colors of the glass—crimson, emerald, burnt yellow, sapphire—so completely filtered natural light even on a bright day that the books were at no risk of sustaining sun damage.

Ethan's Uncle Joe—who'd served as a surrogate dad when Ethan's real father had been too drunk to handle the job—had been a truck driver for a regional bakery. He'd delivered breads and pastries to supermarkets and restaurants, six days a week, eight hours a day. Most of the time, Joe had held down a second job as a night janitor, three days a week.

In his best five years put together, Uncle Joe hadn't made enough to equal the cost of this stained-glass dome.

When he'd first begun to earn a policeman's pay, Ethan had felt rich. Compared to Joe, he had been raking in big dough.

His total income from sixteen years with the LAPD wouldn't have paid the cost of this one room.

"Should've been a movie star," he said as he entered the library to return *Lord Jim* to the shelf from which he'd gotten it.

Every volume in the collection had been arranged in alphabetical order, by author. A third were bound in leather; the rest were regular editions. A significant number were rare, and valuable.

The Face had read none of them.

More than two-thirds of the collection had come with the house. At her employer's instructions, once each month, Mrs. McBee purchased the most talked-about and critically acclaimed current novels and volumes of nonfiction, which were at once catalogued and added to the library.

These new books were acquired for the sole purpose of display. They impressed houseguests, dinner guests, and other visitors with the breadth of Channing Manheim's intellectual interests.

When asked for his opinion of any book, the Face elicited the visitor's judgment first, then agreed with it in such a charming fashion that he seemed both erudite and every bit a kindred spirit.

As Ethan slid *Lord Jim* onto a shelf between two other Conrad titles, a small reedy voice behind him said, "Is there magic in it?"

Turning, he discovered ten-year-old Aelfric Manheim all but swallowed alive by one of the larger armchairs.

According to Laura Moonves, Aelfric (pronounced *elf-rick*) was an Old English word meaning "elf-ruled" or "ruled by elves," which had first been used to describe wise and clever actions, but had in time come to refer to those who acted wisely and cleverly.

Aelfric.

The boy's mother—Fredericka "Freddie" Nielander—a supermodel who had married and divorced the Face all in one year, had read at least three books in her life. *The Lord of the Rings* trilogy. In fact she had read them repeatedly.

She had been prepared to name the boy Frodo. Fortunately, or not, one month before Freddie's due date, her best girlfriend, an actress, had discovered the name Aelfric in the script for a cheesy fantasy film in which she had agreed to play a three-breasted Amazon alchemist.

If Freddie's friend had landed a supporting role in *The Silence of the Lambs*, Aelfric would probably now be Hannibal Manheim.

The boy preferred to be called Fric, and no one but his mother insisted on using his full name. Fortunately, or not, she wasn't around much to torture him with it.

Reliable scuttlebutt had it that Freddie had not seen Fric in over seventeen months. Even the career of an aging supermodel could be demanding.

"Is there magic in what?" Ethan asked.

"That book you just put away."

"Magic of a sort, but probably not the kind of magic you mean."

"This one has a shitload of magic in it," Fric said, displaying a paperback with dragons and wizards on the cover.

"Is that advisable language for a wise and clever person?" Ethan asked.

"Heck, all my old man's friends in the biz talk worse stuff than *shitload*. So does my old man."

"Not when he knows you're around."

Fric cocked his head. "Are you calling my dad a hypocrite?"

"If I ever call your dad such a thing, I'll cut my tongue out."

"The evil wizard in this book would use it in a potion. One of his most difficult tasks is to find the tongue of an honest man."

"What makes you think I'm honest?"

"Get real. You've got a triple shitload of honesty."

"What're you going to do if Mrs. McBee hears you using words like that?"

"She's somewhere else."

"Oh, she is?" Ethan asked, suggesting that he knew something regarding Mrs. McBee's current whereabouts that would make the boy wish he'd been more discreet.

Unable to repress a guilty expression, Fric sat up straight and surveyed the library.

The boy was small for his age, and thin. At times, glimpsed from a distance as he walked along one of the vast halls or across a room scaled for kings and their entourages, he seemed almost wispy.

"I think she has secret passages," Fric whispered. "You know, pathways in the walls."

"Mrs. McBee?"

The boy nodded. "We've lived here six years, but she's been here *forever*."

Mrs. McBee and Mr. McBee—both in their middle fifties—had been employed by the previous owner of the property and had stayed on at the request of the Face.

"It's hard to picture Mrs. McBee skulking about in the walls," said Ethan. "She's not exactly a dastardly sort."

"But if she *was* dastardly," Fric said hopefully, "things would be more interesting around here."

Unlike his father's golden locks, which with a shake of the head always fell perfectly into place, Fric's brown mop achieved perpetual disarray. Here was hair that foiled brushes and broke good combs.

Fric might grow into his looks and prove equal to his pedigree, but currently he appeared to be an average ten-year-old boy.

"Why aren't you in class?" Ethan wondered.

"You an atheist or something? Don't you know it's the week before Christmas? Even home-schooled Hollywood brats get a break."

A cadre of tutors visited five days a week. The private school that Fric attended for a while had not proved to be a suitable environment for him.

With the famous Channing Manheim for a father, with the famous and *notorious* Freddie Nielander for a mother, Fric became an object of envy and ridicule even among the children of other celebrities. Being the skinny son of a buffed star adored for heroic roles also made him a figure of fun to crueler kids. The severity of his asthma further argued for schooling at home, in a controlled environment.

"Have any idea what you'll get Christmas morning?" Ethan asked.

"Yeah. I had to submit my list to Mrs. McBee by December fifth. I told her not to bother wrapping the stuff, but she will. She always does. She says it's not Christmas morning without *some* mystery."

"I'd have to agree with that."

The boy shrugged, and slumped in his chair again.

Although the Face was currently on location for a film, he would return from Florida the day before Christmas.

"It'll be good to have your dad home for the holidays. You guys have any special plans once he gets back?"

The boy shrugged again, attempting to convey lack of knowledge or indifference, but instead—and unwittingly—revealing a misery that made Ethan feel uncharacteristically helpless.

Fric had inherited luminous green eyes to match his mother's. In the singular depths of those eyes, enough could be read about the boy's loneliness to fill a library shelf or two.

"Well," Ethan said, "maybe Christmas morning this year you'll have a couple surprises."

Sitting forward in his chair, eager for the sense of mystery that he had so recently dismissed as unimportant, Fric said, "What—you heard something?"

"If I heard something, which I'm not saying I did or didn't, I couldn't tell you what I heard, assuming I heard anything at all, and still keep the surprise a surprise, by which I don't mean to imply that there is a surprise or that there isn't one."

The boy stared in silence for a moment. "Now you don't sound cop honest, you sound like the head of a studio."

"You know what heads of studios sound like, huh?"

"They come around here sometimes," the boy said in a tone of worldly wisdom. "I recognize their rap."

Ethan parked across the street from the apartment house in West Hollywood, switched off the windshield wipers, but left the engine running to power the heater. He sat in the Ford Expedition awhile, watching the place, deciding upon the best approach to Rolf Reynerd.

The Expedition was one of a collection of vehicles available for both job-related and personal use by the eight live-in members of the twenty-five-person estate staff. Among other wheels, a Mercedes ML500 SUV had been in the lower garage, but that might have drawn too much attention during a stakeout if the day required surveillance work.

The three-story apartment house appeared to be in good but not excellent repair. The cream-colored stucco wasn't pocked or cracked, but the place looked to be at least a year overdue for painting. One of the address numbers above the front door hung askew.

Camellia bushes laden with heavy red blooms, a variety of ferns, and phoenix palms with enormous crowns provided the lushness of high-end landscaping; but everything had needed a trim months ago. The shaggy grass suggested that it was mown not weekly but twice a month.

The landlord shaved his costs, but the building nevertheless looked like a nice place to live.

No one rented here on a welfare check. Reynerd must have a job, but the fact that he'd been delivering death threats at three-thirty in the morning suggested that he didn't have to get up early to go to work. He might be home now.

When Ethan tracked down his suspect's place of employment and began to make inquiries about him with fellow workers and neighbors, Reynerd almost certainly would be alerted by someone. Thereafter, he would grow too wary to be approached directly.

Ethan preferred to start with the man himself and work outward from that initial contact.

He closed his eyes, tipped his head back against the headrest, and brooded about how to proceed.

The engine roar of an approaching car grew so loud that Ethan opened his eyes, half expecting to hear a sudden siren and to see a police chase in progress. Traveling far too fast for a residential street, a cherry-red Ferrari Testarossa exploded past, as though the driver were in fact hoping to run down a darting child or an old lady slowed by orthopedic shoes and a cane.

A tire-thrown plume spewed up from the puddled street, drenching the Expedition. The glass in the driver's door briefly clouded with ripples of dirty water.

Across the street, the apartment house appeared to shimmer as if it were a place in a dream. Some aspect of that transient distortion seemed to trigger a vague memory of a long-forgotten nightmare, and the sight of the building in this warped condition caused the hairs to rise inexplicably on the back of Ethan's neck.

Then the last gouts of the plume drained off the window. Falling rain quickly cleared the murky residue from the glass. The apartment house was nothing more than what it had been when he'd first seen it: a nice place to live.

After judging that the rain was falling only hard enough to make an umbrella more trouble than it was worth, he got out of the SUV and dashed across the street.

In southern California during the late autumn and early winter, Mother Nature suffered unpredictable mood swings. From one year to the next, and even from day to day in the same year, the week before Christmas could vary from balmy to bone-chilling. This air was cool, the rain colder than the air, and the sky as dead gray as it might have been in any truly wintry clime much farther north.

The main door of the building featured no buzz-through security lock. The neighborhood remained safe enough that apartment lobbies did not absolutely require fortification.

Dripping, he entered a small space, less a lobby than a foyer, with a Mexican-tile floor. An elevator and a set of stairs served the upper stories.

The foyer air curdled with the lingering meaty scent of Canadian bacon, cooked hours ago, and the musty smell of stale pot smoke. Weed had a singular aroma. Someone had stood here this morning, finishing a joint, before stepping out to meet the dreary day.

From the bank of mailboxes, Ethan counted four apartments on the ground floor, six on the second, and six on the third. Reynerd lived in the middle of the building, in 2B.

Only the last names of the current tenants were printed on the mailboxes. Ethan needed more information than these stick-on labels provided.

An open communal receptacle, recessed in the wall, had been provided for magazines and other publications on those occasions when the volume of other mail didn't permit the postman to put all items in the boxes.

Two magazines lay in the tray. Both were for George Keesner in Apartment 2E.

Ethan rapped a knuckle against the aluminum doors on several of the mailboxes for the apartments in which he had no interest. The hollow sound suggested they were empty. Most likely the daily mail had not yet been delivered.

When he rapped on Keesner's box, it sounded as though it was packed full of mail. Evidently the man had been away from home for at least a couple days.

Ethan climbed the stairs to the second floor. One long hall, three doors on each side. At 2E, he rang the bell and waited.

Reynerd's unit, 2B, lay directly across from 2E.

When no one answered the bell at Keesner's apartment, Ethan rang it again, twice. After a pause, he knocked loudly.

Each door had been fitted with a fisheye lens to allow the resident to examine a caller before deciding whether or not to admit him. Perhaps from across the hall, Reynerd was watching the back of Ethan's head right now.

Receiving no response to his knock, Ethan turned away from Keesner's door and made a show of frustration. He wiped his rain-wet face with one hand. He pushed that hand through his damp hair. He shook his head. He looked up and down the hall.

When Ethan rang the bell at 2B, the apple man answered almost at once, without the protection of a security chain.

Although an unmistakable match for the image captured by the security camera, he proved to be more handsome than he'd been in the rain the previous night. He resembled Ben Affleck, the actor.

In addition to the Affleck aspect, however, he had a welcome-to-the-Bates-Motel edge to him that any fan of Anthony Perkins would have recognized. The tightness at the corners of his mouth, the rapid pulse visible in his right temple, and especially the hard shine in his eyes suggested that he might be on methamphetamine, not fully amped but clipping along at high altitude.

"Sir," Ethan said even as the door was still opening, "I'm sorry to bother you, but I'm sort of desperate to get in touch with George Keesner over there in 2E. Do you know George?"

Reynerd shook his head. He had a bull's neck. Lots of time spent on weight machines at the gym.

"I know him to say hello in the hall," Reynerd said, "and how's the weather. That's all."

If that was true, Ethan felt secure enough to say, "I'm his brother. Name's Ricky Keesner."

That scam ought to work as long as Keesner was somewhere between twenty and fifty years old.

"Our Uncle Harry's on his deathbed in the ICU," Ethan lied. "Not going to hold on much longer. Since yesterday morning, I been calling George at every number I've got for him. He doesn't get back to me. Doesn't answer the door now."

"I think he's away," said Reynerd.

"Away? He didn't say anything about it to me. You know where he might've gone?"

Reynerd shook his head. "He was going out with a little suitcase the night before last, as I was coming in."

"He tell you when he'd be back?"

"We just said how it looked like rain coming, and then he went out," Reynerd replied.

"Man, he's so close to Uncle Harry—we both are—he's going to be upset he didn't get a chance to say good-bye. Maybe I could leave him a note, so he sees it first thing he gets back."

Reynerd just stared at Ethan. An artery began throbbing in his neck. His speed-cycled brain was racing, but although meth ensured frenetically fast thinking, it didn't assist *clear* thinking.

"The thing is," Ethan said, "I don't have any paper. Or a pen, for that matter."

"Oh. Sure, I got those," said Reynerd.

"I really hate to bother you—"

"No bother," Reynerd assured him, turning away from the open door, going off to find a notepad, a pen.

Left at the threshold, Ethan chafed to get into the apartment. He wanted a better look at Reynerd's nest than he could obtain from the doorway.

Just as Ethan decided to risk being rude and to enter without an invitation, Reynerd halted, turned, and said, "Come on in. Sit down."

Now that the invitation had been extended, Ethan could afford to inject a little authenticity into this charade by demurring. "Thanks, but I just came in from the rain—"

"Can't hurt this furniture," Reynerd assured him.

Leaving the door open behind himself, Ethan went inside.

The living room and dining area comprised one large space. The kitchen was open to this front room, but separated from it by a bar with two stools.

Reynerd proceeded into the kitchen, to a counter under a wall phone, while Ethan perched on the edge of an armchair in the living room.

The apartment was sparsely furnished. One sofa, one armchair, a coffee table, and a television set. The dining area contained a small table and two chairs.

On the television, the MGM lion roared. The sound was low, the roar soft.

On the walls were several framed photographs: large sixteen-by-twenty-inch, black-and-white art prints. Birds were the subject of every photo.

Reynerd returned with a notepad and a pencil. "This do?"

"Perfect," Ethan said, accepting the items.

Reynerd had a dispenser of Scotch tape, as well. "To fix the note on George's door." He put the tape on the coffee table.

"Thanks," Ethan said. "I like the photographs."

"Birds are all about being free," Reynerd said.

"I guess they are, aren't they? The freedom of flight. You take the photos?"

"No. I just collect."

In one of the prints, a flock of pigeons erupted in a swirl of feathered frenzy from a cobblestone plaza in front of a backdrop of old European buildings. In another, geese flew in formation across a somber sky.

Indicating the black-and-white movie on the TV, Reynerd said, "I was just getting some snacks for the show. You mind . . . ?"

"Huh? Oh, sure, I'm sorry, forget about me. I'll jot this down and be gone."

In one of the pictures, the birds had flown directly at the photographer. The shot presented a close-up montage of overlapping wings, crying beaks, and beady black eyes.

"Potato chips are gonna kill me one day," Reynerd said as he returned to the kitchen.

"With me it's ice cream. More of it in my arteries than blood."

Ethan printed DEAR GEORGE in block letters, then paused as if in thought, and looked around the room.

From the kitchen, Reynerd continued: "They say you can't ever eat just one potato chip, but I can't ever eat just one *bag*."

Two crows perched on an iron fence. A strop of sunlight laid a sharp edge on their beaks.

White carpet as pristine as winter snow lay wall to wall. The furniture had been upholstered in a black fabric. From a distance, the Formica surface of the dinette table appeared to be black.

Everything in the apartment was black-and-white.

Ethan printed UNCLE HARRY IS DYING and then paused again, as if a simple message taxed his powers of composition.

The movie music, though soft, had a melodramatic flair. A crime picture from the thirties or forties.

Reynerd continued to rummage in kitchen cabinets.

Here, two doves appeared to clash in midflight. There, an owl stared wide-eyed, as if shocked by what it saw.

Outside, wind had returned to the day. A dice-rattle of rain drew Ethan's attention to the window.

From the kitchen came the distinctive rustle of a foil potato-chip bag.

PLEASE CALL ME, Ethan printed.

Returning to the living room, Reynerd said, "If you've got to eat chips, these are the worst because they're higher in oil."

Ethan looked up and saw a bag of Hawaiian-style chips. Reynerd had inserted his right hand into the open bag.

The way that the bag gloved the apple man's hand struck Ethan as *wrong*. The guy might have been reaching in for some chips, of course; but an oddness of attitude, a tenseness in him, suggested otherwise.

Stopping beside the sofa, not six feet away, Reynerd said, "You work for the Face, don't you?"

At a disadvantage in the armchair, Ethan pretended confusion. "For who?"

When the hand came out of the bag, it held a gun.

A licensed private investigator and certified bodyguard, Ethan had a permit to carry a concealed weapon. Except in the company of Channing Manheim, when he armed himself as a matter of routine, he seldom bothered to strap on his piece.

Reynerd's weapon was a 9-mm pistol.

This morning, disturbed by the eye in the apple and by the wolfish grin that this man had revealed on the security tape, Ethan had put on his shoulder holster. He hadn't expected to need a gun, not really, and in fact he'd felt a little silly for packing it without greater provocation. Now he thanked God that he was armed.

"I don't understand," he said, trying to look equally bewildered and afraid.

"I've seen your picture," Reynerd told him.

Ethan glanced toward the open door, the hallway beyond.

"I don't care who sees or hears," Reynerd told him. "It's all over anyhow, isn't it?"

"Listen, if my brother George did something to piss you off," Ethan said, trying to buy a little time.

Reynerd wasn't selling. Even as Ethan dropped the notepad and reached for the 9-mm Glock under his jacket, the apple man shot him point-blank in the gut.

For a moment, Ethan felt no pain, but only for a moment. He rocked back in the chair and gaped at the gush of blood. Then agony.

He heard the first shot, but he didn't hear the second. The slug hammered him dead-center in the chest.

Everything in the black-and-white apartment went black.

Ethan knew the birds still gathered on the walls, watching him die. He could feel the tension of their wings frozen in flight.

He heard a dicelike rattle again. Not rain against the window this time. His breath rattling in a broken throat.

No Christmas.

CHAPTER 3

ETHAN OPENED HIS EYES.
Traveling far too fast for a residential street, a cherry-red Ferrari Testarossa exploded past, casting up a plume of dirty water from the puddled pavement.

Through the side window of the Expedition, the apartment house blurred and tweaked into strange geometry, like a place in a nightmare.

As if he'd sustained an electrical shock, he twitched violently, and inhaled with the desperation of a drowning man. The air tasted sweet, fresh and sweet and clean. He exhaled explosively.

No gut wound. No chest wound. His hair wasn't wet with rain.

His heart knocked, knocked like a lunatic fist on the padded door of a padded room.

Never in his life had Ethan Truman experienced a dream of such clarity, such intensity, nor any nightmare so crisply detailed as the experience in Reynerd's apartment.

He consulted his wristwatch. If he'd been asleep, he had been dreaming for no more than a minute.

He couldn't have explored the convolutions of such an elaborate dream in a mere minute. Impossible.

Rain washed the last of the murky residue off the glass. Beyond the dripping fronds of the phoenix palms, the apartment house waited, no longer distorted, but now forever strange.

When he'd leaned back against the headrest and closed his eyes, the better to formulate his approach to Rolf Reynerd, Ethan had not been in the least sleepy. Or even tired.

He was certain that he had not taken a one-minute nap. He had not taken a five-second nap, for that matter.

If the first Ferrari had been a figment of a dream, the second sports car suggested that reality now followed precisely in the path of the nightmare.

Although his explosive breathing had quieted, his heart clumped with undiminished speed, galloping after reason, which set an even faster pace, steadily receding beyond reach.

Intuition told him to leave now, to find a Starbucks and have a large cup of coffee. Order a blend strong enough to dissolve the swizzle stick.

Given time and distance from the event, he would discover the key that unlocked the mystery and allowed understanding. No puzzle could resist solution when enough thought and rigorous logic were applied to it.

Even though years of police work had taught him to trust his intuition as a baby trusts its mother, he switched off the engine and got out of the Expedition.

No argument: Intuition was an essential survival tool. Honesty with himself, however, was more important than heeding intuition. In a spirit of honesty, he had to admit that he wanted to drive away not to find a place and time for quiet reflection, not to engage in Sherlockian deduction, but because fear had him in a pincer grip.

Fear must never be allowed to win. Surrender to it once, and you were finished as a cop.

Of course he wasn't a cop anymore. He had left the force more than a year ago. The work that had given his life meaning while Hannah was alive had meant steadily less to him in the years after her death. He had ceased to believe that he could make a difference in the world. He had wanted to withdraw, to turn his back on the ugly reality of the human condition so evident in the daily work of a homicide detective. Channing Manheim's world was as far as he could get from reality and still earn a living.

Although he didn't carry a badge, although he might not be a cop in any official sense, he remained a cop in essence. We are what we are, no matter what we might wish to be, or pretend to be.

Hands shoved in the pockets of his leather jacket, shoulders hunched as if the rain were a burden, he dashed across the street to the apartment house.

Dripping, he entered the foyer. Mexican-tile floor. Elevator. Stairs. As it should be. As it had been.

Stale with the greasy scent of cooked breakfast meat and pot smoke, the air felt thick, seemed to cloy like mucus in his throat.

Two magazines lay in the tray. On each mailing label was the name George Keesner.

Ethan climbed the stairs. His legs felt weak, and his hands trembled. At the landing, he paused to take a few deep breaths, to knit the raveled fabric of his nerve.

The apartment house lay quiet. No voices muffled by the walls, no music for a melancholy Monday.

He imagined that he heard the faint tick and scrape of crow claws on an iron fence, the flap and rustle of pigeons taking flight, the *tick-tick-tick* of insistently pecking beaks. In truth, he knew that these were only the many voices of the rain.

Although he could feel the weight of the pistol in his shoulder holster, he reached under his coat and placed his right hand on the weapon to be certain that he had brought it. With one fingertip, he traced the checking on the grip.

He withdrew his hand from under his jacket, leaving the pistol in the holster.

Having collected hair by hair along the back of his head, rain reached a trickling finger down the nape of his neck, teasing a shudder from him.

When Ethan reached the second-floor hallway, he barely glanced at Apartment 2E, where George Keesner would fail to respond to either the bell or a knock, and he went directly to the door of 2B, where he lost his nerve, but only briefly.

The apple man answered the bell almost at once. Tall, strong, self-confident, he didn't bother engaging the security chain.

He didn't seem to be in the least surprised to see Ethan again or alive, as if their first encounter had never happened.

"Is Jim here?" Ethan asked.

"You've got the wrong apartment," Reynerd said.

"Jim Briscoe? Really? I'm sure this was his place."

"I've been here more than six months."

Beyond Reynerd lay a black-and-white room.

"Six months? Has it been that long since I was here?" Ethan sounded false to himself, but he pressed forward. "Yeah, I guess that's what it's been, six or seven."

On the wall opposite the door, an owl stared with immense eyes, in expectation of a gunshot.

Ethan said, "Hey, did Jim leave a forwarding address?"

"I never met the previous tenant."

The hard shine in Reynerd's eyes, the quick throbbing in his temple, the tightness at the corners of his mouth this time warned Ethan off.

"Sorry to have bothered you," he said.

When he heard Reynerd's television at low volume, the soft roar of the MGM lion, he hesitated no longer and headed directly for the stairs. He realized that he was retreating with suspicious haste, and he tried not to run.

Halfway down the stairs, at the landing, Ethan trusted instinct, turned, looked up, and saw Rolf Reynerd at the head of the stairs, silently watching him. The apple man had in his hand neither a gun nor a bag of potato chips.

Without another word, Ethan descended the last flight to the foyer. Opening the outer door, he glanced back, but Reynerd had not followed him to the lower floor.

Lazy no more, rain chased rain along the street, and cold wind blustered in the palms.

Behind the steering wheel of the Expedition again, Ethan started the engine, locked the doors, switched on the heater.

A strong double coffee at Starbucks no longer seemed adequate. He didn't know where to go.

Premonition. Precognition. Psychic vision. Clairvoyance. The *Twilight Zone Dictionary* turned its own pages in the library of his mind, but no possibility that it presented to him seemed to explain his experience.

According to the calendar, winter would not officially arrive for another day, but it entered early in his bones. He contained a coldness unknown in southern California.

He raised his hands to look at them, never having known them to shake like this. His fingers were pale, each nail as entirely white as the crescent at its base.

Neither the paleness nor the tremors troubled Ethan half as much as what he saw beneath the fingernails of his right hand. A dark substance, reddish-black.

He stared at this material for a long time, reluctant to take steps to determine if it was real or hallucinated.

Finally he used the thumbnail of his left hand to scrape out a small portion of the matter that was trapped under the nail of his right thumb. The stuff proved slightly moist, gummy.

Hesitantly, he brought the smear to his nose. He sniffed it once, twice, and though the scent was faint, he didn't need to smell it again.

Ethan had blood under all five nails of his right hand. With a certainty seldom given to any man who understood the world to be a most uncertain place, he knew that this would prove to be his own blood.

CHAPTER 4

PALOMAR LABORATORIES IN NORTH HOLLY-
wood occupied a sprawling single-story concrete-slab building
with such small and widely spaced windows and with such a low and
slightly pitched sheet-metal roof that it resembled a bunker in the
storm.

The medical-lab division of Palomar analyzed blood samples, Pap
smears, biopsies, and other organic materials. In their industrial division, they performed chemical analyses of every variety for both
private-sector and government clients.

Each year, fans of the Face sent over a quarter of a million pieces of
mail to him, mostly in care of his studio, which forwarded weekly
batches of this correspondence to the publicity firm that responded
to it in the star's name. Among those letters were gifts, including
more than a few homemade foods: cookies, cakes, fudge. Fewer than
one in a thousand fans might be sufficiently deranged to send poisoned brownies, but Ethan nevertheless operated on the better-safe-
than-sorry principle: All foodstuffs must be disposed of without
sampling by anyone.

Occasionally, when a homemade treat from a fan arrived with a
particularly suspicious letter, the edible goodie would not be at once

destroyed but would be passed along to Ethan for a closer look. If he suspected contamination, he brought the item here to Palomar to be analyzed.

When a total stranger could work up sufficient hatred to attempt to poison the Face, Ethan wanted to know that the bastard existed. He subsequently cooperated with authorities in the poisoner's hometown to bring whatever criminal charges might be sustained in court.

Now, proceeding first to the public reception lounge, he signed a form authorizing them to draw his blood. Lacking a doctor's order for tests, he paid cash for the analyses he required.

He requested a basic DNA profile. "And I want to know if any drugs are present in my body."

"What drugs are you taking?" the receptionist asked.

"Nothing but aspirin. But I want you to test for every possible substance, in case I've been drugged without my knowledge."

Perhaps in North Hollywood they were accustomed to encounters with full-blown paranoids. The receptionist didn't roll her eyes, raise an eyebrow, or in any other way appear to be surprised to hear him suggest that he might be the victim of a wicked conspiracy.

The medical technician who drew his sample was a petite and lovely Vietnamese woman with an angel's touch. He never felt the needle pierce the vein.

In another reception lounge provided for the delivery of samples unrelated to standard medical tests, he filled out a second form and paid another fee. This receptionist did give him an odd look when he explained what he wanted to have analyzed.

At a lab table, under harsh fluorescent lights, a technician who resembled Britney Spears used a thin but blunt steel blade to scrape the blood from under the fingernails of his right hand, onto a square of acid-free white paper. Ethan hadn't trimmed his nails in over a week, so she retrieved a significant number of shavings, some of which still appeared to be gummy.

His hand trembled throughout the process. She probably thought her beauty made him nervous.

The material from under his fingernails would first be tested to determine if it was indeed blood. Thereafter it would be conveyed to the medical-lab division to be typed and to have the DNA profile compared to the blood sample that the Vietnamese technician had drawn. Full toxicological results wouldn't be ready until Wednesday afternoon.

Ethan didn't understand how he could have his own blood under his fingernails when he had not, after all, been shot in the gut and the chest. Yet as migrating geese know south from north without the aid of a compass, he knew this blood was his.

CHAPTER 5

IN THE PALOMAR PARKING LOT, AS THE RAIN and the wind painted a procession of colorless spirit shapes on the windshield of the Expedition, Ethan placed a call to Hazard Yancy's cell phone.

Hazard had been born Lester, but he loathed his given name. He didn't like Les any better. He thought the shortened version sounded like an insult.

"I'm not *less* of anything than you are," he'd once said to Ethan, but affably.

Indeed, at six feet four and 240 pounds, with a shaved head that appeared to be as big as a basketball and a neck only slightly narrower than the span of his ears, Hazard Yancy was nobody's idea of a poster child for minimalism.

"Fact is, I'm *more* of a lot of things than some people. Like more determined, more fun, more colorful, more likely to make stupid choices in women, more likely to be shot in the ass. My folks should have named me More Yancy. I could've lived with that."

When he had been a teenager and a young man, his friends had called him Brick, a reference to the fact that he was built like a brick wall.

Nobody in Robbery/Homicide had called him Brick in twenty years. On the force, he was known as Hazard because working a case in tandem with him could be as hazardous as driving a dynamite truck.

Gumshoe duty in Robbery/Homicide might be more dangerous than a career as a greengrocer, but detectives were less likely to die on the job than were night clerks in convenience stores. If you wanted the thrill of being shot at on a regular basis, the Gang Activities Section, the Narcotics Division, and certainly the Strategic Weapons and Tactics teams were better bets than cleaning up after murderers.

Even just staying in uniform promised more violence than hitting the streets in a suit.

Hazard's career was an exception to the rule. People shot at him with regularity.

He professed surprise not at the frequency with which bullets were directed at him, but at the fact that the shooters were people who didn't know him personally. "Being a friend of mine," he once said, "you'd think it would be the other way around, wouldn't you?"

Hazard's uncanny attraction for high-velocity projectiles wasn't a consequence of either recklessness or poor investigative technique. He was a careful, first-rate detective.

In Ethan's experience, the universe didn't always operate like the clockwork mechanism of cause and effect that the scientists so confidently described. Anomalies abounded. Deviations from the common rule, strange conditions, incongruities.

You could make yourself a little crazy, even certifiable, if you insisted that life always proceed according to some this-because-that system of logic. Occasionally you had to accept the inexplicable.

Hazard didn't choose his cases. Like other detectives, he fielded what fate threw at him. For reasons known only to the secret master of the universe, he caught more investigations involving perps who were trigger-happy wackos than he caught cases in which genteel elderly women served poisoned tea to their gentlemen friends.

Fortunately, most shots fired at him missed. He'd been hit just twice: both minor wounds. Two of his partners had sustained injuries more serious than Hazard's, but neither had died or been crippled.

Ethan had worked cases with Hazard during four years of his time on the force. That period constituted the most satisfying police work he'd ever done.

Now, when Yancy answered his cell phone on the third ring, Ethan said, "You still sleeping with an inflatable woman?"

"You applying for the position?"

"Hey, Hazard, you busy right now?"

"Got my foot on a snot-wad's neck."

"Literally?" Ethan asked.

"Figuratively. Was it literally, I'd be stomping his windpipe, and you'd have been forwarded to voice mail."

"If you're about to make a collar—"

"I'm waiting for a comeback from the lab. Won't get it until tomorrow morning."

"How about you and I have lunch, and Channing Manheim pays?"

"As long as that doesn't oblige me to watch any of his shitcan movies."

"Everyone's a critic." Ethan named a famous west-side restaurant where the Face had a standing reservation.

"They have real food or just interior decoration on a plate?" Hazard asked.

"There's going to be fancy carved zucchini cups full of vegetable mousseline, baby asparagus, and patterns drawn with sauces," Ethan admitted. "Would you rather go Armenian?"

"Do I have a tongue? Armenian at one o'clock?"

"I'll be the guy looks like an ex-cop trying to pass for smart."

When he pressed END, terminating the call, Ethan was surprised that he had managed to sound entirely normal.

His hands no longer trembled, but cold greasy fear still crawled restlessly through every turning of his guts. In the rearview mirror, his eyes weren't entirely familiar to him.

Ethan engaged the windshield wipers. He drove out of the Palomar Laboratories parking lot.

In the witches' cauldron of the sky, late-morning light brewed into a thick gloom more suitable to a winter dusk.

Most drivers had switched on their headlights. Bright phantom serpents wriggled across the wet black pavement.

With an hour and fifteen minutes to kill before lunch, Ethan decided to pay a visit to the living dead.

CHAPTER 6

OUR LADY OF ANGELS HOSPITAL WAS A TALL white structure with ziggurat-style step-backs in its higher floors, crowned with a series of diminishing plinths that supported a final column. Aglow in the storm, a dome light capped the high column and was itself surmounted by a radio mast with a winking red aircraft-warning beacon.

The hospital seemed to signal mercy to sick souls across the Angelean hills and into the densely populated flatlands. Its tapered shape suggested a rocket ship that might carry to Heaven those whose lives could not be saved either by medicine or by prayer.

Ethan first stopped in the men's lavatory off the ground-floor lobby, where he washed his hands vigorously at one of the sinks. The lab technician had not scraped every trace of blood from under his fingernails.

The liquid soap in the dispenser proved to have a strong orange fragrance. The lavatory smelled like a citrus orchard by the time that he finished.

Much hot water and much rubbing left his skin a boiled red. He could see no slightest stain remaining. Nevertheless Ethan felt that his hands were still unclean.

He was troubled by the disturbing notion that as long as even a few molecules of that stigmatic residue of his foretold death clung to his hands, the Reaper would track him down by smell and cancel the reprieve that had been granted to him.

Studying his reflection in the mirror, he half expected to see through his body, as through a sheer curtain, but he was solid.

Sensing in himself the potential for obsession, concerned that he might wash his hands without surcease, until they were scrubbed raw, he quickly dried them on paper towels and left the men's room.

He shared an elevator with a solemn young couple holding hands for mutual strength. "She'll be all right," the man murmured, and the woman nodded, eyes bright with repressed tears.

When Ethan got off at the seventh floor, the young couple rode farther up to higher misery.

Duncan "Dunny" Whistler had been abed here on the seventh floor for three months. Between confinements to the intensive care unit—also on this floor—he was assigned to different rooms. During the five weeks since his most recent crisis, he'd been in Room 742.

A nun with a kind Irish face made eye contact with Ethan, smiled, and passed by with nary a swish of her voluminous habit.

The order of sisters that operated Our Lady of Angels rejected the modern garb of many nuns, which resembled the uniforms of airline flight attendants. They favored instead the traditional floor-length habits with commodious sleeves, guimpes, and winged wimples.

Their habits were radiant white, rather than white and black. When Ethan saw them gliding ethereally along these halls, seeming less to walk than to drift like spirits, he could almost believe that the hospital did not occupy only Los Angeles real estate, but bridged this world and the next.

Dunny had existed in a limbo of sorts, between worlds, ever since four angry men shoved his head in a toilet bowl once too often and held him under too long. The paramedics had pumped the water out of his lungs, but the doctors hadn't been able to stir him from his coma.

When Ethan arrived at Room 742, he found it in deep shadow. An old man rested in the bed nearest the door: unconscious, hooked to a ventilator that pumped air into him with a rhythmic wheeze.

The bed nearest the window, where Dunny had spent the past five weeks, stood unoccupied. The sheets were crisp, fresh, luminous in the gloom.

Drowned daylight projected vague gray images of ameboid rain tracks from the window glass onto the bed. The sheets appeared to be acrawl with transparent spiders.

When he saw that the patient's chart was missing, Ethan figured that Dunny had been moved to another room or transferred to the ICU yet again.

At the seventh-floor nurses' station, when he inquired as to where he might find Duncan Whistler, a young nurse asked him to wait for the shift supervisor, whom she paged.

Ethan knew the supervisor, Nurse Jordan, from previous visits. A black woman with a drill sergeant's purposeful carriage and the soft smoky voice of a chanteuse, she arrived at the nurses' station with the news that Dunny had passed away that morning.

"I'm so sorry, Mr. Truman, but I called both numbers you gave us and left voice-mail messages."

"When would this have been?" he asked.

"He passed away at ten-twenty this morning. I phoned you about fifteen or twenty minutes later."

At approximately ten-forty, Ethan had been at Rolf Reynerd's apartment door, trembling with the memory of his foreseen death, pretending to be looking for the nonexistent Jim Briscoe. He'd left his cell phone in the Expedition.

"I know you weren't that close to Mr. Whistler," said Nurse Jordan, "but it's still something of a shock, I'm sure. Sorry you had to learn this way—the empty bed."

"Was the body taken down to the hospital garden room?" Ethan asked.

Nurse Jordan regarded him with new respect. "I didn't realize you were a police officer, Mr. Truman."

Garden room was cop lingo for *morgue.* All those corpses waiting to be planted.

"Robbery/Homicide," he replied, not bothering to explain that he had left the force, or why.

"My husband's worn out enough uniforms to retire in March. I'm workin' overtime so I don't go crazy."

Ethan understood. Cops often went through long law-enforcement careers without worrying much about the dust-to-dust-ashes-to-ashes business, only to tighten with tension so much in the last months before retirement that they needed to eat Metamucil by the pound to stop retaining. The worry could be even worse for spouses.

"The doctor signed a certification of death," Nurse Jordan said, "and Mr. Whistler went down to cold holding pending mortuary pickup. Oh . . . actually, it won't be a mortuary, will it?"

"It's a murder now," Ethan said. "The medical examiner's office will want him for an autopsy."

"Then they'll have been called. We've got a foolproof system." Checking her watch, she said, "But they probably haven't had time to take custody of the body yet, if that's what you're wondering."

Ethan rode the elevator all the way down to the dead. The garden room was in the third and lowest level of the basement, adjacent to the ambulance garage.

Descending, he was serenaded by an orchestrated version of an old Sheryl Crow tune with all the sex squeezed out of it and with a perkiness squeezed in, retaining only the skin of the melody to wrap a different and less tasty variety of sausage. In this fallen world, even the most insignificant things, like pop tunes, were inevitably corrupted.

He and Dunny, both thirty-seven now, had been each other's best friends from the age of five until they were twenty. Raised in the same worn-down neighborhood of crumbling stucco bungalows, each had been an only child, and they'd been as close as brothers.

Shared deprivation had bonded them, as had the emotional and the physical pain of living under the thumb of alcoholic fathers with fiery tempers. And a fierce desire to prove that even the sons of drunks, of poverty, could *be* someone, someday.

Seventeen years of estrangement, during which they had rarely spoken, dulled Ethan's sense of loss. Yet even with everything else that weighed on his mind right now, he was drawn into a melancholy consideration of what might have been.

Dunny Whistler cut the bond between them with his choice of a life outside the law even as Ethan had been training to enforce it. Poverty and the chaos of living under the rule of a selfish drunk had given birth in Ethan to a respect for self-discipline, for order, and for the rewards of a life lived in service to others. The same experiences had made Dunny yearn for buckets of money and for power sufficient to ensure that no one would ever again dare to tell him what to do or ever again make him live by rules other than his own.

In retrospect, their responses to the same stresses had been diverging since their early teens. Maybe friendship had too long blinded Ethan to the growing differences between them. One had chosen to seek respect through accomplishment. The other wanted that respect which comes with being feared.

Furthermore, they had been in love with the same woman, which might have split up even blood brothers. Hannah had come into their lives when they were all seven years old. First she had been one of the guys, the only kid they admitted to their previously two-boy games. The three had been inseparable. Then Hannah gradually became both friend *and* surrogate sister, and the boys swore to protect her. Ethan could never mark the day when she ceased to be just a friend, just a sister, and became for both him and Dunny . . . beloved.

Dunny desperately wanted Hannah, but lost her. Ethan didn't merely want Hannah; he cherished her, won her heart, married her.

For twelve years, he and Dunny had not spoken, not until the night that Hannah died in this same hospital.

Leaving the ruination of Sheryl Crow in the elevator, Ethan followed a wide and brightly lighted corridor with white painted-concrete walls. In place of ersatz music, the only sound was the faint but authentic buzz of the fluorescent tubes overhead.

Double doors with square portholes opened onto the reception area of the garden room.

At a battered desk sat a fortyish, acne-scarred man in hospital greens. A desk plaque identified him as VIN TOLEDANO. He looked up from a paperback novel that featured a grotesque corpse on the cover.

Ethan asked how he was doing, and the attendant said he was alive so he must be doing all right, and Ethan said, "Little over an hour ago, you received a Duncan Whistler from the seventh floor."

"Got him on ice," Toledano confirmed. "Can't release him to a mortuary. Coroner gets him first 'cause it's a homicide."

Only one chair was provided for visitors. Transactions involving perishable cadavers were generally conducted expeditiously, with no need of waiting-room comfort and dog-eared old magazines.

"I'm not with a mortuary," said Ethan. "I was a friend of the deceased. I wasn't here when he died."

"Sorry, but I can't let you see the body right now."

Sitting in the visitors' chair, Ethan said, "Yeah, I know."

To prevent defense attorneys from challenging autopsy results in court, an official chain of custody for the cadaver had to be maintained, ensuring that no outsider could tamper with it.

"There's no family left to ID him, and I'm the executor of the estate," Ethan explained. "So if they're going to want me to confirm identity, I'd rather do it here than later at the city morgue."

Putting aside his paperback, Toledano said, "This guy I grew up with, last year he gets himself thrown out of a car at like ninety miles an hour. It's hard losing a good friend young."

Ethan couldn't pretend to grieve, but he was grateful for any conversation that took his mind off Rolf Reynerd. "We hadn't been close in a long time. Didn't talk for twelve years, then only three times in the past five."

"But he made you executor?"

"Go figure. I didn't know about that till Dunny was here two days in the ICU. Got a call from his lawyer, tells me not only I'm the executor if Dunny dies, but meanwhile I have power of attorney to handle his affairs and make medical decisions on his behalf."

"Must've still been something special there between you."

Ethan shook his head. "Nothing."

"Must've been something," Vin Toledano insisted. "Childhood friendships, they're deeper than you know. You don't see each other forever, then you meet, and it's like no time passed."

"Wasn't that way with us." But Ethan knew that the something special between him and Dunny had been Hannah and their love for her. To change the subject, he said, "So how does your friend come to be pushed out of a car doing ninety?"

"He was a great guy, but he always thought more with his little head than his big one."

"That's not an exclusive club."

"He's in a bar, sees three hotties, no guys with them, so he moves in. All three come on to him, say let's go back to our place, and he figures he's so Brad Pitt they want to three-on-one him."

"But it's a robbery setup," Ethan guessed.

"Worse. He leaves his car, rides in theirs. Two girls get him hot in the backseat, half undress him—then push him out for fun."

"So the hotties were hopped on something."

"Maybe so, maybe not," said Toledano. "Turns out they'd done it twice before. This time they got caught."

Ethan said, "I came across this old movie on TV the other night. Frankie Avalon, Annette Funicello. One of those beach-party flicks. Women sure were different back then."

"So was everybody. Nobody's got better or nicer since the mid-sixties. Wish I'd been born thirty years sooner. So how'd yours die?"

"Four guys thought he'd cheated them out of some money, so they thumped him a little, taped his wrists behind his back, and submerged his head in a toilet long enough to cause brain damage."

"Man, that's ugly."

"It's not Agatha Christie," Ethan agreed.

"But you're dealing with all this, it proves there must've been something left between you and your buddy. Nobody has to be executor of an estate, they don't want to be."

Two meat haulers from the medical examiner's office pushed open the double doors and entered the garden-room reception area.

The first guy was tall, in his fifties, and obviously proud about having kept all his hair. He wore it in a pompadour elaborate enough that it should have been finished with bows.

Ethan knew Pomp's partner. Jose Ramirez was a stocky Mexican-American with myopic eyes and with the sweet dreamy smile of a koala bear.

Jose lived for his wife and four children. While Pomp dealt with the paperwork supplied by the attendant, Ethan asked Jose to see the latest wallet photographs of Maria and the kids.

Once formalities were completed, Toledano led them through an inner door, into the garden room. Instead of a vinyl-tile floor as in the reception area, this chamber featured white ceramic tile with only sixteenth-inch grout joints: an easy surface to sterilize in the event that it became contaminated with bodily fluids.

Although continually cycled through sophisticated filters, the cold air carried a faint but unpleasant scent. Most people didn't die smelling of shampoo, soap, and cologne.

Four standard stainless-steel morgue drawers might have held bodies, but two cadavers on gurneys made an immediate impression. Both were draped with sheets.

A third gurney stood empty, trailing a tangled shroud, and to this one Toledano proceeded with a stupefied expression. "This was him. Right here."

Frowning with confusion, Toledano peeled the sheets back from the heads of the other two cadavers. Neither was Dunny Whistler.

One at a time, he pulled open the four stainless-steel drawers. They were empty.

Because the hospital sent the vast majority of its patients home rather than to funeral services, this garden room was small by the standards of the city morgue. All possible hiding places had already been explored.

CHAPTER 7

I N THIS WINDOWLESS CHAMBER THREE STORIES underground, the four living and the two dead were for a moment so silent that Ethan imagined he could hear rain falling in the streets far above.

Then the meat hauler with the pompadour said, "You mean you released Whistler to the wrong people?"

The attendant, Toledano, shook his head adamantly. "No way. Never did in fourteen years, not startin' today."

A wide door allowed bodies on gurneys to be conveyed directly from the garden room into the ambulance garage. Two deadbolts should have secured it. Both were disengaged.

"I left them locked," Toledano insisted. "They're always locked, *always*, 'cept when I'm overseeing a dispatch, and then I'm always here, right here, watching."

"Who'd want to steal a stiff?" Pomp asked.

"Even some perv wanted to steal one, he couldn't," Vin Toledano said, pulling open the door to the garage to reveal that it lacked keyholes on the outside. "Two blind locks. No keys ever made for it. Can't unlock this door unless you're already here in this room, then you use the thumb-turns."

The attendant's voice had been quickly worn thin by worry. Ethan figured that Toledano saw his job going down the drain as surely as blood was drawn by gravity down the gutters of an inclined autopsy table.

Jose Ramirez said, "Maybe he wasn't dead, you know, so he walked out himself."

"He's deader than dead," Toledano said. "Total damn dead."

With a slump-shouldered shrug and a koala smile, Jose said, "Mistakes happen."

"Not in this hospital, they don't," the attendant insisted. "Not since once fifteen years ago, when this old lady was in cold holding almost an hour, certified dead, and then she sits up and screams."

"Hey, I remember hearing about that," said Pomp. "Some nun had herself a heart attack over it."

"Who had the heart attack was the guy in this job before me, and it was the nun chewin' him out that gave it to him."

Stooping, Ethan extracted a white plastic bag from under the gurney that had held Dunny's body. The bag featured drawstrings, to one of which had been tied a tag that bore the name DUNCAN EUGENE WHISTLER, his date of birth, and his social-security number.

With a wheeze of panic in his voice, Toledano said, "That held the clothes he was wearing when he was admitted to the hospital."

Now the bag proved empty. Ethan put it on top of the gurney. "Ever since the old lady woke up fifteen years ago, you double-check the doctors?"

"Triple-check, quadruple-check," Toledano declared. "First thing a deader comes in here, I stethoscope him, listen for heart and lung action. Use the diaphragm side to hear high-pitched sounds, bell side for low-pitched." He nodded continually, as though while he talked he were mentally reviewing a checklist of steps he'd taken on receipt of Dunny's body. "Do a mirror test for breath. Then establish internal body temp, take it again a half-hour later, then a half-hour after that, to see is it dropping like it should if what you've got is really a deader."

Pomp found this amusing. "Internal temperature? You mean you spend your time shovin' thermometers up dead people's butts?"

Unamused, Jose said, "Have some respect," and crossed himself.

Ethan's palms were damp. He blotted them on his shirt. "Well, if nobody could get in here to take him, and if he was dead—where is he now?"

"Probably one of the sisters jerking your chain," Pomp told the morgue attendant. "Those nuns are jokers."

Cold air, snow-white ceramic tile, stainless-steel drawer fronts glistening like ice: None of it accounted for the depth of Ethan's chill.

He suspected that the subtle scent of death had saturated his clothing.

Places like this had never in the past disturbed him. He was disturbed now.

In the space labeled NEXT OF KIN OR RESPONSIBLE PARTY, the hospital paperwork listed Ethan's name and telephone numbers; nevertheless, he gave the harried attendant a card with the same information.

Ascending in the elevator, he half listened to one of Barenaked Ladies' best songs reduced to nap music.

He went all the way up to the seventh floor, where Dunny had died. When the elevator doors opened, he realized that he had needed to go only as high as the garage on the first subterranean level, where he'd parked the Expedition, just two floors above the garden room.

After pressing the button for the main garage level, he rode up to the fifteenth floor before the cab started down again. People got on the elevator, got off, but Ethan hardly noticed them.

His racing mind took him elsewhere. The incident at Reynerd's apartment. Dead Dunny's disappearance.

Badgeless, Ethan nonetheless retained a cop's intuition. He understood that two such extraordinary events, occurring in the same morning, could not be coincidental.

The power of intuition alone, however, wasn't sufficient to suggest the nature of the link between these uncanny occurrences. He might as well try to perform brain surgery by intuition.

Logic didn't offer immediate answers, either. In this case, even Sherlock Holmes might have despaired at the odds of discovering the truth through deductive reasoning.

In the garage, an arriving car traveled the rows in search of a parking space, turned a corner onto a down ramp, and another car came up out of the concrete abyss, behind headlights, like a deep-salvage submersible ascending from an ocean trench, and drove toward the exit, but Ethan alone was on foot.

Mottled by years of sooty exhaust fumes that formed enigmatic and taunting Rorschach blots, the low gray ceiling appeared to press lower, lower, as he walked farther into the garage. Like the hull of a submarine, the walls seemed barely able to hold back a devastating weight of sea, a crushing pressure.

Step by step, Ethan expected to discover that he wasn't after all alone on foot. Beyond each SUV, behind every concrete column, an old friend might wait, his condition mysterious and his purpose unknowable.

Ethan reached the Expedition without incident.

No one waited for him in the vehicle.

Behind the steering wheel, even before he started the engine, he locked the doors.

CHAPTER 8

THE ARMENIAN RESTAURANT ON PICO BOULE-
vard had the atmosphere of a Jewish delicatessen, a menu featuring food so delicious that it would inspire a condemned man to
smile through his last meal, and more plainclothes cops and film-
industry types together in one place than you would find anywhere
outside of the courtroom devoted to the trial of the latest spouse-
murdering celebrity.

When Ethan arrived, Hazard Yancy waited in a booth by a window.
Even seated, he loomed so large that he would have been well advised
to audition for the title role in *The Incredible Hulk* if Hollywood ever
made a black version.

Hazard had already been served a double order of the kibby appe-
tizer with cucumbers, tomatoes, and pickled turnip on the side.

As Ethan sat across the table from the big detective, Hazard said,
"Somebody told me they saw in the news your boss got twenty-seven
million bucks for his last two movies."

"Twenty-seven million *each*. He's the first to break through the
twenty-five-million ceiling."

"Up from poverty," Hazard said.

"Plus he's got a piece of the back end."

"That kind of money, he can get a piece of anybody's back end he wants."

"It's an industry phrase. Means if the picture is a big hit, he gets a share of the profits, sometimes even a percentage of gross."

"How much might that amount to?"

"According to *Daily Variety,* he's had worldwide hits so big he sometimes walks away with fifty million, thereabouts."

"You read the show-biz press now?" Hazard asked.

"Helps me stay aware of how big a target he's making himself."

"You got your work cut out for you, all right. How many movies does the man do a year?"

"Never fewer than two. Sometimes three."

"I was planning to chow down so much on his dime, Mr. Channing Manheim himself would notice, and you'd get fired for abusing your credit-card privileges."

"Even you can't eat a hundred thousand bucks' worth of kibby."

Hazard shook his head. "Chan the Man. Maybe I'm not hip anymore, but I don't see him being fifty million cool."

"He also owns a TV-production company with three shows currently on major networks, four on cable. He pulls in a few million a year from Japan, doing TV commercials for their top-selling beer. He has a line of sports clothes. Lots more. His agents call the nonacting income 'additional revenue streams.' "

"People just pissing money on him, huh?"

"He'll never need to shop for bargains."

When the waitress came to the table, Ethan ordered Moroccan salmon with couscous, and iced tea.

Taking Hazard's order, she wore the point off her pencil: lebne with string cheese and extra cucumbers, hummus, stuffed grape leaves, lahmajoon flatbread, seafood tagine. . . . "Plus give me two of those little bottles of Orangina."

"Only person I ever saw eat that much," Ethan said, "was this bulimic ballerina. She went to the john to puke after every course."

"I'm just sampling, and I never wear a tutu." Hazard cut his last kibby in two. "So how big an asshole is Chan the Man?"

The masking roar of other lunchtime conversations provided Ethan and Hazard with privacy nearly equal to that on a remote Mojave hill.

"It's impossible to hate him," Ethan said.

"That's your best compliment?"

"It's just that in person he doesn't have the impact he does on the screen. He doesn't stir your emotions one way or the other."

Hazard forked half a kibby into his mouth and made a small sound of pleasure. "So he's all image, no substance."

"That's not quite it. He's so . . . bland. Generous to employees. Not arrogant. But there's this . . . this weightlessness about him. He's sort of careless how he treats people, even his own son, but it's a *benign* indifference. He's not an actively bad guy."

"That money, that much adoration, you expect a monster."

"With him, you don't get it. You get . . ."

Ethan paused to think. In the months he'd worked for Manheim, he had not spoken this much or this frankly about the man to anyone.

He and Hazard had been shot at together, and each had trusted his life to the other. He could speak his mind and know that nothing he said would be repeated.

With such a confidential sounding board, he wanted to describe the Face not only as honestly as possible but as perceptively. In explaining Manheim to Hazard, he also might be able more fully to explain the actor to himself.

After the waitress brought iced tea and the Oranginas, Ethan at last said, "He's self-absorbed but not in the usual movie-star way, not in any way that makes him appear egotistical. He cares about the money, I guess, but I don't think he cares what anyone thinks of him or that he's famous. He's self-absorbed, all right, totally self-absorbed, but it's like this . . . this Zen state of self-absorption."

"Zen state?"

"Yeah. Like life is about him and nature, him and the cosmos, not him and other people. He always seems to be half in a meditative state, not entirely here with you, like some con-man yogi pretending to be otherworldly, except he's sincere. If he's always contemplating the universe, then he's also confident the universe is contemplating him, that their fascination is mutual."

Having finished the last of his kibby, Hazard said, "Spencer Tracy, Clark Gable, Jimmy Stewart, Bogart—were they all airheads, and nobody knew it, or in those days were movie stars real men with their feet on the ground?"

"Some real people are still in the business. I met Jodie Foster, Sandra Bullock. They seem real."

"They seem like they could kick ass, too," Hazard said.

Two waitresses were required to bring all the food to the table.

Hazard grinned and nodded as each dish was placed before him: "Nice. Nice. That's nice. Real nice. Oh, very nice."

The memory of being shot in the gut spoiled Ethan's appetite. As he picked at his Moroccan salmon and couscous, he delayed bringing up the issue of Rolf Reynerd. "So you said you've got one foot on some snot-wad's neck. What's the case?"

"Twenty-two-year-old blond cutie strangled, dumped in a sewage-treatment slough. We call it Blonde in the Pond."

Any cop who works homicides is changed forever by his job. The victims haunt him with the quiet insistence of spirochetes spinning poison in the blood.

Humor is your best and often only defense against the horror. Early in the investigation, every killing is given a droll name, which is thereafter used within the Homicide Division.

Your ranking officer would never ask, *Are you making progress on the Ermitrude Pottlesby murder?* It would always be, *Anything new with Blonde in the Pond?*

When Ethan and Hazard worked the brutal murders of two lesbians of Middle Eastern descent, the case had been called Lezzes in Fezzes. Another young woman, tied to a kitchen table, had choked to death on steel-wool pads and Pine-Sol-soaked sponges that her killer had forced into her mouth and down her throat; her case was Scrub Lady.

Outsiders would probably be offended to hear the unofficial case names. Civilians didn't realize that detectives often dreamed about the dead for whom they sought justice, or that a detective could occasionally become so attached to a victim that the loss felt personal. No disrespect was ever intended by these case names—and sometimes they expressed a strange, melancholy affection.

"Strangled," Ethan said, referring to Blonde in the Pond. "Which suggests passion, a good chance it was someone romantically involved with her."

"Ah. So you haven't gone entirely soft in your expensive leather jackets and your Gucci loafers."

"I'm wearing Rockports, not loafers. Dumping her in a sewage slough probably means he caught her screwing around, so he considers her filthy, a worthless piece of crap."

"Plus maybe he had knowledge of the treatment plant, knew an easy way to get the body in there. Is that a cashmere sweater?"

"Cotton. So your perp works at the plant?"

Hazard shook his head. "He's a member of the city council."

At once losing his appetite altogether, Ethan put down his fork. "A politician? Why don't you just find a cliff and jump?"

Shoving a stuffed grape leaf in his maw, Hazard managed to grin while he chewed, without once opening his mouth. After swallowing, he said, "I've already got a cliff, and I'm pushing *him* off."

"Anybody winds up broken on the rocks, it'll be you."

"You've just taken the cliff metaphor one step too far," said Hazard, spooning hummus into a pita wedge.

After a half-century of squeaky-clean public officials and honest administration, California itself had lately become a deep sewage slough not seen since the 1930s and '40s when Raymond Chandler had written about its dark side. Here in the early years of the new millennium, on a state level and in too many local jurisdictions, corruption had attained a degree of rot seldom seen outside a banana republic, though in this case a banana republic without bananas and with pretensions to glamour.

A significant percentage of the politicians here operated like thugs. If the thugs saw you going after one of their own, they would assume you'd come after them next, and they would use their power to ruin you one way or another.

In another gangster-ridden era, in a crusade against corruption, Eliot Ness had led a force of law-enforcement agents so beyond reach by bribery and so undeterred by bullets that they became known as the Untouchables. In contemporary California, even Ness and his exemplary crew would be destroyed not by bribes or bullets, but by bureaucracy wielded as ruthlessly as an ax and by slander eagerly converted to libel by a feeding-frenzy media with a sentimental affection for the thugs, both the elected and unelected varieties, upon whom they daily reported.

"If you were still doing real work like me," Hazard said, "you'd handle this no different than I'm handling it."

"Yeah. But I sure wouldn't sit there grinning about it."

Indicating Ethan's sweater, Hazard said, "Cotton—like Rodeo Drive cotton?"

"Cotton like Macy's on-sale cotton."

"How much you pay for a pair of socks these days?"

Ethan said, "Ten thousand dollars."

He'd been hesitant to bring up the Rolf Reynerd situation. Now he figured he could do nothing better for Hazard than distract him from this suicidal mission to nail a city councilman for murder.

"Take a look at these." He opened a nine-by-twelve manila envelope, withdrew the contents, and passed them across the table.

As Hazard reviewed what he'd been given, Ethan told him about the five black boxes delivered by Federal Express and the sixth thrown over the gate.

"They came by Federal Express, so you know who sent them."

"No. The return addresses were fake. They were dropped off at different mom-and-pop mailbox shops that collect for FedEx and UPS. The sender paid cash."

"How much mail does Channing get a week?"

"Maybe five thousand pieces. But almost all of it is sent to the studio where it's known he has offices. A publicity firm reviews it and responds. His home address isn't a secret, but it's not widely known, either."

In the envelope were high-resolution computer printouts of six digital photographs taken in Ethan's study, the first of which showed a small jar standing on a white cloth. Beside the jar lay the lid. Spread across the cloth were what had been the contents of the jar: twenty-two beetles with black-spotted orange shells.

"Ladybugs?" Hazard asked.

"The entomological name is *Hippodamia convergens*, of the family Coccinellidae. Not that I think it matters, but I looked it up."

Hazard's shrewd expression spoke clearly enough without words, but he said, "You're stumped worse than a quadruple amputee."

"This guy thinks I'm Batman, he's the Riddler."

"Why twenty-two bugs? Is the number significant?"

"I don't know."

"They alive when you received them?" Hazard asked.

"All dead. Whether they were alive when he sent them, I don't know, but they looked like they'd been dead for a while. The shells were intact, but the more delicate bug parts were withered, crumbly."

In the second photo, a collection of different, spirally coiled, light brown shells were canted at angles in a gray pile of sludge that had been emptied from a black box onto a sheet of waxed paper.

"Ten dead snails," Ethan said. "Well, actually, two were alive but feeble when I opened the box."

"That's a fragrance Chanel won't be bottling."

Hazard paused to fork up some seafood tagine.

The third photo was of a small, clear-glass, screw-top jar. The label had been removed, but the lid indicated that the container had once held pickle relish.

Because the photograph wasn't clear enough to reveal the murky contents of the jar, Ethan said, "Floating in formaldehyde were these ten pieces of translucent tissue with a pale pinkish tint. Tubelike structures. Hard to describe. Like tiny exotic jellyfish."

"You took 'em to a lab?"

"Yeah. When they gave me the analysis, they also gave me a weird look. What I had in the jar were foreskins."

Hazard's jaws locked in midchew, as if the seafood tagine had hardened like a dental mold.

"Ten foreskins from grown men, not infants," Ethan amplified.

After chewing mechanically, not with his former relish, and after swallowing with a grimace, Hazard said, "Ouch. How many grown men get themselves circumcised?"

"They're not standing in line for it," Ethan agreed.

CHAPTER 9

CORKY LAPUTA THRIVED IN THE RAIN.
He wore a long shiny yellow slicker and a droopy yellow rain
hat. He was as bright as a dandelion.

The slicker had many inside pockets, deep and weatherproof.

In his tall black rubber boots, two layers of socks kept his feet
pleasantly warm.

He yearned for thunder.

He ached for lightning.

Storms in southern California, usually lacking crash and flash,
were too quiet for his taste.

He liked the wind, however. Hissing, hooting, a champion of disorder, it lent a sting to the rain and promised chaos.

Ficus and pine trees shivered, shuddered. Palm fronds clicked and
clattered.

Stripped leaves whirled in ragged green conjurations, short-lived
demons that blew down into gutters.

Eventually, clogging drain grills, the leaves would be the cause of
flooded streets, stalled cars, delayed ambulances, and many small but
welcome miseries.

Here in the blustery, dripping midday, Corky walked a charming residential neighborhood in Studio City. Sowing disorder.

He didn't live here. He never would.

This was a working-class neighborhood, managerial-class at best. Intellectual stimulation in such a place would be hard to find.

He had driven here to take a walk.

Emergency-yellow, blazing canary, he nevertheless passed along these streets with complete anonymity, drawing as little notice as might a ghost whose substance was but a twist of ectoplasmic mist.

He had yet to encounter anyone on foot. Few cars traveled the quiet streets.

The weather kept most people snug indoors.

The glorious rotten weather was Corky's fine conspirator.

At this hour, of course, most residents of these houses were away at work. Toiling, toiling, with stupid purpose.

Because this was a holiday week, children had not gone to school. Today: Monday. Christmas: Friday. Deck the halls.

Some children would be in the company of siblings. A lesser number would be under the protection of a nonworking mother.

Others were home alone.

In this instance, however, children were not Corky's avenue of expression. Here, they were safe from the yellow ghost passing among them.

Anyway, Corky was forty-two. Kids these days were too savvy to open their doors to strange men.

Welcome disorder and lovely decadence had deeply infected the world in recent years. Now the lambs of all ages were growing wary.

He contented himself with lesser outrages, just happy to be out in the storm and doing a little damage.

In one of his capacious inner pockets, he carried a plastic bag of glittering blue crystals. A wickedly powerful chemical defoliant.

The Chinese military had developed it. Prior to a war, their agents would sow this stuff in their enemy's farms.

The blue crystals withered crops through a twelve-month growing cycle. An enemy unable to feed itself cannot fight.

One of Corky's colleagues at the university had accepted a grant to study the crystals for the Department of Defense. They felt an urgent need to find a way to protect against the chemical in advance of its use.

In his lab, the colleague had a fifty-pound drum of the stuff. Corky had stolen one pound.

He wore thin protective latex gloves, which he could easily hide in the great winglike sleeves of his slicker.

The slicker was as much a serape as a coat. The sleeves were so voluminous that he could withdraw his arms from them, search his interior pockets, and slip into the sleeves again with fistfuls of one poison or another.

He scattered blue crystals over primrose and liriope, over star jasmine and bougainvillea. Azaleas and ferns. Carpet roses, lantana.

The rain swiftly dissolved the crystals. The chemical seeped into the roots.

In a week, the plants would yellow, drop leaves. In two weeks, they would collapse in a muck of reeking rot.

Large trees would not be affected by the quantities that Corky could scatter. Lawns, flowers, shrubs, vines, and smaller trees would succumb, however, in satisfying numbers.

He didn't sow death in the landscaping of every house. One out of three, in no apparent pattern.

If an entire block of homes were blighted, neighbors might be drawn closer by the shared catastrophe. If some were untouched, they would become the envy of the afflicted. And might arouse suspicion.

Corky's mission was not merely to cause destruction. Any fool could wreck things. He intended also to spread dissension, distrust, discord, and despair.

Occasionally a dog barked or growled from the shelter of a porch where it was tethered or from within a doghouse behind a board fence or a stone wall.

Corky liked dogs. They were man's best friend, though why they would want to fill that role remained a mystery, considering the vile nature of humanity.

Now and then, when he heard a dog, he fished tasty biscuits from an inner pocket. He tossed them onto porches, over fences.

In the interest of societal deconstruction, he could put aside his love of dogs and do what must be done. Sacrifices must be made.

You can't make an omelet without breaking eggs, and all that.

The dog biscuits were treated with cyanide. The animals would die far faster than the plants.

Few things would spread despair so effectively as the untimely death of a beloved pet.

Corky was sad. Sad for the luckless dogs.

He was happy, too. Happy that in a thousand little ways he daily contributed to the fall of a corrupt order—and therefore to the rise of a better world.

For the same reason that he didn't damage the landscaping at every house, he didn't kill every dog. Let neighbor suspect neighbor.

He wasn't concerned that he would be caught in these poisonings. Entropy, the most powerful force in the universe, was his ally and his protecting god.

Besides, the at-home parents would be watching sleazy daytime talk shows on which daughters revealed to their mothers that they were whores, on which wives revealed to their husbands that they were having affairs with their brothers-in-law.

With school out, the kids would be busy learning homicidal skills from video games. Better yet, the pubescent boys would be surfing the Net for pornography, sharing it with innocent younger brothers, and scheming to rape the little girl next door.

Because he approved of those activities, Corky went about his work as discreetly as possible, so as not to distract these people from their self-destruction.

Corky Laputa was not merely a dreary poisoner. He was a man of many talents and weapons.

From time to time, as he plodded along the puddled walkways, under the drizzling trees, he indulged in melody. He sang "Singin' in the Rain," of course, which might be trite, but which amused him.

He did not dance.

Not that he *couldn't* dance. Although not as limber and as right with rhythm as Gene Kelly, he could dazzle on any dance floor.

Capering along a street in a yellow slicker as roomy as any nun's habit was, however, not wise behavior for an anarchist who preferred anonymity.

The streetside mailbox in front of each house always sported a number. Some boxes featured family names, as well.

Sometimes a name appeared to be Jewish. Stein. Levy. Glickman.

At each of these boxes, Corky paused briefly. He inserted one of the letter-size white envelopes that he carried by the score in another slicker pocket.

On each envelope, a black swastika. In each, two sheets of folded paper certain to instill fear and stoke anger.

On the first page, in bold block letters, were printed the words DEATH TO ALL DIRTY JEWS.

The photo on the second page showed bodies stacked ten deep in the furnace yard of a Nazi concentration camp. Under it in red block letters blazed the message YOU'RE NEXT.

Corky had no prejudice against the Jewish people. He held all races, religions, and ethnic groups in equal contempt.

At other special venues, he had distributed DEATH TO ALL DIRTY CATHOLICS notices, DEATH TO ALL BLACKS, and IMPRISON ALL GUN OWNERS.

For decades, politicians had been controlling the people by dividing them into groups and turning them against one another. All a good anarchist could do was try to intensify the existing hatreds and pour gasoline on the fires that the politicians had built.

Currently, hatred of Israel—and, by extension, all Jews—was the fashionable intellectual position among the most glamorous of media figures, including many nonreligious Jews. Corky was simply giving the people what they wanted.

Azalea to lantana to jasmine vine, dog to dog to mailbox, he journeyed through the rain-swept day. Seeding chaos.

Determined conspirators might be able to blow up skyscrapers and cause breathtaking destruction. Their work was helpful.

Ten thousand Corky Laputas—inventive, diligent—would in their quiet persistent way do more, however, to undermine the foundations of this society than all the suicide pilots and bombers combined.

For every thousand gunmen, Corky thought, *I'd rather have one hate-filled teacher subtly propagandizing in a schoolroom, one day-care worker with an unslakable thirst for cruelty, one atheist priest hiding in cassock and alb and chasuble.*

By a circuitous route, he came within sight of the BMW where he had parked it an hour and a half earlier. Right on schedule.

Spending too much time in a single neighborhood could be risky. The wise anarchist keeps moving because entropy favors the rambler, and motion foils the law.

The dirty-milk clouds had churned lower during his stroll, coagulating into sooty curds. In the storm gloom, in the wet shade of the oak tree, his silver sedan waited as dark as iron.

Trailers of bougainvillea lashed the air, casting off scarlet petals, raking thorny nails against the stucco wall of a house, making sgraffito sounds: *scratch-scratch, screek-screek.*

Wind threw sheets, lashed whips, spun funnels of rain. Rain hissed, sizzled, chuckled, splashed.

Corky's phone rang.

He was still half a block from his car. He would miss the call if he waited to answer it in the BMW.

He slipped his right arm out of its sleeve, under his slicker, and unclipped the phone from his belt.

Arm in sleeve again, phone to ear, toddling along as buttercup-yellow and as smile-evoking as any character in any TV program for children, Corky Laputa was in such a good mood that he answered the call by saying, "Brighten the corner where you are."

The caller was Rolf Reynerd. As thick as Corky was yellow, Rolf thought he'd gotten a wrong number.

"It's me," Corky said quickly, before Reynerd could hang up.

By the time he reached the BMW, he wished he had never answered the phone. Reynerd had done something stupid.

CHAPTER 10

BEYOND THE RESTAURANT WINDOW, FALLING rain as clear as a baby's conscience met the city pavement and flooded the gutters with filthy churning currents.

Studying the photo of the jar full of foreskins, Hazard said, "Ten little hats from ten little proud heads? You think they could be trophies?"

"From men he's murdered? Possible but unlikely. Anybody with that many kills isn't the kind to taunt his victims first with freaky gifts in black boxes. He just *does the job*."

"And if they were trophies, he wouldn't give them away so easy."

"Yeah. They'd be the central theme of his home decor. What I think is he works with stiffs. Maybe in a funeral home or a morgue."

"Postmortem circumcisions." Hazard twisted some string cheese onto his fork as he might have spun up a bite of spaghetti. "Kinky, but it's got to be the answer, 'cause I haven't heard about ten unsolved homicides where it looks like the perp might be a lunatic rabbi." He dunked the string cheese in lebne and continued with lunch.

Ethan said, "I think he harvested these from cadavers for the sole purpose of sending them to Channing Manheim."

"To convey what—that Chan the Man is a prick?"

"I doubt the message is that simple."

"Fame doesn't seem so appealing anymore."

The fourth black box had been larger than the others. Two photos were required to document the contents.

In the first picture stood a honey-colored ceramic cat. The cat stood on its hind paws and held a ceramic cookie in each forepaw. Red letters on its chest and tummy spelled COOKIE KITTEN.

"It's a cookie jar," Ethan said.

"I'm such a good detective, I figured that out all by myself."

"It was filled with Scrabble tiles."

The second photo showed a pile of tiles. In front of the pile, Ethan had used six pieces to spell OWE and WOE.

"The jar contained ninety of each letter: *O, W, E*. Either word could be spelled ninety times, or both words forty-five times side by side. I don't know which he intended."

"So the nutball is saying, 'I owe you woe.' He thinks somehow Manheim has done him wrong, and now it's payback time."

"Maybe. But why in a cookie jar?"

"You could also spell *wow*," Hazard noted.

"Yeah, but then you're left with half the *O*s and all the *E*s not used, and they don't make anything together. Only *owe* or *woe* uses all the letters."

"What about two-word combinations?"

"The first one is *wee woo*. Which could mean 'little love,' I guess, but I don't get the message in that one. The second is *E-W-E*, and *woo* again."

"Sheep love, huh?"

"Seems like a dead end to me. I think *owe woe* is what he intended, one or the other, or both."

Smearing lebne on a slice of lahmajoon flatbread, Hazard said, "Maybe after this we can play Monopoly."

The fifth black box had contained a hardcover book titled *Paws for Reflection*. The cover featured a photo of an adorable golden retriever puppy.

"It's a memoir," Ethan said. "The guy who wrote it—Donald Gainsworth—spent thirty years training guide dogs for the blind and service dogs for people confined to wheelchairs."

"No bugs or foreskins pressed between the pages?"

"Nope. And I checked every page for underlining, but nothing was highlighted."

"It's out of character with the rest. An innocuous little book, even sweet."

"Box number six was thrown over the gate a little after three-thirty this morning."

Hazard studied the last two photos. First, the sutured apple. Then the eye inside. "Is the peeper real?"

"He pried it out of a doll."

"Nevertheless, this one disturbs me most of all."

"Me too. Why you?"

"The apple's the most crafted of the six. It took a lot of care, so it's probably the one he finds most meaningful."

"So far it doesn't mean much to me," Ethan lamented.

Stapled to the last photograph was a Xerox of the typewritten message that had been folded in the seed pocket, under the eye. After reading it twice, Hazard said, "He didn't send anything like this with the first five packages?"

"No."

"Then this is probably the last thing he's sending. He's said everything he wants to say, in symbols and now in words. Now he moves from threats to action."

"I think you're right. But the words are as much of a riddle as the symbols, the objects."

With silvery insistence, headlights cleaved the afternoon gloom.

Radiant wings of water flew up from the puddled pavement, obscuring the tires and lending an aura of supernatural mission to the vehicles that plied the currents of Pico Boulevard.

After a brooding silence, Hazard said, "An apple might symbolize dangerous or forbidden knowledge. The original sin he mentions."

Ethan tried his salmon and couscous again. He might as well have been eating paste. He put down his fork.

"The *seeds* of knowledge have been replaced by the eye," Hazard said, almost more to himself than to Ethan.

A flock of pedestrians hurried past the restaurant windows, bent forward as if resisting a wind greater than the one that the December day exhaled, under the inadequate protection of black umbrellas, like mourners quickening to a grave.

"Maybe he's saying, 'I see your secrets, the source—the seeds—of your evil.' "

"I had a similar thought. But it doesn't feel entirely right, and it doesn't lead me anywhere useful."

"Whatever he means by it," Hazard said, "it bothers me that you have this eye in the apple come just after this book about a guy who raised guide dogs for the blind."

"If he's threatening to blind Manheim, that's bad enough," said Ethan, "but I think he intends worse."

After shuffling through the photos once more, Hazard returned them to Ethan and again addressed the seafood tagine with gusto. "I assume you've got your man well covered."

"He's filming in Florida. Five bodyguards travel with him."

"You don't?"

"Not usually. I oversee all security operations from Bel Air. I talk to the head road warrior at least once a day."

"Road warrior?"

"That's Manheim's little joke. It's what he calls the bodyguards who travel with him."

"That's a joke? I fart funnier than he talks."

"I never claimed he was the king of comedy."

"When somebody tossed the sixth box over the gate last night," Hazard asked, "who was the somebody? Any security tape?"

"Plenty. Including a clear shot of his license plate."

Ethan told him about Rolf Reynerd—though he didn't mention his encounters with the man, neither the one that he knew to be real nor the one that he seemed to have dreamed.

"And what do you want from me?" Hazard asked.

"Maybe you could check him out."

"Check him out? How far? You want me to hold his privates while he turns his head and coughs?"

"Maybe not that far."

"You want I should look for polyps in his lower colon?"

"I already know he doesn't have any criminal priors—"

"So I'm not the first one you're calling in a favor from."

Ethan shrugged. "You know me, I'm a user. No one's safe. It'd be useful to know, does Reynerd have any legally registered firearms."

"You been talking to Laura Moonves over in Support Division?"

"She was helpful," Ethan admitted.

"You should marry her."

"She didn't give me *that* much on Reynerd."

"Even all us morons can see you and her would be as right as bread and butter."

"We haven't even dated in eighteen months," Ethan said.

"That's because you're not as smart as us morons. You're just an idiot. So don't jive me. Moonves could get firearm registrations for you. That's not what you want from me."

While Hazard concentrated on lunch, Ethan gazed into the false twilight of the storm.

After two winters of below-average rainfall, the climatological experts had warned that California was in for a long and disastrous dry spell. As usual, the ensuing dire stories of drought, flooding the media, had proved to be sure predictors of a drowning deluge.

The pregnant belly of the sky hung low and gray and fat, and water broke to announce the birth of still more water.

"I guess what I want from you," Ethan said at last, "is to take a look at the guy up close and tell me what you think of him."

As perceptive as ever, Hazard said, "You've already knocked on his door, haven't you?"

"Yeah. Pretended I'd come to see who lived there before him."

"He creeped you out. Something way different about him."

"You'll see it or you won't," Ethan said evasively.

"I'm a homicide cop. He's not a suspect in any killing. How do I justify this?"

"I'm not asking for an official visit."

"If I don't wave a badge, I won't get past the doorstep, not as mean as I look."

"If you can't, you can't. That's okay."

When the waitress arrived to ask if they wanted anything more, Hazard said, "I love those walnut mamouls. Give me six dozen to go."

"I like a man with a big appetite," she said coyly.

"You, young lady, I could gobble up in one bite," Hazard said, eliciting from her a flush of erotic interest and a nervous laugh.

When the waitress went away, Ethan said, "Six dozen?"

"I like cookies. So where does this Reynerd live?"

Earlier, Ethan had written the address on a slip of paper. He passed it across the table. "If you go, don't go easy."

"Go what—in a tank?"

"Just go ready."

"For what?"

"Probably nothing, maybe something. He's either high wired or a natural-born headcase. And he's got a pistol."

Hazard's gaze tracked across Ethan's face as though reading his secrets as readily as an optical scanner could decipher any bar pattern of Universal Product Code. "Thought you wanted me to check for gun registration."

"A neighbor told me," Ethan lied. "Says Reynerd's a little paranoid, keeps the piece close to himself most of the time."

While Ethan returned the computer-printed photos to the manila envelope, Hazard stared at him.

The papers didn't seem to fit in the envelope at first. Then for a moment the metal clasp was too large to slip through the hole in the flap.

"You have a shaky envelope there," said Hazard.

"Too much coffee this morning," Ethan said, and to avoid meeting Hazard's eyes, he surveyed the lunchtime crowd.

The flogged air of human voices flailed through the restaurant, beat against the walls, and what seemed, on casual attention, to be a celebratory roar sounded sinister when listened to with a more attentive ear, sounded now like the barely throttled rage of a mob, and now like the torment of legions under some cruel oppression.

Ethan realized that he was searching face to face for one face in particular. He half expected to see toilet-drowned Dunny Whistler, dead but eating lunch.

"You've hardly touched your salmon," Hazard said in a tone of voice as close as he could ever get to motherly concern.

"It's off," Ethan said.

"Why didn't you send it back?"

"I'm not that hungry, anyway."

Hazard used his well-worn fork to sample salmon. "It's not off."

"It tastes off to me," Ethan insisted.

The waitress returned with the lunch check and with pink bakery boxes full of walnut mamouls packed in a clear plastic bag bearing the restaurant's logo.

While Ethan fished a credit card from his wallet, the woman waited, her face a clear window to her thoughts. She wanted to flirt more with Hazard, but his daunting appearance made her wary.

As Ethan returned the check with his American Express plastic, the waitress thanked him and glanced at Hazard, who licked his lips with theatrical pleasure, causing her to scurry off like a rabbit that had been so flattered by a fox's admiration that she had almost offered herself for dinner before recovering her survival instinct.

"Thanks for picking up the check," Hazard said. "Now I can say Chan the Man took me to lunch. Though I think these mamouls are going to turn out to be the most expensive cookies I ever ate."

"This was just lunch. No obligations. Like I said, if you can't, you can't. Reynerd's my problem, not yours."

"Yeah, but you've got me intrigued now. You're a better flirt than the waitress."

Midst a clutter of darker emotions, Ethan found a genuine smile.

A sudden change in the direction of the wind threw shatters of rain against the big windows.

Beyond the hard-washed glass, pedestrians and passing traffic appeared to melt into ruin as though subjected to an Armageddon of flameless heat, a holocaust of caustic acid.

Ethan said, "If he's carrying a potato-chip bag, corn chips, anything like that, there might be more than snack food in it."

"This the paranoid part? You said he keeps his piece close."

"That's what I heard. In a potato-chip bag, places like that, where he can reach for it, and you don't realize what he's doing."

Hazard stared at him, saying nothing.

"Maybe it's a nine-millimeter Glock," Ethan added.

"He have a nuclear weapon, too?"

"Not that I know of."

"Probably keeps the nuke in a box of Cheez-Its."

"Just take a bagful of mamouls, and you can handle anything."

"Hell, yeah. Throw one of these, you'd crack a guy's skull."

"Then eat the evidence."

The waitress returned with his credit card and the voucher.

As Ethan added the gratuity and signed the form, Hazard seemed almost oblivious of the woman and did not once look at her.

With needles of rain, the blustering wind tattooed ephemeral patterns on the window, and Hazard said, "Looks cold out there."

That was exactly what Ethan had been thinking.

CHAPTER 11

S LICKERED AND BOOTED, WEARING THE SAME
jeans and wool sweater as before, sitting behind the wheel of his silver BMW, Corky Laputa felt stifled by a frustration as heavy and suffocating as a fur coat.

Although his shirt wasn't buttoned to the top, anger pinched his throat as tight as if he'd squeezed his sixteen-inch neck into a fifteen-inch collar.

He wanted to drive to West Hollywood and kill Reynerd.

Such impulses must be resisted, of course, for though he dreamed of a societal collapse into complete lawlessness, from which a new order would arise, the laws against murder remained in effect. They were still enforced.

Corky was a revolutionary, but not a martyr.

He understood the need to balance radical action with patience.

He recognized the effective limits of anarchic rage.

To calm himself, he ate a candy bar.

Contrary to the claims of organized medicine, both the greed-corrupted Western variety and the spiritually smug Eastern brand, refined sugar did not make Corky hyperkinetic. Sucrose soothed him.

Very old people, nerves rubbed to an excruciating sensitivity by life and its disappointments, had long known about the mollifying effect of excess sugar. The farther their hopes and dreams receded from their grasp, the more their diets sweetened to include ice cream by the quart, rich cookies in giant economy-size boxes, and chocolate in every form from nonpareils to Hershey's Kisses, even to Easter-basket bunnies that they could brutally dismember and consume for a double enjoyment.

In her later years, his mother had been an ice-cream junkie. Ice cream for breakfast, lunch, dinner. Ice cream in parfait glasses, in huge bowls, eaten directly from the carton.

She hogged down enough ice cream to clog a network of arteries stretching from California to the moon and back. For a while Corky had assumed that she was committing suicide by cholesterol.

Instead of spooning herself into heart failure, she appeared to grow healthier. She acquired a glow in the face and a brightness in the eyes that she'd never had before, not even in her youth.

Gallons, barrels, troughs of Chocolate Mint Madness, Peanut-Butter-and-Chocolate Fantasy, Maple Walnut Delight, and a double dozen other flavors seemed to turn back her biological clock as the waters of a thousand fountains had failed to turn back that of Ponce de Leon.

Corky had begun to think that in the case of his mother's unique metabolism, the key to immortality might be butterfat. So he killed her.

If she had been willing to share some of her money while still alive, he would have allowed her to live. He wasn't greedy.

She had not been a believer in generosity or even in parental responsibility, however, and she cared not at all about his comfort or his needs. He'd been concerned that eventually she would change her will and stiff him forever, sheerly for the pleasure of doing so.

In her working years, his mother had been a university professor of economics, specializing in Marxist economic models and the vicious departmental politics of academia.

She had believed in nothing more than the righteousness of envy and the power of hatred. When both beliefs proved hollow, she had not abandoned either, but had supplemented them with ice cream.

Corky didn't hate his mother. He didn't hate anyone.

He didn't envy anyone, either.

Having seen those gods fail his mother, he had rejected both. He did not wish to grow old with no comfort but his favorite premium brand of coconut fudge.

Four years ago, paying her a secret visit with the intention of quickly and mercifully smothering her in her sleep, he had instead beaten her to death with a fireplace poker, as if he were acting out a story begun by Anne Tyler in an ironic mood and roughly finished by a furious Norman Mailer.

Though unplanned, the exercise with the poker proved cathartic. Not that he'd taken pleasure in the violence. He had not.

The decision to murder her had really been as unemotional as any decision to purchase the stock of a blue-chip corporation, and the killing itself had been conducted with the same cool efficiency with which he would have executed any stock-market investment.

Being an economist, his mother surely had understood.

His alibi had been unassailable. He inherited her estate. Life went on. His life, anyway.

Now, as he finished the candy bar, he felt sugar-soothed and chocolate-coddled.

He still wanted to kill Reynerd, but the unwise urgency of the compulsion had passed. He would take time to plan the hit.

When he acted, he would follow his scheme faithfully. This time, pillow would not become poker.

Noticing that the yellow slicker had shed a lot of water on the seat, he sighed but did nothing. Corky was too committed an anarchist to care about the upholstery.

Besides, he had Reynerd to brood about. A perpetual adolescent inside a dour exterior, Rolf had been unable to resist the temptation to deliver the sixth box in person. Looking for a thrill.

The fool had thought that perimeter security cameras did not exist solely because he himself could not spot them.

Are there no other planets in the solar system, Corky had asked him, *just because you can't locate them in the sky?*

When Ethan Truman, Manheim's security chief, came calling, Reynerd had been stunned. By his admission, he behaved suspiciously.

As Corky wadded up the candy wrapper and stuffed it into the trash bag, he wished that he could dispose of Reynerd as easily.

Suddenly rain fell more heavily than at any previous moment of the storm. The deluge knocked stubborn acorns from the oak under which he had parked, and cast them across the BMW. They rattled off the paint work and surely marred it, snapped off the windshield but did not crack it.

He didn't have to sit here, in a danger of acorns, plotting Reynerd's demise, until a rotting thousand-pound limb broke free, fell on the car, and crushed him for his trouble. He could get on with his day and mentally draw up blueprints for the murder while he attended to other business.

Corky drove a few miles to a popular upscale shopping mall and parked in the underground garage.

He got out of the BMW, stripped off his slicker and his droopy rain hat, which he tossed onto the floor of the car. He shrugged into a tweed sports coat that complemented his sweater and jeans.

An elevator carried him from subterranean realms to the highest of two floors of shops, restaurants, and attractions. The arcade was on this top level.

With school out, kids crowded around the arcade games. Most were in their early teens.

The machines beeped, rang, tolled, chimed, bleated, tweedled, whistled, rattattooed, boomed, shrieked, squealed, ululated, roared like gunning engines, emitted scraps of bombastic music, the screams of virtual victims, twinkled, flashed, strobed, and scintillated in all known colors, and swallowed quarters, dollars, more voraciously even than the iconic Pac-Man had once gobbled cookies off a million arcade screens in an era now quaint if not unknown to the current crowd.

Wandering among the machines, Corky distributed free drugs to the kids.

These small plastic bags each contained eight doses of Ecstasy—or Extasy, if you'd gone to a public school—with a block-lettered label that promised FREE X, and then suggested, JUST REMEMBER WHO YOUR FRIEND IS.

He was pretending to be a dealer drumming up business. He never expected to see any of these brats again.

Some kids accepted the packets, thought it was cool.

Others showed no interest. Of those who declined, none made an effort to report him to anyone; nobody liked a rat.

In a few instances, Corky slipped the bags into kids' jacket pockets without their knowledge. Let them find it later, be amazed.

Some would take the stuff. Some would throw it away or give it away. In the end, he would have succeeded in contaminating a few more brains.

Truth: He wasn't interested in creating addicts. He would have given away heroin or even crack cocaine if that had been his goal.

Scientific studies of Ecstasy revealed that five years after taking just a single dose, the user continued to exhibit lingering changes in brain chemistry. After regular use, permanent brain damage could ensue.

Some oncologists and neurologists suggested that in the decades to come, the current high incidence of Ecstasy use would produce a dramatic increase in early-onset cancerous brain tumors, as well as a decrease in the cognitive abilities of hundreds of thousands if not millions of citizens.

Eight-dose giveaways like this would not facilitate the collapse of civilization overnight. Corky was committed to long-term effect.

He never carried more than fifteen bags, and once he started to hand them out, he made a point of ridding himself of them quickly. Too clever to get caught holding, he was in and out of the arcade in three minutes.

Because he didn't need to pause to make a sale, the staff didn't have an opportunity to notice him. By the time he left the arcade, he was just another shopper: nothing incriminating in his pockets.

At a Starbucks, he bought a double latte, and sipped it at one of their tables on the promenade, watching the parade of humanity in all its absurdity.

After finishing the coffee, he went to a department store. He needed socks.

CHAPTER 12

THE TREES, A GROVE OF EIGHT, ROSE ON beautifully gnarled trunks, lifted high their exquisitely twisted branches, shook their graceful gray-green tresses in the wet wind, seeming both to defy the storm and to celebrate it. Fruitless in this season, they cast off no olives, only leaves, upon the cobbled walkway.

Twining through the branches, Christmas lights were unlit at this hour, bulbs of dull color waiting to brighten in the night.

This five-story Westwood condominium, less than one block from Wilshire Boulevard, was neither as grand as some in the neighborhood nor large enough to require a doorman. Nevertheless, the purchase price of an apartment here would gag a sword swallower.

Ethan trod the leaves of peace, passed under the extinguished lights of Christmas, and entered a marble-floored and marble-paneled public foyer. He used a key to let himself through the inner security door.

Past the foyer, the secure lobby was small but cozy, with an area rug to soften the marble, two Art Deco armchairs, and a table with a faux Tiffany lamp in red, amber, and green stained glass.

Although stairs served the five-story building, Ethan took the slow-moving elevator. Dunny Whistler lived—had lived—on the fifth floor.

Each of the first four floors held four large apartments, but the highest was divided into only two penthouse units.

A faint unpleasant odor lingered in the elevator from a recent passenger. Complex and subtle, the scent teased memory, but Ethan could not quite identify it.

As he ascended past the second floor, the elevator cab suddenly impressed him as being smaller than he remembered from previous visits. The ceiling loomed low, like a lid on a cook pot.

Passing the third floor, he realized that he was breathing faster than he should be, as though he were a man on a brisk walk. The air seemed to have grown thin, inadequate.

By the time he reached the fourth floor, he became convinced that he detected a *wrongness* in the sound of the elevator motor, in the hum of cables drawn through guide wheels. This creak, that tick, this squeak might be the sound of a linchpin pulling loose in the heart of the machinery.

The air grew thinner still, the walls closer, the ceiling lower, the machinery more suspect.

Perhaps the doors wouldn't open. The emergency phone might be out of order. His cell phone might not work in here.

In an earthquake, the shaft might collapse, crushing the cab to the dimensions of a coffin.

Nearing the fifth floor, he realized that these symptoms of claustrophobia, which he had never previously experienced, were a mask that concealed another fear, to which he, being a rational man, was loath to admit.

He half expected Rolf Reynerd to be waiting on the fifth floor.

How Reynerd would have known about Dunny or where Dunny lived, how he would have known when Ethan intended to come here—these were questions unanswerable without extensive investigation and perhaps without the abandonment of logic.

Nevertheless, Ethan stepped to the side of the cab, to make a smaller target of himself. He drew his pistol.

The elevator doors opened on a ten-by-twelve foyer paneled in honey-toned, figured anigre. Deserted.

Ethan didn't holster his weapon. Identical doors served two penthouse units, and he went directly to the Whistler apartment.

With the key provided by Dunny's attorney, he unlocked the door, eased it open, and entered cautiously.

The security alarm was not engaged. On his most recent visit, eight days ago, Ethan had set the alarm when he'd left.

The housekeeper, Mrs. Hernandez, had visited in the interim. Before Dunny landed in a hospital, in a coma, she had worked here three days a week; but now she came only on Wednesday.

In all likelihood, Mrs. Hernandez had forgotten to enter the alarm code when she'd departed last week. Yet as likely as this explanation might be, Ethan didn't believe it. Juanita Hernandez was a responsible woman, methodically attentive to detail.

Just inside the threshold, he stood listening. He left the door open at his back.

Rain drummed on the roof, a distant rumble like the marching feet of legions gone to war in some far, hollow kingdom.

Otherwise, only silence rewarded his keen attention. Maybe instinct warned him or maybe imagination misled him, but he sensed that this was not a slack silence, that it was instead a coiled quiet as full of potential energy as a cobra, rattler, or black mamba.

Because he preferred not to draw the attention of a neighbor and didn't want to facilitate any exit but his own, he closed the door. Locked it.

From scams, from drugs, from worse, Duncan Whistler had made himself rich. Criminals routinely grab big money, but few keep it or keep the freedom to spend it. Dunny had been clever enough to avoid arrest, to launder his money, and to pay his taxes.

Consequently, his apartment was enormous, with two connecting hallways, rooms leading into rooms, rooms that ordinarily did not spiral as they seemed to spiral now like nautilus shell into nautilus shell.

Searching in a hostile situation of the usual kind, Ethan would have proceeded with both hands on the gun, with arms out straight, maintaining a measured pressure on the trigger. He would have cleared doorways quick and low.

Instead, he gripped the pistol in his right hand, aimed at the ceiling. He proceeded cautiously but not with the full drama inherent in police-academy style.

To keep his back always to a wall, to avoid turning his back to a doorway, to move fast while scanning left-right-left, to be ever aware of his footing, of the need to stay sufficiently well balanced to assume, in an instant, a shooting stance: Doing all that, he would have had to admit that he was afraid of a dead man.

And there was the truth. Evaded, now acknowledged.

The claustrophobia in the elevator and the expectation that he would find Rolf Reynerd on the fifth floor had been nothing but attempts to deflect himself from consideration of his true fear, from the even less rational conviction that dead Dunny had risen from the morgue gurney and had wandered home with unknowable intent.

Ethan didn't believe that dead men could walk.

He doubted that Dunny, dead or alive, would harm him.

His anxiety arose from the possibility that Duncan Whistler, if indeed he'd left the hospital garden room under his own power, might be Dunny in name only. Having nearly drowned, having spent three months in a coma, he might be suffering brain damage that made him dangerous.

Although Dunny had his good qualities, not least of all the sense to recognize in Hannah a woman of exceptional virtues, he had been capable of ruthless violence. His success in the criminal life had not resulted from polished people skills and a nice smile.

He could break heads when he needed to break them. And sometimes he'd broken them when skull cracking wasn't necessary.

If Dunny were half the man that he'd once been, and the *wrong* half, Ethan preferred not to come face to face with him. Over the years, their relationship had taken peculiar turns; one final and still darker twist in the road could not be ruled out.

The huge living room featured high-end contemporary sofas and chairs, upholstered in wheat-colored silk. Tables, cabinets, and decorative objects were all Chinese antiques.

Either Dunny had discovered a genie-stuffed lamp and had wished himself exquisite taste, or he'd employed a pricey interior designer.

Here high above the olive trees, the big windows revealed the buildings across the street and a sky that looked like the soggy char and ashes of a vast, extinguished fire.

Outside: a car horn in the distance, the low somber grumble of traffic up on Wilshire Boulevard.

The June-bug jitter, scarab click, tumblebug tap of the beetle-voiced rain spoke at the window, *click-click-click.*

In the living room, stillness distilled. Only his breathing. His heart.

Ethan went into the study to seek the source of a soft light.

On the chinoiserie desk stood a bronze lamp with an alabaster shade. The buttery-yellow glow struck iridescent colors from the border of mother-of-pearl inlays.

Previously a framed photograph of Hannah had been displayed on the desk. It was missing.

Ethan recalled his surprise on discovering the photo during his first visit to the apartment, eleven weeks ago, after he had learned that he held authority over Dunny's affairs.

Surprise had been matched by dismay. Although Hannah had been gone for five years, the presence of the picture seemed to be an act of emotional aggression, and somehow an insult to her memory that she should be an object of affection—and once an object of desire—to a man steeped in a life of crime and violence.

Ethan had left the photograph untouched, for even with a power of attorney covering all of Dunny's affairs, he had felt that the picture in the handsome silver frame hadn't been his property either to dispose of or to claim.

At the hospital on the night of Hannah's death, again at the funeral, following twelve years of estrangement, Ethan and Dunny had spoken. Their mutual grief had not, however, brought them together otherwise. They had not exchanged a word for three years.

On the third anniversary of Hannah's passing, Dunny had phoned to say that over those thirty-six months, he had brooded long and hard on her untimely death at thirty-two. Gradually but profoundly, the loss of her—just knowing that she was no longer out there somewhere in the world—had affected him, had changed him forever.

Dunny claimed that he was going to go straight, extract himself from all his criminal enterprises. Ethan had not believed him, but had wished him luck. They had never spoken again.

Later, he heard through third parties that Dunny had gotten out of the life, that old friends and associates never saw him anymore, that he had become something of a hermit, bookish and withdrawn.

With those rumors, Ethan had taken enough salt to work up a thirst for truth. He remained certain that eventually he would learn Duncan Whistler had fallen back into old habits—or had never truly forsaken them.

Later still, he heard that Dunny had returned to the Church, attended Mass each week, and carried himself with a humility that had never before characterized him.

Whether this was true or not, the fact remained that Dunny had held fast to the fortune that he amassed through fraud, theft, and dealing drugs. Living in luxury paid for with such dirty money, any genuinely reformed man might have been racked with guilt until at last he put his riches to a cleansing use.

More than the photograph of Hannah had been taken from the study. An atmosphere of bookish innocence was gone, as well.

A double score of hardcover volumes were stacked on the floor, in a corner. They had been removed from two shelves of the wall-to-wall bookcase.

One of the shelves, which had seemed to be fixed like all the others, had been removed. A section of the bookcase backing, which also had appeared fixed, had been slid aside, revealing a wall safe.

The twelve-inch diameter door of the safe stood open. Ethan felt inside. The spacious box proved empty.

He hadn't known that the study contained a safe. Logic suggested that no one but Dunny—and the installer—would have been aware of its existence.

Brain-damaged man dresses himself. Finds his way home. Remembers the combination to his safe.

Or . . . dead man comes home. In a mood to party, he picks up some spending money.

Dunny dead made nearly as much sense as Dunny with severe brain damage.

CHAPTER 13

FRIC IN A FRACAS: TWO TRAINS CLACKETY-clacking and whistling at key crossroads, Nazis in the villages, American troops fighting their way down from the hills, dead soldiers everywhere, and villainous SS officers in black uniforms herding Jews into the boxcars of a third train stopped at a station, more SS bastards shooting Catholics and burying their bodies in a mass grave here by a pine woods.

Few people knew that the Nazis had killed not only Jews but also millions of Christians. Most of the higher-echelon Nazis had adhered to a strange and informal pagan creed, worshiping land and race and myths of ancient Saxony, worshiping blood and power.

Few people knew, but Fric knew. He liked knowing things that other people didn't. Odd bits of history. Secrets. The mysteries of alchemy. Scientific curiosities.

Like how to power an electric clock with a potato. You needed a copper peg, a zinc nail, and some wire. A potato-powered clock looked stupid, but it worked.

Like the truncated pyramid on the back of the one-dollar bill. It represents the unfinished Temple of Solomon. The eye floating above the pyramid is symbolic of the Grand Architect of the Universe.

Like who built the first elevator. Using alternatively human, animal, and water power, Roman architect Vitruvius constructed the first elevators circa 50 B.C.

Fric knew.

A lot of the weird stuff he knew didn't have much application in daily life, didn't alter the fact that he was short for his age, and thin for his age, or that he had a geeky neck and the huge unreal green eyes that magazine writers slobbered about when describing his mother but that made him look like a cross between a hoot owl and an alien. He liked knowing these weird things anyway, even if they did not lift him out of the mire of Fricdom.

Having exotic knowledge rare in other people made Fric feel like a wizard. Or at least like a wizard's apprentice.

Aside from Mr. Jurgens, who came to the estate two days every month to clean and maintain the large collection of contemporary and antique electric trains, only Fric knew *everything* about the train room and its operation.

The trains belonged to that world-renowned movie star, Channing Manheim, who also happened to be his father. In the private world of Fric, the movie star had long been known as Ghost Dad because he was usually only here in spirit.

Ghost Dad knew very little about the train room. He had spent enough money on the collection to purchase the entire nation of Tuvalu, but he rarely played here.

Most people had never heard of the nation of Tuvalu. On nine islands in the South Pacific Ocean, with a population of just ten thousand, its major exports were copra and coconuts.

Most people had no idea what copra might be. Neither did Fric. He'd been meaning to look it up ever since he'd learned about Tuvalu.

The train room was in the higher of two basements, adjacent to the upper garage. It measured sixty-eight feet by forty-four feet, which amounted to more square footage than in the average home.

The lack of windows ensured that the real world could not intrude. The railroad fantasy ruled.

Along the two short walls, floor-to-ceiling shelves housed the train collection, except for whatever models were currently in use.

On the two long walls hung fabulous paintings of trains. Here, a locomotive exploded through thick luminous masses of fog, headlamp blazing. There, a train traveled a moonlit prairie. Trains of every vintage raced through forests, crossed rivers, climbed mountains in rain and sleet and snow and fog and dark of night, clouds billowing from their smokestacks, sparks flying from their wheels.

At the center of this great space, on a massive table with many legs, stood a sculptured landscape of green hills, fields, forests, valleys, ravines, rivers, lakes. Seven miniature villages comprised of hundreds of intricately detailed structures were served by country lanes, eighteen bridges, nine tunnels. Convex curves, concave curves, horseshoe curves, straightaways, descending grades, and ascending grades featured more train track than there were coconuts in Tuvalu.

This amazing construction measured fifty feet by thirty-two, and you could either walk around it or, by lifting a gate, enter into it and take a tour on an inner racetrack walkway, as though you were a giant vacationing in the land of Lilliput.

Fric was in the thick of it.

He had distributed armies of toy soldiers across this landscape and had been playing trains and war at the same time. Considering the resources at his command for the game, it should have been more fun than it was.

Telephones were located at both the exterior and the interior control stations. When they rang with his personal tone, the sound startled him. He seldom received calls.

Twenty-four phone lines served the estate. Two of these were dedicated to the security system, another to the off-site monitoring of the hotel-type heating and air-conditioning system. Two were fax lines, and two were dedicated Internet lines.

Sixteen of the remaining seventeen lines were rationed to family and staff. Line 24 had a higher purpose.

Fric's father enjoyed the use of four lines because everyone in the world—once even the President of the United States—wanted to talk to him. Calls for Channing—or Chan or Channi, or even (in the case of one infatuated actress) Chi-Chi—often came in even when he wasn't in residence.

Mrs. McBee had four lines, although this didn't mean, as the Ghost Dad sometimes joked, that Mrs. McBee should start to think that she was as important as her boss.

Ha, ha, ha.

One of those four lines served Mr. and Mrs. McBee's apartment. The other three were her business phones.

On an ordinary day, management of the house didn't require those three lines. When Mrs. McBee had to plan and execute a party for four or five hundred Hollywood nitwits, however, three telephones were not always sufficient to deal with the event designer, the food caterer, the florist, the talent bookers, and the uncountable other mysterious agencies and forces that she had to marshal in order to produce an unforgettable evening.

Fric wondered if all that effort and expense was worthwhile. At the end of the night, half the guests departed so drunk or so drug-fried that in the morning they wouldn't remember where they had been.

If you sat them in lawn chairs, gave them bags of burgers, and provided tanker trucks of wine, they would get wasted as usual. Then they'd go home and puke their guts out as usual, collapse into unconsciousness as usual, and wake up the next day none the wiser.

Because he was chief of security, Mr. Truman had two lines in his apartment, one personal and one business.

Only two of the six maids lived on the estate, and they shared a phone line with the chauffeur.

The groundskeeper had a line of his own, but the totally scary chef, Mr. Hachette, and the happy cook, Mr. Baptiste, shared one of Mrs. McBee's lines.

Ms. Hepplewhite, personal assistant to Ghost Dad, had two lines for her use.

Freddie Nielander, the famous supermodel known in Fricsylvania as Nominal Mom, had a dedicated phone line here, although she had divorced Ghost Dad nearly ten years ago and had stayed overnight less than ten times since then.

Ghost Dad once told Freddie that he called her line every now and then, hoping she would answer and would tell him that she had come back to him at last and was home forever.

Ha, ha, ha. Ha, ha, ha.

Fric had enjoyed his own line since he was six. He never called anyone, except once when he'd used his father's contacts to get the unlisted home number for Mr. Mike Myers, the actor, who had dubbed the voice of the title character in *Shrek*, to tell him that *Shrek* absolutely, no doubt about it, *rocked*.

Mr. Myers had been very nice, had done the Shrek voice for him, and lots of other voices, and had made him laugh until his stomach hurt. This injury to his abdominal muscles resulted partly from the fact that Mr. Myers was wickedly funny and partly because Fric had not recently exercised his laugh-muscle group as much as he would have liked.

Fric's father, a believer in a shitload of paranormal phenomena, had set aside the last telephone line to receive calls from the dead. That was a story in itself.

Now, for the first time in eight days, since the Ghost Dad's most recent call, Fric heard his signature tone coming from the train-room phones.

Everyone on the estate had been assigned a different sound for the line or lines that were dedicated to him or her. Each of Ghost Dad's lines produced a simple *brrrrrrr*. Mrs. McBee's signature tone was a series of musical chimes. Mr. Truman's lines played the first nine notes from the theme song of an ancient TV cop show, *Dragnet,* which was stupid, and Mr. Truman thought so, too, but he endured it.

This highly sophisticated telephone system could produce up to twelve different signature tones. Eight were standard. Four—like *Dragnet*—could be custom-designed for the client.

Fric had been assigned the dumbest of the standard tones, which the phone manufacturer described as "a cheerful child-pleasing sound suitable for the nursery or the bedrooms of younger children." Why infants in nurseries or toddlers in cribs ought to have their own telephones remained a mystery to Fric.

Were they going to call Babies R Us and order lobster-flavored teething rings? Maybe they would phone their mommies and say, *Yuch. I crapped in my diaper, and it don't feel good.*

Stupid.

Ooodelee-ooodelee-oo, said the train-room phones.

Fric hated the sound. He had hated it when he'd been six, and he hated it even worse now.

Ooodelee-ooodelee-oo.

This was the annoying sound that might be made by some furry, roly-poly, pink, half-bear, half-dog, half-wit character in a video made for preschoolers who thought stupid shows like *Teletubbies* were the pinnacle of humor and sophistication.

Humiliated even though he was alone, Fric pushed two transformer switches to kill power to the trains, and he answered the phone on the fourth ring. "Bob's Burger Barn and Cockroach Farm," he said. "Our special today is salmonella on toast with coleslaw for a buck."

"Hello, Aelfric," a man said.

Fric had expected to hear his father's voice. If instead he had heard the voice of Nominal Mom, he would have suffered cardiac arrest and dropped dead into the train controls.

The entire estate staff, with the possible exception of Chef Hachette, would have mourned for him. They would have been deeply, terribly sad. Deeply, deeply, terribly, terribly. For about forty minutes. Then they would have been busy, busy, busy preparing for the post-funeral gala to which would be invited perhaps a thousand famous and near-famous drunks, druggies, and butt-kissers eager to plant their lips on Ghost Dad's golden ass.

"Who's this?" Fric asked.

"Are you enjoying the trains, Fric?"

Fric had never heard this voice before. No one on the staff. Definitely a stranger.

Most of the people in the house didn't know that Fric was in the train room, and no one outside the estate could possibly know.

"How do you know about the trains?"

The man said, "Oh, I know lots of things other people don't. Just like you, Fric. Just like you."

The talented hairs on the back of Fric's neck did impressions of scurrying spiders.

"Who are you?"

"You don't know me," the man said. "When does your father return from Florida?"

"If you know so much, why don't you tell me?"

"December twenty-fourth. In the early afternoon. Christmas Eve," the stranger said.

Fric wasn't impressed. Millions of people knew his old man's whereabouts and his Christmas plans. Just a week ago, Ghost Dad had done a spot on *Entertainment Tonight,* talking about the film that he was shooting and about how much he looked forward to going home for the holidays.

"Fric, I'd like to be your friend."

"What're you, a pervert?"

Fric had heard about perverts. Heck, he'd probably met hundreds of them. He didn't know all the things they might do to a kid, and he wasn't *exactly* sure what thing they liked most to do, but he knew they were out there with their collections of kids' eyeballs, wearing necklaces made out of their victims' bones.

"I have no desire to hurt you," said the stranger, which was no doubt what any pervert would have said. "Quite the opposite. I want to help you, Fric."

"Help me do what?"

"Survive."

"What's your name?"

"I don't have a name."

"Everyone has to have a name, even if it's just one, like Cher or Godzilla."

"Not me. I'm only one among multitudes, nameless now. There's trouble coming, young Fric, and you need to be ready for it."

"What trouble?"

"Do you know of a place in your house where you could hide and never be found?" the stranger asked.

"That's a weird-ass question."

"You're going to need a place to hide where no one can find you, Fric. A deep and special secret place."

"Hide from who?"

"I can't tell you that. Let's just call him the Beast in Yellow. But you're going to need a secret place real soon."

Fric knew that he should hang up, that it might be dangerous to play along with this nutball. Most likely he was a pathetic pervert loser who got lucky with a phone number and would sooner or later start with the dirty talk. But the guy might also be a sorcerer who could cast a spell long distance, or he might be an evil psychologist who could hypnotize a boy over the telephone and make him rob liquor stores and then make him turn over all the money while clucking like a chicken.

Aware of those risks and many more, Fric nevertheless stayed on the line. This was by far the most interesting phone conversation he'd ever had.

Just in case this guy with no name happened to be the one from whom he might need to hide, Fric said, "Anyway, I've got bodyguards, and they carry submachine guns."

"That's not true, Aelfric. Lying won't get you anything but misery. There's heavy security on the estate, but it won't be good enough when the time comes, when the Beast in Yellow shows up."

"It is true," Fric deceitfully insisted. "My bodyguards are former Delta Force commandos, and one of them was even Mr. Universe before that. They can for sure kick major ass."

The stranger didn't respond.

After a couple seconds, Fric said, "Hello? You there?"

The man spoke in a whisper now. "Seems like I have a visitor, Fric. I'll call you again later." His whisper subsided to a murmur that Fric had to strain to hear. "Meanwhile, you start looking for that deep and special hiding place. There's not much time."

"Wait," Fric said, but the line went dead.

CHAPTER 14

G UN READY, MUZZLE UP, CHAMBER BY HALL by chamber, through Dunny Whistler's nautilus apartment, Ethan came to the bedroom.

One nightstand lamp had been left on. Against the headboard of the Chinese sleigh bed, decorative silk pillows fashioned from cheongsam fabrics had been artfully arranged by the housekeeper.

Also on the bed, cast off with evident haste, lay articles of men's clothing. Wrinkled, stained, still damp from the rain. Slacks, shirt, socks, underwear.

Tumbled in a corner were a pair of shoes.

Ethan didn't know what Dunny had been wearing when he had left the morgue at Our Lady of Angels Hospital. However, he wouldn't have wagered a penny against the proposition that these were the very clothes.

Moving closer to the bed, he detected the faint malodor that he'd first smelled in the elevator. Some of the components of the scent were more easily identified than they had been earlier: stale perspiration, a whiff of rancid ointment with a sulfate base, thin fumes of sour urine. The smell of illness, of being long abed and bathed only with basin and sponge.

Ethan became aware of a background sizzle, which he initially mistook for a new manifestation of the rain. Then he realized that he was listening to the fall of water in the master-bathroom shower.

The bathroom door stood ajar. Past the jamb and through the gap, with the sizzle came a wedge of light and wisps of steam.

He eased the door all the way open.

Golden marble sheathed the floor, the walls. In the black granite countertop, two black ceramic sinks were served by brushed-gold spouts and faucets.

Above the counter, a long expanse of beveled mirror, hazed with condensation, failed to present a clear reflection. His distorted shape moved under that frosted surface, like a strange pale something glimpsed swimming just beneath the shadow-dappled surface of a pond.

Veils of steam floated in the air.

Within the bathroom was a water closet. The door stood open, the toilet visible. No one in there.

Dunny had nearly been drowned in this toilet.

Neighbors in a fourth-floor apartment had heard him struggling furiously for his life, shouting for help.

Police arrived quickly and caught the assailants in desperate flight. They found Dunny lying on his side in front of the toilet, semiconscious and coughing up water.

By the time the ambulance arrived, he had fallen into a coma.

His attackers—who'd come for money, vengeance, or both—had not been cheated recently by Dunny. They had been in prison for six years and, only recently released, had come to settle a long-overdue account.

Dunny might have hoped to journey far from his life of crime, but old sins had caught up with him that night.

Now on the bathroom floor lay two rumpled, damp black towels. Two dry towels still hung on the rack.

The shower was in the far-right corner from the entrance to the bathroom. Even if the steam-opaqued glass door had been clear, Ethan couldn't have seen into that cubicle from any distance.

Approaching the stall, he had an image in his mind of the Dunny Whistler whom he expected to encounter. Skin sickly pale where not a lifeless gray, impervious to the pinking effect of hot water. Gray eyes, the whites now pure crimson with hemorrhages.

Still holding the gun in his right hand, he gripped the door with his left and, after a hesitation, pulled it open.

The stall was unoccupied. Water beat upon the marble floor and swirled down the drain.

Leaning into the stall, he reached behind the cascade, to the single control, and turned off the flow.

The sudden silence in the wake of the watery sizzle seemed to announce his presence as clearly as if he had triggered an air horn.

Nervously, he turned toward the bathroom entrance, expecting some response, but not sure what that might be.

Even with the water turned off, steam continued to escape the shower, though in thinner veils, pouring over the top of the glass door and around Ethan.

In spite of the moist air, his mouth had gone dry. Pressed together, tongue and palate came apart as reluctantly as two strips of Velcro.

When he started toward the bathroom door, his attention was drawn again to the movement of his vague and distorted reflection in the clouded mirror above the sinks.

Then he saw the impossible shape, which brought him to a halt.

In the mirror, under the skin of condensation, loomed a pale form as blurred as Ethan's veiled image but nonetheless recognizable as a figure, man or woman.

Ethan was alone. A quick survey of the bathroom failed to reveal any object or any fluke of architecture that the misted mirror might trick into a ghostly human shape.

So he closed his eyes. Opened them. Still the shape.

He could hear only his heart now, only his heart, not fast, but faster, sledgehammer heavy, pounding and pounding, slamming blood to his brain to flush out unreason.

Of course his imagination had given meaning to a meaningless blur in a mirror, in the same way that he might have found men and dragons and all kinds of fanciful creatures among the clouds in a summer sky. Imagination. Of course.

But then this man, this dragon, whatever—it moved in the mirror. Not much: a little, enough to make Ethan's sledgehammer heart stutter between blows.

Maybe the movement also was imaginary.

Hesitantly he approached the mirror. He didn't step directly in front of the phantom form, for in spite of the strong rush of blood that ought to have clarified his thinking, Ethan suffered from the superstitious conviction that something terrible would happen to him if his reflection were to overlay the ghostly shape.

Surely the movement of the misted apparition had been imaginary, but if it had been, then he imagined it *again*. The figure seemed to be motioning for him to come forward, closer.

Ethan would not have admitted to Hazard Yancy or to any other cop from the old days, perhaps not even to Hannah if she were alive, that when he put his hand to the mirror, he half expected to feel not wet glass, but the hand of another, making contact from a cold and forbidding Elsewhere.

He swabbed away an arc of mist, leaving a glimmering smear of water.

Even as Ethan's hand moved, so did the phantom in the mirror, sliding away from the cleansing swipe. Cunningly elusive, it remained behind the shielding condensation—and moved directly in front of him.

With the exception of his face, Ethan's vague reflection in the misted glass had been dark because his clothes were dark, his hair. The steam-frosted shape now before him rose as pale as moonlight and moth wings, impossibly supplanting his own image.

Fear knocked on his heart, but he wouldn't let it in, as when he'd been a cop under fire and dared not panic.

Anyway, he felt as though he were half in a trance, accepting the impossible here as he might easily accept it in a dream.

The apparition leaned toward him, as if trying to discern his nature from the far side of the silvered glass, in much the same way that he himself leaned forward to study it.

Raising his hand once more, Ethan tentatively wiped away a narrow swath of mist, fully expecting that when he came eye to eye with his reflection, the eyes would not be his, but gray like Dunny Whistler's eyes.

Again the mystery in the mirror moved, quicker than Ethan's hand, remaining blurred behind the frosting of condensation.

Only when breath exploded from Ethan did he realize that he had been holding it.

On the inhale, he heard a crash in a far room of the apartment, the brittle music of shattering glass.

CHAPTER 15

ETHAN HAD TOLD PALOMAR LABORATORIES to analyze his blood for traces of illicit chemicals, in case he'd been drugged without his knowledge. During the events at Reynerd's apartment house, he had almost seemed to be in an altered state of consciousness.

Now, leaving the steamy bathroom, he felt no less disoriented than when, after being gut shot, he had found himself behind the wheel of the Expedition once more, unharmed.

Whatever had happened—or had only seemed to happen—at the mirror, he no longer entirely trusted his senses. As a consequence, he proceeded with greater caution than before, assuming that yet again things might not be as they appeared to be.

He passed through rooms he'd already searched and then into new territory, arriving at last in the kitchen. Shattered glass sparkled on the breakfast table and littered the floor.

Also on the floor lay the silver picture frame missing from the desk in the study. The photo of Hannah had been stripped out of it.

Whoever had taken the picture had been in too great a hurry to release the four fasteners on the back of the frame, and had instead smashed the glass.

The rear door of the apartment stood open.

Beyond lay a wide hall that served the back of both penthouse units. At the nearer end, an exit sign marked a stairwell. Toward the farther end was a freight elevator big enough to carry refrigerators and large pieces of furniture.

If someone had taken the freight route down, he had already completed his descent. No sound issued from the elevator machinery.

Ethan hurried to the stairs. Opened the fire door. Paused on the threshold, listening.

Groan or moan, or melancholy sigh, or clank of chains: Even a ghost ought to make a sound, but only a cold hollow silence rose out of the stairwell.

He went down quickly, ten flights to the ground floor, then another two flights to the garage. He encountered neither a flesh-and-blood resident nor a spirit.

The scent of sickness and fever sweats, first detected in the elevator, didn't linger here. Instead, he smelled a faint soapy odor, as if someone fresh from a bath had passed this way. And a trace of spicy aftershave.

Pushing open the steel fire door, stepping into the garage, he heard an engine, smelled exhaust fumes. Of the forty parking stalls, many were empty at this hour on a work day.

Toward the front of the garage, a car backed out of a stall. Ethan recognized Dunny's midnight-blue Mercedes sedan.

Triggered by remote control, the garage gate was already rising with a steely clack and clatter.

Pistol still in hand, Ethan ran toward the car as it pulled away from him. The gate rose slowly, and the Mercedes had to stop for it. Through the rear window, he could see the silhouette of a man behind the steering wheel, but not clearly enough to make an identification.

Drawing near to the Mercedes, he swung wide of it. He intended to go directly to the driver's door.

The car shot forward while the barrier continued to rise, before it was fully out of the way. The roof of the Mercedes came within a fraction of an inch of leaving a generous paint sample on the bottom rail of the ascending gate, and raced up the steep exit ramp to the street.

The driver thumbed CLOSE on his remote even as he passed under the gate, which was clattering down again when Ethan reached it. Already the Mercedes had turned out of sight into the street above.

He stood there for a moment, peering through the gate into the gray storm light.

Rainwater streamed down the driveway ramp. Foaming, it vanished through the slots of a drain in the pavement immediately outside the garage.

On that concrete incline, a small lizard, back broken by a car tire, but still alive, struggled gamely against the sluicing water. So persistently did it twitch upward inch by inch that it seemed to believe all its needs could be satisfied and all its injuries healed by some power at the summit.

Not wanting to see the little creature inevitably defeated and washed down to die upon the drain grate, Ethan turned away from the sight of it.

He returned the pistol to his shoulder holster.

He studied his hands. They were trembling.

On the back stairs once more, climbing to the fifth floor, he encountered the lingering soapy smell, the trace of aftershave. This time, he also detected another odor less clean than the first two, elusive but disturbing.

Whatever else he might be, Dunny Whistler was surely a living man, not an animated corpse. Why would one of the walking dead come home to shower, shave, and dress in clean clothes? Absurd.

In the apartment kitchen, Ethan used a DustBuster to vacuum up the fragments of picture-frame glass.

He found a spoon and an open half-gallon container of ice cream in the sink. Apparently, those who were recently resurrected enjoyed chocolate caramel swirl.

He put the ice cream in the freezer and returned the empty picture frame to the study.

In the master bedroom, he stopped short of the bathroom doorway. He had intended to check the mirror once more, to see if it was still misted and if, in the glass, anything moved that shouldn't be there.

Actively seeking that phantom suddenly seemed to be a bad idea. Instead, he left the apartment, turning off the lights and locking the door behind him.

In the main elevator, as Ethan descended, he thought, *For the same reason that the proverbial wolf put on a sheep's skin to move undetected among the lambs.*

That was why one of the walking dead would shower, shave, and put on a good suit.

As the elevator conveyed Ethan to the ground floor, he knew how Alice must have felt in free fall down the rabbit hole.

CHAPTER 16

AFTER SHUTTING DOWN THE RAILROADS, Fric left the dirty Nazis to their evil schemes, departed the unreality of the train room for the unreality of the multimillion-dollar car collection in the garage, and ran for the stairs.

He should have taken the elevator. That cableless mechanism, which raised and lowered the cab on a powerful hydraulic ram, would be too slow, however, for his current mood.

Fric's engine raced, raced. The telephone conversation with the weird stranger—whom he had dubbed Mysterious Caller—was high-octane fuel for a boy with a boring life, a feverish imagination, and empty hours to fill.

He didn't climb the stairs; he *assaulted* them. Legs pumping, grabbing at the handrail, Fric flung himself up from the basement, conquering two, four, six, eight long flights, to the top of Palazzo Rospo, where he had rooms on the third floor.

Only Fric seemed to know the meaning of the name given to the great house by its first owner: Palazzo Rospo. Nearly everyone knew that *palazzo* was Italian for "palace," but no one except perhaps a few sneeringly superior European film directors seemed to have any idea what *rospo* meant.

To be fair, most people who visited the estate didn't give a rip what it was called or what its grand name actually meant. They had more important issues on their minds—such as the weekend box-office numbers, the overnight TV ratings, the latest executive shuffles at the studios and networks, who to screw in the new deal that they were putting together, how much to screw them out of, how to bedazzle them so they wouldn't realize they were being screwed, how to find a new source for cocaine, and whether their careers might have been even bigger if they had begun having face-lifts when they were eighteen.

Among the few who had ever given a thought to the name of the estate, there were competing theories.

Some believed the house had been named after a famous Italian statesman or philosopher, or architect. The number of people in the film industry who knew anything about statesmen, philosophers, and architects was almost as small as the number who'd be able to give a lecture regarding the structure of matter on a subatomic level; consequently, this theory was easily embraced and never challenged.

Others were certain that Rospo had been either the maiden name of the original owner's beloved mother or the name of a snow sled that he had ridden with great delight in childhood, when he had been truly happy for the last time in his life.

Still others assumed that it had been named after the original owner's secret love, a young actress named Vera Jean Rospo.

Vera Jean Rospo had actually existed back in the 1930s, though her real name had been Hilda May Glorkal.

The producer, agent, or whoever had renamed her Rospo must have secretly despised poor Hilda. *Rospo* was Italian for "toad."

Only Fric seemed to know that Palazzo Rospo was as close as you could get, in Italian, to naming a house Toad Hall.

Fric had done some research. He liked knowing things.

Evidently, the film mogul who built the estate more than sixty years ago had possessed a sense of humor and had read *The Wind in the Willows.* In that book, a character named Toad lived in a grand house named Toad Hall.

These days, no one in the film business read books.

In Fric's experience, no one in the business had a sense of humor anymore, either.

He climbed the stairs so fast that he was breathing hard by the time that he reached the north hallway on the third floor. This wasn't good. He should have stopped. He should have rested.

Instead, he hurried along the north hall to the east hall, where his private rooms were located. The antiques that he passed on the top floor were spectacular, although not of the museum quality to be found on the two lower levels.

Fric's rooms had been refurnished a year ago. Ghost Dad's interior designer had taken Fric shopping. To redo the furniture in these quarters, his father had provided him with a budget of thirty-five thousand dollars.

Fric had not asked for fancy new furniture. He never asked for anything—except at Christmas, when he was required to fill out the childish Dear Santa form that his father insisted be provided by Mrs. McBee. The idea of refurnishing was entirely Ghost Dad's.

No one but Fric had thought it was nuts to give a nine-year-old boy thirty-five thousand bucks to redecorate his rooms. The designer and the salespeople acted as if this were the usual drill, that every nine-year-old had an equal amount to spend on a room makeover.

Lunatics.

Fric often suspected that the soft-spoken, seemingly reasonable people surrounding him were in fact all BIG-TIME CRAZY.

Every item in his remade rooms was modern, sleek, and bright.

He had nothing against the furniture and artworks of distant times. He liked all that stuff. But sixty thousand square feet of fine antiques was enough already.

In his own private space, he wanted to feel like a kid, not like an old French dwarf, which sometimes he seemed to be among all these French antiques. He wanted to believe that such a thing as the future actually existed.

An entire suite had been set aside for his use. Living room, bedroom, bathroom, walk-in closet.

Still breathing hard, Fric hurried through his living room. Breathing harder still, he crossed his bedroom to the walk-in closet.

Walk-in was a seriously inadequate description. If Fric had owned a Porsche, he could have *driven* into the closet.

Were he to add a Porsche to his Dear Santa list, one would most likely be parked in the driveway come Christmas morn, with a giant gift bow on the roof.

Lunatics.

Although Fric had more clothes than he needed, more than he wanted, his wardrobe required only a quarter of the closet. The rest of the space had been fitted out with shelves on which were stored collections of toy soldiers, which he cherished, boxed games to which he was indifferent—as well as videos and DVDs of every stupid boring movie for kids made in the past five years, which were sent to him free by studio executives and by others who wanted to score points with his father.

At the back of the closet, the nineteen-foot width was divided into three sections of floor-to-ceiling shelves. Reaching under the third shelf in the right-hand section, he pressed a concealed button.

The middle section proved to be a secret door that swung open on a centrally mounted pivot hinge. The shelving unit measured ten inches deep, which left a passageway of about two and a half feet to either side.

Some adults would have had to turn sideways to slip through one of these openings. Fric, however, could walk straight into the secret realm beyond the closet.

Behind the shelves lay a six-by-six space and a stainless-steel door.

Although not solid steel, it was four inches thick and looked formidable.

The door had been unlocked when Fric discovered it three years ago. It was unlocked now. He had never found the key.

In addition to the regular lever handle at the right side, the door featured a second handle in the center. This one turned a full 360 degrees and in fact was not a handle, but a crank, similar to those featured on casement windows throughout the house.

Flanking the crank were two curious items that appeared to be valves of some kind.

He opened the door, switched on the light, and stepped into a room measuring sixteen feet by twelve. An odd place in many ways.

A series of steel plates formed the floor. The walls and the ceiling also were covered in sheets of steel.

These plates and panels had been welded meticulously at every joint. During his study of the room, Fric had never been able to find the smallest crack or pinhole in the welds.

The door featured a rubber gasket. Now old and dried and cracked, the rubber had probably once made an airtight seal with the jamb.

Built into the inner face of the door was a fine-mesh screen behind which lay a mechanism that Fric had examined more than once with a flashlight. Through the screen, he could see fan blades, gears, dusty ball bearings, and other parts that he couldn't name.

He suspected that the crank on the outside of the door had once turned the suction fan, drawing all the air out of the room through the valves, until something like a vacuum had been created.

He remained mystified as to the purpose of the place.

For a while, he'd thought it might have been a suffacatorium.

Suffacatorium was a word of Fric's invention. He imagined an evil genius forcing his terrified prey into the suffacatorium at gunpoint, slamming the door, and gleefully cranking the air out of the chamber, until the victim gradually suffocated.

In fiction, villains sometimes engineered elaborate devices and schemes to kill people when a knife or gun would be much quicker and cheaper. Evil minds were apparently as complex as anthill mazes.

Or maybe some psycho killers were squeamish about blood. Maybe they enjoyed killing, but not if they were left with a mess to clean. Such murderous types might install a secret suffacatorium.

Certain elements of the room design, however, argued against this creepily appealing explanation.

For one thing, a lever handle on the inside of the door overrode the deadbolt lock operated by a key from the outside. Clearly, the intention had been to guard against anyone being trapped in the room by accident, but it also ensured that no one could be locked in here on purpose, either.

The stainless-steel hooks in the ceiling were another issue. Two rows of them extended the length of the room, each row about two feet from a wall.

Gazing up at the gleaming hooks, Fric heard himself breathing as hard now as when he'd just finished racing up eight flights of stairs. The sound of every inhalation and exhalation rushed and reverberated along the metal walls.

An itching between his shoulders spread quickly to the back of his neck. He knew what *that* meant.

This wasn't merely rapid respiration, either. He'd begun to wheeze.

Suddenly his chest tightened, and he grew short of breath. The wheezing became louder on the exhale than on the inhale, leaving no doubt that he was having an asthmatic attack. He could feel his airways narrowing.

He could get air in more easily than he could get it out. But he had to expel the stale to draw in the fresh.

Hunching his shoulders, leaning forward, he used the muscles of his chest walls and of his neck to try to squeeze out his trapped breath. He didn't succeed.

As asthma attacks went, this was a bad one.

He clutched at the medicinal inhaler clipped to his belt.

On three occasions that he could remember, Fric had been so severely deprived of air that his skin had taken on a bluish tint, and he had required emergency treatment. The sight of a blue Fric had scared the piss out of everyone.

Freed from his belt, the inhaler slipped out of his fingers. It fell to the floor, clattered against the steel plates.

Wheezing, he stooped to retrieve the device, grew dizzy, dropped to his knees.

Breath had become so hard to draw that a killer might as well have had both hands around Fric's throat, throttling him.

Anxious but not yet desperate, he crawled forward, groping for the inhaler. The device squirted between his suddenly sweaty fingers and rattled farther across the floor.

Vision swam, vision blurred, vision darkened at the edges.

No one had ever taken a photo of him in a blue phase. He'd long been curious about what he looked like when lavender, when indigo.

His airways tightened further. His wheezing grew higher pitched. He sounded as if he had swallowed a whistle that had lodged in his throat.

When he put his hand on the inhaler again, he held fast to it and rolled onto his back. No good. He couldn't breathe at all on his back. He wasn't in a proper position to use the inhaler, either.

Overhead: the hooks, gleaming, gleaming.

Not a good place to have a severe asthma attack. He didn't have enough wind to cry out. No one would hear a shout, anyway. Palazzo Rospo was well built; sound didn't travel through these walls.

Now he was desperate.

CHAPTER 17

IN A MEN'S-ROOM STALL AT THE SHOPPING mall, Corky Laputa used a felt-tip marker to write vicious racial epithets on the walls.

He himself was not a racist. He harbored no malice toward any particular group, but regarded humanity in general with disdain. Indeed, he didn't know anyone who entertained racist sentiments.

People existed, however, who believed that closet racists were everywhere around them. They needed to believe this in order to have purpose and meaning in their lives, and to have someone to hate.

For a significant portion of humanity, having someone to hate was as necessary as having bread, as breathing.

Some people needed to be *furious* about something, anything. Corky was happy to scrawl these messages that, when seen by certain restroom visitors, would fan their simmering anger and add a new measure of bile to their bitterness.

As he worked, Corky hummed along with the music on the public-address system.

Here on December 21, the Muzak play list included no Christmas tunes. Most likely, the mall management worried that "Hark the Herald Angels Sing" or even "Jingle Bell Rock" would deeply offend those shoppers who were of non-Christian faiths, as well as alienate any highly sensitized atheists with money to spend.

Currently, the system broadcast an old Pearl Jam number. This particular arrangement of the song had been performed by an orchestra with a large string section. Minus the shrieking vocal, the tune was as mind-numbing as the original, though more pleasantly so.

By the time that Corky finished composing pungent racist slurs in the stall, flushed the toilet, and washed his hands at one of the sinks, he was alone in the men's room. Unobserved.

He prided himself on taking advantage of every opportunity to serve chaos, regardless of how minor the damage he might be able to inflict on social order.

None of the restroom sinks had stoppers. He tore handfuls of paper towels from one of the dispensers. After wetting the towels, he quickly wadded them into tightly compressed balls and crammed them into the drain holes in three of the six sinks.

These days, most public restrooms featured push-down faucets that gushed water in timed bursts, and then shut off automatically. Here, however, the faucets were old-fashioned turnable handles.

At each of the three plugged sinks, he cranked on the water as fast as it would flow.

A drain in the center of the floor could have foiled him. He moved the large waste can, half full of used paper towels, and blocked the drain with it.

He picked up his shopping bag—which contained new socks, linens, and a leather wallet purchased at a department store, as well as a fine piece of cutlery acquired at a kitchen shop catering to the crowd that tuned in regularly to the Food Network—and he watched the sinks fill rapidly with water.

Set in the wall, four inches above the floor, was a large air-intake vent. If the water rose that high, spilling into the heating system and traveling through walls, a mere mess might turn into an expensive disaster. Several businesses in the mall and the lives of their employees might be disrupted.

One, two, three, the sinks brimmed. Water cascaded to the floor.

To the music of splash and splatter—and thinly spread Pearl Jam—Corky Laputa departed the restroom, smiling.

The hall serving the men's and women's lavatories was deserted, so he put down the shopping bag.

From a sports-coat pocket, he withdrew a roll of electrician's tape. He never failed to be prepared for adventure.

He used the tape to seal off the eighth-inch gap between the bottom of the door and the threshold. At the sides of the jamb, the door met the stop tightly enough to hold back the mounting water, so he didn't need to apply additional tape.

From his wallet, he extracted a folded three-inch-by-six-inch sticker. He unfolded this item, peeled the protective paper off the adhesive back, and applied it to the door.

Red letters on a white background declared OUT OF ORDER.

The sticker would trigger suspicion in any mall security guard, but shoppers would turn away without further investigation and would seek out another lavatory.

Corky's work here had been completed. The ultimate extent of the water damage now lay in the hands of fate.

Security cameras were banned from restrooms and from approaches to them. Thus far he'd not been captured on videotape near the crime.

The L-shaped corridor serving the restrooms led to the second-floor mall promenade, which was under constant security surveillance. Previously, Corky had scoped out the positions of the cameras that covered the approaches to the lavatory hallway.

Departing now, he casually averted his face from those lenses. Keeping his head down, he quickly blended into the crowd of shoppers.

When security guards later reviewed the tapes, they might focus on Corky as having entered and departed the lavatory corridor in the approximate time frame of the vandalism. But they would not be able to obtain a useful image of his face.

He had intentionally worn nondescript clothes, the better to fade into the rabble. On videotapes recorded elsewhere in the mall, he wouldn't be easily identifiable as the same man who had visited the restroom just prior to the flood.

A gorgeous excess of spangled and frosted holiday decorations further compromised the usefulness of the cameras, infringing upon the established angles of view.

The winter-wonderland theme avoided both direct and symbolic references to Christmas: no angels, no mangers, no images of Santa Claus, no busy elves, no reindeer, no traditional ornaments—and no festive lengths of colored lights, only tiny white twinkle bulbs. Festoons of plastic and shiny aluminum-foil icicles, measured in miles, glimmered everywhere. Thousands of large, sequined Styrofoam snowflakes hung on strings from the ceiling. In the central rotunda, ten life-size ice skaters, all mechanical figures moving on tracks, glided around a fake frozen pond in an elaborate re-creation of a winter landscape complete with snowmen, snow forts, robot children threatening one another with plastic snowballs, and animated figures of polar bears in comical poses.

Corky Laputa was enchanted by the pure, blissful vacuousness of it all.

On the first escalator to the ground floor, on the second to the garage, he brooded over a few details of his scheme to kill Rolf Reynerd. Both as he had shopped and as he had enjoyed his destructive escapades in the mall, Corky had carefully laid a bold and simple plan for murder.

He was a natural-born multitasker.

To those who had never studied political strategy and who also lacked a solid grounding in philosophy, Corky's capers in the men's room might have seemed at best to be childish larks. A society could seldom be brought down solely by acts of violence, however, and every thoughtful anarchist must be dedicated to his mission every minute of the day, wreaking havoc by actions both small and large.

Illiterate punks defacing public property with spray-painted graffiti, suicide bombers, semicoherent pop stars selling rage and nihilism set to an infectious beat, attorneys specializing in tort law and filing massive class-action suits with the express intention of destroying major corporations and age-old institutions, serial killers, drug dealers, crooked cops, corrupted corporate executives cooking the books and stealing from pension funds, faithless priests molesting children, politicians riding to reelection by the agitation of class envy: All these and numerous others, working at different levels, some as destructive as runaway freight trains hurtling off the tracks, others quietly chewing like termites at the fabric of civility and reason, were necessary to cause the current order to collapse into ruin.

If somehow Corky could have carried the black plague without risking his own life, he would have enthusiastically passed that disease to everyone he met by way of sneezes, coughs, touches, and kisses. If sometimes all he could do was flush a cherry bomb down a public toilet, he would advance chaos by that tiny increment while he awaited opportunities to do greater damage.

In the garage, when he reached his BMW, he shrugged out of his sports coat. Before settling behind the steering wheel, he donned the yellow slicker once more. He put the droopy yellow rain hat on the front passenger's seat, within easy reach.

Besides providing superb protection in even a hard-driving rain, the slicker was the ideal gear in which to commit homicide. Blood could be easily washed off the shiny vinyl surface, leaving no stain.

According to the Bible, to every season there is a purpose, a time to kill and a time to heal.

Not much of a healer, Corky believed there was a time to kill and a time not to kill. The time to kill had arrived.

Corky's death list contained more than one name, and Reynerd was not at the top. Anarchy could be a demanding faith.

CHAPTER 18

FRIC IN THE SUFFACATORIUM, ANXIOUS AND wheezing, and no doubt bluer than a blue moon, dragged himself out of the middle of the room and sat with his back against a steel wall.

The medicinal inhaler in his right hand weighed slightly more than a Mercedes 500 M-Class SUV.

If he'd been his father, he would have been surrounded by an entourage big enough to help him lift the stupid thing. Yet another disadvantage of being a geek loner.

For lack of oxygen, his thoughts grew muddled. For a moment he believed that his right hand was trapped on the floor under a heavy shotgun, that it was a shotgun he wanted to lift, put in his mouth.

Fric almost cast the device away in terror. Then in a moment of clarity, he recognized the inhaler and held fast to it.

He couldn't breathe, couldn't think, could only wheeze and cough and wheeze, and seemed to be spiraling into one of those rare attacks that were severe enough to require hospital emergency-room treatment. Doctors would poke him and prod him, bend him and fold him, babbling about their favorite Manheim movies. The scene with the elephants! The airplane-to-airplane midair jump with no parachute! The sinking ship! The alien snake king! The funny monkeys! Nurses would gush over him, telling him how lucky he was and how exciting it must be to have a father who was a star, a hero, a hunk, a genius.

He might as well die here, die now.

Although he was not Clark Kent or Peter Parker, Fric raised the gazillion-pound device to his face. He slipped the mouthpiece between his lips and administered a dose of medication, sucking in the deepest breath that he could manage, which wasn't deep at all.

In his throat: a hard-boiled egg or a stone, or a huge wad of phlegm worthy of the Guinness book of world records, a plug of some kind, allowing only thin wisps of air to enter, to exit.

He leaned forward. Clenching and relaxing neck muscles, chest and abdominal muscles. Struggling to draw cool medicated air into his lungs, to exhale the hot stale breath pooled like syrup in his chest.

Two puffs. That was the prescribed dosage.

He triggered puff two.

He might have gagged on the faint metallic taste if his inflamed and swollen airways could have executed a gag, but the tissues were able only to contract, not expand, flexing tighter, tighter, tighter.

A yellow-gray soot seemed to sift down through his eyes, the slow fall of an interior twilight.

Dizzy. Sitting here on the floor, back against the wall, legs straight out in front of him, he felt as if he were balanced on one foot on a high wire, teetering, about to take a death plunge.

Two puffs. He'd taken two doses.

Overmedicating was inadvisable. Dangerous.

Two puffs. That ought to be enough. Usually was. Sometimes just one dose allowed him to slip out of this invisible hangman's noose.

Don't overmedicate. Doctor's orders.

Don't panic. Doctor's advice.

Give the medication a chance to work. Doctor's instruction.

Screw the doctor.

He triggered a third puff.

A bone-click sound like dice on a game board rattled out of his throat, and his wheezing became less shrill, less of a whistle, more of a raw windy rasping.

Hot air exploding out. Cool air going down. Fric on the mend.

He dropped the inhaler on his lap.

Fifteen minutes was the average time required to recover from an asthma attack. Nothing could be done but wait it out.

Darkness faded from the edges of his vision. Blur gradually gave way to clarity.

Fric on the floor in an empty steel room, with nothing to distract him but hooks in the ceiling, naturally looked at those peculiar curved forms, and thought about them.

When he'd first discovered the room, he'd been reminded of movie scenes set in meat lockers, cow carcasses hanging from ceiling hooks.

He had wondered if a mad criminal genius had hung the bodies of his human victims in *this* meat locker. Perhaps the room had once been refrigerated.

The hooks weren't set far enough apart to accommodate the bodies of grown men and women. Initially, Fric had sprung to the grim conclusion that the killer had collected dead, refrigerated *children*.

On closer inspection, he had seen that the stainless-steel hooks were not sharp. They were too blunt to pierce either kids or cows.

That's when he'd set the matter of the hooks aside for later contemplation and had come to the determination that the room had been a suffacatorium. The existence of the interior lock release, however, had proved this theory wrong.

As his wheezing quieted, as breath came more easily, as the tightness in his chest loosened, Fric studied the hooks, the brushed-steel walls, trying to arrive at a third theory regarding the purpose of this place. He remained mystified.

He'd told no one about the pivoting section of closet shelving or about the hidden room. What made the hidey-hole so cool was less its exotic nature than the fact that only he knew it existed.

This space could serve as the "deep and special secret place" that, according to Mysterious Caller, would soon be needed.

Maybe he should stock it with supplies. Two or three six-packs of Pepsi. Several packages of peanut-butter-and-cracker sandwiches. A couple flashlights with spare batteries.

Warm cola would never be his first choice of beverage, but it would be preferable to dying of thirst. And even warm cola was better than being stranded in the Mojave with no source of water, forced to save and drink your own urine.

Peanut-butter-and-cracker sandwiches, tasty under ordinary circumstances, would be unspeakably vile if accompanied by urine.

Maybe he should stock *four* six-packs of cola.

Even though he wouldn't be drinking his urine, he would need something in which to pee, supposing that he would be required to hide out longer than a few hours. A pot with a lid. Better yet, a jar with a screw top.

Mysterious Caller hadn't said how long Fric should expect to be under siege. They would have to discuss that in their next chat.

The stranger had promised that he would be in touch again. If he was a pervert, he would call for sure, drooling all over his phone. If he wasn't a pervert, then he might be a sincere friend, in which case he would still call, but for better reasons.

Time passed, the asthma relented, and Fric got to his feet. He clipped the inhaler to his belt.

A little woozy, he balanced himself with one hand against the cold steel wall as he went to the door.

A minute later, in his bedroom, he sat on the edge of the bed and lifted the handset from the telephone. An indicator light on the keyboard appeared at his private line.

No one had phoned him since he'd answered his *Ooodelee-*

ooodelee-oo in the train room. After pressing *69, he listened while his phone automatically entered the number of his most recent caller.

If he'd been a brainiac trained in the skills required to be an enormously dangerous spy, and if he'd had the supernaturally attuned ear of Beethoven before Beethoven went deaf, or if one of his parents had been an extraterrestrial sent to Earth to crossbreed with humans, perhaps Fric could have translated those rapidly sounded telephone tones into numerals. He could have memorized Mysterious Caller's phone number for future use.

He was nothing more, however, than the son of the biggest movie star in the world. That position came with lots of perks, like a free Xbox from Microsoft and a lifetime pass to Disneyland, but it didn't confer upon him either astonishing genius or paranormal powers.

After waiting through twelve rings, he engaged the speakerphone feature. He went to a window while the number continued to ring.

The billiards-table smoothness of the east lawn sloped away through oaks, through cedars, to rose gardens, vanishing into gray rain and silver mist.

Fric wondered if he should tell anyone about Mysterious Caller and the warning of impending danger.

If he called Ghost Dad's global cell-phone number, it would be answered either by a bodyguard or by his father's personal makeup artist. Or by his personal hair stylist. Or by the masseur who always traveled with him. Or by his spiritual adviser, Ming du Lac, or by any of a dozen other flunkies orbiting the Fourth Most Admired Man in the World.

The phone would be handed from one to another of them, across unknowable vertical and horizontal distances, until after ten minutes or fifteen, Ghost Dad would come on the line. He would say, "Hey, my main man, guess who's here with me and wants to talk to you."

Then before Fric could say a word, Ghost Dad would pass the

phone to Julia Roberts or Arnold Schwarzenegger, or to Tobey Maguire, or to Kirsten Dunst, or to Winnie the Wonder Horse, probably to all of them, and they would be sweet to Fric. They would ask him how he was doing in school, whether he wanted to be the biggest movie star in the world when he grew up, what variety of oats he preferred in his feed bag. . . .

By the time that the phone had been passed around to Ghost Dad again, a reporter from *Entertainment Weekly,* using the wrong end of a pencil, would be taking notes for a feature piece about the father-son chat. When the story hit print, every fact would be wrong, and Fric would be made to look like either a whiny moron or a spoiled sissy.

Worse, a giggly young actress with no serious credits but with a little industry buzz—what they used to call a starlet—might answer Ghost Dad's phone, as often one of them did. She would be tickled by the name Fric because these girls were always tickled by everything. He'd talked to scores of them, hundreds, over the years, and they seemed to be as alike as ears of corn picked in the same field, as if some farmer *grew* them out in Iowa and shipped them to Hollywood in railroad cars.

Fric wasn't able to phone his Nominal Mom, Freddie Nielander, because she would be in some far and fabulously glamorous place like Monte Carlo, being gorgeous. He didn't have a reliable phone number for her.

Mrs. McBee, and by extension Mr. McBee, were kind to Fric. They seemed to have his best interests always in mind.

Nevertheless, Fric was reluctant to turn to them in a case like this. Mr. McBee was just a little . . . daffy. And Mrs. McBee was an all-knowing, all-seeing, rule-making, formidable woman whose soft-spoken words and mere looks of disapproval were powerful enough to cause the object of her reprimand to suffer internal bleeding.

Mr. and Mrs. McBee served *in loco parentis.* This was a Latin legal phrase that meant they had been given the authority of Fric's parents when his parents were absent, which was nearly always.

When he'd first heard *in loco parentis,* he'd thought it meant that his parents were loco.

The McBees, however, had come with the house, which they had managed long before Ghost Dad had owned it. To Fric, their deeper allegiance seemed to be to Palazzo Rospo, to place and to tradition, more than to any single employer or his family.

Mr. Baptiste, the happy cook, was a friendly acquaintance, not actually a friend, and certainly not a confidant.

Mr. Hachette, the fearsome and possibly insane chef, was not a person to whom *anyone* would turn in time of need, except perhaps Satan. The Prince of Hell would value the chef's advice.

Fric carefully planned every foray into the kitchen so as to avoid Mr. Hachette. Garlic wouldn't repel the chef, because he loved garlic, but a crucifix pressed to his flesh would surely cause him to burst into flames and, screaming, to take flight like a bat.

The possibility existed that the psychotic chef was the very danger about which Mysterious Caller had been warning Fric.

Indeed, virtually any of the twenty-five staff members might be a scheming homicidal nutjob cunningly concealed behind a smiley mask. An ax murderer. An ice-pick killer. A silk-scarf strangler.

Maybe *all twenty-five* were ax murderers waiting to strike. Maybe the next full moon would stir tides of madness in their heads, and they would explode simultaneously, committing hideous acts of bloody violence, attacking one another with guns, hatchets, and high-speed food processors.

If you couldn't know the full truth of what your father and your mother thought of you, if you couldn't *really* know who they were and what went on inside their heads, then you couldn't expect to know for sure anything about other people who were even less close to you.

Fric pretty much trusted Mr. Truman not to be a psychopath with a chain-saw obsession. Mr. Truman had once been a cop, after all.

Besides, something about Ethan Truman was so *right*. Fric didn't have the words to describe it, but he recognized it. Mr. Truman was solid. When he came into a room, he was *there*. When he talked to you, he was *connected* to you.

Fric had never known anyone quite like him.

Nevertheless, he wouldn't tell even Mr. Truman about Mysterious Caller and the need to find a hiding place.

For one thing, he feared not being believed. Boys his age often made up wild stories. Not Fric. But other boys did. Fric didn't want Mr. Truman to think he was a lying sack of kid crap.

Neither did he want Mr. Truman to think that he was a fraidy-cat, a spineless jellyfish, a chicken-hearted coward.

No one would ever believe that Fric could save the world twenty times over, the way they believed his father had done, but he didn't want anyone to think he was a timid baby. Especially not Mr. Truman.

Besides, he sort of liked having this secret. It was better than trains.

He watched the wet day, half expecting to catch a brief glimpse of a villain skulking across the estate, obscured by rain and mist.

After Mysterious Caller's number had rung maybe a hundred times without being answered, Fric returned to the phone and terminated the call.

He had work to do. Preparations to make.

A bad thing was coming. Fric intended to be ready to meet it, greet it, defeat it.

CHAPTER 19

UNDER A BLACK UMBRELLA, ETHAN TRUMAN walked the grassy avenue of graves, his shoes squishing in the saturated turf.

Giant drooping cedars mourned with the weeping day, and birds, like spirits risen, stirred in the cloistered branches when he passed near enough to worry them.

As far as he could see, he alone walked in these mortal fields. Respect for the loved and lost was usually paid on sunny days, with remembrances as bright as the weather. No one would choose to visit a cemetery in a storm.

No one but a cop whose mainspring of curiosity had been wound tight, who had been born with a compulsive need to know the truth. A clockwork mechanism in his heart and soul, designed by fate and granted as a birthright, compelled him to follow wherever suspicion and logic might lead.

In this case, suspicion, logic, and dread.

Intuition wove in him the strange conviction that he would prove to be not the first visitor of the day and that in this bastion of the dead, he would discover something disturbing, though he had no idea what it might be.

Headstones of time-eaten granite, mausoleums crusted with lichen and stained by settled smog, memorial columns and obelisks tilted by ground subsidence: None of that traditional architecture identified this as a cemetery. The marker at each of these graves—a bronze plaque on a pale granite plinth—had been set flush with the grass. From a distance the burial ground appeared to be an ordinary park.

Radiant and unique in life, Hannah was here remembered with the same drab bronze that memorialized the thousands of others who slept eternal in these fields.

Ethan visited her grave six or seven times a year, including once at Christmas. And always on their anniversary.

He didn't know why he came that often. Hannah didn't lie here, only her bones. She lived in his heart, always with him.

Sometimes he thought he traveled to this place less to remember her—for she was not in the least forgotten—than to gaze at the empty plot beside her, at the blank granite tablet on which a cast-bronze plaque with his name would one day be fixed.

At thirty-seven, he was too young a man to welcome death, and life continued to hold the greater promise for him. Nevertheless, five years after losing Hannah, Ethan still felt that something of himself had died, as well.

Through twelve years of marriage, they delayed having children. They had been so young. No need to hurry.

No one expected a vibrant, beautiful, thirty-two-year-old woman to be diagnosed with a virulent cancer, to be dead four months later. When it took her, the malignancy also claimed the children they might have brought into the world, and the grandchildren thereafter.

In a sense, Ethan *had* died with her: the Ethan who would have been a loving father to the children blessed with her grace, the Ethan who would have known the joy of her company for decades yet to come, who would have known the peace and the purpose of growing old at her side.

Perhaps he would have been surprised to find her grave torn open, empty.

What he found instead of grave robbery, though unexpected, did not surprise him.

At the base of her bronze plaque lay two dozen fresh long-stemmed roses. The florist had wrapped them in a cone of stiff cellophane that partly protected the blooms from the pelting rain.

These were hybrid tea roses, a golden-red variety named Broadway. Of all the roses that Hannah loved and grew, Broadway had been her favorite.

Ethan turned slowly in a full circle, studying the cemetery. No figure moved anywhere on those gently sloped green acres.

He peered with special suspicion at every cedar, every oak. As best he could tell, those trunks didn't shelter a lurking observer.

No traffic moved on the narrow winding road that served the cemetery. Ethan's Expedition—white as winter, glimmering like ice—was the only vehicle parked along the lane.

Beyond the boundaries of the cemetery, urban vistas loomed in veils of rain and fog, less like a real city than like a metropolis in a dream. No rumble of traffic, no bleat of horn penetrated from its maze of streets, as though all its citizens had long ago gone horizontal in these silent grassy acres surrounding Ethan.

He looked down at the bouquet once more. In addition to bright color, the Broadway rose offers a fine fragrance. It flourishes in any sun-drenched garden and is more resistant to mildew than are many other varieties.

Two dozen roses found on a grave would not be admitted as evidence in a court of law. Yet Ethan regarded these colorful blooms as proof enough of a strange courtship of the dead, by the dead.

CHAPTER 20

E ATING A MAMOUL, WASHING IT DOWN WITH coffee from a thermos, Hazard Yancy sat in an unmarked sedan directly in front of Rolf Reynerd's apartment house in West Hollywood.

The early winter twilight would not descend for another thirty minutes, but under the pall of the storm, the city had an hour ago settled into a prolonged dusk. Activated by photoelectric sensors, streetlamps glowed, painting a steely sheen on the needles of rain that stitched the gauzy gray sky ever closer to the earth.

Although it might appear that Hazard lingered over cookies on the city's time, he was considering his approach to Reynerd.

After lunch with Ethan, he had returned to his desk in Homicide. In a couple hours, on the Internet and off, working both the keyboard and the phone, he had learned more than a little about his subject.

Rolf Reynerd was an actor who only intermittently made a living at his craft. Between occasional multi-episode supporting roles as a bad boy on one cheesy soap opera or another, he endured long periods of unemployment.

In an episode of *The X-Files*, he'd played a federal agent driven psychotic by an alien brain leech. In an episode of *Law & Order*, he had been a psychotic personal trainer who killed himself and his wife near the end of the first act. In a TV commercial for a deodorant, he had been cast as a psychotic guard in a Soviet gulag; the spot had never gone national, and he'd made only a little money from it.

An actor unlucky enough to be typecast usually didn't fall into that career trap until he'd experienced great success in a memorable role. Thereafter, the public had difficulty accepting him as any character type other than the one that had made him famous.

In Reynerd's case, however, he seemed to have been typecast even in failure. This suggested to Hazard that certain qualities of the man's personality and demeanor allowed him to portray only mentally unbalanced characters, that he played screw-loose well because several of his own screws had stripped threads.

Despite an unreliable flow of income, Rolf Reynerd lived in a spacious apartment in a handsome building, in a good neighborhood. He dressed well, frequented the hottest nightclubs with young actresses who had a taste for Dom Perignon, and drove a new Jaguar.

According to former friends of Reynerd's widowed mother, Mina, she doted on her son, believed that one day he would be a star, and subsidized him with a fat monthly check.

They were her *former* friends because Mina Reynerd had died four months ago. She'd first been shot in the foot, then beaten to death with a marble lamp encrusted with ornate ormolu mountings.

Her killer remained unknown. Detectives had turned up no leads in her case.

Not surprisingly, the sole heir to her estate had been her only child, poor typecast Rolf.

The actor had a dead-solid perfect alibi for the evening of his mother's murder.

This didn't either surprise Hazard or convince him of Reynerd's innocence. Sole heirs usually had airtight alibis.

According to the medical examiner, Mina had been bludgeoned to death between 9:00 and 11:00 P.M. She'd been struck with such brutal force that patterns of the bronze ormolu had been deeply imprinted on her flesh, even crushed into the bone of her forehead.

Rolf had been partying with his current girlfriend and four other couples from seven o'clock that evening until two o'clock in the morning. They had been a flashy, noisy, memorable group at the two trendy nightclubs between which they had divided their time.

Anyway, even though Mina's murder remained unsolved, and even if Rolf's alibi had been only that he'd stayed home alone, playing with himself, Hazard would have had no excuse to give the man a once-over. The case belonged to another detective.

By happy chance, one of Reynerd's party pals that night—Jerry Nemo—was known to Hazard from another case, which opened a door.

Two months ago, a drug dealer named Carter Cook had been shot in the head. Apparently the murder had been incidental to robbery; Cook had been loaded with merchandise and cash.

Reynerd's buddy, Jerry Nemo, had placed a call to Cook's cell phone an hour before the murder. Nemo was a customer, a cokehead. He set up a meet with Cook to score some blow.

Nemo was no longer under suspicion. No one in Los Angeles or anywhere on Planet Earth was still under suspicion. The Cook murder qualified as classic shitcan, a case unlikely ever to be solved.

Nevertheless, by pretending that Nemo remained a suspect, Hazard had an excuse to approach Reynerd and scope him out for Ethan.

He didn't need an excuse for the purpose of satisfying Reynerd. Using just badge and bluster, Hazard could spin a hundred stories convincing enough to persuade the party boy to open the door and answer questions.

Should Reynerd directly or indirectly disclose his obsession with Channing Manheim, however, or in the unlikely event that Reynerd revealed an intent to harm the movie star, Hazard would have to refer the situation outside the Homicide Division for investigation. Then he would need a credible intradepartmental explanation as to why he had been interviewing Reynerd in the first place, when information regarding Manheim had fallen into his lap.

By pretending that Reynerd's snow-blowing buddy, Nemo, remained a suspect in the Carter Cook murder, Hazard could cover his ass.

After licking powdered sugar and mamoul crumbs from his fingers, he got out of the car.

He didn't bother with an umbrella. Considering that he presented nearly two linebackers' worth of surface area to the rain, he would have needed a bumbershoot the size of a beach umbrella to shelter himself completely.

Approaching the apartment house, he proceeded briskly but did not run through the downpour. The building didn't set far back from the street.

Besides, Hazard seldom accommodated himself to the world, for the world usually moved out of his way. He hardly noticed the rain.

Inside, he ignored the elevator and climbed the stairs.

He'd once been shot at in an elevator. He'd ridden up to the sixth floor, the doors had slid aside, and the perp had been waiting.

Targeted in an elevator, you don't have much room to dodge: As a place in which to be shot at, only a telephone booth and a parked car offered worse circumstances.

Hazard had been shot at while sitting in a parked car, but never while standing in a telephone booth. He expected that it was only a matter of time.

Waiting outside the elevator, the shooter had been packing a 9-mm pistol. And he'd been pants-wetting nervous.

If the freak had been either calm or armed with a shotgun, the outcome for Hazard would have been much bleaker than what happened.

The first round had slammed into the cabin ceiling. The second blew a hole in the back wall. The third winged the stranger who had shared the elevator with Hazard.

As it turned out, the stranger, an IRS agent, was the intended target. Hazard had just been in the wrong place at an inconvenient time, marked for death only because he was a witness.

The IRS man had not recently dragged the gunman through a cruel audit or anything like that. He'd been jumping the shooter's wife.

Instead of returning fire, Hazard had gone in under the pistol. He wrenched it away from the assailant, drove him across the hallway, hammered him into the wall, and compacted his testicles with a knee. Not accidentally, he broke the guy's arm.

Later, for a few months during the divorce proceedings, he dated the shooter's wife. She wasn't a bad woman. She'd just gotten mixed up with bad men.

Now, Hazard climbed to the second floor of the apartment house, not entirely comfortable with the confining nature of the stairwell.

At Apartment 2B, he rang the bell without hesitation.

When Rolf Reynerd opened the door, he proved to be a perfect match for Ethan's description, down to the methamphetamine shine in his cold blue eyes and to the tiny flecks of foamy spittle in the corners of his mouth, which suggested that he was so routinely amped that he might, in a moment of toxic psychosis, spin wildly around his apartment under the misapprehension that he was Spiderman squirting silky filaments from his wrists.

Hazard flashed his ID, spread a garden-growing load of crap about Jerry Nemo being a suspect in the death of Carter Cook, and got into the apartment so fast that rain still dripped from his earlobes.

A product of weight training and protein powders, Reynerd looked as if he would have to eat a dozen raw eggs every morning merely to sustain the muscle mass in his right triceps.

Of the two of them, Hazard Yancy was the bigger and no doubt the smarter, but he cautioned himself to remain wary, alert.

Reynerd closed the apartment door and escorted Hazard into the living room, expressing a sincere desire to cooperate, as well as a sincere conviction that his good friend Jerry Nemo was incapable of harming a fly.

Regardless of how fly-loving Nemo might or might not be, Reynerd troweled on the sincerity as thickly as he might have done had he been wearing a purple-dinosaur costume, teaching little life lessons to preschoolers on an early-morning TV program.

If his acting had been this dreadful when he'd appeared on those soap operas, the writers must have been frantic to script Reynerd into a deadly car accident or a lightning-quick terminal brain tumor. The audience might have preferred a bloody end for him, by shotgun in an elevator.

Furniture, carpet, blinds, photographs of birds: Everything in the apartment was black-and-white. On the TV, in an old black-and-white movie, Clark Gable and Claudette Colbert showed Reynerd how it ought to be done.

In black slacks and a black-and-white sport shirt, the sincere friend of Jerry Nemo had coordinated his wardrobe with the decor.

At the suggestion of his host, Hazard settled in an armchair. He perched on the edge, the better to get up fast.

Reynerd plucked the remote control off the coffee table, pausing Gable in midspeech and Colbert in reaction. He sat on the sofa.

The only color in the room was provided by Reynerd's blue eyes and by the bright designs that enlivened the two bags of potato chips that flanked him on the sofa.

The bag to his left offered Hawaiian-style chips. The bag to his right held a sour-cream-and-chive variety. Mr. Gourmet.

Hazard had not forgotten Ethan's enigmatic but intense warning about snack-food containers.

Both bags were open, standing upright, plump enough to be full. Hazard detected the faint oily aroma of the chips.

If the bags contained handguns as well as chips, Hazard wasn't able to smell the weapons. He couldn't see them, either, because the bags, made of foil, were not transparent.

Reynerd sat with his hands palms-down on his thighs, licking his lips, as though he might reach for a salty treat at any moment.

With a nod to indicate the frozen image on the TV, the actor said, "That's the perfect medium for me. I was born too late. I should have lived back then."

"When's that?" Hazard asked, for he knew that suspects often revealed the most when they seemed to be rambling.

"The 1930s and '40s. When all films were black-and-white. I'd have been a star in those days."

"Is that right?"

"I'm too strong a personality for color films. I explode off the screen. I overwhelm the medium, the audience."

"I can see where that would be a problem."

"In the color era, the most successful stars have all been flat personalities, shallow. They're an inch wide, half an inch deep."

"And why is that?"

"The color, the depth of field made possible by modern cameras, surround-sound technology—all that stuff makes flat personalities bigger than life, provides them with a powerful illusion of substance and complexity."

"You, on the other hand—"

"I, on the other hand, am wide and deep and so *alive* to begin with that the further enhancement of modern film technology puts me over the top, makes a caricature of me."

"That must be frustrating," Hazard commiserated.

"You can't imagine. In black-and-white film, I would fill the screen without overwhelming the audience. Where are the Bogarts and Bacalls of our age, the Tracys and Hepburns, the Cary Grants and the Gary Coopers and the John Waynes?"

"We don't have them," Hazard acknowledged.

"They couldn't succeed today," Reynerd assured him. "They would be too powerful for modern film, too deep, entirely too glamorous. What did you think of *Moonshaker*?"

Hazard frowned. "Of what?"

"*Moonshaker*. Channing Manheim's latest hit. Two hundred million dollars at the box office."

Perhaps Reynerd was so obsessed with Manheim that sooner or later in *any* conversation, he would bring the subject around to the star.

Wary nonetheless, Hazard said, "I don't go to the movies."

"Everybody goes."

"Not really. Fewer than thirty million tickets have to be sold to generate two hundred million bucks. Maybe just ten percent of the country."

"All right, but other people see it on TV, on DVD."

"Maybe another thirty million. Pick any particular movie—at least eighty percent of the country never sees it. They have lives to live."

Reynerd seemed to boggle at the notion that movies were not the hub of the world. Although he didn't reach for a gun in either of the chip-bag holsters, his displeasure with this turn in the conversation was evident.

Hazard got back in the actor's good graces by saying, "Now, in the black-and-white era you're talking about, half the country went to the movies once a week. Stars were *stars* in those days. Everybody knew Clark Gable's movies, Jimmy Stewart's."

"Exactly," Reynerd agreed. "Manheim would have faded away in the black-and-white era. He would have been too thin for the medium, too flat. He'd be forgotten now. Worse than forgotten—he'd be *unknown*."

The doorbell rang.

Sounding puzzled and mildly annoyed, Reynerd said, "I'm not expecting anyone."

"Me neither," Hazard said dryly.

Reynerd glanced at the windows, where the sodden gray twilight slowly expired beyond the glass.

He shifted his attention to the television. Gable and Colbert remained frozen in flirtatious argument.

At last Reynerd rose from the sofa, but then hesitated, looking down at the bags of potato chips.

Watching this peculiar performance, Hazard wondered if the actor was approaching that amped-out condition in which a meth freak can slide precipitously from a peak of hyperacute awareness down into a haze of disorientation, into crushing exhaustion.

When the bell rang again, Reynerd finally crossed the living room. "These geeks are always coming around selling Jesus," he said irritably, wearily, and opened the door.

From the armchair, Hazard couldn't see who fired the shots. The hard *boom, boom, boom* of three rapid reports, however, told him that the killer was packing a high-caliber piece, maybe a .357, or bigger.

Unless Seventh Day Adventists had adopted hard-sell techniques, Reynerd had been mistaken about the purpose of the caller.

Hazard came up from the armchair on the second *boom*, reached for his holstered pistol on the third.

As mortal now as even Gable and Bogart had proved to be, Reynerd jolted backward, went down, casting a Technicolor splatter across the black-and-white apartment in which he had been so wide, so deep, so *alive*.

Moving toward the actor, Hazard heard running footsteps in the public hall.

Reynerd had taken three rounds point-blank in his broad chest, including one that must have punched significant scraps of his heart muscle through an exit wound in his back. He'd been mortuary material even as he fell.

The death-blinded blue of the actor's shock-widened eyes seemed less cold than they had been in life. He looked as if he needed some Jesus now.

Hazard stepped over the body, out of the apartment. He saw the shooter reach the end of the hallway. The guy leaped down the stairs two at a time. Hazard went after him.

CHAPTER 21

ABOVE THE CITY, AS THE RETREATING DAY shed its grizzled beard in wet ravelings of mist and drab drizzles, the hard face of night had not quite yet appeared.

On a west-side street of art galleries, of high-end shops, of restaurants in which elitist attitude was served more efficiently than the food, Ethan tucked the Expedition tight up against a red curb, two wheels in a flooded gutter, confident that the parking patrol issued tickets far less enthusiastically in foul weather than in fair.

The businesses in this neighborhood, seeking a sophisticated and exclusive clientele, stood behind shop fronts without flash, relying on subdued signage. Mere money shouts; wealth whispers.

The retail shops were not yet closed, and most restaurants were an hour away from opening their doors. Early lamplight gilded the dripping leaves of curbside trees and transformed the wet sidewalk into a path paved with pirates' treasure.

Without umbrella, Ethan moved in the shelter of shop awnings, all of which were tan or forest-green, silver or black, except for that in front of Forever Roses, which was a deep coral-pink.

The florist's shop might as aptly have been named Only Roses, for beyond the glass doors of the coolers that lined the big front room, no flowers other than roses could be seen, along with supplies of cut ferns and other greenery that were used to soften bright bouquets and arrangements.

Because of Hannah's gardening interests, now even five years after she had been laid to rest under mounded roses, Ethan could identify many of the varieties in the coolers.

Here was a rose so dark red that it almost appeared to be black, with petals that looked like velvet, earning its name: Black Magic.

And here, the John F. Kennedy rose: white petals so thick and glossy that they resembled sculpted wax.

The Charlotte Armstrong: large, fragrant, deep pink blooms. The Jardins de Bagatelle, the Rio Samba, the Paul McCartney rose, the Auguste Renoir, the Barbara Bush, the Voodoo, and the Bride's Dream.

Behind the customer counter stood an exceptional rose who looked as Hannah might have looked had she lived to be sixty. Thick salt-and-pepper hair cut short and shaggy. Large dark eyes brimming with life and delight. Time had not faded this woman's beauty, but had enriched it with a patina of experience.

Reading the name tag on the clerk's blouse, Ethan said, "Rowena, most of what I see in these coolers are hybrid tea varieties. Do you also like climbing roses?"

"Oh, yes, all kinds of roses," Rowena said, her voice musical and warm. "But we seldom use climbing roses. Varieties with longer stems work better in arrangements."

He introduced himself and, as was his habit in such situations, explained that he'd once been a homicide detective but recently had gone to work as an assistant to a high-profile celebrity.

Los Angeles and environs were acrawl with poseurs and frauds who claimed association with the rich and famous. Yet even those who had been made cynical by this city of deception nevertheless believed what Ethan told them, or pretended that they did.

Hannah had said that people trusted him easily because combined in him were the quiet steely strength of Dirty Harry Callahan and the earnest innocence of Huck Finn. *That,* he had replied, was a movie he *never* wanted to see.

Rowena, whether responding to the Harry-Huck of him or to other qualities, seemed to accept Ethan for who and what he claimed to be.

"If I guess your favorite variety of climbing rose," he said, "will you answer a few questions about a customer you served earlier this afternoon?"

"Is this police or celebrity business?"

"Both."

"Oh, delicious. I love running a rose shop, but there's more fragrance than excitement in it. Make your guess."

Because in Rowena he saw Hannah as she might have been at sixty, he spoke the name of the climbing rose that his lost wife had loved best: "Saint Joseph's Coat."

Rowena seemed genuinely surprised and pleased. "That's exactly right! You put Sherlock to shame."

"Now your half of the bargain," Ethan said, leaning with both arms on the counter. "This afternoon a man came in here and bought a bouquet of Broadway roses."

The dazzling golden-red blooms on Hannah's grave had been wrapped in a cone of stiff cellophane. Instead of Scotch tape or staples, a series of six peel-and-press stickers had been applied to seal cellophane to cellophane and thus ensure that the cone kept its shape. Each fancy foil sticker bore the name and address of Forever Roses.

"We had just two dozen," Rowena said, "and he took them all."

"You remember him then?"

"Oh, yes. He was . . . quite memorable."

"Would you describe him for me?"

"Tall, athletic but a bit on the thin side, wearing an exquisite gray suit."

Duncan Whistler owned uncounted fine suits, all custom-tailored at great cost.

"He was a handsome man," Rowena continued, "but terribly pale, as though he hadn't seen the sun in months."

Comatose for twelve weeks, Dunny had developed a hospital pallor subsequently seasoned by at least an hour of morgue time.

"He had the most magnetic gray eyes," Rowena said, "with flecks of green. Beautiful."

She had given a perfect description of Dunny's eyes.

"He said that he wanted the roses for a special woman."

At her funeral, Dunny had seen the Broadway roses.

Rowena smiled. "He said an old friend would be around before long, asking what kind of roses he'd bought. I gather you're in competition for the same girl."

Neither the winter day outside nor the cool air here in the flower shop was responsible for the chill that might have rattled Ethan's teeth if he hadn't clenched them.

He suddenly realized that Rowena's smile had a curious tilt, as though tempered by uncertainty or uneasiness.

When she recognized how deeply her revelation troubled him, her tentative smile faltered, vanished.

"He was a strange man," she said.

"Did he say anything else?"

Rowena broke eye contact and looked toward the windows at the front of the shop, as though expecting to see someone familiar—and unwelcome—at the door.

Ethan gave her an opportunity to consider her words, and at last she spoke: "He said you think he's dead."

Images swelled to the foreground of memory: the empty gurney and the tangled shroud in the hospital morgue; the elusive phantom in the steam-blurred bathroom mirror; the lizard on the driveway, struggling to ascend in spite of its broken back, confronted by a cruel degree of incline and by sluicing water as cold and insistent as the flow of time. . . .

"He said you think he's dead," Rowena repeated, shifting her gaze from the shop door to Ethan once more. "And he said I should tell you that you're right."

CHAPTER 22

HAZARD IN THE HALLWAY, HAZARD ON THE stairs, acutely aware of what an easy target a big man made in a narrow space, threw himself nonetheless into the hot pursuit. When you took the job, you knew it wasn't part of the deal that you could pick and choose the places where you would put your life on the line.

Besides, like most cops, he operated on the superstitious conviction that the greatest risk came with hesitation, came in the moment when nerve was briefly lost. Survival depended on boldness seasoned with just enough fear to discourage outright recklessness.

Or so it was easy to believe until a bit of boldness got you killed.

In the movies, cops were always yelling "Halt! Police!" when they knew that the dirtbags running away from them weren't going to obey, but also when a shout would reveal their presence before absolutely necessary and even before every bad guy on the game board realized that badges were in play.

Hazard Yancy, who had recently escaped being shot at while in an armchair, didn't bellow either a command or a threat at the gunman who had killed Rolf Reynerd. He just plunged down the stairs after the guy.

By the time Hazard reached the midfloor landing, the shooter had thundered to the bottom of the lower flight, losing his balance as he flew off the last step into the public foyer. He slipped on the Mexican-tile floor, windmilled his arms, but avoided a fall.

Running, the perp never looked back, suggesting that he was oblivious of being pursued.

As he gave chase, Hazard was in the guy's head. Expecting Reynerd to be home alone, the rent-a-killer gink comes in to do a quick pop, he drops the sucker with a heart-buster, manages to avoid getting lit up in the process, breaks hard for the street, and now he's already thinking about smoking some good bo with some long-legged fresh who's waiting for him in his crib.

The shooter hit the front door, and at the same moment, Hazard landed in the foyer, but the shooter was making too much noise to hear doom closing from behind, and Hazard didn't slip as his quarry had done, so he was gaining.

When Hazard reached the door, the shooter was already out in the night, down the exterior steps, maybe thinking about spending some of his hit money on fancy chrome laces for the wheels on his bucket, some on 24-carat flash to drape his lady.

Not much wind, cold rain, Hazard on the steps, shooter on the walk: The gap between them closed as inevitably as that between a speeding truck and a brick wall.

Then the car horn blared. One long bleat, two short.

A signal. Prearranged.

In the street, not at the curb, stood a dark Mercedes-Benz, headlights on, engine running, exhaust pluming from the tailpipe. The front passenger door stood open to welcome the shooter. This was a getaway bucket with style, maybe a G-ride, a gangster ride, stolen out of a driveway in Beverly Hills, and behind the wheel sat the shooter's ace kool, his backup homey, ready to shave the tires bald in a pedal-jammed escape.

The one long bleat followed by two short must have signaled the rabbit that he had a wolf on his ass, because he made a sudden break to the left, off the sidewalk. He torqued himself around so hard that he should have stumbled, should have fallen, but didn't, and instead brought up the piece with which he'd popped Reynerd.

Having lost the advantage of surprise, Hazard finally shouted "Police! Drop it!" just like in the movies, but of course the shooter had already earned life without possibility of parole, maybe even the death penalty, by chilling Reynerd, and he had nothing to lose. He would be no more likely to drop his weapon than he would be likely to drop his pants and bend over.

The piece looked big, not a trey-eight or a .357, but a four-five. Loaded with wicked ammo, a four-five would reliably bust bone and tenderize meat for the undertaker, but it required stability and calculation to compensate for the kick.

In a bad stance, from panic rather than poise, the perp squeezed off a shot. His pull was actually more jerk than squeeze, and the round went so wild that Hazard stood at less risk of being drilled by this bullet than of being pulverized by an asteroid.

The instant he saw the muzzle spit fire into the rain and heard the slug shatter a window in the apartment house behind him, however, Hazard was only partly driven by training, partly by duty, and mostly by blood. The shooter wouldn't be sloppy twice. All the sensitivity instruction, all the earnest lectures in social policy and political consequences, all the police-commission directives to meet violence with patience, understanding, and measured response were impediments to survival when, in the quick, you had to kill or be killed.

The sound of bullet-battered glass was still ringing through the rain when Hazard got a two-hand grip on his gun, assumed the stance, and answered fire with fire. He placed two rounds with little concern for the stern judgment of the *Los Angeles Times* in matters of police deportment, but with every concern for the safety of Mother Yancy's favorite baby boy.

The first shot took the killer down, and the second rapped him hammer-hard even as his knees were still buckling.

Reflexively, the perp fired the .45 not at Hazard, but into the grass in front of his own feet. The recoil broke his weakened grip, and the gun flew from his hand.

He met the ground with one knee, in the briefest genuflection, then with two knees, then with his face.

Hazard kicked the dropped .45 away from the killer, into shrubs and shadows, and he ran toward the street, toward the Mercedes.

The driver gunned the engine an instant before he let up on the brakes. Shrieking tires spun off clouds of vaporized rain, and smoke that stank of burnt rubber.

Maybe Hazard was at risk of being shot by the driver, who could get a line on him through the open front passenger's door, but that was a risk worth taking. An ace-kool wheelman specialized in flight, not fight, and although the guy would be packing heat for use in a cornered-rat situation, he wouldn't likely draw down on anyone when he had an open street, gas in the tank, and ignition.

Splashing along the puddled pavement, Hazard reached his sedan. Before he could get around that parked vehicle, into the street, the spinning tires of the getaway car bit blacktop and bolted forward with a bark. Momentum slammed shut the passenger's door.

He hadn't gotten a look at the driver.

The figure behind the wheel had been little more than a shadow. Hunched, distorted, somehow . . . *wrong.*

To Hazard's surprise, the ragged fingernails of superstition scratched at the inner hollows of his bones, where usually it lay buried, quiet, forgotten. But he didn't know what had stirred his fear or why a sense of the uncanny suddenly possessed him.

As the Mercedes roared away, Hazard didn't squeeze off a few shots at it, as a movie cop would have done. This was a peaceful residential neighborhood in which people watching reruns of *Seinfeld* and other people cleaning vegetables for dinner had every right not to expect to be shot dead over their TV remotes and their cutting boards by the stray rounds of a reckless detective.

He ran after the car, however, because he couldn't get a clear take on the license number. Exhaust vapors, street spray, falling rain, and the gloom of day's end conspired to shroud the rear plate.

He persisted, anyway, glad that he regularly used a treadmill. Although the Mercedes soon pulled away from him, a couple street-lamps and a clearing crosswind revealed the plate number in pieces.

Most likely the car had been stolen. The driver would dump it. Nevertheless, having the number was better than not having it.

Giving up the chase, Hazard headed back to the front lawn at the apartment house. He hoped that he'd shot the shooter dead instead of merely wounding him.

Minutes from now, an Officer Involved Shooting team would be on the scene. Depending on the personal philosophies of team members, they would either vigorously build a defense of Hazard's actions and strive to exonerate him without any genuine search for the truth, which was fine by him, or they would seek the tiniest of meaningless inconsistencies and screw him to a cross of bogus evidence, haul him into the court of public opinion, and encourage the media to build a fire at his feet and give him the Saint Joan treatment.

The third possibility was that the OIS team might arrive without preconceptions, might examine the facts analytically, and might come to a dispassionate conclusion based on logic and reason, which would be jake with Hazard because he'd done nothing wrong.

Of course, he'd never heard of such a thing actually occurring, and he considered it far less likely than being eyewitness to eight flying reindeer and an elf-piloted sleigh three nights hence.

If the shooter was alive, he might assert that Hazard had killed Reynerd and then tried to frame him for it. Or that he'd been in the neighborhood, collecting donations to Toys for Tots, when he'd been caught in a cross fire, giving the *real* shooter a chance to escape.

Whatever he claimed, cop haters and aggressively brainless citizens would believe him.

More important, the shooter would find an attorney to file suit against the city, eager to feed at the public trough. A settlement would be reached, regardless of the merits of the case, and Hazard would probably be sacrificed as part of the package. Politicians were no more protective of good law-enforcement officers than they were of the young interns whom they regularly abused and sometimes killed.

The shooter posed far less of a problem dead than alive.

Hazard could have *moseyed* back to the scene, giving the perp a chance to bleed out another critical pint, but he ran.

The killer lay where he'd fallen, face planted in the wet grass. A snail had ascended the back of his neck.

People were at windows, looking down, expressions blank, like dead sentinels at the gates of Hell. Hazard expected to see Reynerd at one of the panes, black-and-white, too glamorous for his time.

He turned the shooter faceup. Somebody's son, somebody's homey, in his early twenties, with a shaved head, wearing a tiny coke spoon for an earring.

Hazard was glad to see the mouth stretched in a death rictus and the eyes full of eternity, but at the same time he was sickened by the sense of relief that flooded through him.

Standing in the storm, swallowing a hard-to-repress sludge of half-digested mamoul that burned in his throat, he used his cell phone to call the division and report the situation.

After making the call, he could have gone inside to watch from the foyer, but he waited in the downpour.

City lights reflected in every storm-glazed surface, yet when night swallowed twilight, darkness swelled in threatening coils, like a well-fed snake.

The rat-feet tap of palm-pelting rain suggested that legions of tree rodents scurried through the masses of arching fronds overhead.

Hazard saw two snails on the dead man's face. He wanted to flick them off, but he hesitated to do so.

Some onlookers at the windows would suspect him of tampering with evidence. Their sinister assumptions might charm the OIS team.

That scratching in his bones again. That sense of *wrongness*.

One dead upstairs, one dead here, sirens in the distance.

What the hell is going on? What the hell?

CHAPTER 23

ROWENA, MISTRESS OF THE ROSES, RECALLED Dunny Whistler's words again, but obviously more for her consideration than for Ethan's: "He said you think he's dead, and that you're right."

A rattle of hinges, a faint jingle of shop bells turned Ethan toward the front door. No one had entered.

The vagrant wind, having wandered out of the storm for a while, had here returned, blustering at the entrance to Forever Roses, trembling the door.

Behind the counter, the woman wondered, "What on earth could he mean by such a bizarre statement?"

"Did you ask him?"

"He said it after he paid for the roses, on his way out of the shop. I didn't have a chance to ask. Is it a joke between the two of you?"

"Did he smile when he said it?"

Rowena considered, shook her head. "No."

From the corner of his eye, Ethan glimpsed a figure that had silently appeared. Turning toward it, breath caught in his throat, he discovered that he had been tricked by his own reflection in the glass door of a cooler.

In pails of water, on tiered racks, the chilled roses bloomed so gloriously that you could easily forget they were in fact already dead, and in a few days would be wilted, spotted brown, and rotting.

These coolers, where Death concealed himself in petals bright, reminded Ethan of morgue drawers, in which the deceased lay much as they had looked in life, and in whom Death dwelt but did not yet manifest himself in all the gaudy details of corruption.

Although Rowena was personable and lovely, although this realm of roses ought to have been pleasant, Ethan grew anxious to leave. "Did my . . . my friend have any other message for me?"

"No. That was all of it, I think."

"Thank you, Rowena. You've been helpful."

"Have I really?" she asked, looking at him strangely, perhaps as puzzled by this odd encounter as by her conversation with Dunny Whistler.

"Yes," he assured her. "Yes, you have."

Wind rattled the door again as Ethan put his hand upon the knob, and behind him Rowena said, "One more thing."

When he turned to her, although they were now almost forty feet apart, he saw that his questioning had left her more pensive than she had been when he'd first approached her.

"As your friend was leaving," she said, "he stopped in the open doorway, on the threshold there, and said to me, 'God bless you and your roses.' "

Perhaps this had been a peculiar thing for a man like Dunny to have said, but nothing in those six words seemed to explain why the memory of them clouded Rowena's face with uneasiness.

She said, "Just as he finished speaking, the lights pulsed and dimmed, went off—but then came on again. I didn't think anything about it at the time, not with the storm, but now it somehow seems . . . significant. I don't know why."

Years of experience with interrogations told Ethan that Rowena had not finished, and that his patient silence would draw her out more surely and more quickly than anything he could say.

"When the lights dimmed and went off, your friend laughed. Just a little laugh, not long, not loud. He glanced at the ceiling as the lights flickered, and he laughed, and then he left."

Ethan waited.

Rowena appeared to be surprised that she had said this much about such a small moment, but then she added, "There was something terrible about that laugh."

The beautiful dead roses behind walls of glass.

A beast of wind snuffling at the door.

Rain gnashing at the windows.

Ethan said, "Terrible?"

"I don't have the words to explain it. No humor in that laugh, but some terrible . . . quality."

Self-conscious, she brushed at the spotless countertop with one hand, as if she saw dust, debris, a stain.

Clearly, she had said all that she wished to say, or could.

"God bless you and your roses," Ethan told her, as though he were countering a curse.

He didn't know what he would have done had the lights flickered, but they burned steadily.

Rowena smiled uncertainly.

Turning to the door again, Ethan encountered his reflection and closed his eyes, perhaps to guard against the sight of an impossible phantom figure sharing the glass with him. He opened the door, then opened his eyes.

In a growl of wind and a jingle of overhead bells, he stepped out of the shop into the cold teeth of the December night, and drew the door shut behind him.

He waited in the entry alcove, between the display windows, as a young couple in raincoats and hoods passed on the sidewalk, led by a golden retriever on a leash.

Relishing the rain and wind, the soaked retriever pranced on webbed paws, snout lifted to savor mysterious scents upon the chilly air. Before it fully passed, it looked up, and its eyes were as wise as they were liquid and dark.

The dog halted, pricked its floppy ears as much as they would prick, and cocked its head as though not entirely sure what kind of man stood here in the shelter of the coral-pink awning, between the roses and the rain. The tail wagged, but only twice, and tentatively.

Stopped by their canine companion, the young couple said, "Good evening," and Ethan replied, and the woman spoke to the dog, "Tink, let's go."

Tink hesitated, searching Ethan's eyes, and only moved on when the woman repeated the command.

Because the couple and the dog were headed in the direction of his SUV, Ethan waited briefly, to avoid following on their heels.

The leaves of the curbside trees were still gilded by lamplight, and from their pointed tips flowed drips and drizzles as glimmerous as molten gold.

In the street, the traffic appeared to be lighter than it should have been at this hour, moving faster than the weather warranted.

Awning by awning, Ethan approached the Expedition, fishing keys from his jacket pocket.

Ahead, Tink twice slowed to an amble, looked back at Ethan, but didn't stop.

The ozone-scented cascades of rain couldn't rinse away the yeasty aroma of freshly baked bread, which issued from one of the glittery restaurants preparing to open their doors for dinner.

At the end of the block, the dog halted once more, turning its head to stare.

Though her voice was muffled by distance, screened by the sizzle of rain and the swish of passing traffic, the woman could be heard saying, "Tink, let's go." She repeated the command twice before the dog began to move again, picking up the slack in its leash.

The trio disappeared around the corner.

Arriving at the red zone near the end of the block, where he had parked illegally, Ethan hesitated under the last awning. He monitored the approaching traffic until he saw a long gap between vehicles.

He stepped into the rain and crossed the sidewalk. He jumped over the dirty racing current in the gutter.

Behind his SUV, he thumbed the lock-release button on his key fob. The Expedition chirruped at him.

Having waited until there was no passing traffic to splash him, he rounded the back of the vehicle while a chance remained that he could avoid an immediate need for a dry cleaner.

Approaching the driver's door, he realized that he had not taken a close look at the SUV itself from the shelter of the final awning, and suddenly he was convinced that *this* time, when he got behind the wheel, he would discover Dunny Whistler, dead or alive, waiting for him in the passenger's seat.

The real threat lay elsewhere.

Entering from the cross street at too high a speed, a Chrysler PT Cruiser fishtailed in the intersection. The driver tried to resist the slide instead of steering into it, the wheels locked, and the Cruiser spun out.

In the spin, the left front bumper rapped Ethan hard. Clipped, flipped, he slammed into the Expedition, shattering the side window with his face.

He wasn't aware of ricocheting off the SUV, collapsing to the pavement, but then he was down on the wet blacktop, tumbling, with the smell of exhaust fumes, with the taste of blood.

He heard brakes shriek, but not the Cruiser. Air brakes. Loud and shrill.

Something loomed, huge, a truck, loomed and immediately *arrived*, tremendous weight on his legs, hideous pressure, bones snapping like dry sticks.

CHAPTER 24

BUNKED THREE-HIGH ALONG THE WALLS, LIKE travelers in a railroad sleeping car, the corpses lay in open berths, the journey from death to grave having been delayed by this unscheduled stop.

After switching on the light, Corky Laputa quietly closed the door behind him.

"Good evening, ladies and gentlemen," he said to the assembled cadavers.

In any circumstances, he could reliably amuse himself.

"The next station on this line is Hell, with cozy beds of nails, hot and cold running cockroaches, and a free continental breakfast of molten sulfur."

To his left were eight bodies and one empty berth. Seven bodies and two empty berths to his right. Five bodies and one empty berth at the end of the room. Twenty cadavers, with accommodations available to serve four more.

These dreamless sleepers lay not on mattresses but on stainless-steel pans. The bunks were actually open racks designed to facilitate air circulation.

This refrigerated chamber provided a dry environment no colder than five—and no higher than eight—degrees above freezing. Corky's exhalations issued from his nostrils in twin ribbons of pale vapor.

A sophisticated ventilation system continuously drew air out of the room through exhausts near the floor. Fresh air pumped in through wall vents just below the ceiling.

Although the smell wasn't conducive to a romantic candlelight dinner, it wasn't instantly repulsive, either. You could half deceive yourself that this odor was not significantly different in character from the stale-sweat, foot-fungus, shower-mold bouquet common to many high-school locker rooms.

None of the resident dead was bagged. The low temperature and the strictly controlled humidity slowed decomposition almost to a halt, but the inevitable process *did* continue at a much reduced rate. A vinyl bag would trap the slowly released gases, becoming a heat-filled balloon and defeating the purpose of the refrigeration.

Instead of vinyl cocoons, loose white cotton shrouds draped the reclining dead. Except for the chill and the smell, they might have been the pampered guests at an exclusive health spa, taking a group nap in a sauna.

In life, few if any of them had ever been pampered. If one had seen the inside of a health spa, he had surely at once been ejected by security guards and warned never to trespass again.

These were life's losers. They had died alone and unknown.

Those who perished at the hand of another were required by law to undergo autopsy. So were those who died by accident, by apparent suicide, from an illness not confidently diagnosed, and from causes that were not apparent and that were, therefore, suspicious.

In any big city, especially in one as dysfunctional as current-day Los Angeles, bodies often arrived at the morgue faster than the medical examiner's overworked staff could deal with them. Priority was given to victims of violence, to possible victims of medical malpractice, and to those among the deceased who had families waiting to receive their remains for burial.

Vagrants without families, often without identification, whose bodies had been discovered in alleyways, in parks, under bridges, who might have succumbed from drug overdoses or from exposure to the elements, or from simple liver failure, were parked here for a few days, for a week, maybe even longer, until the medical examiner's staff had time to conduct at least cursory postmortems.

In death, as in life, these castaways were served last.

A telephone hung on the wall to the right of the door, as though considerately provided to enable the deceased to order pizza.

Most lines permitted only in-facility communication, functioning as intercom links. The last of six lines allowed outgoing calls.

Corky keyed in Roman Castevet's cell-phone number.

Roman, a pathologist on the medical examiner's staff, had just come on duty for the evening shift. He was probably in an autopsy room elsewhere in the building, preparing to cut.

More than a year ago, they had met at an anarchists' mixer at the university where Corky taught. The catered food had been second-rate, the drinks slightly watered down, and the flower arrangements less than inspired, but the company had been engaging.

On the third ring, Roman answered, and after Corky identified himself, he said, "Guess where I am?"

"You've crawled up your own ass and can't get out," Roman said.

He had an unconventional sense of humor.

"It's a good thing this isn't a pay phone," Corky said. "I don't have any change, and none of the cheap stiffs here will lend me a quarter."

"Then it must be a faculty function. Nobody's more miserly than a bunch of anticapitalist academics wallowing in the high life with fat checks from the taxpayers."

"Some might see a wide vein of meanness in your humor," Corky said with a severe note that wasn't characteristic of him.

"They wouldn't be mistaken. Cruelty is my creed, remember?"

Roman was a Satanist. Hail the Prince of Darkness, that kind of stuff. Not all anarchists were also Satanists, but many Satanists were also anarchists.

Corky knew one Buddhist who was an anarchist—a conflicted young woman. Otherwise, in his experience, the vast majority of anarchists were atheists.

In his considered opinion, pure anarchists didn't believe in the supernatural, neither in the powers of Darkness nor in the powers of Light. They put all their faith in the power of destruction and in the new and better order that might arise from ruin.

"Considering your backlog of work," said Corky, "it seems to me academics aren't the only ones who don't always earn their fat checks from the taxpayers. What do you guys do here on the evening shift—just play poker, swap ghost stories?"

Roman must have been only half listening. He didn't pick up on the word *here.* "Banter isn't your strong suit. Get to the point. What do you want? You always want something."

"And I always pay well for it, don't I?"

"The ability to pay cash in full is the virtue I admire most."

"I see you people have solved the rat problem."

"What rat problem?"

Two years ago, the media had given extensive grisly coverage to the fact that sanitary and pest-control conditions in this very room and elsewhere in this facility had been deplorable.

"The place must be rat-proof now. I'm looking around," Corky said, "and I don't see any lowbrow cousins of Mickey Mouse noshing on anyone's nose."

The silence of shocked disbelief greeted this statement. When Roman Castevet could speak, he said, "You can't be where I think you are."

"I'm exactly where you think I am."

The smug self-satisfaction and sarcasm in Roman's voice abruptly vaporized into a whisper fierce with self-concern. "What're you doing to me, coming here? You're not authorized. You don't belong anywhere in the morgue, and especially not in *there*."

"I have credentials."

"The hell you do."

"I could leave here and come to you. Are you in one of the autopsy rooms or still at your desk?"

Roman's whisper grew softer but even more intense: "Are you nuts? Are you trying to get me fired?"

"I just want to place an order," Corky said.

Recently Roman had supplied him with a jar containing tissue preservative and ten foreskins harvested from cadavers destined for cremation.

Corky had given the jar to Rolf Reynerd with instructions. In spite of his congenital stupidity, Reynerd had managed to pack the container in a black gift box and send it to Channing Manheim.

"I need another ten," Corky said.

"You don't come *here* to talk about it. You *never* come here, you moron. You call me at home."

"I thought this would be a hoot, give you a laugh."

Shakily, Roman said, "Dear Jesus."

"You're a Satanist," Corky reminded him.

"Idiot."

"Listen, Roman, where exactly are you? How do I get to you from here? We need to do some business."

"Stay right where you are."

"I don't know. I'm getting a little claustrophobic. This place is beginning to spook me."

"*Stay right where you are!* I'll be there in two minutes."

"I just heard something weird. I think one of these corpses might be alive."

"None of them is alive."

"I'm sure this one guy, over toward the corner, just said something."

"Then he said you're an idiot."

"Maybe you've got a live one in here by mistake. I'm really starting to get creeped out."

"Two minutes," Roman insisted. "You wait right where you are. Don't come blundering out of there, drawing attention to yourself, or I'll harvest *your* foreskin."

Roman terminated the call.

In the vault of the unknown and penniless dead, Corky hung up the phone.

Surveying his shrouded audience, he said, "With all humility, I could teach Channing Manheim a thing or two about acting."

He expected and needed no applause. A perfect performance was its own reward.

CHAPTER 25

SNOW FELL ON THE CITY OF ANGELS.
Unprecedented, the shepherd wind drove white flocks out of the dark meadows above the world, gently harried them between ficus trees and palms, along avenues that had never known a snowy Christmas.

Dazzled, Ethan gazed up into the fleecy night.

Abed in his room, he realized that the roof must have been lifted off the house by a prying wind. Snowdrifts would bury the furniture, ruin the carpet.

Soon he would have to rise, go along the hall to his parents' room. Dad would know what to do about the missing roof.

First, however, Ethan wanted to enjoy this spectacle: Above him, the snowfall hung an infinite crystal chandelier, its beautiful swags of cut beads and beveled pendants in perpetual glittering movement.

His eyelashes were frosted.

Flakes delivered cold kisses to his face, melted on his cheeks.

When his vision fully focused, he discovered that in truth the December night was full of raindrops, to which his troubled eyes had imparted crystalline structures and mysterious hieroglyphic forms.

Once soft, his bed had been spellcast into blacktop.

He felt no discomfort, except that his feather pillow pressed like hard pavement against the back of his head.

The rain on his face fell as cold as snow, imparting an equal chill to his upturned left hand.

His right hand lay exposed, as well, but with it he could not feel the cold or the tap-and-trickle of the rain.

He couldn't feel his legs, either. Couldn't move them. Could not move anything other than his head and left hand.

If his roofless room filled with rain, and if he were unable to move, he might drown.

In the pool of dreamy speculation on which Ethan had been drifting, sudden terror darted sharklike through the depths beneath him, rising.

He closed his eyes to avoid seeing a bigger and more terrible truth than that the snowflakes were actually raindrops.

Voices approached. Dad and Mom must be coming to put the roof back where it belonged, to fluff his stone pillow into comfortable plumpness once more, and to set all wrongness right.

He surrendered himself to their loving care, and like a feather, he drifted down into darkness, toward the Land of Nod, not the Nod to which Cain had fled after killing Abel, but the Nod to which dreaming children journeyed to find adventure and from which they woke safely in the golden dawn.

Still descending through the darkness north of Nod, he heard the words "spinal injury."

Opening his eyes a minute or ten minutes later, he discovered the night aswarm with pulsing-revolving red and yellow lights, and blue, as if he were in an open-air discotheque, and he knew that he would never dance again, or walk.

To the tuneless broken songs of police-radio crackle, flanked by paramedics, Ethan glided through the rain on a gurney toward an ambulance.

On the white van, in red letters trimmed in gold, under the bold word AMBULANCE, glowed the smaller words OUR LADY OF ANGELS HOSPITAL.

Maybe they would give him a bed in Dunny's old room.

That prospect filled him with a choking dread.

He closed his eyes for what seemed a blink, heard men warning one another "careful" and "easy, easy," and when he looked again, he had blinked himself into the ambulance.

He became aware that a needle already pierced his right arm, served by an IV tube and a dangling bag of plasma.

For the first time, he heard his breathing—full of wheeze and rush and rattle—whereupon he knew that more than his legs had been crushed. He suspected that one or both of his lungs struggled against the confinement of a partially collapsed rib cage.

He wished for pain. Anything but this terrible lack of feeling.

The paramedic at Ethan's side spoke urgently to his teammate, who stood in the rain, beyond the open doors: "We're gonna need speed."

"I'll burn asphalt," the rain-lashed medic promised, and he slammed shut the doors.

Along both side walls, near the ceiling, taut garlands of red tinsel sparkled. At the ends and in the middle of each garland, small silver bells, three per set, dangled brightly. Christmas decorations.

The bells in each group were strung concentrically on the same string. The top bell, also the largest, overhung the middle bell, which overhung the third—which was also the smallest—in the set.

When the door slammed, the tiny bells on each string jiggled against one another, producing a silvery ringing as faint as fairy music.

The paramedic fitted Ethan with an oxygen mask.

As cool as autumn, as sweet as springtime, a rich blend of air soothed his hot throat, but his wheezing did not in the least abate.

Having climbed behind the steering wheel in the front of the ambulance, the driver slammed his door, again causing the red tinsel to shimmer and the bells to ring.

"Bells," Ethan said, but the oxygen mask muffled the word.

In the process of fitting the binaurals of a stethoscope to his ears, the paramedic paused. "What did you say?"

The sight of the stethoscope inspired in Ethan the realization that he could hear his heartbeat, and that what he heard was ragged, uneven, alarming.

Listening, he knew that he was hearing not just his heart, but also the knock-hoofed canter of Death's horse approaching.

"Bells," he repeated, as throughout his mind the doors to a thousand fears flew open.

The ambulance began to move, and as it rolled, the siren found its shrill voice.

Ethan couldn't hear the bells above the banshee wail, but he could see the nearest three trembling on their string. Trembling.

He raised his left hand toward the dangling cluster but couldn't reach that far. His hand grasped at empty air.

This terrible intensity of fear brought with it a clouding confusion, and perhaps he was utterly delirious; nevertheless, the bells seemed to be more than mere decorations, seemed mystical in their shiny smoothness, in their glimmering curves, the embodiment of hope, and he desperately needed to hold them.

Apparently the paramedic understood the urgency of Ethan's need to have the bells, if not the reason for it. He plucked a small pair of scissors from a kit, and swaying with the movement of the vehicle, he clipped the knot that secured the nearest cluster to the garland of tinsel.

Given the string of bells, Ethan clutched them in his left hand with a grip both tender and ferocious.

He was exhausted, but he dared not close his eyes again, for he feared that when he opened them, darkness would remain and never go away, that he would henceforth see nothing of this world.

The paramedic picked up the stethoscope once more. He inserted the binaural tips in his ears.

With the fingers of his left hand, Ethan counted the bells on the string, from tiniest to largest, to tiniest again.

He realized that he held these ornaments as he'd held a rosary in the hushed hospital room during the last few nights of Hannah's life: with equal measures of despair and hope, with an unexpected awe that sustained the heart and with a stoicism that armored it. His hope had been unrealized, his stoicism essential, when he had found it necessary to survive her loss.

Between thumb and forefinger, he had tried to pinch mercy from the rosary beads. Now he smoothed the curvatures of bell, bell, and bell, seeking mercy less than understanding, seeking a revelation deaf to the ear but resonant in the heart.

Although Ethan did not close his eyes and bring the darkness down, seeping shadows encroached from the periphery of vision, like ink spreading through the fibers of a blotter.

Apparently the stethoscope captured rhythms that alarmed the paramedic. He loomed close, but his voice came from a distance, and though his face was a mask of calm professionalism, he spoke with an urgency that revealed the depth of his concern for his patient. "Ethan, don't leave us here. Hang tight. Hold on, damn it."

Cinched by a knot of darkness, Ethan's vision narrowed as the cords pulled tighter, tighter.

He detected the astringent scent of rubbing alcohol. A coolness below the crook of his left arm preceded the sting of a needle.

Within him, the knocking hooves of one-horse Death gave way to the thunder of an apocalyptic herd in chaotic gallop.

The ambulance still rocketed toward Our Lady of Angels, but the driver gave the siren a rest, evidently trusting to the swiveling beacons on the roof.

In the absence of the banshee shriek, Ethan thought he heard bells again.

These were not the worry-bead bells that in his hand he smoothed and smoothed, nor were they the strings of ornamental bells suspended from the red sparkling tinsel. These chimes arose at some distance, calling him with a silvery insistence.

His vision irised to a dim spot of light, and then the mortal knot drew tighter still, blinding him completely. Accepting the inevitability of death and endless darkness, at last he closed his eyelids.

He opened the door, then opened his eyes.

In a growl of wind and a jingle of overhead bells, he stepped out of Forever Roses into the cold teeth of the December night, and drew the door shut behind him.

In shock to find himself alive, in disbelief that he stood on legs unbroken, he waited in the entry alcove, between the display windows, as a young couple in raincoats and hoods strolled by on the sidewalk, led by a golden retriever on a leash.

The dog looked up at Ethan, its eyes as wise as they were liquid and dark.

"Good evening," the couple said.

Unable to speak, Ethan nodded.

"Tink, let's go," the woman urged, and then repeated the command when the dog hesitated.

The soaked retriever pranced away, snout lifted to savor the chilly air, followed by its companions.

Ethan turned to peer at the florist who still stood behind the counter, past the glass coffins full of roses.

Rowena had been staring after him. Now she quickly looked down as though attending to a task.

On legs as shaky as his reason, Ethan retraced the route that he had taken to this place, under the sheltering awnings of shops and restaurants, toward the Expedition in the red zone.

Ahead, Tink twice glanced back, but didn't stop.

Passing a restaurant bejeweled with candlelight and sparkling tableware, breathing in the yeasty fragrance of freshly baked bread, Ethan thought, *The staff of life.*

At the end of the block, the dog looked back once more. Then the trio disappeared around the corner.

In the street, the traffic was lighter than usual at this hour, moving faster than the weather warranted.

Arriving at the red zone near the end of the block, Ethan stood under the last awning—and thought that he might stand there, well and safely back from the street, until dawn reclaimed the city from the night.

A long gap appeared in the approaching traffic.

With his trembling right hand, he fished his keys from a jacket pocket and thumbed the lock-release button on the fob. The Expedition chirruped at him, but he didn't approach it.

Turning his attention toward the intersection, Ethan saw the headlights of the PT Cruiser as the vehicle approached at far too high a speed on the cross street.

The Cruiser fishtailed in the intersection, and its wheels locked. In the spinout, the car rotated past the parked Expedition, mere inches from a collision.

Had Ethan stood there, he would have been battered between the vehicles, like a pinball between warring flippers.

Here came the crushing truck, the shrill blast of air brakes.

With a sharp stuttering bark of tires against wet blacktop, the Cruiser spun into the far lanes where it belonged.

Parting the rain where the Cruiser had just whipped through it, the truck shook and shuddered to a stop.

When the driver of the Cruiser regained control, he raced away, at a lower but still reckless speed.

The agitated trucker blew his horn. Then he continued on the route that he'd been following before the near miss, toward whatever destination unhindered fate had planned for him.

In the wake of the truck, the gap in traffic had closed.

The signal light changed at the intersection. In two directions, traffic came to a halt, but in two others, it began to move again.

Drenching the night: the delicious aroma of baking bread.

Golden lamplight spending doubloons upon the pavement.

The rush and rustle of the rain.

Perhaps the signal light changed twice again or even three times before Ethan became aware of an aching in his left hand. The cramping pain had begun to spread into the muscles of his forearm.

Tangled through the fiercely clenched fingers of his fist was the string of three small silvery bells clipped from the ambulance tinsel and given to him by a compassionate paramedic.

CHAPTER 26

A S IF THEY WERE THE DEGENERATE ELITE OF ancient Rome, reclining in midbacchanal, their togas scandalously disarranged, the nameless dead revealed here a smooth and creamy shoulder, here the pale curve of a breast, here a blue-veined thigh, here a hand with the fingers curled in a subtle obscene gesture, here a delicate foot and slender ankle, and here half a profile in which one open eye stared with milky lust.

The least-superstitious witness to this grotesque display might be inclined to suspect that in the absence of a living observer, these unidentified vagrants and teenage runaways would visit bunk to bunk. In the most lonely hours after midnight, might not the restless dead pair up in a cold and hideous parody of passion?

If Corky Laputa had believed in a moral code or even if he had believed that good taste required certain universal rules of social conduct, he might have passed his two-minute wait by rearranging these carelessly draped shrouds, insisting upon modesty even among the deceased.

Instead, he enjoyed the scene because in this chamber was the ultimate fruit of anarchy. Besides, with considerable excitement, he anticipated the arrival of the usually unflappable Roman Castevet, who would be fully flapped on this occasion.

Almost two minutes to the tick, the lever-action door handle clicked, creaked, and eased down. The door cracked open, but only an inch.

As though he expected to discover that Corky awaited him with a camera crew and a pack of muckraking reporters, Roman peered through the gap, his one revealed eye as wide as that of a startled owl.

"Come in, come, come," Corky encouraged. "You're among friends here, even though it *is* your intention eventually to dissect some of them."

Opening the door only wide enough to accommodate his thin frame, Roman slipped into the cadaver vault, pausing to peer back worriedly at the hallway before closing himself in with Corky and the twenty naughty members of the toga party.

"What the hell are you wearing?" asked the nervous pathologist.

Corky turned in place, flaring the skirt of his yellow slicker. "Fashionable rain gear. Do you like the hat?"

"How did you slip by security in that ludicrous outfit? How did you slip by security at all?"

"No slipping necessary. I presented my credentials."

"What credentials? You teach empty-calorie modern fiction to a bunch of self-important sluts and brain-dead, snot-nosed wonder-boys."

Like many in the sciences, Roman Castevet held a dim view of the liberal-arts departments in contemporary universities and of those students who sought, first, truth through literature and, second, a delayed entry into the job market.

Taking no offense, in fact approving of Roman's nasty antisocial vitriol, Corky explained: "The pleasant fellows at your security desk think I'm a visiting pathologist from Indianapolis, here to discuss with you certain deeply puzzling entomological details related to the victims of a serial killer operating throughout the Midwest."

"Huh? Why would they think that?"

"I have a source for excellent forged documents."

Roman boggled. *"You?"*

"Frequently, it's advisable for me to carry first-rate false identification."

"Are you delusional or merely stupid?"

"As I've explained previously, I'm not just an effete professor who gets a thrill from hanging out with anarchists."

"Yeah, right," Roman said scornfully.

"I promote anarchy at every opportunity in my daily life, often at the risk of arrest and imprisonment."

"You're a regular Che Guevara."

"Many of my operations are as clever and shocking as they are unconventional. You didn't think I wanted those ten foreskins just for some sick personal use, did you?"

"Yeah, that's exactly what I thought. When we met at that boring university mixer, you seemed like the grand pooh-bah of the demented, a moral and mental mutant of classic proportions."

"Coming from a Satanist," Corky said with a smile, "that could be taken as a compliment."

"It's not meant as one," Roman replied impatiently, angrily.

At his best, groomed and togged and breath-freshened for serious socializing, Castevet was an unattractive man. Anger made him uglier than usual.

Slat-thin, all bony hips and elbows and sharp shoulders, with an Adam's apple more prominent than his nose and with a nose sharper than any Corky had ever seen on another member of the human species, with gaunt cheeks and with a fleshless chin that resembled the knob of a femur, Roman appeared to have a serious eating disorder.

Every time that he met Castevet's bird-keen, reptile-intense eyes, however, and whenever he caught the pathologist, for no apparent reason, sensuously licking his lips, which were the only ripe feature

of that scarecrow face and form, Corky suspected that a fearsome
erotic need spun the wheels of the man's metabolism almost fast
enough to cause smoke to issue from various orifices. Had there been
a betting pool regarding the average number of calories that Roman
burned up every day in obsessive self-abuse alone, Corky would have
wagered heavily on at least three thousand—and he would no doubt
have ensured a comfortable retirement with his winnings.

"Well, whatever you think of me," Corky said, "nevertheless, I
would like to place an order for another ten foreskins."

"Hey, get it through your head—I'm not doing business with you
anymore. You're reckless, coming here like this."

Partly as a profitable sideline, but also partly from a sense of religious duty and as an expression of his abiding faith in the King of
Hell, Roman Castevet provided—only from cadavers—selected body
parts, internal organs, blood, malignant tumors, occasionally even
entire brains to other Satanists. His customers, other than Corky, had
both a theological and a practical interest in arcane rituals designed
to petition His Satanic Majesty for special favors or to summon actual demons out of the fiery pit. Frequently, after all, the most essential ingredients in a black-magic formula could not be purchased at
the nearest Wal-Mart.

"You're overreacting," Corky said.

"I'm *not* overreacting. You're imprudent, you're foolhardy."

"*Foolhardy?*" Corky smiled, nearly laughed. "All of a sudden you
seem awfully prissy for a man who believes plunder, torture, rape,
and murder will be rewarded in the afterlife."

"Lower your voice," Roman demanded in a fierce whisper, though
Corky had continued to speak in a pleasant conversational tone. "If
somebody finds you here with me, it could mean my job."

"Not at all. I'm a visiting pathologist from Indianapolis, and we're
discussing your current manpower shortage and this deplorable backlog of unidentified cadavers."

"You'll ruin me," Roman moaned.

"All I've come here to do," Corky lied, "is to order ten more foreskins. I don't expect you to collect them while I wait. I just placed the order in person because I thought it would give you a chuckle."

Although Roman Castevet appeared too emaciated, too juiceless to produce tears, his feverish black eyes grew watery with frustration.

"Anyway," Corky continued, "there's a bigger threat to your job than being caught here with me—if someone discovers you people have mistakenly penned up a living man in this place with all these dead bodies."

"Are you wired on something?"

"I already told you on the phone, a few minutes ago. One of these unfortunate souls is still alive."

"What kind of mind game is this?" Roman demanded.

"It's not a game. It's true. I heard him murmuring '*Help me, help me,*' so soft, barely loud enough to hear."

"Heard who?"

"I tracked him down, peeled the shroud back from his face. He's paralyzed. Facial muscles distorted by a stroke."

Hunching closer, bristling like the collection of dry sticks in a bindle of kindling, Roman *insisted* on eye-to-eye conversation, as if he believed the fierceness of his gaze would convey the message that his words had failed to deliver.

Corky blithely continued: "The poor guy was probably comatose when they brought him in here, then he regained consciousness. But he's awfully weak."

A crack of uncertainty breached Roman Castevet's armor of disbelief. He broke eye contact and swept the bunks with his gaze. "Who?"

"Over there," Corky said brightly, indicating the back of the vault, where the light from the overhead fixture barely reached, leaving the recumbent dead shrouded in gloom as well as in white cotton cloth.

"Seems to me I'm saving *all* your jobs by alerting you to this, so you ought to fill my order for free, out of gratitude."

Moving toward the back of the vault, Roman said, "Which one?"

Stepping close behind the pathologist, Corky replied, "On the left, the second from the bottom."

As Roman bent to peel the shroud off the face of the corpse, Corky raised his right arm, revealing the hand that until now had been concealed in the sleeve of his yellow slicker, and the ice pick in the hand. With judicious aim, great force, and utter confidence, he drove the weapon into the pathologist's back.

Placed with precision, an ice pick can penetrate atriums and ventricles, causing such a convulsive shock in cardiac muscle that the heart stops in an instant and forever.

With a rustle of clothes and a quiet knockety-knock of folding limbs, Roman Castevet collapsed without a cry to the floor.

Corky didn't need to check for a pulse. The gaping mouth, from which no breath escaped, and the eyes, as fixed as the glass orbs in a fine work of taxidermy, confirmed the perfection of his aim.

Preparation paid off. At home, using this same ice pick, Corky had practiced on a CPR dummy that he had stolen from the university medical school.

If he'd needed to stab twice, three, four times, or if Roman's heart had continued to pump for even a short while, the assault could have proved messy. For that reason, he'd worn the stainproof slicker.

In the unlikely event that one of the vault's properly chilled treasures sprung an unfortunate leak, the tile floor featured a large drain. Near the door, a collapsible vinyl hose on a reel was attached to a wall spigot.

Corky knew about this janitorial equipment from the articles that he had read two years ago, when the rat scandal had made the front page. Happily, he didn't need the hose.

He lifted Roman into one of the empty bunks along the back wall of the vault, where the shadows served his scheme.

From a deep inner pocket of his slicker, he withdrew the sheet that earlier he'd purchased in a department store at the mall. He draped the sheet over Roman, being careful to cover him entirely, for he needed to conceal both the identity of the corpse and the fact that, unlike the others here, it was fully clothed.

Because death had been instantaneous and the wound had been minute, no blood seeped forth to stain the sheet and thus call attention to the freshness of this carcass.

In a day or two, or three, Roman would most likely be found by a morgue employee taking inventory or withdrawing a cadaver for an overdue autopsy. Another front-page story for the medical examiner.

Corky regretted having to kill a man like Roman Castevet. As a good Satanist and a committed anarchist, the pathologist had served well in the campaign to destabilize the social order and hasten its collapse.

Soon, however, ghastly events at Channing Manheim's estate would make big headlines worldwide. Authorities would commit extraordinary resources to discover the identity of the man who'd sent the taunting gifts in the black boxes.

Logic would send them to private mortuaries and public morgues, in search of the source of the ten foreskins. If Roman had come under suspicion during that investigation, he would have tried to save his own hide by fingering Corky.

Anarchists labored under no obligation of loyalty to one another, which was as it should be among champions of disorder.

Indeed, Corky had other loose ends to tie up before the yuletide celebrations could begin.

Considering that his hands were sheathed in latex gloves, which had been hidden from his victim in the roomy sleeves of his slicker, he could have left the ice pick in the vault without worrying that he might provide police with incriminating fingerprints. Instead, he returned it to its sheath and then to a pocket not only because it might serve him well again, but also because it now had sentimental value.

Leaving the morgue, he said a friendly good-bye to the night security men. They had a thankless job, protecting the dead from the living. He even paused long enough to share with them an obscene joke about an attorney and a chicken.

He had no fear that eventually they would be able to provide the police with a useful description of his face. In his droopy hat and tent-like slicker, he was an eccentric and amusing figure about whom no one would remember more than his costume.

Later, in a fireplace at home, while he enjoyed a brandy, he would burn all the ID that had established him as a pathologist from Indianapolis. He possessed numerous additional sets of documentation for other identities if and when he needed them.

Now he returned to the night, the rain.

And so the time had come to deal with Rolf Reynerd, who by his actions had shown himself to be every bit as unfit for life as he had proved to be unfit for soap-opera stardom.

CHAPTER 27

I F AELFRIC MANHEIM'S MONDAY-EVENING DIN-
ner had been reported upon in *Daily Variety*, the colorful trade paper of the film industry, the headline might have been FRIC CLICKS
WITH CHICK.

On the grill, the plump breast had been basted with olive oil and
sprinkled with sea salt, pepper, and a delicious mixture of exotic
herbs known around Palazzo Rospo as the McBee McSecret. In addition to the chicken, he had been served pasta, not with tomato sauce,
but with butter, basil, pine nuts, and Parmesan cheese.

Mr. Hachette, the Cordon Bleu–trained chef who was a direct de-
scendent of Jack the Ripper, didn't work Sundays and Mondays, so
that he might stalk and slash innocent women, toss rabid cats into
baby carriages, and indulge in whatever other personal interests currently appealed to him.

Mr. Baptiste, the happy cook, was off Mondays and Tuesdays;
therefore, on Mondays the kitchen was, in show-biz lingo, dark. Mrs.
McBee had prepared these delicacies herself.

By the softly pulsing light of electric fixtures tricked up to look
like antique oil lamps, Fric ate in the wine cellar, alone at the refectory table for eight in the cozy tasting room, which was separated

from the temperature-controlled portion of the cellar by a glass wall. Beyond the glass, in aisles of shelves, were fourteen thousand bottles of what his father sometimes identified as "Cabernet Sauvignon, Merlot, Pinot Noir, claret, port, Burgundy—and the blood of critics, which is a bitter vintage."

Ha, ha, ha.

When Ghost Dad was home, they usually ate in the dining room, unless the dinner guests—the old man's buddies, business associates, or various personal advisers from his spiritual counselor to his clairvoyance instructor—felt uncomfortable having a ten-year-old kid listening to their gossip and rolling his eyes at their trash talk.

In Ghost Dad's absence, which was most of the time, Fric could choose to have dinner not just in his private rooms, where he usually ate, but virtually anywhere on the estate.

In good weather, he might dine outdoors by the swimming pool, grateful that in his father's absence no hopelessly dense, tiresomely giggly, embarrassingly half-naked starlets were there to pester him with questions about his favorite subject in school, his favorite food, his favorite color, his favorite world-famous movie star.

They were always trying to cadge some Ritalin or antidepressants from Fric. They refused to believe that his only prescription was for asthma medication.

If not by the pool, he might dine dangerously with fine china and antique silverware at a table in the rose garden, keeping his inhaler ready on a dessert plate in the event that a breeze stirred up enough pollen to trigger an asthma attack.

Sometimes he ate from a lap tray while ensconced in one of the sixty comfortable armchairs in the screening room, which had recently been remodeled using the ornate Art Deco–style Pantages Theater, in Los Angeles, as inspiration.

The screening-room equipment could handle film, all formats of videotape, DVDs, and broadcast-television signals, projecting them onto a screen larger than many in the average suburban multiplex.

To watch videos and DVDs, Fric didn't need the assistance of a projectionist. Sitting in the center seat in the center row, adjacent to the control console, he could run his own show.

Sometimes, when he knew that no cleaning had been scheduled in the theater, when he was certain that no one would come looking for him, he locked the door to ensure privacy, and he loaded the DVD player with one of his father's movies.

Being *seen* watching a Ghost Dad movie was unthinkable.

Not that they sucked. Some of them sucked, of course, because no star rang the big bell every time. But some were all right. Some were cool. A few were even amazing.

If anyone were to *see* him watching his father's movies under these circumstances, however, he would be the National Academy of Nerds' choice for Greatest Nerd of the Decade. Maybe of the century. The Pathetic Losers Club would vote him a free lifetime membership.

Mr. Hachette, the psychopathic chef related to the Frankenstein family, would mock him with sneers and by drawing sly comparisons between Fric's sticklike physique and his father's maximum buffness.

Anyway, in the only occupied seat of sixty, with the ornate Art Deco ceiling soaring thirty-four feet overhead, Fric sometimes sat in the dark and ran Ghost Dad's movies on the huge screen. Drenched in Dolby surround sound.

He watched certain films for the stories, though he'd seen them many times. He watched others for blow-out-the-walls special effects.

And always in his father's performances, Fric looked for the qualities, the charms, the expressions, and the bits of business that made millions of people all over the world love Channing Manheim.

In the better films, such moments abounded. Even in the suckiest of the sucky, however, there were scenes in which you couldn't help but like the guy, admire him, want so much to hang out with him.

When citing the brightest moments in his finest films, critics had said that Fric's father was magical. "Magical" sounded stupid, like gooey girl gush, embarrassing, but it was the right word.

Sometimes you watched him on the big screen, and he seemed more colorful, more *real* than anyone you'd ever known. Or ever would know.

This super-real quality couldn't be explained by the giant size of his projected image or by the visual genius of the cameraman. Nor by the brilliance of the director—most being no more brilliant than a boiled potato—nor by the layered details achieved through digital technology. Most actors, including stars, didn't have the Manheim magic even when they worked with the best directors and technicians.

You watched him up there, and he seemed to have been everywhere, to have seen everything, to know all that could be known. He seemed to be wiser, more caring, funnier, and braver than anyone, anywhere, ever—as though he lived in six dimensions while everyone else had to live in only three.

Fric had studied certain scenes over and over again, scores of times, maybe a hundred times in some cases, until they seemed as real to him as any moments he had actually spent with his father.

Once in a while, when he went to bed drag-ass tired, but was able to settle only on the twilight edge of sleep, or when he woke incompletely in the middle of the night yet continued to skate upon the surface of a temporarily frozen dream, those special movie scenes with his father *did* seem real to Fric. They played in memory not as though he'd viewed them from a theater seat, but as though they were true-life experiences that he and his father had shared.

These dreamy spells of half-sleep were some of the happiest moments of Fric's life.

Of course, if he ever *told* anyone that those were some of the happiest moments of his life, the Pathetic Losers Club would erect a thirty-foot statue of him, emphasizing his uncombable hair and his skinny neck, and they would spotlight it on the same hill that held the HOLLYWOOD sign.

So on this Monday evening, though Fric might have preferred to eat in the theater while watching his father beat the crap out of bad guys and save an entire orphanage full of waifs, he dined in the wine cellar because in the pre-Christmas bustle, little privacy could be found elsewhere in Palazzo Rospo.

Ms. Sanchez and Ms. Norbert, the maids who lived on the estate, had been away on an early Christmas leave for the past ten days. They would not return until Thursday morning, December 24.

Mrs. McBee and Mr. McBee would be gone Tuesday and Wednesday, to have an early Christmas with their son and his family in Santa Barbara. They, too, would return to Palazzo Rospo on December 24, to ensure that the biggest movie star in the world was met with the proper pomp when he arrived from Florida later that afternoon.

Consequently, here on Monday evening, the other four maids and the porters were working late, under the firm direction of the busy McBees, alongside a few outsourced services that included a six-man floor-cleaning crew specializing in the care of marble and limestone, an eight-person holiday-decorating team, and an emergency feng-shui facilitator who would make certain that various Christmas trees and other seasonal displays were arranged and festooned in such a way as not to interfere with the proper energy flow of the great house.

Madness.

Far from the hum of floor-polishing machines and the jolly laughter of the Christmas-besotted decorating team, Fric took refuge deep underground in the wine cellar. Within these brick walls, under this low, vaulted brick ceiling, the only sounds were those he made swallowing and the clink of his fork against his plate.

And then: *Ooodelee-ooodelee-oo.*

Muffled but audible, the phone rang inside a keg.

Because the temperature in the tasting room was too high for wine storage, the barrels and bottles in this chamber, on the warmer side of the glass wall, were strictly decorative.

Ooodelee-ooodelee-oo.

Stacked floor to ceiling along one brick wall, several of the enormous barrels featured hinged bottoms that could be swung open, doorlike. Some barrels had shelves inside, on which were stored wineglasses, linen napkins, corkscrews, other items. Four contained televisions, allowing a wine connoisseur to view multiple channels simultaneously.

Ooodelee-ooodelee-oo.

Fric opened the phone keg and answered his private line in the usual Frician style, determined not to sound intimidated. "Pete's Pest Control and School of Home Canning. We'll rid your house of rats and teach you how to preserve them for future holiday feasts."

"Hello, Aelfric."

"Do you have a name yet?" Fric asked.

"Lost."

"Is that a first name or last name?"

"Both. Are you enjoying your dinner?"

"I'm not eating dinner."

"What did I tell you about lying, Aelfric?"

"That it won't get me anything but misery."

"Do you eat in the wine cellar often?"

"I'm in the attic."

"Don't seek misery, boy. Enough of it will find you without your help."

"In the movie business," Fric said, "people lie twenty-four hours a day, and all it gets them is rich."

"Sometimes the misery follows swiftly," Mysterious Caller assured him. "More often it takes a lifetime to arrive, and then at the end, there's a great roaring *sea* of it."

Fric was silent.

The stranger matched his silence.

At last Fric drew a deep breath and said, "I've got to admit, you're a spooky son of a bitch."

"That's progress, Aelfric. A little truth."

"I found a place where I can hide and never be found."

"Do you mean the secret room behind your closet?"

Fric had never imagined that any creepy creatures lived in the hollows of his bones, but now he seemed to feel them crawling through his marrow.

Mysterious Caller said, "The place with steel walls and all the hooks in the ceiling—is that where you think you can hide?"

CHAPTER 28

WITH MURDER ON HIS MIND BUT NOT ON HIS conscience, Corky Laputa, fresh from the vault of the nameless dead, crossed the city in the night rain.

As he drove, he thought about his father, perhaps because Henry James Laputa had squandered his life as surely as the vagrants and teenage runaways bunking at the morgue had squandered theirs.

Corky's mother, the economist, had believed in the righteousness of envy, in the power of hatred. Her life had been consumed by both, and she had worn bitterness as though it were a crown.

His father believed in the *necessity* of envy as a motivator. His perpetual envy led inevitably to chronic hatred whether he believed in the power of hatred or not.

Henry James Laputa had been a professor of American literature. He had also been a novelist with dreams of worthy fame.

He chose the most acclaimed writers of his time to envy. With fierce diligence, he begrudged them every good review, every word of praise, every honor and award. He seethed at news of their successes.

Thus motivated, he produced novels in a white-hot passion, works meant to make the fiction of his contemporaries appear shallow and pallid and puerile by comparison. He wanted to humble other writers, humiliate them by example, inspire in them an envy greater than any he'd directed against them, for only then could he let go of his own envy and at last enjoy his accomplishments.

He believed that one day these literati would be so jealous of him that they'd be unable to take any pleasure in their own careers. When they coveted his literary reputation with such intensity that they were *avaricious* for it, when they burned with shame that their greatest efforts were fading embers compared to the bonfire of his talent, then Henry Laputa would be happy, fulfilled.

Year after year, however, his novels had received only lukewarm praise, and much of this had flowed from the pens of critics who were not of the highest tier. The expected award nominations never came. The deserved honors were not conferred. His genius went unrecognized.

Indeed, he detected that many of his literary contemporaries patronized him, which led him to recognize, at long last, that they were all members of a club from which he'd been blackballed. They *did* recognize the superiority of his talent, but they conspired to deny him the laurels that he had earned, for they were intent on keeping the pieces of the pie that they had cut for themselves.

Pie. Henry realized that even in the literary community, the god of gods was money. Their dirty little secret. They handed awards back and forth, blathering about art, but were interested only in using these honors to pump their careers and get rich.

This insight into the conspiratorial greed of the literati was fertilizer, water, and sunshine to the garden of Henry's hatred. The black flowers of antipathy flourished as never before.

Frustrated by their refusal to accord him the acclaim that he desired, Henry set out to earn their envy by writing a novel that would be an enormous commercial success. He believed that he knew all the tricks of plotting and the many uses of treacly sentimentality by which such hacks as Dickens manipulated the unwashed masses. He would write an irresistible tale, make millions, and let the phony literati be consumed by jealousy.

This commercial epic found a publisher but not an audience. The royalties were meager. Instead of showering him with money, the god of mammon left him standing in a manure storm, which was exactly what one major critic called his novel.

As more years passed, Henry's hatred thickened into a malignity of pure, persistent, and singularly venomous quality. He cherished this malignity, and in time it soured and festered into rancor as virulent and implacable as pancreatic cancer.

At the age of fifty-three, while delivering a caustic speech full of fire and outrage to an indifferent crowd of academics at the Modern Language Association's annual convention, Henry James Laputa suffered a massive heart attack. He fell instantly dead with such authority that some audience members thought he'd daringly punctuated a point with a pratfall, and they applauded briefly before realizing that here was death indeed, not shtick.

Corky had learned so much from his parents. He had learned that envy alone does not constitute a philosophy. He'd learned that a fun lifestyle and cheerful optimism cannot exist in the face of all-consuming, all-embracing hatred without surcease.

He'd also learned not to trust in laws, idealism, or art.

His mother had trusted in the laws of economics, in the ideals of Marxism. She ended as a bitter old woman, without hope or purpose, who seemed almost relieved when her own son had beaten her to death with a fireplace poker.

Corky's father had believed that he could use art like a hammer to beat the world into submission. The world still turned, but Dad had gone to ashes, scattered in the sea, dispersed, as if he'd never existed.

Chaos.

Chaos was the only dependable force in the universe, and Corky served it with the confidence that it would, in turn, always serve him.

Across the glistening city, through the night and unrelenting rain, he drove to West Hollywood, where the undependable Rolf Reynerd needed to die.

Both ends of the block where Reynerd lived were closed off by police barricades. Officers in black rain slickers with fluorescent yellow stripes used chemical-light torches to redirect traffic.

In the basic colors of emergency, bright skeins of rain raveled through the pulsing ambulance beacons and knitted urgent patterns on the puddled pavement.

Corky drove past the barricade. Within two blocks, he found a parking place.

Perhaps the official bustle on Rolf Reynerd's street had no connection with the actor, but Corky's intuition insisted otherwise.

He wasn't worried. Whatever mess Rolf Reynerd had gotten himself into, Corky would find a way to use the situation to further his own agenda. Tumble and tumult were his friends, and he was confident that in the church of chaos, he was a favored child.

CHAPTER 29

F RIC FELT THAT BY SOME MAGICAL INFLUENCE of the brick floor under his feet and the brick walls around him and the low brick vaults overhead, he had been transformed into brick himself as he listened to the soft voice of this stranger.

"The secret room concealed behind your closet isn't as secret as you think, Aelfric. You won't be safe there when Robin Goodfellow pays a visit."

"Who?"

"Previously I called him the Beast in Yellow. He styles himself Robin Goodfellow, but he's darker than that. In truth, he's Moloch, with the splintered bones of babies stuck between his teeth."

"That'll take some heavy-duty dental floss," said Fric, though a tremor in his voice belied the flippancy of his words. He hurried on, hoping that Mysterious Caller had failed to detect his fear. "Robin Goodfellow, Moloch, baby bones—you aren't making any sense."

"You have a great library in your house, don't you, Aelfric?"

"Yeah."

"And you must have a good dictionary in that library."

"We have a whole shelf of dictionaries," said Fric, "just to prove how scholarly we are."

"Then look it all up. Know your enemy, prepare yourself for what is coming, Aelfric."

"Why don't you *tell* me what's coming? I mean just plain, simple, easy to understand."

"That's not within my power. I'm not licensed to take any direct action."

"So you aren't James Bond."

"I'm authorized to work only by indirection. Encourage, inspire, terrify, cajole, advise. I influence events by every means that is sly, slippery, and seductive."

"What're you—an attorney or something?"

"You're an interesting young man, Aelfric. I'll genuinely be sorry if you're disemboweled and nailed to the front door of Palazzo Rospo."

Fric almost hung up.

Wrapped around the handset of the phone, his palm became greasy with perspiration.

He would not have been surprised if the man on the far end of the line had smelled this sweat and had commented on the salty scent.

Returning to the subject of a deep and special secret place, Fric mustered a steady voice. "We have a panic room in the house," he said, referring to a hidden high-security haven armored to keep out even the most determined kidnappers or terrorists.

"Because the house is so large, you actually have two panic rooms," Mysterious Caller said, which was true. "Both are known, and neither will keep you safe on the night."

"And when is the night?"

Enigmatically, the man said, "It's a fur vault, you know."

"A what?"

"Long ago, your nice suite of rooms was occupied by the original owner's mother."

"How do you know which rooms are mine?"

"She had a collection of expensive fur coats. Several minks, sable, white fox, black fox, chinchilla."

"Did you know her?"

"That steel-lined room was meant to keep the fur coats safe from burglars, moths, and rodents."

"Have you been in our house?"

"The fur vault is a bad place to have an asthma attack—"

Stunned, Fric said, "How could you know about that?"

"—but it'll be an even worse place to be trapped by Moloch when he comes. Time is running out, Aelfric."

The line went dead, and Fric stood alone in the wine room, surely alone, but feeling watched.

CHAPTER 30

I F THE SKY OPENED TO DISGORGE A DELUGE OF fanged and poisonous toads, if the wind blew hard enough to flay the skin to bloody ruin and to blind the unprotected eye, even such cataclysmic weather would fail to dissuade ghouls and gossips from gathering at the scenes of spectacular accidents and shocking crimes. By comparison, a steady drizzle on a cool December night was picnic weather to this crowd that followed misery as others might follow baseball.

On the front lawn of an apartment house, catercorner across the intersection from the police barricade, twenty to thirty neighborhood residents gathered to share misinformation and gory details. The majority were adults, but half a dozen energized children capered among them.

Most of these sociable vultures were outfitted in rain gear or carried umbrellas. Two bare-chested and barefoot young men, however, wore only blue jeans and appeared to be so steeped in a marinade of illegal substances that the night could not chill them, as though they were being cooked flamelessly like fish fillets in lime juice.

An air of carnival had settled upon this gathering, expectations of fireworks and freaks.

In all his glistening yellowness, Corky Laputa moved among the onlookers, like a buzzless bumblebee patiently gathering a morsel of nectar here, a morsel there. From time to time, to blend better with the swarm and to win friends, he offered a taste of ersatz honey, inventing florid details of the vicious crime that he claimed to have heard from cops manning the second barricade at the farther end of the block.

He quickly learned that Rolf Reynerd had been killed.

The gossips and the ghouls weren't sure if the victim's first name was Ralph or Rafe, Dolph or Randolph. Or Bob.

They were pretty sure that the luckless fellow's last name was either Reinhardt or Kleinhard, or Reiner like the film director, or maybe Spielberg like another famous director, or Nerdoff, or possibly Nordoff.

One of the bare-chested young men insisted that everyone had confused the victim's first name, surname, and nickname. According to this wizard of deductive reasoning, the dead man's true identity was Ray "the Nerd" Rolf.

All agreed that the murdered man had been an actor whose career had recently rocketed toward stardom. He had just completed a film in which he played Tom Cruise's best buddy or younger brother. Paramount or DreamWorks had hired him to costar with Reese Witherspoon. Warner Brothers offered him the title role in a new series of Batman movies, Miramax wanted him to play a transvestite sheriff in a sensitive drama about anti-gay bigotry in Texas circa 1890, and Universal hoped he would sign a ten-million-dollar deal for two films that he would also write and direct.

Evidently, in this new millennium and in the popular imagination of those who dwelt on the glamorous west side of L.A., no failure ever died young, and Death came early only to the famous, the rich, the adored. Call it the Princess Di Principle.

Whether the man who had killed Ray "the Nerd" Rolf had also

been an actor on the brink of superstardom, no one knew for certain. The murderer's name remained unknown, unmangled.

Indisputably, the killer himself had been gunned down. His body lay on the lawn in front of Rolf's apartment house.

Two pairs of binoculars circulated among the onlookers. Corky borrowed one pair to study Rolf's apparent executioner.

In the darkness and the rain, even with magnification, he was unable to discern any identifying details of the corpse sprawled on the grass.

Crime-scene investigators, busy with scientific instruments and cameras, crouched alongside the cadaver. In black raincoats draped like folded wings, they had the posture and the intensity of crows pecking at carrion.

In every version of the story viewed with credibility among the gossips, the killer himself had been killed by a police officer. The cop had been passing by in the street at the right moment, by sheer happenstance, or he had lived in Rolf's building, or he'd come there to visit his girlfriend or his mother.

Whatever had occurred here this evening, Corky was reasonably confident that it would not compromise his plans or cause the police to turn a gimlet eye on him. He had kept his association with Reynerd secret from everyone he knew.

He believed that Reynerd had been likewise discreet. They had committed crimes together and had conspired to commit others. Neither of them had anything to gain—and much to lose—by revealing their relationship to anyone.

Stupid in uncounted ways, Rolf had not been entirely reckless. To impress a woman or his witless friends, he might wish to reveal that he'd had his mother killed by proxy or that he was partner to a murderous conspiracy involving the biggest movie star in the world, but he would never go that far. He would just invent a colorful lie.

Although Ethan Truman, incognito, had visited earlier this very day, the possibility that Reynerd's death was connected in any way to Channing Manheim and the six gifts in black boxes remained unlikely.

Being an apostle of anarchy, Corky understood that chaos ruled the world and that in the rough and disorderly jumble-tumble of daily events, meaningless coincidences like this frequently occurred. Such apparent synchronisms encouraged lesser men than he to see patterns, design, and meaning in life.

He had wagered his future and, in fact, his existence, on the belief that life was meaningless. He owned a lot of stock in chaos, and at this late date, he wasn't going to second-guess his investment by selling chaos short.

Reynerd had fancied himself not only a potential movie star of historic proportions, but also something of a bad boy, and bad boys made enemies. For one thing, more in search of thrills than profits, he had dealt drugs to a refined list of entertainment-industry clients, mostly cocaine and meth and Ecstasy.

More likely than not, tougher men than pretty-boy Reynerd had decided that he was poaching in their fields. With a bullet in the head, he'd been discouraged from further competition.

Corky had needed Reynerd dead.

Chaos had obliged.

No more, no less.

Time to move on.

Time, in fact, for dinner. Aside from a candy bar in the car and a double latte at the mall, he had eaten nothing since breakfast.

On good days filled with worthwhile endeavors, his work provided nourishment enough, and he often skipped lunch. Now, after busy hours of useful enterprise, he was famished.

Nevertheless, he tarried long enough to serve chaos. The six children were a temptation that he could not resist.

All were six to eight years old. Some were better dressed for the

rain and the cold than others were, but all remained unflaggingly exuberant, dancing-playing-chasing in the nasty night, as though they
were storm petrels born to wet wind and turbulent skies.

Focused on the hubbub of cops and ambulances, the adults stood
oblivious of their offspring. The kids were wise enough to understand
that as long as they played on the lawn behind their elders and kept
their chatter below a certain volume, they could prolong their night
adventure indefinitely.

In this paranoid age, a stranger dared not offer candy to any child.
Even the most gullible among them would shriek for the cops at the
offer of a lollipop.

Corky had no lollipops, but he traveled with a bag of luscious,
chewy caramels.

He waited until the kids' attention turned elsewhere, whereupon
he extracted the bag from a deep inner pocket of his slicker. He
dropped it on the grass where the children were sure to find it when
their games brought them in this direction again.

He hadn't laced the candy with poison, but only with a potent hallucinogenic. Terror and disorder could be spread through society by
means more subtle than extreme violence.

The amount of drug infused in each sweet morsel was small
enough that even a child who greedily stuffed his face with six or
eight of them would not risk toxic overdose. By the third piece, the
waking nightmares would begin.

Corky mingled a while longer with the adults, surreptitiously ob-
serving the children, until two girls found the bag. Being girls, they at
once generously shared the contents with the four boys.

This particular drug, unless taken in concert with a mellowing an-
tidepressant like Prozac, was known to cause hallucinations so hor-
rific that they tested the user's sanity. Soon, the kids would believe
that mouths, bristling with sharp teeth and serpent tongues, had
opened in the earth to swallow them, that alien parasites were burst-

ing from their chests, and that everyone they knew and loved now intended to rend them limb from limb. Even after they recovered, flashbacks would trouble them for months, possibly for years.

Having sown these seeds of chaos, he returned to his car through the refreshingly cool night and cleansing rain.

If he had been born in an earlier century, Corky Laputa would have followed the original trail of Johnny Appleseed, killing one by one all the trees that the fabled orchardist had planted on this continent.

CHAPTER 31

IF FRIC HAD SUSPECTED THAT THE WINE CELLAR was haunted or that something less than human prowled its channels and chambers, he would have eaten dinner in his bedroom.

He proceeded without caution.

Likening the separation noise of the rubber seal to the sucking sound made by popping the lid off a vacuum-packed can of peanuts, Fric opened the thick glass door in the insulated-glass wall.

He stepped out of the wine-tasting room into the wine cellar proper. Here the temperature was maintained at a constant fifty-five degrees.

Fourteen thousand bottles required a lot of racks—a *maze* of racks. These weren't simply arranged like aisles in a supermarket. Instead, they lined a cozy brick labyrinth of vaulted passageways that intersected at circular grottoes ringed by more racks.

Four times each year, every bottle in the collection was gently rotated a quarter turn—ninety degrees—in its niche. This ensured that no edge of any cork would dry out and that the sediment would settle properly to the bottom of each punt.

The two porters, Mr. Worthy and Mr. Phan, were able to attend to the turning of the wine bottles for only four hours a day due to the tediousness of the work, the measured care that it required, and the havoc that it caused with neck and shoulder muscles. Each man could properly rotate between twelve hundred and thirteen hundred bottles per four-hour session.

Through a flow of cool dry air that pumped ceaselessly from ceiling vents, Fric followed a narrow dome-vaulted passageway of Pinot Noir to a wider groin-vaulted corridor of Cabernet, circled a curiously coved grotto of Lafitte Rothschild stocked with various vintages, continued through a tunnel of Merlot, in search of a place where he would be able to hide without fear of discovery.

Arriving in an elongated-oval gallery stocked with French Burgundy, he thought he heard footsteps other than his own, elsewhere in the maze. He froze, listened.

Nothing. Just the whispery voice of the perpetual wine-cooling draft lazily entering the gallery by one passageway, leaving by a second.

The fluttering false flames of the fake gas lamps, which were wall-mounted in some places but also hung from grotto ceilings where height allowed, caused shimmers of light to chase twists of shadow along the racks and brickwork. This meaningless but spooky movement teased the mind into hearing footsteps that probably weren't there.

Probably.

Proceeding less boldly than before, occasionally glancing over his shoulder, he moved on with the gentle draft.

Other wine cellars might be musty dens in which time shed skin after skin of dust, leaving a record of its unending progress. In fact a dusty film on the bottles was often considered good ambience.

Fric's father had an almost obsessive aversion to dust, however, and none could be found in this place. Taking special care not to disturb the bottles, the staff vacuumed the racks once a month, as well as the ceiling, walls, and floor.

Here and there in the corners of the passageways and more often in the shadowed curves of the masonry ceiling vaults were delicate spider webs. Some were simple, others elaborate.

No eight-legged architects could be glimpsed at home in these constructions. Spiders were not tolerated.

When at work, the housekeepers kept the vacuum cleaner away from these gossamer architectures, which had been made not by spiders but by a specialist in set decoration from Ghost Dad's favorite film studio. Nevertheless, the webs deteriorated. Twice a year, Mr. Knute, the set decorator, swabbed them off the bricks and then rebuilt them as good as new.

The wine itself was real.

Turn by turn through the labyrinth, Fric calculated how long his father could stay blind drunk on wine before exhausting the contents of this cellar.

Certain assumptions had to be made, the first being that Ghost Dad would sleep eight hours a night. Perpetually soused, he might sleep longer; however, in the interest of keeping these calculations simple, an arbitrary number must be selected. Eight.

Also assume that a grown man could stay seriously drunk by consuming one bottle of wine every three hours. To establish a state of inebriation, the first bottle might have to be slugged down in an hour or two, but after that, one every three hours.

This was actually not an assumption but hard knowledge. Fric had on numerous occasions been in a position to observe actors, writers, rock stars, directors, and other famous drunks with a taste for fine wine, and while some could pour it down faster than one bottle every three hours, those aggressive drinkers always passed out.

Okay. Five bottles spread over each sixteen-hour day. Divide fourteen thousand by five. Twenty-eight hundred.

The contents of this cellar ought to keep Ghost Dad shitfaced for twenty-eight hundred days. So then divide 2,800 by 365 . . .

Over seven and a half years. The old man could stay blind drunk until Fric had graduated from high school and had run away to join the United States Marine Corps.

Of course, the biggest movie star in the world never drank more than one glass of wine with dinner. He didn't use drugs at all—not even pot, which everyone else in Hollywood seemed to think was just a health food. "I'm far from perfect," he'd once told a reporter for *Premiere* magazine, "but all my faults and failures and foibles tend to be spiritual in nature."

Fric had no idea what *that* meant, even though he'd spent more than a little time trying to figure it out.

Maybe Ming du Lac, his father's full-time spiritual adviser, could have explained the quote. Fric never dared to ask him for a translation because he found Ming nearly as scary as Mr. Hachette, the extraterrestrial predator disguised as their household chef.

Arriving in the last grotto, the point farthest from the wine-cellar entrance, he heard footsteps again. As before, when he cocked his head and listened intently, he detected nothing suspicious.

Sometimes his imagination went into overdrive.

Three years ago, when he'd been seven, he'd been convinced that something strange and green and scaly crawled out of the toilet bowl in his bathroom every night and waited to devour him if ever he went for a postmidnight pee. For months, when Fric woke in the middle of the night with a bloated bladder, he left his suite and used safe bathrooms elsewhere in the house.

In his own monster-occupied bath, he'd left a cookie on a plate. Night after night, the cookie remained untouched. Eventually he had substituted a chunk of cheese for the cookie, and then a package of lunch meat in place of the cheese. A monster might have no interest in cookies, might even turn its nose up at cheese, but surely no carnivorous beast could resist pimento-loaf bologna.

When the bologna went unmolested for a week, Fric used his own bathroom again. Nothing ate him.

Now nothing followed him into the final grotto. Nothing but the cool draft and the flicker of light and shadow from fake gas lamps.

The entrance and exit passages more or less divided the grotto in half. To Fric's right were yet more racks of wine bottles. To his left, stacked floor to ceiling along the wall, were sealed wooden cases of wine.

According to the stenciled names, the cases contained a fine French Bordeaux. In fact they were filled with cheap vino that only gutter-living bums would drink, and the contents had no doubt turned to vinegar decades before Fric had been born.

The wooden cases had been stacked here partly for decoration and partly to conceal the entrance to the port-wine closet.

Fric pressed a hidden latch-release button. One stack of wooden cases swung inward.

Beyond lay a room the size of a walk-in closet. At the back was a rack of port wines fifty, sixty, and seventy years old.

Ports were dessert wines. Fric preferred chocolate cake.

He assumed that even in the late 1930s, when this house had been built, the nation had not been plagued by gangs of port-wine thieves. The closet had most likely been concealed just for the fun of it.

This secret chamber, smaller than the fur vault, might make an adequate hiding place—depending on how long he would need to remain hidden. The space would be comfortable enough for a few hours.

If he had to stay in here for two or three days, however, he would start to feel that he'd been buried alive. He'd collapse into a screaming fit of claustrophobia and eventually, descending into madness, he would probably eat himself alive, beginning with his toes and working upward.

Unnerved by the direction their second conversation had taken, he'd forgotten to ask Mysterious Caller how long he could expect to be under siege.

He retreated from the port closet and pulled shut the clever wine-case door.

Turning, Fric saw movement in the passageway by which he had entered this last grotto. Not just the throb of fake gas flames.

A large, strange, spiral silhouette wheeled across the racks and vaulted brick ceiling, layering itself over the familiar flicker of small pennants of light and small flags of shadow. It was approaching the grotto.

Quite unlike his father in a big-screen pinch, Fric seized up with fear and could neither attack nor flee.

Eerily shapeless, shifting, gently tumbling, the shadow billowed closer, closer, and then the fearsome source appeared at the mouth of the passageway: a spirit, a ghost, an apparition, ragged and milky, semitransparent and vaguely luminous, drifting slowly toward him by supernatural locomotion.

Fric frantically stepped backward, stumbled, fell hard enough to remind himself that his butt was as scrawny as his biceps.

Out of the passageway and into the grotto came the apparition, gliding like a stingray in ocean depths. Lambent light and pulsing shadow played upon the phantom form, lending it a greater mystery, an aura of veiled or bearded evil.

Fric raised his hands protectively before his face and peered up between his spread fingers as the spirit arrived above him. For a moment, weightless and slowly revolving, the apparition reminded him of the Milky Way galaxy, with its gossamer spiral arms—and then he recognized it for what it was.

Lazily drifting on the cool draft, a fake web, fabricated by Mr. Knute, had come unanchored. Floating with all the ghostly grace of a jellyfish, it followed the air currents across the grotto toward the next passageway.

Mortified, Fric scrambled to his feet.

Passing out of the grotto, the airborne web snared on one of the wall-mounted lamps, tangled upon itself, and hung there, flimsy and aflutter, like something from Tinkerbell's lingerie drawer.

Angry with himself, Fric fled the wine cellar.

He was in the tasting room, closing the heavy glass door behind himself, before he realized that the spider web could not have come loose all by itself. A draft alone would not have spun it free, up, and away.

Someone would have had to brush against it, at the least, and Fric didn't believe that he himself had done so.

He suspected that someone close behind him in the wine maze had patiently worked the web loose from its corner, careful not to shred or wad it, and had set it afloat upon the draft, to taunt him.

On the other hand, he remembered too well the toilet-spawned, scaly, green monster that had not even been real enough to nibble on a slice of bologna.

He stood for a moment, frowning at the refectory table. While he had been wandering the wine cellar, his dinner dishes had been taken away.

One of the maids might have cleaned up after him. Or Mrs. McBee, though as busy as she was this evening, she would probably send the mister.

Why any of them would have followed him into the wine cellar without calling out to him, why they would have set the Knute-spun cobweb afloat, he couldn't begin to understand.

Fric felt that he was at the center of a web not manufactured by Mr. Knute, an invisible web of conspiracy.

CHAPTER 32

UPON RECEIVING THE CALL, DUNNY WHISTLER at once responds to it, driving directly to Beverly Hills.

He doesn't need the car anymore. Nevertheless, he enjoys being behind the wheel of a well-engineered automobile, and even the simple pleasure of driving has a new poignancy in light of recent events.

En route, traffic lights turn green just when needed, gaps in traffic repeatedly open for him, and he makes such speed that dark wings of water plume from his tires most of the way. He should feel exhilarated, but many concerns weigh on his mind.

At the hotel, where the arriving and departing vehicles seem to be those makes that retail for six figures, he leaves his car with valet parking. He tips the attendant twenty bucks, going in, because he's not likely to be around long enough to spend all his cash on pleasures for himself.

The sumptuous luxury of the lobby embraces him with such warmth of color, texture, and form that Dunny could easily forget that the night outside is cold and rainy.

Richly paneled, expensively appointed, lighted for romance, a textbook on glamorous decor, the hotel bar is huge, but crowded in spite of its size.

Every woman in sight, regardless of age, is beautiful, by either the grace of God or the knife of a good surgeon. Half the men are as handsome as movie stars, and the other half *think* they are.

Most of these people work in the entertainment industry. No actors, but agents and studio executives, publicists and producers.

In another hotel, elsewhere in the city, you might hear several foreign tongues, but in this place only English is spoken, and only that narrow but colorful version of English known as the dialect of the deal. Connections are being secured here; money is being made; sexual excesses are being plotted.

These people are energetic, optimistic, flirtatious, loud, and convinced of their immortality.

In the manner that Cary Grant once navigated crowded parties in the movies, as though skating while everyone around him walked with leg weights, Dunny glides past the bar, among the crowded tables, directly to a prized corner table for four where only one man sits.

This man's name is Typhon, or so he would have you believe. He pronounces it *tie-fon*, and tells you on first meeting that he bears the name of a monster from Greek mythology, a beast that traveled in storms and spread terror wherever the rain took it. Then he laughs, perhaps in recognition that his name is dramatically at odds with his appearance, his genteel business style, and his polished manners.

Nothing about Typhon appears the least monstrous or stormy. He is plump, white-haired, with a sweet androgynous face that would serve well in a movie as either that of a beatific nun or that of a saintly friar. His smile comes easily and often, and seems sincere. Soft-spoken, a good listener, irresistibly likable, the man can make a friend in a minute.

He is impeccably dressed in a dark blue suit, white silk shirt, blue-and-red club tie, and red display handkerchief. His thick white hair has been cut by a stylist to stars and royalty. Unblemished skin smoothed by expensive emollients, bleached teeth, and manicured nails suggest that he takes pride in his appearance.

Typhon sits facing the room, pleasantly regal in demeanor, as might be a kindly monarch holding court. Although he must be known to this crowd, no one bothers him, as though it is understood that he prefers to see and be seen rather than to talk with anyone.

Of the four chairs at the table, two face the room. Dunny takes the second.

Typhon is eating oysters and drinking a superb Pinot Grigio. He says, "Dine with me, please, dear boy. Have anything you wish."

As if conjured by a sorcerer, a waiter instantly appears. Dunny orders double oysters and a bottle of Pinot Grigio for himself. He has always been a man of large appetites.

"You have always been a man of large appetites," Typhon notes, and smiles impishly.

"There'll be an end to that soon enough," Dunny says. "While there's still a banquet in front of me, I intend to gorge."

"That's the spirit!" Typhon declares. "You're a man after my own heart, Dunny. By the way, that's a handsome suit."

"You've got an excellent tailor yourself."

"It's a bother having to do business," says Typhon, "so let's get it out of the way first thing."

Dunny says nothing, but steels himself for a reprimand.

Typhon sips his wine, sighs with pleasure. "Am I to understand that you hired a hit man to remove Mr. Reynerd?"

"Yes. I did. A guy called himself Hector X."

"A hit man," Typhon repeats with audible astonishment.

"He was a gangbanger I knew in the old days, a ranking cuzz with the Crips. We manufactured and distributed sherm together back then."

"Sherm?"

"PCP, an animal tranquilizer. Had a Jim Jones production line going. Marijuana joints laced with cocaine and dipped in PCP."

"Do all your associates have such charming resumes?"

Dunny shrugs. "He was who he was."

"Yes, *was*. Both men are dead now."

"Here's the way I see it. Hector had killed before, and Reynerd conspired to have his own mother murdered. I wasn't corrupting an innocent or targeting one, either."

"I'm not concerned about corruption, Dunny. I'm concerned that you seem not to understand the limits of your authority."

"I know ringing in one killer to take out another is somewhat unconventional—"

"Unconventional!" Typhon shakes his head. "No, lad, it's utterly *unacceptable*."

Dunny's oysters and wine arrive. The waiter uncorks the Pinot Grigio, pours a taste, and Dunny approves.

Relying on the pleasant boozy rumble of the glamorous crowd to screen their sensitive conversation, Typhon returns to business. "Dunny, you must conduct yourself with discretion. All right, you've been a rogue much of your life, that's true, but you gave that up in recent years, didn't you?"

"Tried. Mostly succeeded. Listen, Mr. Typhon, I didn't pull the trigger on Reynerd myself. I worked by indirection, like we agreed."

"Hiring a hit man is *not* indirection."

Dunny swallows an oyster. "Then I misunderstood."

"I doubt that," Typhon says. "I believe you knowingly stretched your authority to see if it would snap."

Pretending gluttonous fascination with the oysters, Dunny dares not ask the obvious question.

The most powerful studio chief in the film industry enters the farther end of the room with all the poise and self-assurance of a Caesar. He travels in the company of an entourage of young male and female employees who are as sleek and cool as vampires yet, on closer inspection, appear simultaneously as nervous as Chihuahuas.

At once spotting Typhon, this king of Hollywood waves with a measured but revealing eagerness.

Typhon returns the greeting with a markedly more restrained wave, thus instantly establishing himself as the higher of the two on the pecking order, to the Caesar's controlled but still visible embarrassment.

Typhon now asks the question that Dunny has been reluctant to voice: "In hiring Hector X, did you stretch your authority past the snapping point?" Then he answers it: "Yes. But I'm inclined to give you one more chance."

Dunny swallows another oyster, which slides down his throat more easily than the one before it.

"Many of the men and women in this bar," says Typhon, "daily negotiate contracts with the intention of breaching them. The people with whom they negotiate fully expect to be victimized or to breach certain terms themselves. Eventually angry accusations are exchanged, attorneys are brandished, legal actions are served if not filed, and amidst bitter charges and vehement countercharges, a settlement is arranged out of court. After all this, and sometimes even during it, the same parties are engaged in negotiating other contracts with each other, contracts which they also intend to breach."

"The film business is an asylum," Dunny observes.

"Yes, it is. But, dear boy, that's not my point."

"Sorry."

"My point is that breach of contract—betrayal in general—is an accepted part of their personal and business culture, just as human sacrifice was an accepted practice in the Aztec world. But betrayal isn't something *I* accept. I'm not that cynical. Words, promises, and integrity matter to me. They matter deeply. I can't do business—I simply won't—with people who give their word insincerely."

"I understand," Dunny says. "I'm properly chastised."

Typhon appears to be genuinely pained by Dunny's reaction. His plump face puckers with dismay. His eyes, usually characterized as much by a sparkle of merriment as by their singular blue color, now cloud with sadness.

This man is remarkably easy to read, open with his emotions, not in the least enigmatic, which is one reason that he's so likable.

"Dunny, I'm truly sorry if you feel chastised. That wasn't my intention. I just needed to clear the air. The thing is, I want you to succeed, I really do, lad. But if you're to succeed, you've got to operate according to the high standards we originally discussed."

"All right. You're more than fair. And I'm grateful to have another chance."

"Ah, now, there's no need for gratitude, Dunny." Typhon smiles broadly, his merriment regained. "If you succeed, then *I* succeed. Your interests are my own."

To reassure his benefactor that they are in full understanding of each other, Dunny says, "I'll do everything I possibly can for Ethan Truman—always keeping a low profile, of course. But I won't make any move against Corky Laputa."

"What an appalling piece of work *he* is." Typhon clucks his tongue, but his eyes twinkle. "The world desperately needs God's mercy as long as there are men like Corky in it."

"Amen."

"You know that Corky would most likely have killed Reynerd anyway if you hadn't interfered."

"I know," Dunny says.

"Then why show up with Hector X?"

"Laputa wouldn't have killed him with witnesses, certainly not with Hazard Yancy present. When Reynerd died in front of Yancy, then Yancy was *involved*, and more deeply than he'd have been otherwise. For Ethan's sake, I want him involved."

"Your friend *does* need all the help he can get," Typhon acknowledges.

For a minute or two, they enjoy the oysters and the fine wine in a mutual, comfortable silence.

Then Dunny says, "The incident with the PT Cruiser came as a surprise."

Raising his eyebrows, Typhon says, "You don't think our people were involved with that, do you?"

"No," Dunny says. "I understand how these things work. It came as a surprise, that's all. But I was able to use it to my advantage."

"Leaving him with the three little bells was a clever move," Typhon agrees. "Though you've driven him to drink."

Smiling, nodding, Dunny agrees: "I probably have."

"No 'probably' about it," says Typhon. Pointing, he adds: "Poor Ethan is at the bar right now."

Although Dunny's chair faces most of the room, about a third of the long bar is to his back. He turns to look where Typhon points.

Past intervening tables where breachers of contracts socialize like friends, Ethan Truman sits on a stool at the bar, in profile to Dunny, staring into a glass that might contain high-quality Scotch.

"He'll see me," Dunny worries.

"Most likely not. He's too distracted. In a sense, he doesn't see anyone right now. He might as well be here alone."

"But if he does—"

"If he does," Typhon says reassuringly, "then you'll manage the situation one way or another. I'm here for guidance if you need it."

Dunny stares at Ethan for a moment, then turns his back to him. "You chose this place knowing he was here?"

The only response from Typhon is a winning smile with a sly twist, which seems to say that he knows he's been naughty but simply couldn't resist.

"You chose this place *because* he was here."

Typhon says, "Did you know that Saint Duncan, for whom you were named, is the patron saint of guardians and protectors of many kinds, and that he will help you be steadfast and resourceful in your work if you petition him?"

Smiling thinly, Dunny says, "Is that so? Ironic, huh?"

Patting Dunny on the arm, Typhon reassures him: "From everything I've seen, you're an amazingly resourceful man to begin with."

Dunny communes with the Pinot Grigio for a while, but then says, "Do you think he's going to come through this alive?"

After finishing his last oyster, Typhon says, "Ethan? To some extent, that's up to you."

"But only to some extent."

"Well, you know how these things work, Dunny. More likely than not, he'll be dead before Christmas. But his situation isn't entirely hopeless. No one's ever is."

"And the people at Palazzo Rospo?"

With his white hair, plump features, and sparkling blue eyes, Typhon is but a beard away from being Santa Claus. His sweet face isn't made for grim expressions. He appears disconcertingly merry when he says, "I don't think any experienced oddsmaker would give them much of a chance, do you? Not against the likes of Mr. Laputa. He has the violent temperament and the reckless determination to get what he wants."

"Even the boy?"

"Especially the boy," says Typhon. "Especially him."

CHAPTER 33

FED, FRIGHTENED, AND FRUSTRATED, FRIC WENT directly from the wine cellar to the library, proceeding by an indirect route least likely to result in an encounter with a member of the house staff.

Like a spirit, like a phantom, like a boy wearing a cloak of invisibility, he passed room to hall to stair to room, and no one in the great house registered his passage, in part because he carried a rare gene for catlike stealth, but in part because no one, with the possible exception of Mrs. McBee, cared where the hell he was or ever wondered what the hell he was up to.

Being small, thin, and ignored was not always a curse. When the forces of evil were rising up against you in vast dark battalions, having a low profile improved your chances of avoiding evisceration, decapitation, induction into the soulless legions of the living dead, or whatever other hideous fate they might have planned for you.

The last time that Nominal Mom had visited, which wasn't quite as far back in the mists of time as mastodons and sabertooths, she had told Fric that he was a mouse: "A sweet little mouse that no one ever realizes is there because he's so quiet, so quick, so quick and so gray, as quick as the gray shadow of a darting bird. You're a little mouse, Aelfric, an almost invisible perfect little mouse."

Freddie Nielander said a lot of stupid things.

Fric didn't hold any of them against her.

She'd been so beautiful for so long that nobody really listened to her. They were overwhelmed by the visuals.

When no one ever listened to you, really listened, you could begin to lose the ability to tell whether or not you were making sense when you talked.

Fric understood this danger because no one really listened to him, either. In his case, they weren't overwhelmed by the visuals. They were underwhelmed.

Without exception, people loved Freddie Nielander on sight, and they wanted her to love them in return. Even if they *had* listened to her, therefore, they wouldn't have disagreed with her, and even when she made no sense whatsoever, people praised her wit.

Poor Freddie didn't get any truthful feedback from anything but a mirror. No explanation short of a miracle explained why she hadn't gone as crazy as a nuclear-waste-dump rat a long time ago.

Arriving in the library, Fric discovered that the furniture in the reading area nearest the entrance had been slightly rearranged to accommodate a twelve-foot Christmas tree. The fresh forestal smell of evergreens was so strong that he expected to see squirrels sitting in the armchairs and busily storing acorns in the antique Chinese vases.

This was one of nine massive spruces erected this very evening in key rooms throughout the mansion. Flawlessly shaped, perfectly symmetrical, greener-than-green clone trees.

Each of the nine evergreens would be decorated with a different theme. Here the subject was angels.

Every ornament on the tree was an angel or featured an angel in its design. Baby angels, child angels, adult angels, blond angels with blue eyes, African-American angels, Asian angels, noble-looking American

Indian angels with feathered headdresses as well as halos. Angels smiling, angels laughing, angels using their halos as Hula-Hoops, angels flying, dancing, caroling, praying, and skipping rope. Cute dogs with angel wings. Angel cats, angel toads, an angel pig.

Fric resisted the urge to puke.

Leaving all the angels to glitter and glimmer and dangle and grin, he went into the book stacks, directly to the shelf that held the dictionaries. He sat on the floor with the biggest volume—*The Random House Dictionary of the English Language*—and paged to ROBIN GOODFELLOW, because Mysterious Caller had said that the man from whom Fric would soon need to hide "styles himself as Robin Goodfellow."

The definition was a single word: *Puck.*

To Fric, this appeared to be an obscenity, although he didn't know what it meant.

Dictionaries were full of obscenities. This didn't bother Fric. He assumed that the people who compiled dictionaries weren't just a bunch of foul-mouthed gutter scum, that they had scholarly reasons for including trash talk.

When they started providing one-word obscene definitions that made no sense, however, maybe the time had come for the publisher to start smelling their coffee to see if it was loaded with booze.

Many of his father's associates used so many obscenities per sentence that they probably owned dictionaries that contained nothing but foul language. Yet *Puck* was so obscure none of them had ever spoken it in Fric's presence.

Fric paged forward through the volume, pretty sure he would discover that *Puck* meant "Screw you, we're tired of defining words, make up your own meaning."

Instead, he learned that Puck was a "mischievous sprite" in English folklore and a character in Shakespeare's *A Midsummer Night's Dream.*

Most words had more than one meaning, and that was true of *Puck*. The second definition proved to be less cheerful-sounding than the first: "a malicious or mischievous demon or spirit; a goblin."

Mysterious Caller had said that the guy Fric needed to worry about had a darker side than Robin Goodfellow, alias Puck. A darker side than a malicious demon or goblin.

Ugly clouds were gathering over Friclandia.

Fric paged farther forward in the dictionary, looking for a guy named M-o-e L-o-c-k. Instead, after some searching, he found MOLOCH. He read the definition twice.

Not good.

Moloch had been a deity, mentioned in two books of the Bible, whose worshipers were required to sacrifice children. Obviously, he had not been a Bible-approved deity.

The last four words of the definition particularly disturbed Fric: ". . . the sacrifice of children *by their own parents*."

This seemed to be carrying child sacrifice one step too far.

He didn't for a moment believe that Ghost Dad and Nominal Mom would strap him down on an altar and chop him to pieces for Moloch.

For one thing, with their superstar schedules, they'd probably never again be together in the same place at the same time.

Besides, while they might not be the kind of parents who tucked you in bed at night and taught you how to throw a baseball, they were not monsters, either. They were just people. Confused. Trying to do the best they knew how.

Fric had no doubt they cared about him. They had to care. They'd made him.

They just didn't express their feelings well. Images, not words, were your average supermodel's strength. Naturally, the biggest movie star in the world, being an actor, was better with words than Freddie was, but only when someone wrote them for him.

For a while, just to have something to do that didn't require think-ing about being brutally murdered, Fric looked up obscene words in the dictionary. It was an amazingly dirty book.

Eventually he began to feel ashamed of himself for reading all these filthy definitions in the same room with a tree full of angels.

After returning the dictionary to its shelf, he went to the nearest telephone. Because the library was a humongous space, three phones were distributed among its armchair-furnished reading areas.

On those rare occasions when Ghost Dad invited a magazine jour-nalist to interview him at home rather than on a set or some other neutral ground, he usually noted that the library contained more than twice as many books as there were bottles of wine in the wine cellar. Then he said, "When I'm a has-been, at least I'll be a pleasantly wasted, well-educated has-been."

Ha, ha, ha.

Fric sat on the edge of a chair, picked up the phone beside it, pressed the access button for his private line, and keyed in *69. He had forgotten to do this in the wine-tasting room, after Mysterious Caller had hung up on him.

Previously, when he'd tried this trick, the call-back number had rung and rung, and no one had ever answered it.

This time, someone answered. Someone picked up on the fourth ring, but didn't say anything.

"It's me," said Fric.

Though he didn't receive a reply, Fric knew he wasn't listening to a dead line. He could sense a presence at the other end.

"Are you surprised?" Fric asked.

He could hear breathing.

"I used star sixty-nine."

The breathing grew strange, a little ragged, as though the idea of being tracked down with *69 excited the guy.

"I'm calling you from the crapper in my father's bathroom," he lied, and waited to see if his weird phone buddy would warn him about the misery with which lying was rewarded.

Instead, he just got breathed at some more.

The guy was obviously trying to spook him. Fric refused to give the pervert the satisfaction of knowing that he had succeeded.

"What I forgot to ask you is how long I'll need to hide from this Puck when he shows up."

The longer he listened to the breathing, the more Fric realized that this had peculiar and disturbing qualities far different from the standard pervert-on-the-phone panting that he'd heard in movies.

"I looked up Moloch, too."

This name seemed to excite the freak. The breathing grew rougher and more urgent.

Abruptly Fric became convinced that the heavy breather was not a man, but an animal. Like a bear, maybe, but worse than a bear. Like a bull, but nothing as ordinary as a bull.

Up the coiled cord, into the handset, into the ear piece, into Fric's right ear, the breathing squirmed, a serpent of sound, seeking to coil inside his skull and set its fangs into his brain.

This didn't seem at all like Mysterious Caller. He hung up.

Instantly, his line rang: *Ooodelee-ooodelee-oo.*

He didn't answer it.

Ooodelee-ooodelee-oo.

Fric got up from the armchair. He walked away.

He passed quickly along aisles of bookshelves to the front of the library.

His personal call tone continued to mock him. He paused to stare at the phone in this main reading area, watching as the signal light burned bright with each ring.

Like all the members of the household and the staff who enjoyed dedicated phone lines, Fric had voice mail. If he didn't pick up by the fifth ring, the call would be recorded for him.

Although his voice mail was currently activated, the phone had rung fourteen times, maybe more.

He circled the Christmas tree, opened one of the two tall doors, and stepped out of the library, into the hall.

At last the phone stopped taunting him.

Fric glanced to his left, then to his right. He stood alone in the hall, yet the feeling of being watched had once more settled over him.

In the library, among the hundreds of tiny white lights strung like stars across the dark boughs of the evergreen, the angels sang silently, laughed silently, silently blew heralds' horns, glimmered, glittered, hung from their halos or harps, dangled from their pierced wings, from their hands raised in blessing, from their necks, as if they had broken all the laws of Heaven and, executed in one great throng, had been condemned forever to this hangman's tree.

CHAPTER 34

ETHAN DRANK SCOTCH WITHOUT EFFECT, FOR his metabolism seemed to have been dramatically accelerated by the experience of his own death twice in one day.

This hotel bar, with its crowd of self-polished glitterati, was a favorite of Channing Manheim's, a haunt from the early days of his career. In ordinary circumstances, however, Ethan would have chosen a joint without this flash, and with a comforting soaked-in-beer smell.

The few other bars familiar to him were frequented by off-duty cops. The prospect of running into an old friend from the force, on this evening of all evenings, daunted him.

During just one minute of conversation with any brother in the badge, regardless of how artfully Ethan tried to wear a happy face, he'd reveal himself to be deeply troubled. Then no self-respecting cop would be able to resist working him, either subtly or obviously, for the source of his worry.

Right now he didn't want to talk about what had happened to him. He wanted to *think* about it.

Well, that wasn't entirely true. He would have preferred denial to thought. Just forget it had happened. Turn away from it. Block the memory and get drunk.

Denial wasn't an option, however, not with the three silvery bells from the ambulance glimmering on the bar beside his glass of Scotch. He might as well try to deny the existence of Big Foot with a Sasquatch sitting on his face.

So he had no choice but to dwell on what had happened, which led him immediately into an intellectual dead end. He not only didn't know what to think about these weird events, he also didn't know *how* to think about them.

Obviously he had not been shot in the gut by Rolf Reynerd. Yet he intuitively knew the lab report would confirm that the blood under his fingernails was his own.

The experience of being run down in traffic and broken beyond repair remained so vivid, his memory of paralysis so horrifically detailed, that he could not believe he had merely imagined all of it under the influence of a drug administered without his knowledge.

Ethan asked the bartender for another round, and as the Scotch splashed over fresh ice into a clean glass, he pointed to the bells and said, "You see these?"

"I love that old song," the bartender said.

"What song?"

" 'Silver Bells.' "

"So you see them?"

The bartender cocked one eyebrow. "Yeah. A set of three little bells. How many sets do you see?"

Ethan's mouth cracked into a smile that he hoped looked less demented than it felt. "Just one. Don't worry. I'm not going to be a danger on the highway."

"Really? Then you're unique."

Yeah, Ethan thought, *I'm nothing if not unique. I've died twice today, but I'm still able to handle my booze*, and he wondered how quickly the bartender would snatch the drink from him if he spoke those words aloud.

He sipped the Scotch, seeking clarity from inebriation, since he couldn't find any clarity in sobriety.

Ten or fifteen minutes later, still cold sober, he caught sight of Dunny Whistler in the back-bar mirror.

Ethan spun on his stool, slopping Scotch from his glass.

Threading his way among the tables, Dunny had almost reached the door. He was not a ghost: A waitress paused to let him pass.

Ethan got to his feet, remembered the bells, snatched them off the bar, and hurried toward the exit.

Some patrons were visiting from table to table, standing in the aisles. Ethan had to resist the urge to shove them aside. His "Excuse me" had such a sharp edge that people bristled, but the expression on his face at once made them choke on their unvoiced reprimands.

By the time Ethan stepped out of the bar, Dunny had vanished.

Hurrying into the adjacent lobby, Ethan saw guests standing at the registration desk, others at the concierge desk, people walking toward the elevator alcove. Dunny wasn't among them.

To Ethan's left, the marble-clad lobby opened to an enormous drawing room furnished with sofas and armchairs. There, guests could attend high tea every afternoon; and at this later hour, drinks were being served to those who preferred an atmosphere gentler than that in the bar.

At a glance, Dunny Whistler couldn't be seen among the crowd in the drawing room.

Nearer, to Ethan's right, the revolving door at the hotel's main entrance was slowly turning to a stop, as though someone had recently gone in or out, but its quadrants were deserted now.

He pushed through the door, into the night chill under the roof of the porte-cochere.

Sheltering their charges with umbrellas, the doorman and a busy squad of parking valets escorted visitors to and from arriving and departing vehicles. Cars, SUVs, and limousines jostled for position in the crowded hotel-service lanes.

Dunny wasn't standing with those who were waiting for their cars. Nor did he appear to be hurrying through the downpour in the company of any of the escorts.

Several Mercedes in various dark colors idled among the other vehicles, but Ethan was pretty sure none of them was Dunny's wheels.

The ring of his cell phone might not have been audible above the chatter of the people under the porte-cochere, the car engines, and the hiss and sizzle of the drizzling night. Set for a silent signal, however, it vibrated in a jacket pocket.

Still surveying the night for Dunny, he answered the phone.

Hazard Yancy said, "I've got to see you right now, man, and it's got to be somewhere the elite don't meet."

CHAPTER 35

DUNNY TAKES THE HOTEL ELEVATOR UP TO THE fourth floor in the company of an elderly couple. They hold hands as though they are young lovers.

Overhearing the word "anniversary," Dunny asks how long they have been married.

"Fifty years," the husband says, aglow with pride that his bride has chosen to spend most of her life with him.

They are from Scranton, Pennsylvania, here in Los Angeles to celebrate their anniversary with their daughter and her family. The daughter has paid for the hotel honeymoon suite, which is, according to the wife, "so fancy we're afraid to sit on the furniture."

From L.A., they'll fly to Hawaii, just the two of them, for a romantic week-long idyll in the sun.

They are unaffected, sweet, clearly in love. They have built a life of the kind that Dunny for so long disdained, even mocked.

In recent years, he's come to want their brand of happiness more than anything else. Their devotion and commitment to each other, the family they have built, the life of mutual striving, the memories of shared challenges and hard-won triumphs: Here is what matters, in the end, not the things that he has pursued with single-minded strategy and brutal tactics. Not power, not money, not thrills, not control.

He has tried to change, but he's gone too far along a solitary road to be able to turn back and find the companionship for which he yearns. Hannah is five years gone. Only when she had been on her deathbed had he realized that she'd been the best chance he'd ever had of finding his way from the wrong road to the right one. As a young hothead, he had rejected her counsel, had believed that power and money were more important to him than she was. The shock of her early death forced him to face the hard truth that he'd been wrong.

Only on this strange, rainy day has he come to understand that she was also his *last* chance.

For a man who once believed that the world was clay from which he could make what he wished, Dunny has arrived at a difficult place. He has lost all power, for nothing he does now can change his life.

Of the money he withdrew from the wall safe in his study, he still has twenty thousand dollars. He could give ten of it to this elderly couple from Scranton, tell them to stay a full month in blue Hawaii, to dine well and drink well, with his blessings.

Or he could stop the elevator and kill them.

Neither act would change his future in any meaningful way.

He bitterly envies their happiness. There would be a certain savage satisfaction in robbing them of their remaining years.

Whatever else may be wrong with him—the list of his faults and corruptions is long—he can't kill solely out of envy. Pride alone prevents him, more than mercy.

On the fourth floor, their accommodations are at the opposite end of the hotel from his. He wishes them well and watches them walk away, hand-in-hand.

Dunny is using the presidential suite. This grand space has been booked on a twelve-month basis by Typhon, who will not be needing it for the next few days, as business will take him elsewhere.

Presidential implies an understated democratic grandeur. These large rooms are so rich and so sensual, however, that they are less suitable for a steward of democracy than for royalty or demigods.

Inlaid marble floors, Oushak rugs in tones of gold and red and apricot and indigo, bubinga paneling soaring sixteen feet to coffered ceilings . . .

Dunny wanders room to room, moved by humanity's desire to make beautiful its habitat and thereby bravely to deny that the roughness of the world must be endured. Every palace and every work of art is only dust as yet unrealized, and time is the patient wind that will wither it away. Nevertheless, men and women have given great thought, effort, and care to making these rooms appealing, because they hope, against all evidence, that their lives have meaning and that in their talents lies a purpose larger than themselves.

Until two years ago, Dunny never knew this hope. Three years of anguish over her loss, ironically, made him *want* to believe in God.

Gradually, during the years following her funeral, an unexpected hope grew in him, desperate and fragile but enduring. Yet he remains too much the old Dunny, mired in old habits of thought and action.

Hope is a cloudy radiance. He has not learned how to distill it into something pure, clear, more powerful.

And now he never will.

In the master bedroom, he stands at a rain-washed window, gazing northwest. Beyond the storm-blurred city lights, beyond the lushly landscaped and mansioned slopes of Beverly Hills, lies Bel Air and Palazzo Rospo, that foolish yet nonetheless brave monument to hope. All who ever owned it have died—or will.

He turns from the window and stares at the bed. The maid has removed the spread, turned down the sheets, and left a tiny gold box on one of the pillows.

The box holds four bonbons. Elegantly formed and decorated, they appear to be delicious, but he doesn't sample them.

He could call any of several beautiful women to share the bed with him. Some would expect money; others would not. Among them are women for whom sex is an act of love and grace, but also women who revel in their own debasement. The choice is his, any tenderness or any thrill that he desires.

He cannot recall the taste of the oysters or the bouquet of the Pinot Grigio. The memory has no savor, offers less stimulation to his senses than might a photograph of oysters and wine.

None of the women he could call would leave a greater impression than the food and drink that, still settling in him, seems to be a meal imagined. The silken texture of their skin, the smell of their hair would not linger with him past the moment when, in leaving, they closed the door behind them.

He is like a man living through the night before doomsday, with full knowledge that the sun will go nova in the morning, yet unable to enjoy the precious pleasures of this world because all his energy is devoted to wishing desperately that the foreseen end will not, after all, come to pass.

CHAPTER 36

ETHAN AND HAZARD MET IN A CHURCH, FOR at this hour on a Monday night, the pews were empty, and no chance whatsoever existed that they would be seen here together by politicians, by members of the Officer Involved Shooting team, or by other authorities.

In the otherwise deserted nave, they sat side by side in a pew, near a side aisle where neither the overhead nor the footpath lights were aglow, veiled in shadows. The stale but pleasant spice of long-extinguished incense perfumed air as still as that in a sealed jar.

They spoke less in conspiratorial whispers than in the hushed voices of men humbled by awesome experience.

"So I told the OIS team I went to see Reynerd to ask about his friend Jerry Nemo, who happens to be a suspect in the murder of this coke peddler name of Carter Cook."

"They believe you?" Ethan asked.

"They seem like they want to. But suppose tomorrow I get a lab report that superglues Blonde in the Pond to that city councilman I told you about."

"That girl dumped in the sewage plant."

"Yeah. So the bastard councilman will start looking for a way to get at me. If any guys on the OIS team can be bought or blackmailed, they'll turn that homey hit man with the coke-spoon earring into a crippled choirboy who got shot in the back, and my mug will be on the front pages under the nine-letter headline."

Ethan knew what the nine-letter headline would be—KILLER COP—because they had talked about the power of anti-cop prejudice over the years. When a dirty politician and the sensation-hungry press discovered a shared agenda in any case, truth was stretched tighter than the skin of any Hollywood dowager with four face-lifts, and the blindfold over Lady Justice's eyes was ripped away and shoved into her mouth to shut her up.

Hazard hunched forward, forearms on his thighs, hands clasped almost as if in prayer, staring at the altar. "The media love this councilman. His rep is he's a reformer, got all the right sympathies and positions on the issues. They ought to love me, too, 'cause I'm so lovable, but that crowd would rather cut off their lips than kiss a cop. If they see a chance to save him by crucifying me, every hardware store in the city will be sold out of nails."

"I'm sorry I got you into this."

"You couldn't know some fool would whack Reynerd." Hazard turned his gaze from the altar, and his eyes met Ethan's as though searching for the Judas taint: "Could you?"

"Some ways this looks bad for me."

"Some ways," Hazard agreed. "But even you aren't dumb enough to work for some movie-star asshole who settles business like he's a rap-music mogul."

"Manheim doesn't know about Reynerd or the black boxes. And if he did know, he'd figure all Reynerd needed to improve his psychology was a little aromatherapy."

"But there *is* something you're not telling me," Hazard pressed.

Ethan shook his head, but not in denial. "Oh, man, this has been one long day in a monkey barrel."

"For one thing, Reynerd was sitting on his sofa between two bags of potato chips. Turns out he kept a loaded piece in each bag."

"Yet when the shooter rang the bell, Reynerd answered the door unarmed."

"Maybe 'cause he figured I was the true threat, and already through the door. My point is you were right about the potato chips."

"Like I told you, a neighbor said he was paranoid, kept a pistol close to him, stashed it in odd places like that."

"The talky neighbor—that's bullshit," Hazard said. "There was no talky neighbor. You knew some other way."

They were at a crossroads of trust and suspicion. Unless Ethan spilled more than he had revealed thus far, Hazard wasn't going to follow him one step farther. Their friendship would not be finished, but without greater disclosure, it would never be the same.

"You're gonna think I'm mental," Ethan said.

"Already do."

Ethan inhaled more incense, exhaled inhibition, and told Hazard about being shot in the gut by Reynerd, opening his eyes to discover he wasn't shot after all, and in the absence of a wound, nevertheless finding blood under his fingernails.

Throughout all this, Hazard's eyes neither swam out of focus nor shifted toward some far point of the church, as they would have done if he'd decided that Ethan was either jiving or psychotic. Only when Ethan finished did Hazard look down at his folded hands again.

Eventually the big man said, "Well, for sure I'm not sitting here beside a ghost."

"When you choose an institution for me," Ethan said, "I'd prefer one with a good arts-and-crafts program."

"Other than having your blood tested for drugs, you cooked up any theories about this?"

"You mean, besides I'm in the Twilight Zone? Or I really did die from that gut shot, and this is Hell?"

Hazard took the point. "Aren't a whole lot of theories come to mind, are there?"

"Not the kind you can explore with what the suits at the police academy call 'conventional investigative techniques.' "

"You don't seem nuts to me," Hazard said.

"I don't seem nuts to me, either. But then the nut is always the last to know."

"Besides, you were right about the pistol in the potato chips. So it was at least like . . . a psychic experience."

"Clairvoyance, yeah. Except that doesn't explain the blood under my nails."

Hazard had absorbed this bizarre revelation with quiet trust and remarkable equanimity.

Nevertheless, Ethan had no intention of telling him about being run down by the PT Cruiser and the truck. Or about dying in the ambulance.

If you reported having seen a ghost, you were a regular guy who'd had an uncanny experience. If you reported seeing *another* ghost at another place and time, you were at best an eccentric whose every statement would thereafter be taken with enough salt to crust the rims of a million margarita glasses.

"The shooter who killed Reynerd," Hazard said, "was a gang-banger called himself Hector X. Real name was Calvin Roosevelt. He's a high cuzz in the Crips, so you figure his accomplice must've been driving a set of wheels they boosted right before the hit."

"Standard," Ethan agreed.

"But there's no stolen-car report on the Benz they used. I got the number on the tags, and you won't believe who it belongs to."

Hazard looked up from his folded hands. He met Ethan's eyes.

Although Ethan didn't know what was coming, he knew it couldn't be good. "Who?"

"Your boyhood pal. The notorious Dunny Whistler."

Ethan didn't look away. He didn't dare. "You know what happened to him a few months ago."

"Some guys drowned him in a toilet, but he didn't quite die."

"Few days after that, his lawyer contacted me, told me Dunny's will named me executor, and his *living* will gives me the right to make medical decisions for him."

"You never mentioned this."

"Didn't see any reason. You know what he was. You understand why I didn't want him in my life. But I accepted the situation out of . . . I don't know . . . because of what he meant to me when we were kids."

Hazard nodded. He withdrew a roll of hard caramels from a coat pocket, peeled back the wrapping, and offered to share.

Ethan shook his head. "Dunny died this morning at Our Lady of Angels."

Hazard pried a caramel from the roll, popped it in his mouth.

"They can't find his body," Ethan said, for suddenly he sensed that Hazard already knew all this.

Carefully folding the loose end of the wrapper over the exposed candy, Hazard said nothing.

"They swear he was dead," Ethan continued, "but considering how things work at the hospital morgue, he couldn't have gotten out of there any way but on his own two feet."

Hazard returned the roll to his coat pocket. He sucked on the caramel, moving it around his mouth.

"I'm sure he's alive," Ethan said.

Finally Hazard looked at him again. "All this happened before we had lunch."

"Yeah. Listen, man, I didn't mention it because I didn't see how Dunny could be connected to Reynerd. I *still* don't see how. Do you?"

"You were one self-possessed dude at lunch, considering all this was churning through your head."

"I thought I was going crazy, but I didn't see how you'd be more likely to help me if I virtually *told* you I was losing my mind."

"So what happened *after* lunch?"

Ethan recounted his visit to Dunny's apartment, leaving nothing out except the strange elusive shape in the steam-clouded mirror.

"Why'd he keep a photo of Hannah on his desk?" Hazard asked.

"He'd never gotten over her. Still hasn't. I guess that's why he ripped it out of the frame today and took it with him."

"So he drives out of the garage in his Mercedes—"

"I assumed it was him. I couldn't get a look at the driver."

"And then what?"

"I had to think about it. Then I visited Hannah's grave."

"Why?"

"Gut feeling. Thought I might find something there."

"And what did you find?"

"Roses." He told Hazard about the two dozen Broadways and his subsequent visit to Forever Roses. "The florist described Dunny as good as I could've. That's when I was sure he was alive."

"What'd he mean when he told her that you thought he was dead—and you were right?"

"I don't know."

Hazard crunched the half-finished caramel.

"You can break a tooth that way," Ethan warned.

"Like that's my biggest problem."

"Just friendly advice."

"Whistler wakes up in a morgue, realizes he's been mistaken for dead, so then he puts his clothes on, goes home without saying boo to anyone, takes a shower. That make sense to you?"

"No. But I thought he might be brain-damaged."

"He drives to a florist, buys some roses, visits a grave, hires a hit man. . . . For a guy who comes out of a coma with brain damage, he seems to get around pretty well."

"I've given up the brain-damage theory."

"Good for you. So what happened after you left the florist?"

Operating on the two-ghost theory of credibility, Ethan didn't tell him about the PT Cruiser, but said, "I went to a bar."

"You're not a guy who looks for answers in a glass of gin."

"This was Scotch. Didn't find any answers there either. Might try vodka next."

"So that's everything? You've come clean with me now?"

With all the conviction that he could muster, Ethan said, "What—this whole mess isn't *X-Files* enough already? You want there should be some aliens in it, vampires, werewolves?"

"What're you—dodging the question?"

"I'm not dodging anything," Ethan said, regretting that he was going to be forced to lie boldly rather than by indirection. "Yeah, that was everything, through the flower shop. I was drinking Scotch when I got your call."

"Truth?"

"Yeah. I was drinking Scotch, I got your call."

"Remember, you're in a church here."

"The whole world's a church if you're a believer."

"Are you a believer?"

"I used to be."

"Not since Hannah died, huh?"

Ethan shrugged. "Maybe I am, maybe I'm not. It's a day-to-day thing."

After giving him a look that could have peeled an onion layer by layer to the pearl at the core, Hazard said, "Okay. I believe you."

Feeling low enough to slide under a snake, Ethan said, "Thanks."

Hazard turned in the pew to survey the nave, to be sure that a lost soul had not entered in need of a God fix. "You've come clean, so I'll tell you something, but you've got to forget you heard it."

"Already I don't even remember being here."

"Not much of interest in Reynerd's apartment. Spare furnishings, everything black-and-white."

"He seemed to live like a monk, but a monk with style."

"And drugs. He had a big stash of coke packaged for resale and a notebook of names and numbers that's probably a customer list."

"Famous names?"

"Not really. Some actors. Nobody big. The thing you need to know about is the screenplay he was writing."

"In this town," Ethan said, "guys writing screenplays outnumber those cheating on their wives."

"He had twenty-six pages in a pile beside his computer."

"That's not even enough for a first act."

"You know about screenplays, huh? You writing one?"

"No. I've still got some self-respect."

Hazard said, "Reynerd was writing about this young actor goes to a special acting class, makes what he calls 'a deep intellectual connection' with his professor. They both hate this character named Cameron Mansfield, who happens to be the biggest movie star in the world, so they decide to kill him."

Under a weight of weariness, Ethan had slouched in the corner of the pew. Now he sat up straight. "What's their motivation?"

"That's not clear. Reynerd has lots of handwritten notes in the margin, trying to figure that out. Anyway, sort of to prove to each other that they've got the guts to do this, each agrees to give the other guy the name of someone to kill *before* they do the movie star together. The actor wants the professor to kill his mother."

"Why's this sound so Hitchcock?" Ethan wondered.

"It's sort of like his old film, *Strangers on a Train*. The idea is by swapping killings, each guy can have a perfect alibi for the murder he might otherwise be convicted of."

"Let me guess. Reynerd's mother was actually murdered."

"Four months ago," Hazard confirmed. "On a night when her son had an alibi more airtight than a space-shuttle window."

The church seemed to turn at a lazy six or eight revolutions per minute, as if the Scotch might be having a delayed effect on Ethan, but he knew this vertigo was caused less by the Scotch than by these latest weird revelations. "What kind of idiot does these things, then writes them up in a screenplay?"

"An arrogant idiot actor. Don't tell me you think he's unique."

"And who did the professor want Reynerd to kill?"

"A colleague at the university. But Reynerd hadn't written that part yet. He'd just completed the scene featuring the murder of his mother. In real life, her name was Mina, and she was shot once in the right foot and then beaten to death with a marble-and-bronze lamp. In the script, her name's Rena, and she's stabbed repeatedly, beheaded, dismembered, and incinerated in a furnace."

Ethan winced. "Sounds like his mom's days were numbered whether or not Reynerd ever met the professor."

They were silent. The well-insulated church roof lay so far overhead that the storm's voice was barely audible, less like the drumming of rain than like the whispery wings of some hovering flock.

"So," Hazard eventually said, "even with Reynerd dead, maybe Chan the Man had better be looking over his shoulder. The professor— or whatever he might be in real life—is still out there somewhere."

"Who's working Mina Reynerd's murder?" Ethan wondered. "Anyone I know?"

"Sam Kesselman."

Sam had been a detective with Robbery/Homicide when Ethan still carried a badge.

"What's he make of the screenplay?"

Hazard shrugged. "He hasn't heard about it yet. They probably won't drop a Xerox on him till tomorrow."

"He's a good man. He'll be all over it."

"Maybe not fast enough for you," Hazard predicted.

At the front of the church, teased by a draft, votive-candle flames squirmed in ruby glasses. Chameleons of light and shadow wriggled across a sanctuary wall.

"What're you going to do?" Hazard asked.

"Reynerd's shooting will be in the morning newspaper. They're sure to mention his mother's murder. That'll give me an excuse to go to Kesselman, fill him in on those packages Reynerd has been sending to Manheim. He'll have read the partial screenplay—"

"About which you don't know jack," Hazard reminded him.

"—and he'll realize there's an ongoing threat to Manheim until the professor is identified. That'll accelerate the investigation, and I might even get police protection for my boss in the meantime."

"In a perfect world," Hazard said sourly.

"Sometimes the system works."

"Only when you don't expect it to."

"Yeah. But I don't have the resources to investigate Reynerd's friends and associates fast enough to matter, and I don't have the authority to dig through his personal records and effects. I've got to rely on the system whether I want to or not."

"What about our lunch today?" Hazard asked.

"It never happened."

"Someone might've seen us. And there's a credit-card trail."

"Okay, we had lunch. But I never mentioned Reynerd to you."

"Who's going to believe that?"

Ethan couldn't think of anyone sufficiently gullible.

"You and I have lunch," Hazard said, "I cook up a reason to visit Reynerd the same day, and it just so happens he gets killed while I'm there. *Then* it just so happens the shooter's getaway car belongs to Dunny Whistler, your old buddy."

"My head hurts," Ethan said.

"And I haven't even kicked it yet. Man, they'll expect us to know what's going on here, and when we claim we don't—"

"Which we don't."

"—they're going to be sure we're lying. I was them, *I'd* think we were lying."

"Me too," Ethan admitted.

"So they'll dream up a screwy scenario that sorta-kinda explains things, and we'll wind up accused of offing Reynerd's mother, wasting Reynerd, pinning it on Hector X, then popping him, too. Before it's over, the bastard D.A. will be trying to pin us for the disappearance of the dinosaurs."

The church didn't seem like a sanctuary anymore. Ethan wished he were in another bar, where he might have a chance of finding solace, but not a bar that Dunny, dead or alive, would be likely to visit.

"I can't go to Kesselman," he decided.

Hazard would never sigh with relief and concede the intensity of his concern. A mirror held under his nostrils might have revealed a sudden bloom of condensation, but otherwise his relaxation of tension was marked by only a slight settling of his mountainous shoulders.

Ethan said, "I'm going to have to take extra measures to protect Manheim, and just hope Kesselman finds Mina's killer quickly."

"If the preliminary OIS opinion doesn't move me off the Reynerd case," Hazard said, "I'll turn this city inside out to find Dunny Whistler. I've got to believe he's the key to all this."

"I think Dunny will find me first."

"What do you mean?"

"I don't know." Ethan hesitated, sighed. "Dunny was there."

Hazard frowned. "There where?"

"At the hotel bar. I only noticed him when he left. I went after him, lost him in the crowd outside."

"What was he doing there?"

"Drinking. Maybe watching me. Maybe he followed me there, intended to approach me, then decided against it. I don't know."

"Why didn't you tell me first thing?"

"I don't know. It seemed . . . like one ghost too many."

"You think it all gets too rich, I won't believe it? Have some faith, man. We go back, don't we? We been shot at together."

They chose to leave the church separately.

Hazard got up first and moved away. From the farther end of the pew, in the center aisle, he said, "Like old times, huh?"

Ethan knew what he meant. "Covering each other's ass again."

For such a big man, Hazard made little noise as he walked from the nave to the narthex, and out of the church.

Having a reliable friend to watch your back is a comfort, but the consolation and support provided by even the best of friends is no match for what a loving wife can be to a husband, or a loving husband to a wife. In the architecture of the heart, the rooms of friendship are deeply placed and strongly built, but the warmest and most secure retreat in Ethan's heart was the one that he had shared with Hannah, where these days she lived only as a precious ghost, a sweet haunting memory.

He could have told her everything—about the phantom in the mirror, about his second death outside Forever Roses—and she would have believed him. Together they'd have sought some understanding.

During the five years that she'd been gone, he had never missed her more than he missed her at this moment. Sitting alone in a silent church, keenly aware of the soft beating of the rain on the roof, of the lingering fragrance of incense, of the ruby light of the votive candles, but unable to detect the faintest whisper, whiff, or glimmer of God, Ethan longed not for evidence of his Maker, but for Hannah, for the music of her voice and the beautiful geometry of her smile.

He felt homeless, without hearth or anchor. His apartment in the Manheim house awaited his return, offering many comforts, but it was merely a residence, not a place endeared to him. He had felt the tug of home only once in this long strange day: when he'd stood at Hannah's grave, where she lay beside an empty plot to which he held the deed.

CHAPTER 37

FROM ALTERNATING BRONZE-BALL AND BRONZE-flame finials, from cast panels of arabesques, from darts and twists and frets and scallops and leaves, from griffins and heraldic emblems, black and silver rain dripped and drizzled off the Manheim gate.

Ethan braked to a stop beside the security post: a five-foot-high, square, limestone-clad column in which were embedded a closed-circuit video camera, an intercom speaker, and a keypad. He put down his window and keyed in his six-digit personal code.

Slowly, with the Expedition's headlight beams rippling across its ornate surfaces, the massive gate began to roll aside.

Each employee of the estate had a different code. The security staff maintained computerized records of every entrance.

Remote-control units such as typical garage-door openers or coded transponders, assigned to each vehicle, would have been more convenient than a key-entry system, especially in foul weather; however, such devices would have been accessible to garage mechanics, valet-parking attendants, and anyone else in temporary custody of a vehicle. One dishonest person among them might easily compromise the security of the estate.

If Ethan had been a visitor lacking a personal gate-entry code, he would have pushed the intercom button on the post and would have announced himself to the guard in the security office at the back of the property. If the visitor was expected or was a family friend on the permanent-access list, the guard would open the gate from his command board.

As he waited for the massive bronze barrier to roll out of the way, Ethan was under surveillance by the camera on the security post. Entering the property, he would be scrutinized through a series of tree-mounted cameras angled in such a manner as to reveal anyone who might be lying on the floor of the SUV to avoid detection.

All videocams included night-vision technology that transformed the faintest moonlight into a revealing glow. A sophisticated bit of software filtered out most of the veiling and the distortion effects produced by falling rain, ensuring a clear real-time image on the security-office screens.

Had he been a repairman or deliveryman arriving in an enclosed van or truck, Ethan would have been asked to wait outside the gate until a security guard arrived. The guard would then look inside the vehicle to ensure that the driver was not, under duress, bringing any bad guys with him.

Palazzo Rospo was not a fortress either by modern definition or by the moat-and-drawbridge standards of medieval times. Neither was the estate a cupcake served on a plate to be easily plucked by any hungry thief.

Explosives could bring down the gate. The property wall could be scaled. But the grounds couldn't easily be entered by stealth. Intruders would be identified and tracked almost at once by cameras, motion detectors, heat sensors, and other devices.

The thirty-foot-wide bronze gate, more solid than open, weighed over eight thousand pounds. The motor that operated the chain drive was powerful, however, and the barrier rolled aside with apparent ease and with more speed than one might expect.

A five-acre plot qualified as a large piece of land in most residential communities. In *this* neighborhood, where an acre could bring upwards of ten million dollars, a five-acre property was the equivalent of an English country estate of baronial scale.

The long driveway looped around a reflection pond in front of the great house, which was not Baroque, like the bronze gate, but a limestone-clad, three-story Palladian structure with simple classic ornamentation, huge yet elegant in its proportions.

Just before reaching the pond, the driveway split, and Ethan took the branch that led around to the side of the house. When it split again, one artery led to the groundskeeper's building and the security office, while the other led down a ramp to the underground garage.

The garage had two levels. In the upper, the Face stored thirty-two vehicles in his personal collection, ranging from a new Porsche to a series of Rolls-Royces from the 1930s, to a 1936 Mercedes-Benz 500K, to a 1931 Duesenberg Model J, to a 1933 Cadillac Sixteen.

The lower garage housed the fleet of workaday vehicles owned by the estate and provided parking for cars belonging to employees.

Like the upper garage, the lower featured a beige matte-finish ceramic-tile floor and walls of glossy tile in a matching color. Supporting columns were decorated with free-flowing mosaics in various shades of yellow.

Few high-end automobile sales facilities, catering to the very wealthy, were as beautifully appointed as this lower garage.

The pegboard for car keys hung on the wall outside the elevator, and Fric sat on the floor under the board, holding the same paperback fantasy novel that he'd been reading in the library this morning. He got to his feet as Ethan approached.

To a degree that surprised Ethan, the sight of the boy gladdened him. Nothing else had done so in this long, gray, dismal day.

He wasn't entirely sure why the kid lifted his spirits. Maybe because you expected the son of the Face, raised in such wealth and with such indifference, to be spoiled rotten or to be dysfunctionally neurotic, or both; and because instead Fric was basically decent and shy, tried to cover his shyness with a seen-it-all air, but could not conceal a fundamental modesty as rare in his glamorous world as pity was rare among the scaly denizens of a crocodile swamp.

Indicating the paperback, Ethan said, "Has the evil wizard found the tongue of an honest man for his potion?"

"No luck yet. But he just sent his brutal assistant, Cragmore, to visit a lying politician and harvest his testicles."

Ethan winced. "He *is* an evil wizard."

"Well, it's just a politician. Some of them come around here now and then, you know. After they leave, Mrs. McBee does an inventory of the valuable items in the rooms they visited."

"So . . . what're you doing down here? Planning to go for a drive?"

Fric shook his head. "There's no point making a break for it until I'm sixteen. First I've got to get my driver's license, have enough time to put together a stash of cash big enough to start over with, research the perfect small town to hide in, and design a series of really cool impenetrable disguises."

Ethan smiled. "That's the plan, huh?"

Failing to match Ethan's smile, with bone-dry seriousness, Fric said, "That's the plan."

The boy pressed the button to call the elevator. The machinery hummed into motion, the noise only partly muffled by the shaft walls.

"I've been hiding out from the decorating crew," Fric revealed. "They're still putting up trees and stuff all over the house. This is your first Christmas here, so you don't know, but they all wear these stupid Santa hats, and every time they see you, they shout, 'Merry Christmas,' grinning like lunatics, and they want to give you these sucky little candy canes. They don't just decorate, they like make a performance out of it, which I guess most people want, otherwise they wouldn't have a business, but it's enough to turn you into an atheist."

"Sounds like a memorable holiday tradition."

"It's better than the paid carolers on Christmas Eve. They dress like characters out of Dickens, and between songs they talk to you about Queen Victoria and Mr. Scrooge and whether you're going to have goose and suet pudding for Christmas dinner, and they call you 'm'lord' and 'young master,' and you've got to be there because Ghost . . . because my father thinks it's all so cool. After about half an hour, you're sure you're either going to shit or go blind, and there's *another* half-hour to get through. But then it's okay, because after the carolers is the magician who does this act with dwarfs dressed up like Santa's elves, and he's radically hilarious."

Aelfric seemed to be concealing a nervous and urgent concern that he unintentionally expressed in a flood of words set loose with a quality akin to babble. He wasn't a tight-lipped boy by nature, but neither was he a nonstop talker.

The elevator arrived and the doors opened.

Ethan followed the boy into the wood-paneled cab.

After pushing the button for the ground floor, Fric said, "In your experience, are phone perverts really dangerous or are they just all talk?"

"Phone perverts?"

To this point, the boy had made eye contact. Now he watched the light on the floor-indicator board and didn't even glance at Ethan. "Guys that call up and breathe at you. Do they mainly get their kicks from just that, or do they sometimes actually come around and want to grope you and stuff?"

"Has someone called you, Fric?"

"Yeah. This freak." The boy made heavy, ragged panting sounds, as if Ethan might be able to identify the pervert from the unique signature of his breathing patterns.

"When did this start?"

"Just today. First when I was in the train room. Then he called again when I was in the wine cellar, eating dinner."

"He called on your private line?"

"Yeah."

On the board, the indicator light blinked from the lower garage to the higher garage. The elevator moved slowly upward.

"What did this guy say to you?"

Fric hesitated, shuffling his feet slightly on the inlaid-marble floor. Then: "He just breathed. And made some . . . some almost like animal sounds."

"That's all?"

"Yeah. Animal sounds, but I don't know what they were supposed to be, 'cause he wasn't like *talented* at it or anything."

"You're sure he didn't say something to you? Didn't even use your name?"

Remaining focused on the indicator board, Fric said, "Just that stupid breathing. I star sixty-nined him, figuring maybe the pervert still lives with his mother, see, and she'd answer, and I could tell her what her precious sicko son was up to, but then I just got him breathing at me."

They arrived at the ground floor. The doors opened.

Ethan stepped into the hall, but Fric remained in the elevator.

Blocking the doors with one arm, Ethan said, "Calling him back— that wasn't a good idea, Fric. When someone's trying to harass you, what gives them a kick is knowing they got under your skin. The best thing to do is hang up as soon as you realize who it is, and if the phone rings again right away, don't answer it."

Looking at his wristwatch, adjusting the time with the stem, busying himself, Fric said, "I thought you'd have a way to find out who he is."

"I'll give it a try. And Fric?"

The boy continued to fiddle with the watch. "Yeah?"

"It's important that you tell me everything about this."

"Sure."

"You *are* telling me everything, aren't you?"

Holding the watch to one ear, as if listening for ticking, Fric said, "Sure. It was this breather."

The boy was withholding information, but putting pressure on him at this time would only ensure that he would guard his secret all the more fiercely.

Recalling how he himself had responded to Hazard's interrogation in the church, Ethan relented. "If it's all right with you, when your line rings tonight or anytime tomorrow while I'm here, I'd like to answer it myself."

"Okay."

"Your line doesn't ring in my apartment, but I'll just go into the house computer and change that."

"When?"

"Right now. I'll pick it up on the first few rings, but if a call comes in tomorrow when I'm not here, then just let it go to your voice mail."

The boy made eye contact at last. "Okay. You know what my ring sounds like?"

Ethan smiled. "I'll recognize it."

With a look of consternation, Fric said, "Yeah, it's dorky."

"And you think the first nine notes of 'Dragnet' makes me feel like I'm getting an important call?"

Fric smiled.

"If you need to call me anytime, day or night," Ethan said, "on one of my house lines or my cell phone, don't hesitate, Fric. I don't sleep all that much anyway. You understand?"

The boy nodded. "Thanks, Mr. Truman."

Ethan stepped backward into the hallway once more.

Self-conscious, Fric chewed solemnly on his lower lip as he pushed a control-panel button, probably for the third floor where he had his rooms.

Because of the boy's diminutive stature, the elevator, as big as any in a high-rise building, seemed to be even larger than usual.

Although short and slender for his age, Fric possessed a quiet determination and a courage, apparent in his posture and in his daily attitude, that were surprising for his years and bigger than his small body. The boy's strange and lonely childhood had already begun to steel him for adversity.

In spite of his wealth and wit and growing wisdom, adversity would come to him sooner or later. He was a human being, after all, and therefore heir to his share of misery and misfortune.

The elevator doors slid shut.

As Fric disappeared from view and as machinery purred, Ethan looked at the indicator board above the door. He watched until he saw the light change from the ground floor to the second, listened as the lift mechanism continued to grind.

In his mind's eye, Ethan saw the elevator doors open on the third floor, revealing an empty cab, Fric having vanished forever between floors.

Such peculiar dark imaginings were not common to him. On any day but this one, he would have wondered where such a disturbing twist of thought had come from, and he would have at once smoothed it out of his mind as easily as pressing a wrinkle from a shirt.

This was the day it was, however, so utterly unlike any other that Ethan felt inclined to take seriously even the most unlikely presentiments and possibilities.

The back staircase wrapped the elevator shaft. He was tempted to race up four flights. The elevator rose so slowly that he might beat it to the third floor.

When the doors slid open, revealing Fric unharmed, the boy would be startled to be greeted with such alarm. Breathing hard from his frantic ascent, Ethan wouldn't be able to conceal his concern from Fric—nor would he be able to explain it.

The moment passed.

His clenched throat relaxed. He swallowed, breathed.

The indicator light blinked from the second to the third floor. The elevator motor fell silent.

Surely Fric had arrived safely at the top of the house. He had not been consumed and digested by demonically possessed machinery.

As best he could, Ethan smoothed that bizarre idea from his mind as he went to his apartment in the west wing.

CHAPTER 38

HURRYING THE LENGTH OF THE LONG NORTH hall, Fric more than once looked worriedly over his shoulder, for he had always half believed that ghosts lurked in the lonelier corners of the great house. On *this* night, he was all but certain of their presence.

As he passed a gilded mirror set above an old-as-dirt console, he thought he glimpsed *two* figures in the age-discolored glass: he himself, but also someone taller, darker, hurrying just behind him.

In a tapestry that probably dated from before the last ice age, threatening-looking horsemen on dark steeds seemed to turn their heads to watch him pass. Peripherally, he thought he saw the horses—eyes wild, nostrils flared—begin to gallop through that fabric field and forest, as if intent on bolting out of their woven world and into the third-floor hallway.

Considering his current state of mind, Fric was not suited for work in a graveyard, a mortuary, a morgue, or in a cryogenics facility where gaggles of dead people were frozen in expectation that one day they could be thawed and returned to life.

In a movie, Ghost Dad had played Sherlock Holmes, who had turned out to be the first man ever to have his body scientifically frozen upon death. Holmes was revived in the year 2225, where a utopian society needed his help to solve the first murder in a hundred years.

Deleting either the evil robots or the evil aliens, or the evil mummies, would have made it a better movie. Sometimes a film could be *too* imaginative.

At this moment, however, Fric had no difficulty believing that Palazzo Rospo might be seething with ghosts, robots, aliens, mummies, and some unnameable thing worse than all the others, especially here on the third floor, where he was alone. Not *safely* alone, perhaps, but alone in the sense that he was the only living human presence.

His father's bedroom and the suite of rooms related to it were on this level, in the west wing and along part of the north corridor. With Ghost Dad in residence, Fric had company in this high retreat, but most nights he dwelt alone here on the third floor.

Like now.

At the junction of the north and the east hallways, he stood as still as a corpsicle in a cryogenic vat, listening to the house.

Fric more imagined than heard the patter of rain. The roof was slate, well insulated, and far above even this high hallway.

The faint and inconstant sough of winter wind was but a memory from another time, for this was largely a windless night.

In addition to Fric's suite, along the east hall were other chambers. Seldom-used guest bedrooms. A walk-in linen closet. An electric-utilities room crammed with equipment mysterious to Fric but reminiscent of Frankenstein's laboratory. There was a small sitting room, richly furnished and well maintained, in which no one ever sat.

At the end of the hall lay the door to a set of back stairs that went down five stories, all the way to the lower garage. Another set of stairs, at the end of west hall, also descended to the bottom of Palazzo Rospo. Neither was as wide or as grand, of course, as the main staircase, which featured a crystal chandelier at each landing.

The actress Cassandra Limone—born name, Sandy Leaky—who had lived with Fric's father for five months, staying in the house even when he was absent, had churned up and down every staircase fifteen times a day, as part of her workout regimen. A well-equipped gym on the second floor offered a StairMaster among numerous machines, but Cassandra said the "authentic" stairs were less boring than the make-believe stairs and had a more natural effect on leg and butt muscles.

Slathered in sweat, grunting, squinting, grimacing, cursing like the possessed girl in *The Exorcist*, screeching at Fric if he happened onto the stairs when she was using them, climbing Cassandra would not have been recognizable to the editors at *People* magazine. They had twice selected her as one of the most beautiful people in the world.

Apparently, however, all the effort had been worthwhile. Ghost Dad had more than once told Cassandra that she was a deadly weapon because her calf muscles could crack a man's skull, her thigh muscles could break any heart, and her butt could drive a man crazy.

Ha, ha, ha. Instead of testing your sense of humor, some jokes tested your gag reflex.

One day near the end of her stay, Cassandra had fallen down the back west stairs and broken an ankle.

Genuinely funny.

Now Fric followed the east hall not to his suite, but to the last room on the right before the stairs.

This inelegant space, measuring about twelve feet by fourteen, had a sturdy plank floor and bare white walls. Empty at the moment, it served as a staging point for the transferral of goods in and out of the attic.

A spacious dumbwaiter, driven by an electric motor, could carry up to four hundred pounds, allowing for the storage of heavy boxes and large objects in the vastness above. A door opened to a spiral staircase that also led to the attic.

Fric used the stairs. He climbed carefully, with one hand always on the railing, concerned that his amusement regarding Cassandra's broken ankle would jinx him with a shattered leg of his own.

The attic extended the entire length and breadth of the mansion. The space was finished, not rough: plaster walls, solid plank floor covered with linoleum for easy cleaning.

Colonnades of massive vertical beams supported an elaborate trusswork of rafters that held up the roof. No partitions had been constructed between these beams, so the attic remained one great open room.

In practice, you could not see easily from one end of the high chamber to another, for suspended by wires from the rafters were hundreds of enormous, framed movie posters. Every one of them bore the name and giant image of Channing Manheim.

Fric's father had made just twenty-two films, but he collected career-related items in every language. His movies were big box office worldwide, and any one project produced dozens of posters.

The hanging posters formed walls of a kind, and aisles, as did hundreds of stacked boxes packed full of Channing Manheim memorabilia that included T-shirts bearing his likeness and/or catchphrases from his films, wristwatches on which time ticked across his famous face, coffee mugs bearing *his* mug, hats, caps, jackets, drinking glasses, action figures, dolls, hundreds of different toys, lingerie, lockets, lunchboxes, and more merchandise than Fric could remember or imagine.

At every turn were life-size and larger-than-life, freestanding cardboard figures of Ghost Dad. Here he was a roughneck cowboy, there the captain of a spaceship, here a naval officer, there a jet pilot, a jungle explorer, a nineteenth-century cavalry officer, a doctor, a boxer, a policeman, a firefighter. . . .

More elaborate cardboard dioramas featured the biggest star in the world in whole sets from his movies. These had been displayed in theater lobbies, and many of them, if supplied with batteries, would prove to have moving parts and flashing lights.

Cool props from his films lay on open metal shelves or leaned against the walls. Futuristic weapons, firemen's helmets, soldiers' helmets, a suit of armor, a robot spider the size of an armchair . . .

Larger props, like the time machine from *Future Imperfect*, were stored at a warehouse in Santa Monica. That facility and this attic featured museum-quality heating and humidifying systems to ensure the least possible deterioration of the items in the collection.

Ghost Dad had recently bought the estate next door to Palazzo Rospo. He intended to tear down the existing house on that adjacent property, connect the two parcels of land, and build a museum in the architectural style of Palazzo Rospo, to display his memorabilia.

Although his father had never said as much, Fric suspected that the intention was for the estate to be opened to the public one day, in the manner of Graceland, and that Fric himself would be expected to manage this operation.

If that day ever came, he would, of course, have to blow his brains out or throw himself off a tall building, or both, if he had not already successfully started a new, secret life under an assumed identity in Goose Crotch, Montana, or in some other town so remote and simple that the locals still referred to movies as "magic-lantern shows."

Once in a while when he climbed into the attic to wander the Manheim maze, Fric was enchanted. Sometimes he was even thrilled to be a part of this almost-legendary, nearly magical enterprise.

At other times, he felt at most an inch tall and shrinking, an insignificant bug of a boy, in danger of being stepped on, smashed flat, and forgotten.

This evening, he felt neither inspired nor discouraged by the collection, for he toured it solely in search of a hiding place. In this labyrinth, surely he would discover a pocket of sanctuary among the memorabilia, where he could conceal himself and be protected by his father's omnipresent face and name, which might ward off evil in much the way that garlic and a crucifix discouraged vampires.

He came to a seven-foot-high mirror in a frame of carved and hand-painted snakes writhing in jewel-colored tangles. In *Black Snow*, Fric's father had seen glimpses of his future in this mirror.

Fric saw Fric, and Fric alone, squinting at his reflection as he sometimes did, trying to blur his image into someone taller and tougher than who he really was. As usual, he failed to fool himself into feeling heroic, but he was glad that the mirror didn't reveal scenes from *his* future, confirming what a hopeless geek he would still be at thirty, forty, fifty.

As Fric stepped back from the mirror and began to turn away, the glass appeared to ripple, and a man came *through* it, a big man, looking plenty tough without having to squint. The grinning brute reached for Fric, and Fric ran for his life.

CHAPTER 39

TROUBLED AS NEVER BEFORE BY THE DARKNESS beyond the windows, Ethan went through his apartment, closing the drapes and shutting out the rainy night as if, in fact, it had a thousand eyes.

In his study, at his desk, he switched on the computer and engaged the house-control program. On the screen, icons appeared for the heating-cooling controls, the pool and spa heaters, the landscape watering and lighting, the interior lighting, the interlinked audio-video equipment, the electronic security apparatus, the telephones, and other systems.

Using his mouse, he clicked the telephone icon. A request for his password appeared, and he entered it.

Among everyone on the household staff, only Ethan could access *and* reprogram the security and the telephone systems.

The screen changed, offering him a new set of options.

The phones in his apartment featured all twenty-four lines, but only two were accessible to him. He could not eavesdrop on anyone's calls, and they were likewise unable to overhear his.

Furthermore, when calls came through to other lines in the house,

Ethan heard no ringing in his rooms. The indicator light above the number of each line did, however, flutter when a call was coming in, and it burned steadily when a conversation was being conducted.

Having entered the telephone program, Ethan edited the controls to make Line 23, Fric's line, henceforth accessible to his apartment phones. It would also ring here using Fric's personal tone.

With this task completed, he perused the day's phone log.

Every incoming call to Palazzo Rospo and all outgoing calls as well were automatically logged—although not voice recorded. Note was made of the time that each connection had been effected and of the duration of each conversation.

For every outgoing call, the phone number was also preserved on the computer log. Incoming caller numbers were noted as well, except in those instances when they had Caller ID blocking to protect their privacy.

He entered his name and saw that he had received only one call while he'd been out of the house. The calls he'd made and received on his cell phone were not included in these records.

He snatched up the phone to check his voice mail. The call had been from the hospital, informing him of Dunny's death.

When Ethan cleared his name and typed Aelfric's, the computer reported that the boy had received no calls at any time on this date, Monday, December 21.

According to Fric, the breather had phoned twice. And at least once, the boy had tracked him back with *69. All three occurrences should have been noted.

Ethan jumped from Fric's file to the master log, which listed all phone-line activity since the previous midnight in the order that the calls had been placed and received. The list was long because the staff had been busy making Christmas preparations.

Carefully scrolling through the log, Ethan found no calls to or from Fric's line.

Unless the record-keeping system had erred, which it had never done before in Ethan's experience, the inescapable conclusion had to be that Fric lied about receiving obscene calls.

His respect for the boy motivated Ethan to scroll through the phone log again, bottom to top this time. The result was the same.

As difficult as it might be to believe that the system had failed to note the calls that Fric reported, Ethan found it almost equally hard to accept that the kid had concocted the story of the heavy breather. Fric was not a self-dramatizer and certainly not an attention-seeker.

Besides, he had seemed genuinely disturbed when he'd recounted those calls. *He just breathed. And made some . . . some almost like animal sounds.*

Aware of a winking brightness at the periphery of his vision, Ethan turned from the computer and saw the indicator light fluttering on Line 24. As he watched, the call was answered, a connection made, and the light burned steadily.

Line 24, the last line on the board, was set aside to receive phone calls from the dead.

CHAPTER 40

WHEN A FIERCE-LOOKING GUY COMES OUT of a mirror as though it's a doorway, and when he grabs for you and snags your shirt with his fingertips, you could be excused for wetting your pants or for losing total control of your sphincter, so Fric was amazed that he didn't instantly void from every orifice, that he reacted quickly enough to slip free of the snagging fingers, and that he raced away into the memorabilia maze in a totally dry and stink-free condition.

He turned left, right, right, left, vaulted over a low stack of boxes from one aisle into another, knocking between two huge posters as he went, raced past a life-size Ghost-Dad-as-1930s-detective, pushed between more posters, dodged around a realistic-looking Styrofoam unicorn from the one film in the Manheim credit list that no one dared talk about in his father's presence, turned left, left, right, and halted when he realized that he had lost track of where he'd come from and that he might be returning in a circle to the serpent-embraced mirror.

In his wake, across a significant portion of the wide attic, the framed posters swung like giant pendulums. He had stirred some of them during his flight, but the wind of those dozen fanned others into gentler motion, perpetrating a wider disturbance.

Among all this movement, the approach of the mirror man was more difficult to discern than it would have been in an attic steeped in stillness. Fric couldn't catch a glimpse of him.

Unless you were a skulking fiend with a sympathy for shadows, the lighting here was troublesome. Wall lamps ringed the perimeter of the attic, while others were mounted to some of the columns that supported the trusswork, though the number and brightness of them left much to be desired. The hanging palisades of posters, arrayed like flags from the many nations of Manheim, thwarted the even flow of light from aisle to aisle.

Crouched warily in gloom, Fric drew a deep breath, held it, listened.

At first he could hear nothing but the *didop-da-bidda-boom* of his skipping-drumming heart, but near the useful end of that banked breath, he began to hear, as well, the dash of rain on slate.

Aware that by his every noise he would locate himself for the stalking predator, Fric *eased* out the dead breath, coaxed in a live one, held it.

Higher in the house, he was also higher in the storm. Here the lonely sighing of the rain swelled into the whispers of a multitude exchanging sinister secrets in the sea of night that now submerged Palazzo Rospo.

Yet in the same way that he had focused himself to hear the rain above the drumbeat of his heart, he tuned in to the footsteps of the mirror man. The attic architecture, the pendulum motion of the giant posters, and the whiffle of the rain served to distort the sound, to make it seem that the intruder was going away from Fric, then coming closer, then going, when in fact he most likely made steady progress toward his quarry.

Fric had heeded Mysterious Caller's advice to find a deep and secret hiding place. He had believed that he would need a refuge soon, but he hadn't realized that he would need it *this* soon.

Learning to breathe and listen at the same time, he took to heart his dotty mother's insistence that he was "an almost invisible perfect little mouse." He crept with quiet quickness past the red-and-gold cardboard spires of a futuristic city over which his father—in cardboard—towered with a fearsome laser rifle at the ready.

At an intersection of aisles, Fric looked both ways, turned left. He scurried onward, analyzing the sound of the heavy footsteps as he went, calculating what route might best put distance between him and the man from the mirror.

The intruder made no effort at stealth. He seemed to *want* Fric to hear him, as though confident that the boy couldn't evade capture.

Moloch. This must be Moloch. Looking for a child to take as a sacrifice, a child to kill, perhaps to eat.

He's Moloch, with the splintered bones of babies stuck between his teeth. . . .

Fric refrained from screaming for help, certain that he would not be heard by anyone other than the man-god-beast-thing who stalked him. The walls of the house were thick, the floors thicker than the walls, and no one was nearer than the second floor down in the middle of the mansion.

He might have sought a window and risked a ledge or a three-story drop. The attic had no windows.

A fake stone sarcophagus stood on end, decorated with carved hieroglyphics and the image of a dead pharaoh, no longer inhabited by the evil mummy that had once done battle with the biggest movie star in the world.

A steamer trunk, in which a ruthless and clever murderer (played by Richard Gere) had once crammed the corpse of a gorgeous blonde (actually the live body of the aforementioned Cassandra Limone), now stood empty.

Fric wasn't tempted to hide in those containers, nor in the black-lacquered coffin, nor in the trick box in which a magician's assistant could be made to disappear with the help of angled mirrors. Even the ones that weren't coffins *seemed* like coffins, and he was sure that crawling into any of them would mean certain death.

The wise thing to do would be to keep moving, mouse-quick and mouse-quiet, staying low, staying loose, always several twists and turns ahead of the mirror man. Eventually he could circle back to the spiral staircase, descend from the attic, and flee to lower floors where help could be found.

Suddenly he realized that he could no longer hear the footsteps of his pursuer.

No cardboard Ghost Dad stood more still, no mummy under Egyptian sands rested any more breathless with its shriveled lungs, than Fric as he began to suspect that this new silence was a bad development.

A shadow floated overhead, treading air as though it were water.

Fric gasped, looked up.

The roof-supporting trusses rested atop the attic columns, five feet above his head. From one truss line to another, above the movie posters, a figure flew across the aisle, wingless but more graceful than a bird, leaping with the slow and weightless form exhibited by any astronaut in space, contemptuous of gravity.

This was no caped phantom, but a man in a suit, the one who had stepped out of the mirror, executing an impossible aerial ballet. He landed on a horizontal beam, pivoted toward Fric, and swooped down from his high perch, not like a plummeting stone, but like a feather, grinning exactly as Fric had imagined that evil Moloch, hungry for a child, would grin.

Fric turned and ran.

Although Moloch's descent had been feather-slow, suddenly he was *here*. He seized Fric from behind, one arm around his chest, one hand over his face.

Fric tried desperately to wrench loose but was lifted off his feet as a mouse might be snatched off the ground by the talons of a hunting hawk.

For an instant, he thought that Moloch would fly up into the rafters with him, there to rip at him with fierce appetite.

They remained on the floor, but Moloch was already moving. He strode along as if certain of where each turning of the maze would take him.

Fric struggled, kicked, kicked, but seemed to be fighting nothing more substantial than water, caught in the dreamy currents of a nightmare.

The hand on his face pressed up from beneath his chin, a clamp that jammed teeth to teeth, forcing him to swallow his scream, and pinching shut his nose.

He was overcome by the panic familiar from his worst asthma attacks, the terror of suffocation. He couldn't open his mouth to bite, couldn't land a kick that mattered. Couldn't *breathe.*

And yet a worse fear gripped him, clawed him, tore at his mind as they passed the mummy's sarcophagus, passed a cardboard cop with Ghost Dad's face: the horrifying thought that Moloch would carry him through the mirror and into a world of perpetual night where children were fattened like cattle for the pleasure of cannibal gods, where you wouldn't find even the paid kindness of Mrs. McBee, where there was no hope at all, not even the hope of growing up.

CHAPTER 41

ETHAN GLANCED AT HIS WRISTWATCH, THEN at the indicator light on Line 24, timing the telephone call.

He didn't believe a dead person had dialed up Palazzo Rospo, dropping metaphysical coins into a pay phone on the Other Side. Dependably, this would be either a wrong number or a solicitation from a salesman with such a high-pressure approach that he would rattle out his spiel even to the answering machine that recorded these messages.

When Ming du Lac, spiritual adviser to the Face, had explained Line 24, Ethan had been perceptive enough to realize that Ming would be impatient with even so much as a raised eyebrow, and hostile to any expression of disbelief. He had managed to keep a straight face and a solemn voice.

Only Mrs. McBee on the household staff and only Ming du Lac among Manheim's other associates had the influence to get the great man to fire Ethan. He knew exactly with whom he must tread softly.

Calls from the dead.

Everyone has answered the phone, heard silence, and said "Hello" again, assuming that the caller has been distracted by someone on his end or that there is a problem with the switching equipment. When a third "Hello" draws no response, we hang up, convinced that the call must have been a wrong number or from a crank, or the result of a technical glitch in the system.

Some people, the Face among them, believe that a portion of such calls originate with deceased friends or loved ones trying to reach us from Beyond. For some reason, according to this theory, the dead can make your phone ring, but they can't as easily send their voices across the chasm between life and death; therefore, all you hear is silence or peculiar static, or on rare occasion whispery scraps of words as if from a great distance.

Upon investigating this subject after Ming explained the purpose of Line 24, Ethan had learned that researchers in the paranormal had made recordings on telephone lines left open between test numbers, operating on the assumption that if the dead could initiate a call, they might also take advantage of an open line specifically set aside to detect their communications.

Next, the researchers amplified and enhanced the faint sounds on the recordings. Indeed, they discovered voices that often spoke English, but also that sometimes spoke French, Spanish, Greek, and other languages.

Most of these whispery entities offered only scraps of sentences or disjointed words that made little sense, providing insufficient data for analysis.

Other, more complete "messages" could sometimes be construed as predictions or even dire warnings. They were always short, however, and often enigmatic.

Reason suggested that the recordings had caught only bleed-over conversations from living people using other lines in the telephone system.

In fact, many of the coherent snippets seemed to deal with matters too mundane to motivate the dead to reach out to the living: questions about the weather, about grandchildren's latest report cards from school, bits like "... always loved pecan pie, yours best of

all . . ." and ". . . better put your pennies away for a rainy day . . ." and
". . . at that cafe you like, the owner keeps a dangerously dirty
kitchen . . ."

And yet . . .

And yet a few of the voices were said to be so haunted, so bleak
with despair or so full of desperate love and concern, that they could
not be forgotten, could not be easily explained, especially when the
messages were delivered with urgency: ". . . fumes from the furnace,
fumes, don't go to sleep tonight, fumes . . ." and ". . . I never told you
how much I love you, so much, please look for me when you come
across, remember me . . ." and ". . . a man in a blue truck, don't let
him get near little Laura, don't let him near her . . ."

These most eerie messages reported by paranormal researchers
were what motivated Channing Manheim to maintain Line 24
strictly for the convenience of the chatty dead.

Every day, wherever they were in the world, Manheim and Ming du
Lac used part of their meditation periods to broadcast mentally the area
code plus the seven-digit number for Line 24, casting this baited hook
into the sea of immortality with the hope that it would catch a spirit.

Thus far, over a period of three years, they had recorded only
wrong numbers, sales pitches, and a series of calls from a hoaxer who,
before Ethan's arrival, had proved to be a security guard on the estate.
He had been let go with generous severance pay and, according to
Mrs. McBee, with a lecture from Ming du Lac to the effect that he
would be wise to put his spiritual house in order.

The signal light winked off. This call had lasted one minute and
twelve seconds.

Sometimes Ethan wondered how the Channing Manheim who
managed an acting career so brilliantly and who had proved himself
an investment wizard could be the same man who employed Ming
du Lac and also a feng-shui adviser, a clairvoyance instructor, and a
past-life researcher who spent forty hours a week tracking the actor's
reincarnations backward through the centuries.

On the other hand, the singular events of this day left him less certain of his usual skepticism.

He turned his attention to the computer screen once more, to the telephone log. He frowned, wondering why Fric would have invented the heavy breather.

If someone had in fact made obscene calls to the boy, chances were good that this related to the implied threats against Manheim that had come in those black boxes. Otherwise, there were two sources of threats that had arisen simultaneously. Ethan didn't believe in coincidences.

The heavy breather might be the real-life inspiration for the "professor" mentioned in Reynerd's partial screenplay, the man who had conspired to send the black gift boxes and to kill Manheim. If so, he had somehow acquired at least one of the house's unlisted numbers: a disturbing development.

Yet the phone log had never failed to record any call in the past. And though they might err, machines didn't lie.

The recent incoming call to Line 24 was now the last item on the day's log. As it should be.

Ethan had timed the call at one minute twelve seconds. The monitoring software registered one minute fourteen seconds. He had no doubt that the two-second error was his.

According to the log, Caller ID blocking prevented notation of the point-of-origin number. That was peculiar if the call had been from a phone-sales agent, a breed now forbidden by law to block their ID, not peculiar at all if it had been a wrong number.

Neither was it unusual for a wrong number to have tied up the line for a minute or longer. The outgoing greeting on the special answering machine that serviced Line 24 was not an elaborate hello to those in the spirit world, but a simple "Please leave a message." Some callers, failing to realize that they hadn't reached the desired number, complied with that invitation.

Anyway, whoever called Line 24 wasn't the issue. The question was if the ever-dependable machine had erred or lied in failing to record the calls that the boy claimed to have received.

Logically, Ethan could only conclude that the machine couldn't be faulted. In the morning, he would have a talk with Fric.

On the desk beside the computer were the three silvery bells from the ambulance. He stared at them for a long time.

Beside the bells was a nine-by-twelve manila envelope that had been left here for him by Mrs. McBee. She had printed his name in matchless calligraphy.

As with all things McBee, her graceful penmanship made Ethan smile. She knew the best and most elegant way that every task ought to be performed, and she held herself to her own high standards.

He opened the envelope and confirmed a truth that he already knew: Freddie Nielander, Fric's mother, was a braying jackass.

CHAPTER 42

FANTASTICALLY YELLOW FROM HEAD TO FOOT, Corky Laputa accepted the shocking-pink plastic bag from Mr. Chung.

He was aware that he evoked smiles from other customers, and he supposed that in his yellow-and-pink flamboyance, he must be the most cheerful-looking anarchist in the world.

The bag bulged with containers of Chinese food, and Mr. Chung overflowed with good will. He effusively thanked Corky for his continuing patronage and wished him all the best that fortune had to offer.

After a typically busy day in the pursuit of social collapse, Corky seldom found himself in the mood to make dinner. He got takeout from Mr. Chung as often as three or four times a week.

In a better world, instead of resorting repeatedly to Chinese takeout, he would have preferred to dine frequently in upscale restaurants. If an establishment offered fine cuisine and excellent service, however, there were invariably enough customers to ruin the experience.

With but few exceptions, human beings were tedious, self-deluded bores. He could tolerate them individually or in classroom situations where he set the rules, but in crowds they were not conducive to the enjoyment of a good meal or to proper digestion.

He drove home through the rain with his pink bag, and he left it unopened on the kitchen table. Mouth-watering aromas flooded the room.

After changing into a comfortable Glen-plaid cashmere robe suitable to a drizzly December evening, Corky mixed a martini. Only a trace of vermouth, two olives.

In the sublime afterglow of a day well spent, he often liked to walk his spacious home and admire the richness of its Victorian architecture and ornamentation.

His parents, both from well-to-do families, had purchased the property shortly after their marriage. Had they not been the people they were, the beautiful house would have been alive with wonderful family memories and with a sense of tradition.

Consequently, his only fine family memory, the one that warmed him most, was associated with the living room, especially with the area around the fireplace, where he had separated his mother from his inheritance by the application of an iron poker.

He stood there for only a minute or two, basking in the fire, before going upstairs again. This time, martini in hand, he went to the back guest bedroom, to check on Stinky Cheese Man.

He didn't even bother to lock the door these days. Old Stinky wasn't going anywhere under his own power ever again.

The room would have been dark in daylight, for the two windows were boarded over. The wall switch by the door controlled the lamp on the nightstand.

The tinted bulb and the apricot silk shade provided an appealing glow. Even in this flattering light, Stinky appeared paler than pale, so gray that he seemed to be petrifying into stone.

His head, shoulders, and arms were exposed, but the rest of him remained covered by a sheet and blanket. Later, Corky would enjoy the entire show.

Stinky had once been a trim 200 pounds, in excellent condition. If he could have gotten on a scale now, he probably would have weighed less than 110.

All bone, skin, hair, and pressure sores, he was barely strong enough to lift his head an inch off his pillow, too weak by far to get out of bed and onto a scale, and the depth of his despair had weeks ago broken his will to resist.

Stinky was no longer semi-sedated. His sunken eyes met Corky's, darkly shining with a desperate petition.

On the IV tree, the dangling twelve-hour bag of glucose and saline solution had drained completely. The slow drip of glucose, vitamins, and minerals that kept Stinky alive also infused a drug that ensured mental vagueness and reliable docility.

Corky put down his martini, and from a small refrigerator well stocked with full infusion bags, he plucked a replacement for the empty container. With practiced hands, he removed the collapsed bag and installed the plump one.

The current drip included no drug. Corky wanted his withered guest to have a clear head later.

After picking up his martini and taking a sip, he said, "I'll rejoin you after dinner," and he left the bedroom.

In the living room once more, Corky stopped by the fireplace to finish his drink and to remember Mama.

Unfortunately, the historic poker was not here to be polished, hefted, and admired. Years ago, on the night of the event, police had taken it away with many other items, intent on collecting evidence, and had never brought it back.

Corky had been too wise to request its return, leery that the police might suspect that it had sentimental value to him. All the fireplace tools had been purchased new following his mother's death.

Reluctantly, he had replaced the carpet as well. If the homicide detectives had for any reason returned in the months following the murder, upon seeing the bloodstained carpet still in place, they might have at least raised an eyebrow.

In the kitchen, he heated the Chinese food in the microwave. Moo goo gai pan. Mu shu pork. Beef and red pepper. Rice, of course, and pickled cabbage.

He could not eat all this food himself. Ever since he'd begun methodically to starve Stinky Cheese Man in the guest room, however, Corky had been buying too much takeout.

Evidently, the spectacle of Stinky's ghastly decline was not merely entertaining but subconsciously disturbing. It raised in Corky a deepseated fear of being underfed.

In the interest of good mental health, therefore, he continued to purchase too much takeout and enjoyed the therapeutic pleasure of feeding the excess to the garbage disposal.

This evening, as had been the case more often than not in recent months, Corky ate at the dining-room table, on which were stacked the complete blueprints of Palazzo Rospo. These prints had been produced from a set of diskettes developed by the architectural firm that had overseen the six-million-dollar renovation of the mansion soon after Manheim had purchased the estate.

In addition to receiving new electrical, plumbing, heating, air-conditioning, and audio-video systems, the enormous house had been computerized and fitted with a state-of-the-art security package designed for continual, easy upgrading. According to one source on whom Corky was relying, that package had indeed been upgraded at least once in the past two years.

As if the night were a living thing, and moody, it rose out of its sodden lethargy and worked up a peevish wind, hissing at the windows, clawing at the house walls with prosthetic hands that it fashioned from tree limbs, and by the shaking of its great black coat, rattled barrages of rain against the glass.

In his warm dining room, wrapped in Glen-plaid cashmere, with a Chinese feast before him, with worthwhile and exciting work to occupy his mind, Corky Laputa had seldom felt so cozy or more glad to be alive.

CHAPTER 43

THE MCBEE REPORT WAS DETAILED AND BUSI-
nesslike, as usual, yet also friendly, presented in calligraphy
that made it a minor work of art and lent to it the aura of a historical
document. Sitting at the desk in his study, Ethan could hear in his
mind the musical lilt and the faint Scottish brogue of the housekeeper's voice.

After an initial greeting to the effect that she hoped Ethan had enjoyed a productive day and that the Christmas spirit buoyed him as
much as it did her, Mrs. McBee reminded him that she and Mr.
McBee would be off to Santa Barbara early in the morning. They were
spending two days with their son and his family, and were scheduled
to return at 9:00 A.M. on the twenty-fourth.

She further reminded him that Santa Barbara lay but an hour to the
north and that she remained on call in the event that her counsel was
needed. She supplied her cell-phone number, which Ethan already
knew, and her son's phone number. In addition, she provided her
son's street address and the information that less than three blocks
from his house was a large, lovely park.

*The park features many stately old California live oaks and other
trees of size,* she wrote, *but within its boundaries are also at least*

two generous meadows, either of which will accommodate a heli-
copter in the event there should arise a household emergency of such
dire proportions that I must be ferried home in the style of a battle-
field surgeon.

Ethan would not have believed that anyone could make him laugh out loud at the end of this distressing day. With her dry sense of humor, Mrs. McBee had done so.

She reminded him that in her and Mr. McBee's absence, Ethan would serve *in loco parentis,* with full responsibility for and authority over Fric.

During the day, if Ethan needed to be away from the estate, Mr. Hachette, the chef, would be next in the succession of command. The porters and maids could attend to the boy as needed.

After five o'clock, the day maids and the porters would be gone. Following dinner, Mr. Hachette would depart, as well.

Because the other live-in staff members were off on an advance Christmas holiday, Mrs. McBee advised Ethan that he must be certain to return before Mr. Hachette went home for the day. Otherwise Fric would be alone in the house, with no adults nearer than the two guards in the security office at the back of the estate.

Next, in her memo, the housekeeper addressed the issue central to Christmas morning. Early this day, after speaking with the boy in the library, before driving to West Hollywood to investigate Rolf Reynerd, Ethan had raised with Mrs. McBee the matter of Fric's Christmas gifts.

Any kid would have thrilled to the idea that he could submit a list of wanted items as extensive as he wished and that he would receive on Christmas morning everything he requested, precisely those items, nothing less, but nothing more. Yet it seemed to Ethan that this robbed Christmas morning of its delicious suspense and even of some of its magic. As this would be his first Christmas at Palazzo Rospo, he had approached Mrs. McBee in her office off the kitchen to inquire as to the protocol of leaving an unexpected gift under the tree, for Fric.

"God bless you, Mr. Truman," she had said, "but it's a bad idea. Not quite as bad as shooting yourself in the foot to observe the effect of the bullet, but nearly so."

"Why?" he had wondered.

"Every member of the staff receives a generous Christmas bonus, plus a small item from Neiman Marcus or Cartier, of a more personal nature—"

"Yes, I read that in your *Standards and Practices*," Ethan had said.

"And staff members are thoughtfully forbidden to exchange gifts among themselves because there are so many of us that shopping would take too much time and would impose a financial burden—"

"That's in *Standards and Practices* as well."

"I am flattered that you have it so well memorized. Then you'll also know that the staff is kindly forbidden from presenting gifts to members of the family, primarily because the family is fortunate enough to have everything it could want, but also because Mr. Manheim considers our hard work and our discretion in discussing his private life with outsiders to be gifts for which he is grateful every day."

"But the way the boy has to prepare a list and knows everything on it will be there Christmas morning—it seems so *mechanized*."

"A major celebrity's career and life are often one and the same, Mr. Truman. And in an industry as large and complex as Mr. Manheim, the only alternative to mechanization is chaos."

"I suppose so. But it's cold. And sad."

Speaking more softly and with some affection, Mrs. McBee had taken him into her confidence: "It *is* sad. The boy is a lamb. But the best that all of us can do is be especially sensitive to him, give him counsel and encouragement when he asks for it or when he seems to need it but won't ask. An actual unexpected Christmas gift might be well received by Fric, but I'm afraid his father wouldn't approve."

"I sense you mean he wouldn't approve for some reason other than those in *Standards and Practices*."

Mrs. McBee had brooded for a long moment, as though consulting in memory a version of *Standards and Practices* much longer than the one in the ring-bound notebook that she presented to every employee.

At last she'd said, "Mr. Manheim isn't a bad man, or heartless, just overwhelmed by his life . . . and perhaps too in love with the flash of it. On some level, he recognizes what he's failed to give Fric, and he surely wishes that things were different between them, but he doesn't know how to fix it and still do everything he needs to do to keep being who he is. So he pushes it out of mind. If you were to put a gift under the tree for Fric, Mr. Manheim's guilt would surface, and he'd be hurt by what your gesture implied. Although he's a fair man with employees, I wouldn't be able to predict what he might do."

"Sometimes, when I think about that lonely little kid, I want to shake a little sense into his old man even if—"

Mrs. McBee had raised a warning hand. "Even among ourselves, we don't gossip about those who buy our bread, Mr. Truman. That would be ungrateful and indecent. What I've said here has been by way of friendly advice, because I believe you're a valuable member of the staff and a good example to our Fric, who is more observant of you than you probably realize."

Now, in her memo, Mrs. McBee addressed the gift issue once more. She'd had the day to reconsider her advice: *As to the delicate issue of an unexpected gift, I find that I want to qualify what I told you earlier. A small and very special item, something more magical than expensive, if left not under the tree but elsewhere, and anonymously, would thrill the recipient in the way that you and I recall being thrilled on the Christmas mornings of our youth. I suspect that he would intuitively understand the wisdom of discretion in the matter, and would all but surely keep the existence of the gift to himself if only for the sheer deliciousness of having such a secret. But the item must be truly special, and caution is advised. Indeed, when you have read the last of this, please shred and eat.*

Ethan laughed again.

Simultaneous with his laugh, an indicator light fluttered on the telephone: Line 24. He watched as, on the third ring, the answering machine picked up, whereafter the light burned steadily.

He could not go into the computer and edit the program to allow him to receive Line 24 here in his apartment. Only the first twenty-three lines were accessible to his manipulation. Other than Manheim, only Ming du Lac had access to the sacred twenty-fourth. A request to change that situation would have made Ming as angry as a spiritual guru ever got, which was in fact as furious as a rattlesnake teased with a sharp stick, minus all the hissing.

Even if he'd had access to Line 24, Ethan wouldn't have been able to monitor any call once the answering machine picked it up, because the recorder established an exclusive connection that as a matter of mechanics precluded eavesdropping.

He had never previously been a fraction as interested in Line 24 as he was this evening, and his interest made him uneasy. If he were ever to puzzle his way through what had happened to him on this momentous day, he would need to keep superstition at bay and think logically.

Nevertheless, when he stopped staring at the light on Line 24, he found himself gazing at the three silvery bells on his desk. And could not easily look away.

The last item in Mrs. McBee's memo regarded the magazine that she had enclosed, the latest issue of *Vanity Fair*.

She wrote: *This publication arrived in the mail on Saturday, with several others and was, as usual, put on the proper table in the library. This morning, shortly after the young master had left the library, I discovered the magazine open to the page I've marked. This discovery had much to do with my reconsideration of the advice I'd given you regarding the matter of Christmas gifts.*

Between the second and third pages of an article about Fric's mother, Fredericka Nielander, Mrs. McBee had placed a yellow Post-it. With a pen, she had marked a section of the text.

Ethan read the piece from the beginning. Near the top of the second page, he found a reference to Aelfric. Freddie had told the interviewer that she and her son were "as thick as thieves," and that wherever in the world her glamorous work might take her, they stayed in touch "with long gossipy chats, like two school chums, sharing dreams and more secrets than two spies aligned against the world."

In fact, their entire telephone relationship was so secret that even Fric didn't know about it.

Freddie described Fric as "an exuberant, self-assured boy, very athletic like his father, wonderful with horses, a superb rider."

Horses?

Ethan would have bet a year's pay that if Fric ever had dealings with horses, they had been the kind that never left droppings and ran always to calliope music.

By manufacturing this false Fric, Freddie seemed to suggest that the real qualities of her son either did not impress her or possibly even embarrassed her.

Fric was smart enough and sensitive enough to draw that very conclusion.

The thought of the boy reading this hurtful drivel moved Ethan not to toss the magazine in the trash basket beside his desk, but to throw it angrily toward the fireplace, with the intention of burning it later.

Freddie would probably argue that in an interview with *Vanity Fair*, she needed to calculate each statement to enhance her image. How super could a supermodel be, if from her loins had sprung any but a supernaturally super son?

Burning those pages of the magazine that featured photographs of Freddie would be *especially* satisfying. Make-believe voodoo.

Line 24 was still engaged.

He looked at the computer, where the telephone log continued to be displayed. This call, too, appeared to be from a number screened by Caller ID blocking.

Because the connection had not been broken, the time continued to change in the column headed LENGTH OF CALL. Already it was over four minutes.

That was a long message to leave on an answering machine if the caller was either a salesman or someone who'd unknowingly reached a wrong number. Curious.

The indicator light blinked off.

CHAPTER 44

FRIC WOKE TO THE SIGHT OF A MULTITUDE OF fathers on all sides of him, a guardian army in which every soldier had the same famous face.

He lay flat on his back, and not in bed. Although he remained cautiously still, pressing with something akin to desperation against the hard smooth surface under him, his mind turned lazily, lazily, in a whirlpool of confusion.

Huge they were, these fathers, sometimes full towering figures and sometimes only disembodied heads, but giant heads, like balloons in the Macy's Thanksgiving parade.

Fric had the impression that he'd passed out for lack of air, which meant a terrible asthma attack. When he tried to breathe, however, he experienced no difficulty.

Often these enormous father faces wore noble expressions, expressions of fearless determination, of squint-eyed ferocity, but some smiled. One winked. One laughed soundlessly. A few gazed fondly or dreamily not at Fric but at famous women with equally huge heads.

As his mind turned at a steadily slower speed, toward stability, Fric abruptly remembered the man who had come out of the mirror. He sat straight up on the attic floor.

For a moment, his slowly spinning mind spun faster.

The urge to puke overcame him. He successfully resisted it and felt semiheroic.

Fric dared to tip his head back to scan the rafters for the wingless phantom. He expected a glimpse or more of a gray wool suit in flight, black wing-tip shoes skating across the air with an ice-dancer's grace.

He spied no flying freak, but saw everywhere the guardian fathers in full color, in duochromatic schemes, in black-and-white. They advanced, they receded, they encircled, they loomed.

Paper fathers, all of them.

A daredevil of modest ambition, he got to his feet and stood for a moment as if he were balancing on a high wire.

He listened and heard only the rain. The incessant, besieging, all-dissolving rain.

Too quick for caution, too slow for courage, Fric found his way through the memorabilia maze, seeking the attic stairs. Perhaps inevitably, he came to the serpent-framed mirror.

He intended to give it a wide berth. Yet the silvered glass exerted a dark and powerful attraction.

By turns, his experience with the man from the mirror played in memory like a dream but then as real as the smell of his own fear sweat.

He felt a need to know what was truth and what was not, perhaps because too much of his life seemed unreal, making it impossible to tolerate yet one more uncertainty. Far from brave, but less a coward than he had expected to be, he approached the snake-protected glass.

Convinced by recent events that the universe of Aelfric Manheim and that of Harry Potter were in quiet collision, Fric would have been alarmed but not much surprised if the carved serpents had come magically to life and had struck at him as he approached. The painted scales, the sinuous coils remained motionless, and the green-glass eyes glittered with only inanimate malice.

In the looking glass, he saw only himself and a reversed still life of all that lay behind him. No glimpse of Elsewhere, no hint of Otherwhen.

Tentatively, with his right hand, dismayed to see how severely it trembled, Fric reached toward his image. The glass felt cool and smooth—and undeniably solid—beneath his fingertips.

When he flattened his palm against the silver surface, making full-hand contact, the memory of Moloch seemed less like a real encounter than like a dream.

Then he realized that the eyes in his reflection were not the green that he'd grown up with, the green that he had inherited from Nominal Mom. These eyes were gray, a luminous satiny gray, with only flecks of green.

They were the eyes of the mirror man.

The instant that Fric recognized this terrifying difference in his reflection, a man's two hands came from the mirror, seized him by the wrist, and passed something to him. Then the man's hands closed over his hand and compressed it into a fist, crumpling the bestowed object before shoving him away.

In terror, Fric threw down whatever had been given to him, shuddering at the simultaneously slick and crackled texture of it.

He sprinted along the end aisle, to the attic stairs, around and down the spiral staircase, feet slamming with such panic-powered force that behind him the metal treads thrummed like drumskins quivering with the memory of thunder.

From east hall to north, along the lonely third floor, he quaked as he passed closed doors that might be flung open by any monster the mind could imagine. He cringed from the sight of age-clouded antique mirrors above old-as-dirt consoles.

Repeatedly, he looked back, looked up, in fearful expectation. Surely Moloch would be floating toward him, an unlikely cannibal god in a business suit.

He reached the main stairs without being harmed or pursued, but he was not relieved. The banging of his heart could have drowned out the iron-shod hooves of a hundred horses mounted by a hundred Deaths with a hundred scythes.

Anyway, his enemy didn't need to run him to ground as a fox would chase down a rabbit. If Moloch could travel by way of mirrors, why not by way of window glass? Why not through any surface well enough polished to present even a dim reflection, such as the bowl of that bronze urn, such as the black-lacquered doors of that tall Empire cabinet, such as, such as, such as . . . ?

Before him, the three-story entry rotunda dropped into darkness. The grand stairs that followed the curved wall to the ground floor vanished in the winding gloom.

The evening had waned. The floor polishers and the decorating crew had finished their work and departed, as had the overtime staff. The McBees had gone to bed.

He could not remain here alone on the third floor.

Impossible.

When he pressed a wall switch, the series of crystal chandeliers that followed the curve of stairs were as one illuminated. Hundreds of dangling beveled pendants cast prismatic rainbows of color on the walls.

He descended to the ground floor with such headlong momentum that if Cassandra Limone, the actress with the skull-cracking calf muscles, had been exercising on these stairs, Fric could not have avoided knocking her to worse than a broken ankle.

Leaping off the last step, he skidded to a stop on the marble floor of the rotunda, halted by his first sight of the main Christmas tree. Sixteen or eighteen feet tall, decorated exclusively with red and silver and crystal ornaments, the tree was paralyzingly sensational even when its garlands of electric lights were not switched on.

The dazzling spectacle of the tree alone would not have been sufficient to give him more than the briefest pause in his flight, but as he stared up at the glitter-bedecked evergreen, he realized that he clutched something in his right hand. Opening his fist, he saw the object that had been passed to him from the man within the mirror, the crumpled thing that he had been certain he'd thrown to the attic floor.

Both slick and crackled in texture, light in weight, it was not a dead beetle, not the shed skin of a snake, not a crushed bat wing, not any of the ingredients of a witch's brew that he had imagined it to be. Just a wadded-up photograph.

He unfolded the picture, smoothed it between trembling hands.

Ragged at two edges, as if torn from a frame, the five-by-six portrait showed a pretty lady with dark hair and dark eyes. She was a stranger to him.

Fric knew from considerable experience that the way people look in pictures has nothing to do with the qualities they exhibit in life. Yet from this woman's gentle smile, he inferred a kind heart, and he wished that he knew her.

A cursed amulet, a poultice formulated to draw the immortal soul out of anyone who held it, a voodoo dofunny, a black-magic jiggum-bob, a satanic polywhatsit, or any of the weird and grisly items you might have expected to receive from something that lived inside mirrors would have been less surprising and less mystifying than this creased photograph. He couldn't imagine who this woman was, what her picture was meant to signify, how he could proceed to identify her, or what he might have to gain or lose by learning her name.

His fright had been diluted by the calming effect of the woman's face in the photograph, but when he lifted his gaze from the picture to the evergreen, fear concentrated in him again. Something moved in the tree.

Not branch to branch, not lurking in the green shadows of the boughs: Instead, this movement manifested in the ornaments. Each silver ball, silver trumpet, silver pendant was a three-dimensional mirror. A formless shadowy reflection flowed across those curved and shiny surfaces, back and forth, up the tree, and down.

Only something flying around the rotunda, repeatedly approaching and retreating from the glittering tree, could possibly have cast such a reflection. No great bird, no bat with wings the size of flags, no

Christmas angel, no Moloch plied this air, however, and so it seemed that the swooping darkness flowed *within* the ornaments, rippling up one flank of the tree, cascading down another.

Less bright, murkier than the silver decorations, the red were mirrors, too. The same pulsing shadow traveled through those candy-apple curves and ruby planes, inevitably suggesting the spurt and flow of blood.

Fric sensed that what stalked him now—if in fact anything did—was what had stalked him in the wine cellar earlier in the evening.

The skin tightened on his scalp, puckered on the back of his neck.

In one of the fantasy novels he loved, Fric had read that ghosts could appear by an act of their own will, but could not long sustain material form if you failed to focus on them, that your wonder and your fear empowered and sustained them.

He'd read that vampires could not enter your home unless someone inside invited them to cross the threshold.

He'd read that an evil entity can escape the chains of Hell and enter a person in this world through the trivet of a Ouija board, not if you simply ask questions of the dead, but only if you're careless enough to say something like "come join us" or "come be with us."

He'd read a shitload of stupid things, in fact, and most of them were probably just made up by stupid novelists trying to make a buck while they peddled their stupid screenplays to stupid producers.

Nevertheless, Fric convinced himself that if he didn't look away from the Christmas tree, the apparition in the blown glass would move faster, faster, growing in power by the second until, like bandoliers of grenades, every ornament would at once explode, piercing him with ten thousand splinters, whereupon every jagged shard would carry into his flesh a fragment of this pulsing darkness, which would flourish in his blood and soon become his master.

He ran past the tree, out of the rotunda.

He pressed a light switch in the north hall, and squeaked his rubber-soled sneakers along an avenue of newly polished limestone floor. Past drawing room, tea room, intimate dining room, grand dining room, breakfast room, butler's pantry, kitchen, to the end of the north wing he raced, and did not look back this time, or left, or right.

In addition to the dayroom in which the household staff took breaks and ate their lunch, and also the professionally equipped laundry, the ground-floor west wing housed the rooms and apartments of the live-in staff members.

The maids, Ms. Sanchez and Ms. Norbert, were away until the morning of the twenty-fourth. He wouldn't have gone to them, anyway. They were nice enough, but one had a giggle problem and the other was full of tales of her native North Dakota, which to Fric seemed even less interesting than the island nation of Tuvalu with its thrilling coconut-export industry.

Mrs. McBee and Mr. McBee had put in an especially long hard day. By now they might be asleep, and Fric was reluctant to disturb them.

Arriving at the door of the apartment assigned to Mr. Truman, who had so recently invited him to call for help at any hour of the day or night, and to whom he had intended to go from the moment that he'd fled the attic, Fric abruptly lost his nerve. A man stepping out of a mirror; the same man flying among the attic rafters; some spirit that lived in, watched from, and might explode out of the ornaments on a Christmas tree: Fric could not imagine that such a fantastic and incoherent story would be believed by anyone, especially not by an ex-cop who'd probably grown cynical after listening to a million crazy tales from uncounted lying sleazeballs and deluded fruitcakes.

Fric worried a little about being put in a booby hatch. No one had ever before suggested that he belonged in one. But at least one booby hatch was a part of his family history. Someone would remember a certain experience of Nominal Mom's, and maybe they would look at Fric and think, *Here's a booby in need of a hatch.*

Worse, he had earlier lied to Mr. Truman, and now he would have to admit to that lie.

He had not reported his weird conversations with Mysterious Caller because even *that* stuff had seemed too wickedly strange to be believed. He had hoped that if he just talked about a heavy-breathing pervert, Mr. Truman would track back the calls, find the scumbag—assuming that Mysterious Caller *was* a scumbag—and get to the bottom of this bizarreness.

Mr. Truman had asked if Fric was telling him everything, and Fric had said, "Sure. It was this breather," which is where the lie had been told.

Now Fric would have to admit that he'd not been what cops called "entirely forthcoming," and cops on TV weren't happy with dirtbags who withheld information. From then on, Mr. Truman would be rightly suspicious of him, wondering if the son of the biggest movie star in the world was actually just another sleazeball in the making.

Yet he had to tell Mr. Truman about Mysterious Caller in order to tell him about the Robin Goodfellow who was actually Moloch, and he had to tell him about Moloch in order to prepare him for the story of the totally insane events that had happened in the attic.

This seemed like way too much crazy stuff to explain to anyone in one big load, let alone to a cynical ex-cop who had seen it all twice too often and who hated unforthcoming slopbuckets. By not telling Mr. Truman the full truth earlier in the evening, Fric had dug a hole for himself, just like stupid people in stupid cop shows were always digging holes for themselves, innocent and guilty alike.

Lying won't get you anything but misery.

Yeah, yeah, yeah.

The sole proof of his tale was the crumpled photograph of the pretty lady with the gentle smile, which had been thrust into his hands by the man in the mirror.

He stared at the door to Mr. Truman's apartment.

He looked at the photograph.

The photograph didn't prove anything. He could have gotten it from anyone, from anywhere.

If the man in the mirror had given him a magic ring that allowed him to turn into a cat, or had given him a two-headed toad that spoke English out of one head and French out of the other, and sang Britney Spears tunes out of its butt, *that* would have been proof.

The photo amounted to nothing. Just a crumpled picture. Nothing more than a portrait of a pretty lady with a great smile, a stranger.

If Fric reported what had happened in the attic, Mr. Truman would think that he'd been smoking weed. He would lose whatever credibility he currently had.

Without knocking, he turned away from the door.

In this battle, he stood alone. Standing alone was nothing new, but it sure was getting tiresome.

CHAPTER 45

HAVING EATEN TOO MUCH CHINESE TAKEOUT, having refreshed his knowledge of the more obscure corners of Palazzo Rospo, having fed the leftovers to the garbage disposal, Corky Laputa prepared a second martini and returned upstairs to the guest bedroom at the back of the house, where Stinky Cheese Man lay in a state of such emaciation that even ravenously hungry vultures would have considered him to be slim pickings and would have declined to sit deathwatch.

Corky called him Stinky Cheese Man because after many weeks abed, unbathed, he had acquired a stench reminiscent of many things objectionable, including certain particularly strong cheeses.

A long time had passed since Stinky had produced any solid waste. Odors associated with the bowel had therefore ceased to be an issue.

Upon first taking the man captive, Corky had catheterized him, with the consequence that urine-soaked bedclothes had never been a problem. The catheter line served a one-gallon glass collection jug beside the bed, which was currently only a quarter full.

The sour, biting stink resulted largely from weeks of repeated fear sweats left to dry without attention, and from natural skin oils accumulated so long that they had turned rancid. Sponge baths were not among the services that Corky provided.

Upon entering the bedroom, he put aside his martini and picked up a can of pine-scented disinfectant from the nightstand.

Stinky closed his eyes because he knew what was coming.

Corky pulled the sheet and blanket to the bottom of the bed and liberally sprayed his skeletal captive from head to foot. This was a quick and effective method of reducing the malodor to an acceptable level for the duration of their nightly chat.

Beside the bed stood a bar stool with a comfortably padded seat and back. Corky settled upon this perch.

A tall plant stand, crafted from oak and serving as a table, stood beside the stool. After taking a sip of his martini, Corky put it down on the plant stand.

He studied Stinky for a while, saying nothing.

Of course, Stinky didn't speak because he had learned the hard way that it was not his place to initiate conversations.

Furthermore, his once robust voice had deteriorated until it was weaker than that of any terminal tuberculosis patient, marked by an eerie rasp and rattle: a voice like wind-driven sand scouring across ancient stone, like the brittle whispery click of scuttling scarabs. The sound of his voice scared Stinky these days, and speaking had become painful; evening by evening he said less.

In the early days, to prevent him from crying out loud enough to make the neighbors curious, his mouth had been taped shut. Tape was no longer necessary, for he could not project a worrisome volume of sound.

Initially, although maintained in a state of semiparalysis with drugs, Stinky had been chained to the bed. With the severe withering of his body, with the total collapse of his physical strength, the chains had become superfluous.

In Corky's absence, the captive's glucose drip always included drugs to keep him docile, as insurance against an unlikely escape.

Evenings, he was allowed a clear mind. For their sessions.

Now his fright-stricken eyes alternately avoided Corky and were drawn to him by magnetic dread. He lay in terror of what was to come.

Corky had never struck this man, had never employed physical torture. He never would.

With words and words alone he had broken his captive's heart, had shattered his hope, had crushed his sense of self-worth. With words he would break his mind, as well, if in fact Stinky was not already insane.

Stinky's real name was Maxwell Dalton. He had been a professor of English at the same university where Corky still enjoyed tenure.

Corky taught literature from a deconstructionist perspective, instilling in students the belief that language can never describe reality because words only refer to other words, not to anything real. He taught them that whether a piece of writing is a novel or a law, each person is the sole arbiter of what that writing says and what it means, that all truth is relative, that all moral principles are fraudulent interpretations of religious and philosophical texts that actually have no meaning other than what each person *wants* them to mean. These were deliciously destructive ideas, and Corky took great pride in his work as a teacher.

Professor Maxwell Dalton was a traditionalist. He believed in language, meaning, purpose, and principle.

For decades, Corky's like-minded colleagues had controlled the English Department. In the past few years, Dalton had attempted to mount a revolt against meaninglessness.

He was a nuisance, a pest, a threat to the triumph of chaos. He admired the work of Charles Dickens and T. S. Eliot and Mark Twain. He was an unspeakably vile man.

Thanks to Rolf Reynerd, Dalton had been imprisoned in this bedroom for more than twelve weeks.

When Corky and Reynerd had sworn that together they would

make a statement to the world by making a well-planned assault on Channing Manheim's tightly guarded estate, they had also agreed that to prove the seriousness of their pledge, each would first commit a capital crime on behalf of the other. Corky would murder Reynerd's mother; in return, the actor would kidnap Dalton and deliver him to Corky.

Keeping in mind how his intention to smother his own mother with a minimum of mess had so easily degenerated into a frenzied clubbing with a fireplace poker, Corky had obtained an untraceable handgun with which to despatch Mina Reynerd quickly, professionally, with a shot through the heart to ensure that there would be little blood.

Unfortunately, at that time, he'd not been expert in the use of firearms. His first shot hit her not in the heart, but in the foot.

Mrs. Reynerd had begun to scream in pain. For reasons that Corky still didn't fully understand, instead of proceeding with the gun, he eventually discovered himself flailing away furiously with an antique marble-and-bronze lamp, which he severely damaged.

Later, he had apologized to Rolf for diminishing the value of this lovely heirloom.

True to his word, the actor had subsequently kidnapped Maxwell Dalton. He delivered the professor, unconscious, to this bedroom, where Corky had been waiting with a stock of refrigerated infusion bags and a supply of drugs required to keep his captive docile during the early weeks when Dalton still possessed the physical potential for resistance.

Since then, he had methodically starved his colleague, providing him with only sufficient nutrients, by intravenous drip, to keep him alive. Evening after evening, sometimes in the morning, he subjected Dalton to extreme psychological torment.

The good professor believed that his wife, Rachel, and his ten-year-old daughter, Emily, had been kidnapped as well. He thought that they were being kept in other rooms of this house.

Daily, Corky regaled Dalton with accounts of the indignities, abuses, and torments to which he had most recently subjected lovely Rachel and tender Emily. His reports were graphic, exquisitely crude, gloriously obscene.

His talent for pornographic invention surprised and delighted Corky, but he was more surprised that Dalton so readily accepted his stories as truth, withering with grief and despair when he listened to them. Had he been tending to *three* captives in addition to the demands of daily life, had he committed a fraction of the atrocities on Rachel and Emily that he claimed to have enjoyed, he would have been nearly as thin and weak as the starving man in the bed.

Corky's mother, the economist and vicious academic infighter, would have been astonished to know that her son had proved to be a greater terror to at least one colleague than she had ever dreamed of being to one of hers. She would not have been capable of devising and executing such a complex and clever scheme as the one with which he had brought down Maxwell Dalton.

Mother had been motivated by envy, hatred. Free of envy, free of hatred, Corky was instead motivated by the dream of a better world through anarchy. She wanted to destroy a handful of enemies, while he wished to destroy *everything.*

Success often comes in greater measure to those with a greater vision.

Here at the end of an unusually successful day, Corky sat on his stool, overlooking the shrunken professor, and took small sips of his martini for perhaps ten minutes, saying nothing, letting the suspense build. Even during his busy hours in and out of the rain, he'd found the time to concoct a fabulously brutal story that might at last crack Dalton's sanity as if it were a breadstick.

Corky intended to report that he had murdered Rachel, the wife. Considering Dalton's extremely fragile condition, perhaps that lie, if well told, would precipitate a fatal heart attack.

Should the professor survive this hideous news, he would be informed in the morning that his daughter had been killed as well. Maybe the second shock would finish him.

One way or another, Corky was ready to be done with Maxwell Dalton. He'd squeezed all the entertainment value out of this situation. The time had come to move on.

Besides, soon he would need this room for Aelfric Manheim.

CHAPTER 46

NIGHT ON THE MOON, CRATERED AND COLD, could be no less lonely than this night in the Manheim mansion.

Within, the only sounds were Fric's footsteps, his breathing, the faint creak of hinges when he opened a door.

Outside, a changeable wind, alternately menacing and melancholy, quarreled with the trees, raised lamentations in the eaves, battered the walls, moaned as if in sorrowful protest of its exclusion from the house. Rain rapped angrily against the windows, but then cried silently down the leaded panes.

For a while, Fric believed that he would be safer on the move than settled in any one place, that when he stopped, unseen forces would at once begin to gather around him. Besides, on his feet, in motion, he could break into a run and more readily escape.

His father believed that when a child reached the age of six, an arbitrary bedtime should not be forced on him, but that he should be allowed to find his personal circadian rhythms. Consequently, for years, Fric had been going to bed when he wanted, sometimes at nine o'clock, sometimes after midnight.

Soon, ceaselessly rambling, turning lights on ahead of him and leaving them aglow in his wake, he grew tired. He had thought that the possibility of Moloch, child-eating god, walking out of a mirror at any moment would keep him awake for the rest of his life or at least until he turned eighteen and no longer qualified as a child under most definitions. Fear, however, proved as exhausting as hard labor.

Worried that he might slump upon a sofa or a chair and fall asleep in a place that made him more vulnerable than necessary, he considered returning to the west wing on the ground floor, where he could curl up outside Mr. Truman's apartment. If Mr. Truman or the McBees found him sleeping there, however, he would appear to be a gutless weenie and an embarrassment to the name Manheim.

He decided that the library offered the best refuge. He always felt comfortable among books. And although the library lay on the second floor, which was as lonely as the third, it had no mirrors.

The tree of angels greeted him.

He recoiled from the winged multitude.

Then he realized that this evergreen featured not a single shiny ornament from which an evil other-dimensional entity could pass into this world or watch from another.

Indeed, the dangling angels seemed to suggest that here was a protected place, true sanctuary.

Throughout the massive chamber, the decorative urns and pots and amphorae and figurines were either Wedgwood basalts with Empire-period themes or Han Dynasty porcelains. The basalts were all matte-finish black, not shiny. Two thousand years had worn the luster from the glaze on the Han pieces, and Fric had no concern that an ancient figure of a horse or a water jar made before the birth of Christ might serve as a peephole through which he could be watched by some wicked creature in a neighboring dimension.

At the back of the library, a door led to a powder room. Using a straight-backed chair, Fric wedged this door securely shut without daring to open it, for above the sink in the powder room, a mirror waited.

This sensible precaution presented a minor problem easily resolved. He had to pee, so he relieved himself in a potted palm.

Always he washed his hands after toileting. This time he would
have to risk contamination, disease, and plague.

At least twenty potted palms were distributed throughout the big
room. He made a point of remembering which one he had sprinkled,
to avoid killing off the entire library rainforest.

He returned to the conversation area nearest the Christmas tree
and the battalion of sentinel angels. Surely this was a safe place.

The arrangement of armchairs and footstools included a sofa. Fric
was about to stretch out on this makeshift bed when the silence gave
way to a cheerful child-pleasing sound suitable for the nursery or the
bedrooms of younger children.

Ooodelee-ooodelee-oo.

The telephone stood on a piece of furniture that Mrs. McBee referred to as an "escritoire," but which was still a writing desk to Fric.
He stood beside it, watching the signal light flutter at his private line
each time that the phone rang.

Ooodelee-ooodelee-oo.

He expected Mr. Truman to answer the call by the third ring.

Ooodelee-ooodelee-oo.

Mr. Truman didn't respond.

The phone rang a fourth time. A fifth.

The voice-mail system didn't take the call, either.

Six rings. Seven.

Fric refused to pick up the handset.

Ooodelee-ooodelee-oo.

In his apartment, Ethan had retrieved the six black-box items from
a cabinet and had arranged them on his desk in the order that they
had been received.

He had switched off the computer.

The phone was near at hand, where he could intercept calls to Fric should that line in fact ring, and where he would notice the indicator light on Line 24 if it signaled additional incoming calls. Traffic on this messages-from-the-dead line seemed to be increasing, which disturbed him for reasons he could not articulate, and he wanted to keep an eye on the situation.

Sitting in his desk chair with a can of Coke, he considered the elements of the riddle.

The small jar containing twenty-two dead ladybugs. *Hippodamia convergens*, of the family Coccinellidae.

Another, larger jar into which he had transferred the ten dead snails. An uglier sight by the day.

A pickle-relish jar holding nine foreskins in formaldehyde. The tenth had been destroyed by the lab in the process of analysis.

The closed drapes muffled the snap of rain on glass, the threat of wind enraged.

Beetles, snails, foreskins . . .

For some reason, Ethan's attention drifted to the phone, though it hadn't rung. No indicator light burned on Line 24 or on any of the first twenty-three.

He tipped the Coke can, took a swallow.

Beetles, snails, foreskins . . .

Ooodelee-ooodelee-oo.

Maybe Mr. Truman had slipped and fallen and hit his head, and maybe he lay unconscious, oblivious of the ringing. Or maybe he had been carried off into a land beyond a mirror. Or maybe he had just forgotten to modify the system to receive Fric's private calls.

The caller would not give up. After twenty-one repetitions of the stupid child-pleasing tones, Fric decided that if he didn't pick up the phone, he would have to listen to it ringing all night.

The slight tremor in his voice dismayed him, but he persevered:

"Vinnie's Soda Parlor and Vomitorium, home of the nine-pound ice-cream sundae, where you splurge and then purge."

"Hello, Aelfric," said Mysterious Caller.

"I can't make up my mind whether you're a pervert or a friend like you say. I'm leaning toward pervert."

"You're leaning wrong. Look around you for the truth, Aelfric."

"Look around me at what?"

"At what's there with you in the library."

"I'm in the kitchen."

"By now you ought to realize that you can't lie to me."

"My deep and secret hiding place is going to be one of the bigger ovens. I'll crawl inside and pull the door shut behind me."

"You better baste yourself in butter, because Moloch will just turn on the gas."

"Moloch has already been here," Fric said.

"That wasn't Moloch. That was me."

Receiving this revelation, Fric almost slammed down the phone.

Mysterious Caller said, "I paid you a visit because I wanted you to understand, Aelfric, that you really *are* at risk, and that time really *is* running out. If I'd been Moloch, you'd be toast."

"You came out of a mirror," said Fric, his curiosity and sense of wonder for the moment outweighing his fear.

"And I went back into one."

"How can you come out of a mirror?"

"For the answer, look around you, son."

Fric surveyed the library.

"What do you see?" asked Mysterious Caller.

"Books."

"Oh? You have a lot of books there in the kitchen?"

"I'm in the library."

"Ah, truth. There's hope that you'll avoid at least some misery, af-ter all. What else do you see besides books?"

"A writing desk. Chairs. A sofa."

"Keep looking."

"A Christmas tree."

"There you go."

"There I go where?" asked Fric.

"What dingles and what dangles?"

"Huh?"

"And is spelled almost like *angles*."

"Angels," Fric said, surveying the radiant white flock that gathered with trumpets and harps upon the tree.

"I travel by mirrors, by mist, by smoke, by doorways in water, by stairways made of shadows, on roads of moonlight, by wish and hope and simple expectation. I've given up my car."

Amazed, Fric clenched the phone so hard that his hand ached, as if he might squeeze a few more revealing words from the mirror man.

Mysterious Caller met silence with silence, waited.

Of all the kinds of weirdness Fric had been expecting, this had not been on the list.

Finally, with a tremor of a different quality in his voice, he said, "Are you telling me you're an angel?"

"Do you believe I could be?"

"My . . . guardian angel?"

Instead of answering directly, the mirror man said, "Believing is important in all this, Aelfric. In many ways, the world is what we make it, and our future is ours to shape."

"My father says that our future is in the stars, our fate set when we're born."

"There's much in your old man to admire, son, but as far as his thoughts on fate are concerned, he's full of shit."

"Wow," said Fric, "can angels say 'shit'?"

"I just did. But then I'm new at this, and I'm quite capable of making a mistake now and then."

"You're still wearing your training wings."

"You could say that. Anyway, I don't want to see any harm come to you, Aelfric. But I alone can't guarantee your safety. You've got to help save yourself from Moloch when he comes."

Beetles, snails, foreskins . . .

On Ethan's desk with the other items stood the cookie-jar kitten filled with two hundred seventy tiles, ninety each of *O*, *W*, and *E*.

Owe. Woe. Wee woo. Ewe woo.

Beside the cookie jar lay *Paws for Reflection*, the hardcover book by Donald Gainsworth, who had trained guide dogs for the blind and service dogs for people in wheelchairs.

Beetles, snails, foreskins, cookie jar with tiles, book . . .

Next to the book stood the sutured apple opened to reveal the doll's eye. THE EYE IN THE APPLE? THE WATCHFUL WORM? THE WORM OF ORIGINAL SIN? DO WORDS HAVE ANY PURPOSE OTHER THAN CONFUSION?

Ethan had a headache. He probably ought to be grateful that a headache was all he had, after dying twice.

Leaving the six gifts from Reynerd on the desk, he went into the bathroom. He took a bottle of aspirin from the medicine cabinet and shook a pair of tablets into his hand.

He intended to draw a glass of water from the bathroom sink and take the aspirin. When he glanced in the mirror, however, he found himself looking at his reflection only briefly, then searching for a shadowy form that shouldn't be there, that might slide away from his eyes as he tried to pin it with his stare, as in the bathroom at Dunny's penthouse apartment.

For the glass of water, he went into the kitchen, where no mirrors hung.

Curiously, his attention was drawn to the wall-mounted telephone near the refrigerator. None of the lines was in use. Not Line 24. Not Fric's line.

He thought about the heavy breather. Even if the boy was the type to invent little dramas to focus attention on himself, which he was not, this seemed a pale invention, not worth the effort of a lie. When kids made up stuff, they tended toward flamboyant details.

After taking the aspirin, Ethan went to the phone and picked up the handset. A light appeared at the first of his two private lines.

The house phones doubled as an intercom system. If he pressed the button marked INTERCOM and then the button for Fric's line, he would be able to speak directly to the boy in his room.

He didn't know what he would say or why he felt that he ought to seek out Fric at this late hour rather than in the morning. He stared at the boy's line. He put one finger on the button, but hesitated to press it.

The kid was most likely asleep by now. If not asleep, he ought to be. Ethan racked the handset.

He went to the refrigerator. Earlier, he had not been able to eat. The events of the day had left him with a stomach clenched as tight as a fist. For a while, all he'd wanted was good Scotch. Now, unexpectedly, the thought of a ham sandwich made his mouth water.

You got up every day, hoping for the best, but life threw crap at you, and you were shot in the gut and died, then you got up and went on, and life threw more crap at you, and you were run down in traffic and died again, and when you just tried, for God's sake, *to get on with it,* life threw still more crap at you, so it shouldn't be a surprise that eventually all this strenuous activity gave you the appetite of an Olympic power lifter.

Looking at frosted-glass angels, plastic angels, carved-wood angels, painted-tin angels, while at the same time talking to a maybe-for-real angel on the telephone, Fric said, "How can I ever find a safe place if Moloch can travel by mirrors and moonlight?"

"He can't," said Mysterious Caller. "He doesn't have my powers, Aelfric. He's mortal. But don't think being mortal makes him less dangerous. A demon would be no worse than him."

"Why don't you come here and wait with me till he shows up, and then beat the crap out of him with your holy cudgel?"

"I don't have a holy cudgel, Aelfric."

"You must have something. Cudgel, staff, truncheon, a sanctified broadsword glowing with divine energy. I've read about angels in this fantasy novel. They're not airy-fairy types as fragile as fart gas. They're warriors. They fought Satan's legions and drove them out of Heaven, into Hell. That was a cool scene in the book."

"This isn't Heaven, son. This is Earth. Here, I'm authorized to work only by indirection."

Quoting Mysterious Caller from their previous conversation, when they had spoken on the wine-cellar phone, Fric said, " 'Encourage, inspire, terrify, cajole, advise.' "

"You've a good memory. I know what's coming, but I may influence events only by means that are sly—"

"—slippery, and seductive," Fric finished.

"I may not interfere directly with Moloch's pursuit of his own damnation. Just as I may not interfere with any heroic policeman who is about to sacrifice his life to save another, and therefore raise himself forever high."

"I guess I understand that. You're like a director who doesn't get final cut of the film."

"I'm not even a director. Think of me as just another studio executive who gives notes for suggested revisions of the script."

"The kind of notes that always make screenwriters so pissy and turn them into drunks. They'll bore your butt off talking about that, like a ten-year-old kid could care, like *anyone* could care."

"The difference," said the maybe-angel, "is that my notes are always well intended—and based on a vision of the future that may be too true."

Fric thought about all this for a moment as he pulled the chair out from the kneehole of the desk. Sitting down, he said, "Wow. Being a guardian angel must be frustrating."

"You can't begin to know. *You* control the final cut of your life, Aelfric. It's called free will. You've got it. Everyone here has it. And in the end, I can't act for you. That's what you're here to do . . . to make choices, right or wrong, to be wise or not, to be courageous or not."

"I guess I can try."

"I guess you better. What've you done with the photo I gave you?"

"The pretty lady with the nice smile? She's folded in my back pocket."

"It won't be any good to you there."

"What do you expect me to do with it?"

"Think. Use your brain, Aelfric. Even in your family, that's possible. Think. Be wise."

"I'm too drag-ass tired to think right now. Who is she—the lady in the picture?"

"Why don't you play detective? Make inquiries."

"I did make an inquiry. Who is she?"

"Ask around. That's not a question for me to answer."

"Why isn't it?"

"Because I have to abide by the sly-slippery-seductive rule, which sometimes makes any guardian angel a pain in the ass."

"Okay. Forget it. Am I safe tonight? Can I wait till morning to find that deep and special secret place to hide?"

"First thing in the morning will be all right," the guardian said. "But don't waste any more time. Prepare, Aelfric. Prepare."

"Okay. And, hey, I'm sorry for what I called you."

"You mean earlier—an attorney?"

"Yeah."

"I've been called worse."

"Really?"

"Much worse."

"And I'm sorry for trying to track you back."

"What do you mean?"

"It seems like a sneaky thing to do to an angel. I'm sorry for star sixty-nining you."

Mysterious Caller fell silent.

An indefinable quality of the silence made it different from any hush that Fric had ever heard.

This was a *perfect* silence, for one thing, and it sucked away not only all the noise on the open line but also every whisper of sound in the library, until he seemed to have gone deafer than deaf.

The silence felt deep, too, as though the guardian were calling from the bottom of an oceanic trench. Deep and so *cold*.

Fric shuddered. He could not hear his teeth chatter or his body quake. He could not hear his exhalation, either, although he felt the breath rush from him, hot enough to dry his teeth.

Perfect, deep, cold silence, yes, but more and stranger than simply perfect, deep, and cold.

Fric imagined that such a silence might be cast like a spell by *any* angel with supernatural powers, but that it might be a trick most characteristic of the Angel of Death.

The Mysterious Caller drew a breath, inhaling the very silence and letting sound into the world once more, beginning with his voice, which resonated with an ominous note of concern: "When did you use star sixty-nine, Aelfric?"

"Well, after you called me in the train room."

"And also after I called you in the wine cellar?"

"Yeah. Don't you know all this . . . being who you are?"

"Angels don't know everything, Aelfric. Now and then, some things are . . . slipped by us."

"The first time, your phone just rang and rang—"

"That's because I used the telephone in my old apartment, where I lived before I died. I didn't enter your number, just thought of you, but I *did* pick up the phone. I was still learning . . . learning what I can do now. I'm getting smoother at this by the hour."

Fric wondered if he was more tired even than he realized. The conversation wasn't always making sense. "Your old apartment?"

"I'm a relatively new angel, son. Died this morning. I'm using the body I used to live in, though it's . . . more flexible now, with my new powers. What happened the second time you used star sixty-nine?"

"You really don't know?"

"I'm afraid I might. But tell me."

"I got this pervert."

"What did it say to you?"

"Didn't say anything. He just breathed heavy . . . and then made these like animal sounds."

The Mysterious Caller was quiet, but this proved to be a far different silence from the death-deep stillness of a moment ago. This hush had in it a host of half-heard twitches, the moth-wing vibration of fluttering nerves, the so-soft tensing of muscles.

"At first, I thought he was you," Fric explained. "So I told him I'd looked up Moloch in the dictionary. The name excited him."

"Don't ever use star sixty-nine after I call, Aelfric. Not ever, ever again."

"Why?"

With hard insistence, revealing a degree of alarm that seemed to be too mortal in character for an immortal guardian angel, the caller said, "Not *ever* again. Do you understand?"

"Yes."

"Do you promise me you'll never again try to call me back with star sixty-nine?"

"All right. But why?"

"When I called you in the wine cellar, I didn't use a phone, the way I did the first time. I don't require a phone to ring you up any more than I need a car to travel. I need only the *idea* of a phone."

"The idea of a phone? How's that work?"

"My current position comes with certain supernatural abilities."

"Being a guardian angel, you mean."

"But when I use only the idea of a phone, star sixty-nine might connect you with a place you must not go."

"What place?"

The guardian hesitated. Then he said, "The dark eternity."

"Doesn't sound good," Fric agreed, and uneasily surveyed the library.

In the labyrinth of shelves, monsters both human and not abided between the covers of so many books. Perhaps one beast prowled not in those paper worlds but in this one, breathing not ink fumes but air, waiting for a small boy to find it along one turning or another of those quiet aisles.

"The dark eternity. The bottomless abyss, the darkness visible, and all that dwells there," the guardian elaborated. "You were lucky, son. It didn't talk to you."

"It?"

"What you called 'the pervert.' If they talk to you, they can wheedle, persuade, charm, sometimes even command."

Fric glanced at the tree again. The angels seemed to be watching him, every one.

"When you press star sixty-nine," the guardian said, "you open a door to them."

"Who?"

"Do we need to speak their sulfurous name? We both know who I mean, do we not?"

Being a boy with a taste for fantasy in his reading, with a home theater in which he could watch everything from kid flicks to R-rated monster fests, with an imagination stropped sharp by solitude, Fric was pretty sure he knew who was meant.

The caller said, "You open a door to them, and then, with one wrong word, you might unintentionally . . . invite them in."

"In here, to Palazzo Rospo?"

"You might invite one of them into *you*, Aelfric. When invited, they can travel by the telephone connection, by that fragile link of spirit to spirit, much the way that I can travel through one mirror to another."

"No lie?"

"No lie. Don't you dare use star sixty-nine after I hang up."

"All right."

"Or ever again when I call you."

"Never."

"I'm deadly serious about this, Aelfric."

"I wouldn't expect a guardian angel to do this."

"Do what?"

"Scare the crap out of me."

"Encourage, inspire, *terrify*," the caller reminded him. "Now sleep in peace tonight, while you can. And in the morning, waste no time. Prepare. Prepare to survive, Aelfric, prepare, because when I look forward right now to see how things will most likely unfold . . . I see you dead."

CHAPTER 47

FRIC IN A QUANDARY, LYING FACEDOWN ON the sofa, looked at the telephone on the library floor. He had moved it from the writing desk to the maximum length of its cord.

He'd relocated it for extra security, in the event that he needed to make a quick call for help.

While that was true, it represented only part of the truth. He also toyed with the idea of keying in *69.

Fric didn't embrace self-destruction. He wasn't one of those Hollywood brats who were eager to grow up and become a rich heroin junkie. He had no intention of killing himself with a sports car, a handgun, a shotgun, diet pills, hard liquor, marijuana-induced lung cancer, or women.

Sometimes during a party, when Palazzo Rospo was crawling with hundreds of famous and semifamous and craving-to-be-famous people, Fric made himself invisible, the better to eavesdrop. In a crowd of that kind, you could easily become invisible, because half of the guests were barely aware of anyone but themselves, anyway, and the other half were intently focused on the handful of directors, agents, and studio honchos who could make them either filthy rich or filthier rich than they already were.

During one of these spells of invisibility, Fric had heard it said of the third—or possibly the fourth—biggest movie star in the world that "the stupid prick will kill himself with women, the way he's going." Fric had no slightest idea how one could kill oneself with women, or why a suicidal person would not just buy a pistol.

That intriguing statement had remained with him, however, and he intended to be careful. These days, when he met new women, he studied them surreptitiously for indications that they were the potentially dangerous type.

Until this weird night, he had likewise never imagined that death could be rung up just by pressing *69.

Maybe what came through the phone would not kill him. Maybe it would imprison his soul and take control of his body and make him so miserable that he would *wish* he were dead.

Or perhaps it would take control of him and run him headfirst into a brick wall, into an open cesspool (assuming an open cesspool could be found in Bel Air), off the roof of Palazzo Rospo, or into the arms of a deadly blonde (with which Bel Air apparently was infested).

His quandary was that he didn't know whether to believe anything that Mysterious Caller had said.

On the one hand, the entire rap about being a guardian angel, about moving by mirrors and moonlight—it might all be a shitload of nonsense. A bigger pile even than Ghost Dad's unicorn movie.

On the other hand—and there was always another hand— Mysterious Caller *had* walked out of a mirror. He *had* flown through the rafters. His performance in the attic—and later in the shiny surfaces of the Christmas-tree ornaments—had been so incredible that it had earned him some credibility.

Yet what kind of guardian angel wore a suit and tie straight out of a big-bucks Rodeo Drive shop, had skin as pale as fish flesh, looked a lot less holy than scary, and had gray eyes as cold as ashes in ice?

Possibly Mysterious Caller, for reasons unknown, had been lying, leading Fric toward wrong conclusions, setting him up.

He'd once overheard his father say that virtually everyone in this town was setting someone up for a fall, that if they weren't doing it for money, then they were doing it for sport.

Mysterious Caller said Fric must not use *69 because it would connect him with the dark eternity. Maybe the *truth* was that the guy just didn't want Fric to try tracking him.

Still belly-down on the sofa, leaning out toward the phone, Fric picked up the handset. He pressed the button for his private line.

He listened to the dial tone.

The angels on the tree *looked* like angels. You could trust an angel with a harp, with a trumpet, wearing white, sporting wings.

He pressed * and 6 and 9.

The phone was picked up not on the fourth ring, as it had been previously, but on the first. No one said hello. As before, only silence greeted him.

Then, after a few seconds, he heard breathing.

Fric intended to outwait the breather, make the pervert speak first. After twenty or thirty seconds, however, he grew so nervous that he said, "It's me again."

His concession didn't bring a response.

Trying to strike a light and somewhat jokey tone, but largely failing, Fric asked, "How're things in the dark eternity?"

The breathing grew rougher, heavier.

"You know—the dark eternity?" Fric asked tauntingly but also with a faint tremor that he could not control and that put the lie to his pose of bold self-assurance. "Also known on some maps as the bottomless abyss. Or the darkness visible."

The freak continued to breathe at him.

"You don't sound so good. You have a bad sinus thing going on there," said Fric.

With his head hanging over the edge of the sofa, he began to feel a little dizzy.

"I'll give you my doctor's name. He'll write a prescription. You'll be able to breathe better. You'll thank me."

A croaking-grinding voice, issuing from a throat clogged with razor blades, drier than the ashes of ashes twice burnt, arising from a terrible depth, through crevices in the broken stones of strange ruins, said just one word: *"Boy."*

In Fric's ear, the word crawled as if it were an insect, maybe one of those earwigs that legend said could find its way into your brain and lay eggs in there, transforming you into a walking hive filled with squirming legions.

Remembering all those posters of his father looking noble and brave and full of steely resolve, Fric held fast to the phone. He summoned an iron weight of determination to press the wrinkles of fear from his voice, and he said, "You don't scare me."

"Boy," the other repeated, *"boy,"* and additional voices arose on the phone, initially just four or five, at a lower volume than the first, male and female, punctuating their gabble with *"boy . . . boy."* Their voices were urgent, eager. Desperate. Voices whispery and smooth, voices rough. ". . . who's there?" ". . . the way, he's the way . . ." ". . . sweet flesh . . ." ". . . stupid little piglet, easy for the taking . . ." ". . . ask me in . . ." ". . . ask *me* . . ." ". . . no, ask *me* . . ." In seconds their numbers swelled to a dozen, a score, a crowd. Maybe because they were all talking at once, their speech sounded as though it descended into bestial mutterings and snarls, and what words remained were as often as not obscenities strung together in incoherent sequences. Chilling cries of fear, pain, frustration, and raw anger sewed these rags of raucous noise into a tapestry of *need*.

Fric's strong heart rapped hard against his ribs, pulsed in his throat, throbbed in his temples. He had claimed not to be scared, but he was scared, all right, too scared to come up with a single smart-ass remark or to speak at all.

Yet the churning voices intrigued him, compelled his attention. The hunger in them, the intense yearning, the pitiful desperation, the melancholy longing wove a poignant song that strummed the cords of his abiding loneliness, that *spoke* to him and assured him that he need not suffer solitude, that companionship was his for the asking, that purpose and meaning and family were all his if only he would open his heart to them.

Even when wordless, when bursting with ripe obscenities that ought to have repelled Fric, the guttural chorus, full of growl and hiss, steadily soothed his terror. His heart continued to pound, but moment by moment, the power driving its frenzied hammering was less fear than excitement. Everything could change. Utterly. Completely. Now and forever. Change in an instant. He could have a new life and a better one simply for the asking, a life from which all loneliness would be banished, all uncertainty, all confusion and self-doubt and weakness. . . .

Fric opened his mouth to issue what all but certainly would have been an invitation similar to those that users of a Ouija board were well advised to avoid. Before he could speak, he was distracted by movement at the periphery of his vision.

When he turned to look at what had drawn his attention, Fric saw that the stretchy, coiled cord between the handset and the telephone, once a clean white length of vinyl-coated wires, now appeared to be organic, pink and slick, like that rope of tissue that tied a mother to a newborn baby. A pulse throbbed through the cord, slow and thick, but strong, moving from the phone box on the floor to the handset that he held, toward his ear, as if in anticipation of the invitation that trembled on his tongue.

Sitting at the desk in his study, eating a ham sandwich, trying to puzzle meaning from Reynerd's six taunting gifts, Ethan found his thoughts drifting repeatedly to Duncan Whistler.

In the garden room at Our Lady of Angels, when he had initially learned that Dunny's body had gone missing, he had known intuitively that the uncanny events at Reynerd's apartment and Dunny's dead-man-walking stunt were related. Later, Dunny's apparent involvement in the murder of Reynerd, though unexpected, had been no surprise.

What *did* surprise Ethan, the more he thought about it, was the close encounter with Dunny in the hotel bar.

More than coincidence must be involved. Dunny had been in the bar because Ethan was in the bar. He had been *meant* to see Dunny.

If he'd been meant to see Dunny, then he'd been meant to follow him. Perhaps he had also been meant to catch up with Dunny.

Outside the hotel, in the bustle and the rain, unable to get a glimpse of his quarry, Ethan had received the urgent phone call from Hazard. Now he paused to think what he would have done next, if he had not been obliged to meet Hazard at the church.

He obtained the number of the hotel from information and called it. "I'd like to speak to one of your guests. I don't know his room number. The name's Duncan Whistler."

After a pause to check the hotel computer, the desk clerk said, "I'm sorry, sir, but we have no registration for Mr. Whistler."

Previously, only a few table lamps had been lit here and there throughout the big room, but now all the lamps glowed, as did the ceiling lights, the cove lights, and the looping strings of tiny twinkle bulbs on the Christmas tree. The library had been nearly as purged of shadows as any surgery would have been; but it was still not bright enough for Fric.

He had returned the phone to the desk. He'd unplugged it.

He supposed that the phones were ringing in his third-floor rooms and that they would ring for a long while. He wasn't going to go up there to listen. When Hell was calling, it could be persistent.

He had dragged an armchair close to the Christmas tree. Close to the angels.

Maybe he was being superstitious, childish, stupid. He didn't care. Those desperate people on that phone, those *things* . . .

He sat with his back to the tree because he figured that nothing could come through all those branches full of roosting angels to take him by surprise from behind.

If he had not earlier lied to Mr. Truman, he could now have gone directly down to the security chief's apartment to seek help.

Here in Fricburg, USA, the time was always high noon, and the sheriff could not expect backup from the townsfolk when the gang of outlaws rode in for the showdown.

Ethan concluded his conversation with the hotel desk clerk and picked up the remaining wedge of his ham sandwich, but one of his two phone lines rang before he could take a bite.

When he answered the call, he was met with silence. He said, "Hello," again, but failed to elicit a response.

He wondered if this might be Fric's pervert.

He heard no heavy breathing, suggestive or otherwise. Only the hollowness of an open line and a hiss of static so thin as to be just this side of subaudible.

Ethan rarely received calls this late: nearly midnight. Because of the hour and the events of this day, he found even silence to be significant.

Whether instinct or imagination was at work, he could not be sure, but he sensed a presence on the line.

During the years that he had carried a badge, he'd conducted enough stakeouts to learn patience. He listened to the listener, trading silence for silence.

Time passed. Ham waited. Still hungry, Ethan also grew thirsty for a beer.

Eventually, he heard a cry, repeated three times. The voice was faint neither because it whispered nor because it was feeble but because it arose from a great distance, so fragile that it might have been merely a mirage of sound.

More silence, more time, and then the voice rose again, no less frail than before, so ephemeral that Ethan could not confidently say whether it was the voice of a man or a woman. Indeed, it might have been the mournful cry of a bird or an animal, repeated three times again, with a damped quality similar to that provided by a filter of fog.

He had ceased to expect heavy breathing.

Although no louder than before, the quiet hiss of static had acquired a menacing quality, as though each soft tick represented the impact of a radioactive particle on his eardrum.

When the voice came a third time, it didn't resort to the short cry that it had previously repeated. Ethan detected patterns of sound surely meant to convey meaning. Words. Not quite comprehensible.

As though broadcast from a distant radio station into an ether troubled by storms, these words were distorted by fading, by drift, by scratchy atmospherics. A voice out of time might sound like this, or one sent by spacefarers from the night side of Saturn.

He didn't remember leaning far forward in his chair. Neither did he recall when his arms had slid off the arms of the chair nor when he had propped his elbows on his knees. Yet here he sat in this compacted posture, both hands to his head, one holding the phone, like a man humbled by remorse or bent by despair upon the receipt of terrible news.

Although Ethan strained to capture the content of the faraway speaker's conversation, it continuously sifted through him without sticking, as elusive as cloud shadows projected by moonlight upon a rolling seascape.

Indeed, when he struggled the hardest to find meaning in these might-be words, they receded farther behind a screen of static and distortion. He suspected that if he relaxed, the flow of speech might clarify, the voice grow stronger, but he could not relax. Although he pressed the handset to his head with such force that his ear ached, he was unable to relent, as if a brief moment of less-intense focus would prove to be the very instant when the words would come clearly, but only to he who faithfully attended them.

The voice possessed a plaintive quality. Although unable to grasp the words and deduce their meaning, Ethan detected an urgent and beseeching tone, and perhaps a yearning sadness.

When he assumed that he had spent five minutes striving without success to net those words from the sea of static and silence, Ethan glanced at his wristwatch. 12:26. He had been riveted to the phone for nearly half an hour.

Having been crushed so long against the earpiece, his ear burned and throbbed. His neck felt stiff, his shoulders ached.

Surprised and somewhat disoriented, he sat up straight in his chair. He had never been hypnotized; but he imagined that this must be how it would feel to shake off the lingering effects of a trance.

Reluctantly, he put down the phone.

The suggestion of a voice in the void might have been that and nothing more, merely a suggestion, an audial illusion. Yet he had pursued it with the single-minded sweaty expectation of a submarine sonar operator listening for the *ping* of an approaching battleship as it off-loaded depth charges.

He didn't quite understand what he'd done. Or why.

Although the room was not excessively warm, he blotted his brow with his shirt sleeve.

He expected the phone to ring again. Perhaps he would be wise not to answer it.

That thought disturbed him because he didn't understand it. Why not answer a ringing phone?

His gaze traveled across the six items from Reynerd, but his attention settled longest on the three small bells from the ambulance in which he'd never ridden.

When the phone had not rung after two or three minutes, he switched on the computer and again accessed the telephone log. The most recent entry was the call that he had placed to the hotel to inquire about Dunny Whistler.

Subsequently, the call that he'd received, which had lasted nearly half an hour, had not registered in the log.

Impossible.

He stared at the screen, thinking about Fric's calls from the heavy breather. He'd been too quick to dismiss the boy's story.

When Ethan glanced at the phone, he discovered the indicator light aglow at Line 24.

Sales call. Wrong number. And yet . . .

Had it been easy to satisfy his curiosity, he would have gone up to the third floor where the answering machine serving Line 24 was isolated in a special chamber behind a locked blue door. By the very act of entering that room, however, he would be surrendering his job.

To Ming du Lac and Channing Manheim, the room behind the blue door was a sacred place. Entry by anyone but them had been forbidden.

In the event of an emergency, Ethan was authorized to use his master key anywhere in the house. The only door that it didn't open was the blue one.

A flock of angels, the pleasant smell of spruce, and the comfort of the huge armchair could not lull Fric into sleep.

He got out of the chair, ventured warily to the nearest shelves of books, and selected a novel.

Although ten, he read at a sixteen-year-old level. He took no pride in this, for in his experience, most sixteen-year-olds, these days, weren't whiz kids, probably because no one expected them to be.

Even Ms. Dowd, his English and reading tutor, didn't expect him to *enjoy* books; she doubted they were good for him. She said books were relics; the future would be shaped by images, not by words. In fact, she believed in "memes," which she pronounced *meems* and defined as ideas that arose spontaneously among "informed people" and spread mind-to-mind among the populace, like a mental virus, creating "new ways of thinking."

Ms. Dowd visited Fric four times a week, and after each session, she left behind enough manure to fertilize the lawns and flower beds of the estate for at least a year.

In the armchair once more, Fric discovered that he couldn't concentrate well enough to become involved in the story. This didn't mean that books were obsolete, only that he was tired and scared.

He sat for a while, waiting for a meme to pop into his mind and give him something radically new to think about, something that would blow out of his head all thoughts of Moloch, child sacrifices, and strange men who traveled by mirrors. Apparently, however, there was currently no meme epidemic underway.

As his eyes began to feel hot and grainy but no heavier, he took from a pocket of his jeans the photo that had been passed to him out of a mirror. He unfolded the picture and smoothed it on his leg.

The lady looked even prettier than he remembered. Not supermodel beautiful, but pretty in a *real* way. Kind and gentle.

He wondered who she was. He spun a story for himself about what life would be like if this woman were his mother and if her husband were his father. He felt a little guilty for dumping Nominal Mom and Ghost Dad out of this imaginary life, but they *lived* make-believe, so he didn't think they would begrudge him a fantasy family for one night.

After a while, the smile of the woman in the photo fostered a smile in Fric, which was better than catching a meme.

Later, when Fric was living with his new mom and her husband, whom he had not yet met, in a cozy cottage in Goose Crotch,

Montana, where no one knew who he had once been, the gray-eyed mirror man stepped out of the shine on the side of a toaster, patted the dog on the head, and warned that it would be dangerous to *69 him. "If an angel uses the *idea* of a phone to call me," Fric said, "and then if I star sixty-nine him, why would I be connected to a place like Hell instead of to Heaven?" Instead of answering the question, the man breathed a dragon's snort of fire at him and disappeared back through the shine on the toaster. The flames singed Fric's clothes and caused wisps of smoke to rise from him, but he wasn't set afire. His wonderful new mother poured him another glass of lemonade to cool him off, and they continued to talk about favorite books as he ate a fat slice of the homemade chocolate cake that she had baked for him.

In a tumultuous darkness filled first with gunfire and the roar of approaching engines, then with a voice crying out of a void, Ethan turned and turned, tumbling across wet blacktop, until he turned one last time into a quiet darkness of damp tangled sheets.

Sitting up in bed, he said, "Hannah," for in sleep, where all his psychological defenses were removed, he had recognized her voice as the one that he had heard on the telephone.

Initially, she had repeated the same cry three times, and then three times again. In sleep, he had recognized the word, his name: *"Ethan . . . Ethan . . . Ethan."*

What else she had said to him, the urgent message that she had struggled to convey across the gulf between them, continued to elude him. Even in sleep, that room next door to death, he had not been close enough to Hannah to hear more than his name.

As the shrouds of sleep slipped off him, Ethan was overcome by a conviction that he was being watched.

Every child knows well the feeling of waking from a dream to the perception that the bedroom darkness grants cover to vicious fiends of innumerable descriptions and appetites. The presence of demons seemed so real that many a small hand had hesitated on a lamp switch, for fear that seeing would be even worse than the images that the fevered imagination provided; yet always the terrors evaporated in the light.

Ethan wasn't sure that light would banish unreason this time. He sensed that what watched him were owls and crack-beaked crows, ravens and fierce-eyed hawks, that they perched not on his furniture but in somber black-and-white photographs on the walls, pictures that hadn't hung there when he'd gone to sleep. Although hours ago the night had melted into the predawn blackness of a new day, he had no reason to suppose that Tuesday would be less stained by irrationality than Monday had been.

He didn't reach for the lamp switch. He reclined once more, head upon his pillows, resigned to the presence of whatever the darkness might conceal.

He doubted that he would be able to doze off again. Sooner than later, however, his eyes grew heavy.

On the rim of sleep's whirlpool, as Ethan drifted lazily around, around, he heard from time to time a *tick-tick-tick* that might have been the talons of sentinel crows as they shifted position on an iron fence. Or perhaps it was only claws of cold rain scratching at the windows.

As he began to revolve more rapidly around the relentless pull of black-hole gravity that was sleep, Ethan's eyes fluttered one last time, and he noticed a small light in the lampblack gloom. The phone. Without investigation, he couldn't with certainty identify the number of the indicator light, but he knew instinctively that it must be Line 24.

He slid off the rim of the whirlpool, into the vortex, down into whatever dreams might come.

CHAPTER 48

FREE OF ENVY, FREE OF HATRED, BUOYANT IN the service of chaos, Corky Laputa began his day with a cinnamon-pecan roll, four cups of black coffee, and a pair of caffeine tablets.

Anyone who would bring the social order to ruin must embrace anything that gives him an additional edge, even at the risk of destroying his stomach lining and instigating chronic intestinal inflammation. Fortunately for Corky, periodically consuming massive quantities of caffeine seemed to increase the bitter potency of his bile without causing acid indigestion or other regrettable symptoms.

Washing down caffeine with caffeine, he stood at his kitchen window, smiling at the low somber sky and at the trailing beard of night fog that had not entirely been shorn away by the blunt gray dawn. Bad weather was again his co-conspirator.

The current pause in the rain would be brief. Rushing in fast on the heels of the departing tempest, a new and reportedly stronger storm would wash the city and justify the wearing of rain gear, regardless of how elaborate it might be.

Corky had already reloaded the weatherproof interior pockets of his yellow vinyl slicker, which hung now from a hook in the garage.

He carried his last cup of coffee upstairs to the guest room, where he finished it while informing Stinky Cheese Man that his beloved daughter, Emily, was dead.

The previous night he'd reported the final torture and savage murder of Rachel, Stinky's wife, who was still alive, of course, and not in Corky's custody. The invented details were so imaginative and vivid that Stinky had been reduced to uncontrollable tears, to sobs that sounded weirdly inhuman—and quite disgusting—coming from his withered voice box.

Although crushed by despair, Stinky had not suffered the heart attack for which Corky had been hoping.

Rather than coddle the man with a sedative, Corky had introduced a powerful hallucinogenic through a port in the IV line. His hope was that Stinky would be unable to sleep and would pass the darkest hours between midnight and dawn in a hell of drug-induced visions featuring his brutalized wife.

Now, regaling his guest with an even more outrageous tale of the many crude violations and cruel acts of violence visited upon young Emily, Corky grew weary of the tears and anguish that were replayed here yet again. Under the circumstances, a massive cardiac infarction didn't seem too much to ask, but Stinky would not cooperate.

For a man who supposedly loved his wife and daughter more than life itself, Stinky's determination to survive was unseemly now that he'd been told that his family was nothing more than rotting meat. Like most traditionalists, with all their loudly expressed belief in language and meaning and purpose and principle, Stinky was probably a fraud.

Now and then, Corky glimpsed rage underlying Stinky's grief. Into the man's eyes came hatred hot enough to sear with a look, but then at once vanished under pools of tears.

Perhaps Stinky clung to life only for the hope of revenge. The guy was delusional.

Besides, hatred only destroys the hater. By the example of her wasted life, Corky's mother had proved the truth of that contention.

With facility and efficiency, Corky changed infusion bags after doctoring the new one with a drug that would induce a semiparalytic state. Stinky had so little muscle tissue left that an artificially induced paralysis seemed unnecessary, but Corky was loath to let anything to chance.

Ironically, to serve chaos well, he needed to be well organized. He required a strategy for victory and the carefully planned tactics necessary to fulfill that strategy.

Without strategy and tactics, you weren't a true agent of chaos. You were just Jeffrey Dahmer or some crazy lady who kept a hundred cats and filled her yard with unsightly piles of junk, or a recent governor of California.

Five years ago, Corky had learned how to give injections, how to insert a cannula in a vein, how to handle the equipment related to an IV setup, how to catheterize either a man or a woman. . . . Since then, he had enjoyed a few opportunities, as with Stinky Cheese Man, to practice these skills; consequently, he used these instruments and devices with a facility that any nurse would admire.

In fact, he'd been trained by a nurse, Mary Noone. She had the face of a Botticelli Madonna and the eyes of a ferret.

He'd met Mary at a university mixer for people interested in utilitarian bioethics. Utilitarians believed that every life could be assigned a value to society and that medical care should be rationed according to that assigned value. This philosophy supported the killing, by neglect, of the physically handicapped, Down-syndrome children, people over sixty with medical problems requiring expensive treatment like dialysis and bypass surgery, and many others.

The mixer had been full of fun and witty conversation—and he and Mary Noone had clicked the moment their eyes met. They'd both been drinking Cabernet Sauvignon when they were introduced, and over refills, they had fallen in lust.

Weeks thereafter, when he had asked Mary to teach him the proper way to give an injection and how to maintain a patient on intravenous infusion, Corky had solemnly revealed that his mother's health was rapidly declining. "I dread the day when she'll be bedridden, but I'd rather attend to her myself than turn her over to strangers in a nursing home."

Mary told him that he was a wonderful son, and Corky pretended to accept this compliment with humility, which was an easy pretense to maintain because he was lying about both his mother's health and his intentions. The old bitch had been as healthy as Methuselah still six centuries short of the grave, and Corky had been toying with the idea of injecting her with something lethal while she slept.

He was pretty sure that Mary suspected the truth. Nevertheless, she taught him what he wanted to know.

Initially he believed that her willingness to educate him in these matters could be attributed to the fact that she was hot for him. Jungle cats in heat didn't copulate with the ferocity or the frequency of Mary Noone and Corky in the few months that they had been together.

Eventually he realized that she understood his true motives and didn't disapprove. Furthermore, he began to suspect that Mary was a self-styled Angel of Death who acted upon her utilitarian bioethics by quietly killing the patients whose lives she deemed to be of poor quality and of little value to society.

He dared not remain her sex toy under such circumstances. Sooner or later, she would be arrested and put on trial, as angels of her breed usually were. By virtue of being her lover, Corky was sure to be closely scrutinized by the police, which would put his life's work and possibly his freedom in jeopardy.

Besides, after they had been together more than three months, Corky grew uneasy about sleeping in the same bed with Mary Noone. Although as a lover he might command a high value in horny Mary's estimation, Corky didn't know how much—or how little— she thought he was worth to society.

To his surprise, when he cautiously raised the issue of an amicable breakup, Mary responded with relief. Apparently, she had not been sleeping well, either.

In time he had chosen not to kill his mother by injection, but the effort to educate himself in these aspects of medical care had not been wasted.

During the years since, he had seen Mary only twice, both times at bioethics parties. The old heat was still there between them, but so was the wariness.

With an efficiency and tenderness that Mary Noone would admire, Corky finished ministering to Stinky Cheese Man.

The paralytic drug would incapacitate Stinky without making him drowsy or putting him in an altered state of consciousness. With full mental clarity, he could spend the day agonizing over the deaths of his wife and daughter.

"Now I've got to dispose of Rachel's and Emily's bodies," Corky lied with panache that pleased him. "I'd feed their remains to hogs, if I knew where to find a hog farm."

He remembered a recent news story about a young blonde whose body had been dumped in a sewage-treatment plant. Borrowing details from that crime, he spun for Stinky a story about the ponds of human waste for which his loved ones were bound.

Still no heart attack.

Late this evening, when he returned here with Aelfric Manheim, Corky would introduce the boy to this emaciated wretch, to prime him for the terrors that awaited him. Aelfric's suffering would be of a somewhat different variety from what had been required of this once-arrogant lover of Dickens, Dickinson, Tolstoi, and Twain. If the stubborn drudge hadn't died of a heart attack during the day, Corky would kill him before midnight.

Leaving Stinky to whatever strange thoughts might occupy the odd mind of a traditionalist in these circumstances, Corky donned his amply provisioned yellow slicker, locked the house, and set out into the December day in his BMW.

The new storm had already shouldered into the city. Great dragon herds of black clouds seethed from horizon to horizon, coils tangled in one colossal heaving mass, full of pent-up roars and white fire that might soon be breathed out in dazzling, jagged plumes.

A tentative drizzle fell, but cataracts were sure to follow, vertical rivers, torrents, Niagaras, a deluge.

CHAPTER 49

PROTECTED BY THE TREE OF ANGELS AND BY the photo of the unknown pretty lady, Fric woke unharmed, with his body and soul intact.

Over the center of the library, the elaborate stained-glass dome brightened with the dawn, but the colors were muted because the early light fell weak and gray.

After studying the photograph of his dream mother for a moment, Fric folded it and returned it to a back pocket of his jeans.

He got up from the armchair. He yawned and stretched. He took a moment to be amazed that he was alive.

At the back of the library, he removed the bracing chair from under the knob of the powder-room door. He did not, however, enter that mirrored space to use the facilities.

Following a quick look around to be certain that he remained un-observed, he peed on the potted palm that he had begun to kill the previous evening. The experience was satisfying for him, but surely not for the tree.

He could think of no water closet in the mansion that could be reached without going through a bathroom with mirrors.

This unconventional toileting would be all right for a while, but only as long as he could stand up to do what needed to be done. The moment sitting was required, he would be in trouble.

If the rain ended at last—or if it didn't—he might venture outside to the grouping of deodar cedars beyond the rose garden. There he could do what bears did in the woods, by which he didn't mean hibernate or guzzle honey from bee hives.

Security guards would see him going to and from the cedars. Fortunately, no cameras were positioned inside that little grove.

If anyone asked why he'd gone out in the rain to the woods, he would say without hesitation that he'd been bird watching. He must remember to take with him a pair of binoculars for cover.

No one would doubt his story. People *expected* a geeky-looking kid like him to be a bird watcher, a math whiz, a builder of plastic model-kit monsters, a secret reader of body-building magazines, and a collector of his own boogers, among other things.

With his toilet strategy now devised, he plugged in the library phone, which he had unplugged the previous night. He expected his line to ring at once, but it didn't.

He dragged the armchair away from the Christmas tree and returned it to its proper position. After turning out the lights, he left the library.

As he closed the door, some of the dangling angels glimmered softly in the gloom, barely touched by storm light filtering through the stained-glass dome.

Moloch was coming.

Preparations must be made.

He went down the main stairs, across the rotunda, and along the hall to the kitchen. En route, he switched off the lights that he had left on during the night.

The post-dawn stillness in the great house was deeper even than the silence that, during the long night, had made it seem like such a perfect haunt for ghosts of all intentions.

In the kitchen, passing a window, he noticed a lull in the rain, and he glimpsed the grove of cedars in the distance. At the moment, however, he felt no urge to engage in any bird watching.

Usually Fric avoided the kitchen on days when Mr. Hachette, the diabolical chef, was on the job. Here be the lair of the beast, where the many ovens could not help but bring to mind Hansel and Gretel and their close call, where you were reminded that a rolling pin was also a wicked bludgeon, where you expected to discover that the knives and the cleavers and the meat forks were engraved with the words PROPERTY OF THE BATES MOTEL.

This morning, the territory was safe because Mr. Hachette—late of the Cordon Bleu school of culinary arts and more recently released from an equally prestigious asylum—would not be present to prepare breakfast for either family or staff. He would begin his day skulking from the farmers' market to a series of specialty shops, selecting— and arranging for the delivery of—the fruits, vegetables, meats, delicacies, and no doubt poisons needed to prepare the series of holiday feasts that he had planned with his usual sinister secrecy. Mr. Hachette would not arrive at Palazzo Rospo before noon.

Although short, Fric could nevertheless reach the faucets at the kitchen sink. He adjusted the water until it was pleasantly warm.

If the kitchen had featured a mirror, he wouldn't have dared to bathe here. You were so vulnerable when you were taking a bath, all defenses down.

The stainless-steel fronts of the six refrigerators and the numerous ovens had a brushed rather than a polished finish. They didn't serve as mirrors and were therefore unlikely to offer cheap and easy travel to spirits good or evil.

Fric stripped off his shirt and undershirt, but nothing more. He was not an exhibitionist. Even if he *had* been an exhibitionist, the kitchen didn't seem like a suitable place to exhibit.

Using paper towels and lemon-scented ooze from the liquid-soap dispenser, he washed his arms and upper body, with special attention to his armpits. He used more paper towels to rinse and dry himself.

No sooner had he shut off the water and finished blotting his torso than he heard someone approaching. The footsteps came not from the hall but through the butler's pantry, where the china, crystal, and fine silverware were stored.

Grabbing his shirt and undershirt, Fric dropped to the floor and crawled as fast as a skittering skink, away from the butler's pantry and around the corner of the nearest of three granite-topped center islands.

Atop this particular island were four deep-well French fryers, a griddle large enough to prepare two dozen pancakes side by side, and an acre of work surface. Cowering here, discovered by a grinning Mr. Hachette, Fric could be skinned, gutted, French fried, and eaten while the few people currently in the house snoozed on undisturbed, blissfully unaware that an extraterrestrial gourmet was whipping up a grisly breakfast for itself.

When he dared peek around the corner of the island, he saw not Mr. Hachette but Mrs. McBee.

He was doomed.

Mrs. McBee had dressed for her early-morning drive to Santa Barbara. She crossed the kitchen to her office, entered, and left the door standing open behind her.

She would smell Fric. Smell him, hear him, sense him somehow. She would discover the water beaded in the sink, would open the trash compactor and see the damp paper towels, and would instantly *know* what he'd done and where he now hid.

Nothing escaped the notice of Mrs. McBee or foiled her powers of deduction.

She would not gut him and French fry him, of course, because she was a good person and entirely human. Instead she would insist upon knowing why he was stripped to the waist in the kitchen, freshly washed, and looking as guilty as a stupid cat with canary crumbs on its lips.

Because she was Ghost Dad's employee, Fric could have made the argument that technically she worked for him, too, and that he didn't have to answer her questions. If he resorted to that argument, he would be in deep *merde,* as Mr. Hachette would say with glee. Mrs. McBee knew that she served *in loco parentis,* and while she was not quite power mad with that authority, she took it seriously.

Whether Fric concocted a false explanation or tried to get away with telling only part of the truth, Mrs. McBee would see through his deception as clearly as he himself could see through a window, and she would intuitively know everything that he'd been up to at least since he'd awakened in the armchair. Twenty seconds later, with one of his ears pinched firmly between the thumb and forefinger of Mrs. McBee's right hand, he would find himself standing before the potted palm in the library, sweating like a lowlife scumbag as he tried to explain why he had attempted to assassinate the plant with a double volley of urine.

Minutes thereafter, she would have succeeded in getting him to spill the entire story from Moloch to mirror man to the phone call from Hell. Then there would be no going back.

Even Mrs. McBee, with her scary ability to see through any lie or evasion, would not recognize the truth in this case. His story was too outrageous to be believed. He would sound like a bigger lunatic than any of the uncountable entertainment-industry lunatics who, on visiting Palazzo Rospo, had astonished Mrs. McBee with their lunacy during the past six years.

He didn't want Mrs. McBee to be disappointed in him or to think that he was mentally deranged. Her opinion of Fric mattered to him.

Besides, the more he thought about it, the more he realized that if he tried to convince anyone that he was in communication with a mirror-traveling guardian angel, he'd be hand-carried into a group-therapy session. The group would be six psychiatrists and he would be the only patient.

Ghost Dad was almost as big on shrinks as he was on spiritual advisers.

Now Mrs. McBee stepped out of her office, closed the door, and paused to look around the kitchen.

Fric ducked back behind the fryer-and-griddle island. He held his breath. He wished that he could as easily close down his pores and prevent them from spewing out his scent.

The main kitchen was not quite a maze to rival the labyrinth of memorabilia in the attic, though it boasted not only six large Sub-Zero refrigerators but also two upright freezers, more ovens of more types than you would find in a bakery, three widely separated cooking areas with a total of twenty high-intensity gas burners, a planning station, a baking station, a clean-up station with four sinks and four dishwashers, three islands, prep tables, and a shitload of restaurant-quality equipment.

A Beverly Hills caterer and forty of his employees could work here with Mr. Hachette and the household staff, with little sense of being crowded. At a party, they prepared, plated, and served three hundred sit-down dinners, on a timely basis, from this space. Fric had seen it happen many times, and it never failed to dazzle him.

If two or even three ordinary people had set out to search the kitchen for him, Fric's chances of eluding them would have been good. Mrs. McBee was in no way ordinary.

Holding his breath, he thought that he could hear her sniffing the air. *Fee-fie-fo-fum*.

He was glad that he had not turned on the kitchen lights, though she was certain to smell the fresh water that remained in the central sink.

Footsteps.

Fric almost bolted to his feet, almost announced his presence, which seemed a wiser course of action than waiting here to be found lurking like a sleazeball criminal, stripped to the waist and clearly up to no good.

Then he realized the footsteps were moving away from him.

He heard the butler's-pantry door swing shut.

The footsteps faded into silence.

Stunned and strangely dismayed to discover that Mrs. McBee was fallible, Fric breathed again.

After a while, he crept to the hall door, which he cracked open. He stood listening.

When he heard the distant hum of the service elevator, he knew that Mrs. McBee and Mr. McBee were descending to the lower garage. Soon they would be off to Santa Barbara.

He waited a few minutes before he ventured from the kitchen to the laundry room in the nearby west wing, which also contained the McBees' apartment.

Whereas the kitchen was gigantic, the laundry was only huge.

He liked the smell of this place. Detergent, bleach, starch, the lingering scent of hot cotton under a steam iron . . .

Fric would happily have worn the same jeans and shirt a second day. But he worried that Mr. Truman might notice, and inquire.

Mrs. McBee would have noticed in an instant. She would have insisted on knowing the reason for this slovenliness.

Mr. Truman couldn't help but be slower on the uptake than Mrs. McBee. Still, he *was* an ex-cop, so he wouldn't long overlook day-old, dirty, rumpled clothes.

The possibility might be slim that something evil and supremely slimy was waiting for Fric in his suite, but he didn't intend to find out anytime soon. He would not return there to change clothes.

Monday had been a scheduled wash day. Mrs. Carstairs, one of the day maids and in fact the laundress, processed laundry one day and returned it promptly to family members and to staff the following morning.

Fric found his pressed blue jeans, pants, and shirts hanging from a cart similar to those with which hotel bellmen move suit bags and luggage. His folded underwear and socks were arranged under the hanging items, on the bed of the cart.

Red-faced, feeling like a pervert for sure, he stripped naked right there in the laundry. He changed into fresh underwear, jeans, and a

blue-and-green checkered flannel shirt with a straight-cut tail that allowed it to be worn out, Hawaiian style.

He transferred his wallet and the folded photograph from his old
jeans before dropping the soiled garments into the collection basket
under the laundry chute that served the second and third floors.

Emboldened by having successfully toileted, bathed, and changed
clothes under these desperate wartime conditions, Fric returned to
the kitchen.

He entered cautiously, expecting to find Mrs. McBee waiting for
him: *Ah, laddie, did ya truly think I was such a fool as to be that easily deceived?*

She had not returned.

From the appliance pantry, he fetched a small stainless-steel cart
with two shelves. He traveled the kitchen, loading the cart with
items that he would need in his deep and special secret place.

He considered including a six-pack of Coke among his provisions,
but warm cola didn't taste good. Instead, he selected a four-pack of
Stewart's Diet Orange 'N Cream soda, which was fabulous even at
room temperature, and six twelve-ounce bottles of water.

After he put a few apples and a bag of pretzels on the cart, he realized his mistake. When hiding from a demented psycho killer who
had the sharply honed senses of a stalking panther, eating noisy food
was no wiser than singing Christmas songs to pass the time.

Fric replaced the apples and pretzels with bananas, a box of
chocolate-covered doughnuts, and several chewy granola bars.

He added a quart-size Hefty OneZip plastic bag in which to store
the peels after he ate the fruit. Left in the open air, peels would give
off an intense banana scent as they darkened. According to the
movies, every serial killer had a sense of smell keener than that of a
wolf. Banana peels might be the death of Fric if he didn't stow them
in an airtight container.

A roll of paper towels. Several foil-wrapped moist towelettes. Even
in hiding, he would want to be neat.

From a cupboard filled with Rubbermaid containers, he chose a pair of one-quart, soft-plastic jars with screw-on lids. They would serve in place of the library palm tree.

Mr. Hachette, being a deeply unstable person, had stocked the kitchen with ten times more cutlery than would ever be needed even if the entire staff developed knife-throwing acts and ran off to work in carnival sideshows. Three wall racks and four drawers offered enough blades to arm the entire coconut-rich nation of Tuvalu.

Fric selected a butcher knife. Proportionate to his size, the blade was as large as a machete—scary to look at, but unwieldy.

Instead, he chose a smaller but formidable knife with a six-inch blade, a wickedly pointed tip, and an edge sharp enough to split a human hair. The thought of cutting a person with it made him queasy.

He put the knife on the lower shelf of the cart and covered it with a dishtowel.

For the time being, he could think of nothing additional that he needed from the kitchen. Mr. Hachette—busy shopping and no doubt also shedding his skin for a new set of scales—wasn't due to slither back to Palazzo Rospo for hours yet, but Fric remained eager to get out of the chef's domain.

Using the service elevator would be too dangerous because it was in the west wing, not far from Mr. Truman's apartment. He hoped to avoid the security chief. The public elevator, toward the east end of the north hall, would be safer.

In sudden guilty haste, he pushed the cart through the swinging door into the hallway, turned right, and nearly collided with Mr. Truman.

"You're up early this morning, Fric."

"Ummm, things to do, things, you know, ummm," Fric muttered, silently cursing himself for sounding devious, guilty, and more than a little like an absentminded Hobbit.

"What's all this?" Mr. Truman asked, indicating the stuff piled on the cart.

"Yeah. For my room, things I need, you know, stuff for my room."
Fric shamed himself; he was pathetic, transparent, stupid. "Just some
soda and snacks and stuff," he added, and he wanted to smack himself upside the head.

"You're going to put one of the maids out of work."

"Gee, no, that's not what I want." *Shut up, shut up, shut up!* he
warned himself, yet he couldn't resist adding, "I like the maids."

"Are you all right, Fric?"

"Sure. I'm all right. Are you all right?"

Frowning at the items on the cart, Mr. Truman said, "I'd like to
talk to you a little more about those calls."

Glad that he had covered the knife with a dishtowel, Fric said,
"What calls?"

"From the heavy breather."

"Oh. Yeah. The breather."

"Are you sure he didn't say anything to you?"

"Breathed. He just, you know, breathed."

"The odd thing is—none of the calls you told me about are on the
computerized telephone log."

Well, of course, now that Fric understood these calls were being
made by a supernatural, mirror-walking being who referred to himself as a guardian angel and who only used the *idea* of a telephone, he
was not surprised that they weren't recorded as entries in the log. He
also wasn't any longer puzzled about why Mr. Truman hadn't picked
up on the call the previous night, even though it had rung just about
forever: Mysterious Caller always knew where Fric was—train room,
wine cellar, library—and using his uncanny powers and only the *idea*
of a phone, he made Fric's line ring not throughout the house but
only in the room where Fric could hear it.

Fric longed to explain this crazy situation to Mr. Truman and to reveal all the weird events of the previous evening. Even as he worked
up the courage to spill his guts, however, he thought of the six psychiatrists who would be eager to earn hundreds of thousands of bucks

by keeping him on a couch, talking about the stress of being the only child of the biggest movie star in the world, until he either exploded into bloody pieces or escaped to Goose Crotch.

"Don't get me wrong, Fric. I'm not saying you invented those calls. In fact, I'm sure you didn't."

Clenched tightly around the cart handle, Fric's hands had grown damp. He blotted them on his pants—and realized that he should not have done so. Every crummy, sleazy criminal in the world probably got sweaty palms in the presence of a cop.

"I'm sure you didn't," Mr. Truman continued, "because last night someone rang me up on one of my private lines, and it didn't show on the log, either."

Surprised by this news, Fric stopped blotting his hands and said, "You heard from the breather?"

"Not the breather, no. Someone else."

"Who?"

"Probably a wrong number."

Fric looked at the security chief's hands. He couldn't tell whether or not they were sweaty.

"Evidently," Mr. Truman continued, "something's wrong with the telephone-log software."

"Unless he's like a ghost or something," Fric blurted.

The expression that crossed Mr. Truman's face was hard to read. He said, "Ghost? What makes you say that?"

On the trembling edge of divulging all, Fric remembered that his mother had once been in a booby hatch. She had stayed there only ten days, and she hadn't been chop-'em-up-with-an-ax crazy or anything as bad as that.

Nevertheless, if Fric started babbling about recent freaky events, Mr. Truman would surely recall that Freddie Nielander had spent some time in a clinic for the temporarily wacko. He would think, *Like mother, like son.*

For sure, he would immediately contact the biggest movie star in the world on location in Florida. Then Ghost Dad would send in a powerful SWAT team of psychiatrists.

"Fric," Mr. Truman pressed, "what did you mean—ghost?"

Shoveling manure over the seed of truth that he'd spoken, hoping to grow a half-convincing lie from it, Fric said, "Well, you know, my dad keeps a special phone for messages from ghosts. I just meant like maybe one of them called the wrong line."

Mr. Truman stared at him as though trying to decide whether he could be as stupid as he was pretending to be.

Not as great an actor as his father, Fric knew he couldn't long stand up to interrogation by an ex-cop. He was so nervous that in a minute he'd need to take a leak in one of the Rubbermaid jars.

"Ummm, well, gotta go, things to do, things up in my room, you know," he muttered, once more sounding like a cousin from the feeble-minded branch of the Hobbit clan.

He swung the cart around Mr. Truman and pushed it east along the main hall. He didn't look back.

CHAPTER 50

THE DOME LIGHT ATOP OUR LADY OF ANGELS Hospital was a golden beacon. High above the dome, at the top of the radio mast, the red aircraft-warning lamp winked in the gray mist, as if the storm were a living beast and this were its malevolent Cyclopean eye.

In the elevator, on the way from the garage to the fifth floor, Ethan listened to a lushly orchestrated version of a classic Elvis Costello number tricked up with violins and fulsome French horns. This cable-hung cubicle, ascending and descending twenty-four hours a day, was a little outpost of Hell in perpetual motion.

The physicians' lounge on the fifth floor, to which he'd been given directions by phone, was nothing more than a dreary windowless vending-machine room with a pair of Formica-topped tables in the center. The orange plastic items that surrounded the tables qualified as chairs no more than the room deserved the grand name on its door.

Having arrived five minutes early, Ethan fed coins to one of the machines and selected black coffee. When he sipped the stuff, he knew what death must taste like, but he drank it anyway because he'd slept only four or five hours and needed the kick.

Dr. Kevin O'Brien arrived precisely on time. About forty-five, handsome, he had the vaguely haunted look and the well-suppressed but still-apparent nervous edge of one who had spent two-thirds of his life in arduous scholarship, only to find that the hammers wielded by HMOs, government bureaucracy, and greedy trial attorneys were daily degrading his profession and destroying the medical system to which he'd dedicated his life. His eyes were pinched at the corners. He frequently licked his lips. Stress lent a gray tint to his pallor. Unfortunately for his peace of mind, he seemed to be a bright man who would not much longer be able to delude himself into believing that the quicksand under his feet was actually solid ground.

Although he was not Duncan Whistler's personal internist, Dr. O'Brien had been the physician on duty when Dunny had gone flatline. He had overseen resuscitation procedures and had made the final call to cease heroic efforts. The death certificate carried his signature.

Dr. O'Brien brought with him the complete patient file in three thickly packed folders. During their discussion, he gradually spread the entire contents across one of the tables.

They sat side by side in the orange pseudochairs, the better to review the documents together.

Dunny's coma resulted from cerebral hypoxia, a lack of adequate oxygen to the brain for an extended period of time. Results revealed on EEG scrolls and by brain-imaging tests—angiography, CT scanning, MRI—led inescapably to the conclusion that if he had ever regained consciousness, he would have been profoundly handicapped.

"Even among patients in the deepest comas," O'Brien explained, "where there's little or no apparent activity in the cerebrum, there is usually enough function in the brain stem to allow them to exhibit some automatic responses. They continue to breathe unaided. Once in a while they might cough, blink their eyes, even yawn."

Throughout most of his hospitalization, Dunny had breathed on his own. Three days ago, his declining automatic responses required that he be connected to a ventilator. He'd no longer been able to breathe without mechanical assistance.

In his early weeks at the hospital, although deeply comatose, he had at times coughed, sneezed, yawned, blinked. Occasionally he had even exhibited roving eye movements.

Gradually, those automatic responses declined in frequency until they ceased to be observed at all. This suggested a steady loss of function in the lower brain stem.

The previous morning, Dunny's heart had stopped. Defibrillation and injections of epinephrine restarted the heart, but only briefly.

"The automatic function of the circulatory system is maintained by the lower brain stem," Dr. O'Brien said. "It was clear his heart had failed because brain-stem function failed. There's no coming back from irreparable damage to the brain stem. Death inevitably follows."

In a case like this, the patient would not be connected to a heart-lung machine, providing artificial circulation and respiration, unless his family insisted. The family would need to have the means to pay because insurance companies would disallow such expenditures on the grounds that the patient could never regain consciousness.

"As regards Mr. Whistler," O'Brien said, "you held a power of attorney in matters of health care."

"Yes."

"And you signed a release quite some time ago, specifying that heroic efforts, other than a ventilator, were not to be employed to keep him alive."

"That's right," Ethan said. "And I've no intention of suing."

This sincere assurance caused no visible relief on O'Brien's part. Evidently he believed that even though the conscientious medical care given to Dunny was lawsuit-proof, a plague of lawyers would nonetheless rain down on him.

"Dr. O'Brien, whatever happened to Dunny once his body reached the hospital morgue is another matter altogether, unrelated to you."

"But I'm not any less disturbed about it than you are. I've discussed it twice with the police. I'm . . . bewildered."

"I just want you to know that I don't hold the morgue employees at all responsible for his disappearance, either."

"They're good people," O'Brien said.

"I'm sure they are. Whatever's going on here isn't the fault of the hospital. The explanation is . . . something extraordinary."

The physician dared to let hope tweak a little color into his face. "Extraordinary? And what would that be?"

"I don't know. But amazing things have happened to me in the past twenty-four hours, in some way all related to Dunny, I think. So why I wanted to speak to you this morning . . ."

"Yes?"

Searching for words, Ethan pushed back from the table. He got to his feet, his tongue stilled by a thirty-seven-year-long reliance on reason and rationality.

He wished for a window. Gazing out at the rain would have given him an excuse not to look at O'Brien while he asked what needed to be asked.

"Doctor, you weren't Dunny's primary physician . . ."

Talking while gazing moodily at a vending machine full of candy bars seemed eccentric.

". . . but you were involved with his treatment."

O'Brien said nothing, waited.

Having finished his coffee, Ethan scooped the paper cup off the table, crumpled it in his fist.

"And after what happened yesterday, I'd wager that you know his file better than anyone."

"Backward and forward," O'Brien confirmed.

Taking the paper cup to the waste can, Ethan said, "Is there anything in the file that you'd consider unusual?"

"I can't find a single misstep in diagnosis, treatment, or in the death-certification protocols."

"That's not what I mean." He tossed the crumpled cup in the can and paced, looking at the floor. "I'm sincere when I tell you that I'm convinced you and the hospital are utterly blameless. When I say 'unusual,' what I really mean is . . . strange, uncanny."

"Uncanny?"

"Yeah. I don't know how to put a finer point on it."

Dr. O'Brien remained silent so long that Ethan stopped pacing and looked up from the floor.

The physician chewed on his lower lip, staring at the piles of documents.

"There *was* something," Ethan guessed. He returned to the table, sat in the orange torture device. "Something uncanny, all right."

"It's here in the file. I didn't bring it up. It's meaningless."

"What?"

"It could be misconstrued as evidence that he came out of the coma for a period, but he didn't. Some attributed the problem to a machine malfunction. It wasn't."

"Malfunction? What machine?"

"The EEG."

"The machine that records his brain waves."

O'Brien chewed his lip.

"Doctor?"

The physician met Ethan's eyes. He sighed. He pushed his chair away from the table and got up. "It'll be better if you actually see it yourself."

CHAPTER 51

CORKY PARKED ON THE WRONG STREET AND walked two blocks through the cold rain to the home of the three-eyed freak.

Windier than Monday's storm, this one snapped weak fronds off queen palms, tumbled an empty plastic trash can down the center of the street, tore a window awning and loudly flapped the loose length of forest-green canvas.

Melaleucas lashed their willowy branches as though trying to whip themselves to pieces. Stone pines were stripped of dead brown needles that bristled through the churning air and gave it the power to prick, to blind.

As Corky walked, a dead rat bobbed past him on the racing water in the gutter. The lolling head rolled toward him, revealing one dark empty socket and one milky eye.

The grand and lovely spectacle made him wish that he had time to join in the celebration of disorder, to spread some prankish chaos of his own. He longed to poison a few trees, stuff mailboxes with hate literature, spread nails under the tires of parked cars, set a house afire. . . .

This was a busy day of a different kind, however, and he had numerous scheduled tasks to which he must attend. Monday he had been a devilish rascal, an amusing imp of nihilism, but this day he must be a serious soldier of anarchy.

The neighborhood was an eclectic mix of two-story Craftsman houses with raised front porches and classic single-story California bungalows that borrowed from many styles of architecture. They were maintained with evident pride, enhanced with brick walkways, picket fences, beds of flowers.

By contrast, the bungalow of the three-eyed freak sat behind a half-dead front lawn, skirted by masses of unkempt shrubbery, at the end of a cracked and hoved concrete walkway. Under the Mexican-tile roof, the filthy tangles of long-empty birds' nests dripped from the eaves, and the stucco walls were cracked, chipped, in need of paint.

The structure looked like the residence of a troll who had grown weary of living under bridges, without amenities, but who had neither the knowledge nor the industry, nor the sense of pride, needed to maintain a house.

Corky rang the doorbell, which produced not sweet chimes but the sputtering racket of a broken, corroded mechanism.

He loved this place.

Because Corky had called ahead and promised money, the three-eyed freak was waiting by the door. He answered the tubercular cough of the bell even before the sound finished grating on Corky's ear.

Yanking the door open, looming, one great grizzled grimace with a pendulous gut and size-thirteen bare feet, wearing gray sweat pants and a Megadeth concert T-shirt, Ned Hokenberry said, "You look like a damn mustard pot."

"It's raining," Corky observed.

"You look like a pimple on Godzilla's ass."

"If you're worried about getting the carpet wet—"

"Hell, scuzzy as this carpet is, a bunch of pukin'-drunk hobos with bad bladders couldn't do it any harm."

Hokenberry turned away, lumbering into the living room. Corky stepped inside and closed the door behind himself.

The carpet looked as if previously it had been wall-to-wall in a barn.

Should the day arrive when mahogany-finish Formica furniture with green-and-blue-striped polyester upholstery became prized by collectors and museums, Hokenberry would be a wealthy man. The two best items in the living room were a recliner littered with crushed corn chips and a big-screen TV.

The small windows were half covered by drapes. No lamps were aglow; only the TV screen cast light.

Corky was comfortable with the gloom. In spite of his affinity for chaos, he hoped never to see the interior of this house in bright light.

"The last batch of information you gave me checks out, as far as I'm able to check it," Corky said, "and it's really been helpful."

"Told you I know the estate better than that candy-ass actor knows his own dick."

Until he'd been dismissed, with generous severance pay, for leaving prank messages on the answering machine that his employer had dedicated to phone calls from the dead, Ned Hokenberry had been a security guard at Palazzo Rospo.

"You say they got a new security chief. I can't guarantee he didn't change some procedures."

"I understand."

"You have my twenty thousand?"

"I have it right here." Corky withdrew his right arm from the voluminous sleeve of the slicker, and reached to an interior pocket for the packet of cash, his second payment to Hokenberry.

Even framed by the snugly buttoned yellow collar of his slicker and the drooping yellow brim of his rain hat, Corky's face must have revealed more of his contempt than he intended.

Hokenberry's bloodshot eyes blurred with self-pity, and his doughy face kneaded itself into more and deeper folds as he said, "I wasn't always a sorry damn wreck, you know. Didn't used to have this gut. Shaved every day, cleaned up real nice. Front lawn used to be green. Bein' fired by that son of a bitch is what ruined me."

"I thought you said Manheim gave you lots of severance pay?"

"That was soul-buyin' money, I now understand. Anyway, Manheim wasn't man enough to fire me himself. He had his creepy guru do it."

"Ming du Lac."

"That's the one. Ming, he takes me to the rose garden, pours tea, which I'm polite enough to drink even if it tastes like piss."

"You're a gentleman."

"We're sittin' at this table surrounded by roses, got this white lace cloth and fancy china—"

"Sounds lovely."

"—while he talks at me about gettin' my spiritual house in order. I'm not just bored shitless, but thinkin' he's even a bigger fruitcake than I ever figured, when *after fifteen minutes* I realize I'm bein' fired. If he'd made that clear at the start, I wouldn't have had to drink his piss-poor tea."

"That does sound traumatizing," Corky said, pretending sympathy.

"It wasn't traumatizin', you ass pimple. What do you think I am, some pansy gets his dainties all puckered just 'cause someone looks at him wrong? I wasn't traumatized, I was *hexed*."

"Hexed?"

"Hexed, cursed, hoodooed, diabolized, spellcast by the evil eye— whatever you want to call it. Ming du Lac, he's got hell power in him, the creepy runt, and he ruined me forever in that rose garden. I've been slidin' downhill ever since."

"He sounds like the usual Hollywood fraud to me."

"I'm tellin' you, that little weasel's the real juju, and I been spell-struck."

Corky held out the package of cash, but then pulled it back as the hexed wreckage of a man reached for it. "One more thing."

"Don't screw with me," Hokenberry said, hulking over Corky and glowering as if he'd come down a beanstalk, angry and looking for whoever had stolen his hen's eggs.

"You'll get your money," Corky assured him. "I'd just like to hear how you acquired your third eye."

Hokenberry had only two eyes of his own, but around his neck, on a pendant, hung the eye of a stranger.

"I already told you twice how I got it."

"I just like to hear it," Corky said. "You tell it so well. It tickles me."

Scrunching his face until he resembled a Shar-Pei, Hokenberry considered the concept of himself as a raconteur, and he seemed to like it. "Twenty-five years ago, I started doin' road security for rock groups, tour security. I don't mean I planned it or managed it. That's not my zone."

"You've always been just beef," Corky said, anticipating him.

"Yeah, I've always been just beef, been out front to intimidate the crazier fans, the totally wired meth freaks and PCP spongebrains. Been beef for Rollin' Stones tours, Megadeth, Metallica, Van Halen, Alice Cooper, Meat Loaf, Pink Floyd—"

"Queen, Kiss," Corky added, "even for Michael Jackson when he still was Michael Jackson."

"—Michael Jackson back when he still was Michael Jackson if he ever really was," Hokenberry agreed. "Anyway I had this three-week gig with . . . My memory's fuzzy about this. I think it was either the Eagles or could've been Peaches and Herb."

"Or it could've been the Captain and Tennille."

"Yeah, it could've been. One of them three acts. This crowd gets all jammed up, gonads gone nuclear, too much of some bad juice bein' toked and poked that night."

"You could feel they might rush the stage."

"I could feel they might rush the stage. All you need is one idiot punk with spunk for brains, he decides to bolt for the band, and he starts a riot."

"You've got to anticipate him," Corky encouraged.

"Anticipate him, put him down like the *instant* he makes his move, or another two hundred headcases will follow him."

"So this punk with blue hair—"

"Who's tellin' this story?" Hokenberry grumbled. "Me or you?"

"You are. It's your story. I love this story."

To express his disgust with these interruptions, Hokenberry spat on the carpet. "So this punk with blue hair tenses to make his move, gonna climb the stage, try to get to Peaches and Herb—"

"Or the Captain."

"Or Tennille. So I call him out, move in on him fast, and the little butthead flips me the finger, which gives me absolute license to pop him." Hokenberry raised one fist the size of a ham. "I planted Bullwinkle as deep in his face as it would go."

"You call your right fist Bullwinkle."

"Yeah, and my left is Rocky. Didn't even need Rocky. Bullwinkled him so hard one of his eyes popped out. Startled me, but I caught it in midair. Glass eye. The punk went down cold, and I kept the eye, had it made into this pendant."

"It's a terrific pendant."

"Glass eyes aren't really glass, you know. They're thin plastic shells, and the iris is hand-painted on the inside. Way cool."

"Way," Corky agreed.

"Had an artist friend make this little glass sphere to hold the eye, stop it deteriorating. That's the story, gimme my twenty grand."

Corky passed to him the plastic-wrapped packet of cash.

As he had done with his initial twenty thousand on the first of their three previous meetings, Hokenberry turned away from Corky and took the bundle to the table in the adjacent dinette area to count every crisp hundred-dollar bill.

Corky shot him three times in the back.

When Hokenberry hit the floor, the bungalow shook.

The big man's fall was much louder than the shots because the pistol was fitted with a sound suppressor that Corky had purchased from an anarchic survivalist with deep ties to an aggressive group of anti-veal activists who manufactured the suppressors both for their own use and as a fund-raising activity. Each of the shots made a quiet sound like someone pronouncing the word *supper* with a lisp.

This was the weapon with which he had shot Rolf Reynerd's mother in the foot.

Considering Hokenberry's intimidating size, Corky hadn't trusted the ice pick to do the job.

He moved closer to the beef and shot him three more times, just to be certain no punch remained in Rocky and Bullwinkle.

CHAPTER 52

TWO WINDOWS PRESENTED A SOLVENT SKY and a city dissolving in drips, drizzles, and vapors.

Most of the large records room at Our Lady of Angels was divided into aisles by tall banks of filing cabinets. Near the windows lay a more open area with four work stations, and people were busy at two.

Dr. O'Brien settled at one of the unused stations and switched on the computer. Ethan pulled up a chair beside him.

Inserting a DVD into the computer, the physician said, "Mr. Whistler began to experience difficulty breathing three days ago. He needed to be put on a ventilator, and he was moved into the intensive care unit."

When the DVD was accessed, WHISTLER, DUNCAN EUGENE appeared on the screen with Dunny's patient number and other vital information that had been collected by the admissions office.

"While he was in the ICU," O'Brien continued, "his respiration, heartbeat, and brain function were continuously monitored and sent by telemetry to the unit nurses' station. That's always been standard procedure." He used the mouse to click on a series of icons and numbered choices. "The rest is relatively new. The system digitally records data collected by the electronic monitoring devices during the patient's entire stay in the ICU. For later review."

Ethan figured they kept a digital record as evidence to defend against frivolous lawsuits.

"Here's Whistler's EEG when first admitted to the ICU at four-twenty P.M. last Friday."

An unseen stylus drew a continuous line left to right across an endlessly scrolling graph.

"These are the brain's electrical impulses as measured in micro-volts," O'Brien continued.

A monotonous series of peaks and valleys depicted Dunny's brain activity. The peaks were low and wide; the valleys were compara-tively steep and narrow.

"Delta waves are the typical pattern of normal sleep," O'Brien ex-plained. "These are delta waves but not those associated with an or-dinary night's rest. These peaks are broader and much lower than common delta waves, with a smoother oscillation into and out of the troughs. The electrical impulses are few in number, attenuated, weak. This is Whistler in a deep coma. Okay. Now let's fast-forward to the evening of the day before his death."

"Sunday night."

"Yes."

On the screen, as hours of monitoring flew past in a minute, the uncommon delta waves blurred and jumped slightly, but only slightly because the variation from wave to wave was minuscule. An hour of compressed data, viewed in seconds, closely resembled any minute of the same data studied in real time.

Indeed, the sameness of the patterns was so remarkable that Ethan would not have realized how many hours—days—of data were streaming by if there hadn't been a time display on the screen.

"The event occurred at one minute before midnight, Sunday," O'Brien said.

He clicked back to real-time display, and the fast-forwarding stopped at 11:23:22, Sunday night. He speeded the data again in two quick spurts, until he reached 11:58:09.

"Less than a minute now."

Ethan found himself leaning forward in his chair.

Shatters of rain clattered against the windowpanes, as though the wind, in wounded anger, had spat out broken teeth.

One of the people at the other work stations had left the room.

The remaining woman murmured into her phone. Her voice was soft, singsong, slightly spooky, as might be the voices that left messages on the answering machine that served Line 24.

"Here," said Dr. O'Brien.

At 11:59, the lazy, variant delta waves began to spike violently into something different: sharp, irregular peaks and valleys.

"These are beta waves, quite extreme beta waves. The low, very fast oscillation indicates that the patient is concentrating on an external stimulus."

"What stimulus?" Ethan asked.

"Something he sees, hears, feels."

"External? What can he see, hear, or feel in a coma?"

"This isn't the wave pattern of a man in a coma. This is a fully conscious, alert, and disturbed individual."

"And it's a machine malfunction?"

"A couple people here think it has to be machine error. But . . ."

"You disagree."

O'Brien hesitated, staring at the screen. "Well, I shouldn't get ahead of the story. First . . . when the ICU nurse saw this coming in by telemetry, she went directly to the patient, thinking he'd come out of his coma. But he remained slack, unresponsive."

"Could he have been dreaming?" Ethan asked.

O'Brien shook his head emphatically. "The wave patterns of dreamers are distinctive and easily recognizable. Researchers have identified four stages of sleep, and a different signature wave for each stage. None of them is like this."

The beta waves began to spike higher and lower than before. The peaks and valleys were mere needle points instead of the former rugged plateaus, with precipitous slopes between them.

"The nurse summoned a doctor," O'Brien said. "That doctor called in another. No one observed any physical evidence that Whistler had ascended by any degree from deep coma. The ventilator still handled respiration. Heart was slow, slightly irregular. Yet according to the EEG, his brain produced the beta waves of a conscious, alert person."

"And you said 'disturbed.' "

The beta tracery on the screen jittered wildly up and down, valleys growing narrower, the distance between the apex and nadir of each pattern increasing radically, until it was reminiscent of the patterns produced on a seismograph during a major earthquake.

"At some points you might accurately say he appears 'disturbed,' at others 'excited,' and in this passage you're watching now, I'd say without any concern about being melodramatic, that these are the brain waves of a terrified individual."

"Terrified?"

"Thoroughly."

"Nightmare?" Ethan suggested.

"A nightmare is just a dream of a darker variety. It can produce radical wave patterns, but they're nevertheless recognizable as those of a dream. Nothing like this."

O'Brien speeded the flow of data again, forwarding through eight minutes' worth in a few seconds.

When the screen returned to real-time display, Ethan said, "This looks the same . . . yet different."

"These are still the beta waves of a conscious person, and I would say this guy is still frightened, although the terror may have declined here to high anxiety."

The serpent-voiced wind, singing in a language of hiss-shriek-moan, and the claw-tap of rain on window glass seemed to be the perfect music to accompany the jagged images on the screen.

"Although the overall pattern remains one of conscious anxiety," Dr. O'Brien continued, "within it are these irregular subsets of higher spikes, each followed by a subset of lower spikes."

He pointed at the screen, calling examples to Ethan's attention.

"I see them," Ethan said. "What do they mean?"

"They're indicative of conversation."

"Conversation? He's talking to himself?"

"First of all, he isn't talking *aloud* to anyone, not even to himself, so we shouldn't be seeing these patterns."

"I understand. I think."

"But what these represent is not arguable. During the subsets of higher spikes, the subject should be speaking. During the subsets of lower spikes, he should be listening. A subject having a bit of *mental* give-and-take with himself, even when he's awake, produces no such subsets. After all, for one thing, when you're talking to yourself, conducting a little interior debate—"

"Technically, you're always talking," Ethan said. "You're both sides of the debate. You're never really listening."

"Exactly. These subsets are indicative of *conscious* conversation between this individual and another person."

"What other person?"

"I don't know."

"He's in a coma."

"Yes."

Frowning, Ethan said, "Then how is he talking to anyone? By telepathy?"

"Do we believe in telepathy?" O'Brien asked.

"I don't."

"Neither do I."

"Then why couldn't this be a malfunctioning machine?" Ethan wondered.

O'Brien accelerated the data flow until the brain-wave patterns disappeared from the screen, replaced by the words DATA INTERRUPT.

"They took Whistler off the EEG, the one they thought must be malfunctioning," the doctor said. "They connected him to a different machine. The switchover took six minutes."

He fast-forwarded through the gap, until the patterns appeared once more.

"They look the same on the new machine," Ethan said.

"Yeah, they are. Beta waves representing consciousness, lots of anxiety, and with subsets suggesting vigorous conversation."

"A second malfunctioning machine?"

"There's one holdout who still thinks so. Not me. These wave patterns ran nineteen minutes on the first EEG, apparently for six minutes between hookups, and then thirty-one minutes on the second machine. Fifty-six minutes total before they abruptly stopped."

"How do you explain it?" Ethan asked.

Instead of answering him, O'Brien worked the keyboard, calling up a second display of data, which appeared above the first: another moving white line on the blue background, spiking from left to right. In this case, all the spikes were above the base line, none below.

"This is Whistler's respiration synchronized with the brain-wave data," O'Brien said. "Each spike is an inhalation. Exhalation takes place between spikes."

"Very regular."

"Very. Because the ventilator is breathing for him."

The physician tapped the keys again, and a third display shared the screen with the first two.

"This is heart function. Standard three-phase action. Diastole, atrial systole, ventricular systole. Slow but not too slow. Weak but not too weak. Slight irregularities, but nothing dangerous. Now look here at the brain waves."

The beta waves were doing the earthquake jitterbug once more.

Ethan said, "He's terrified again."

"In my opinion, yes. Yet there's no change in heart function. It's the same slow, somewhat weak beat with tolerable irregularities, exactly his deep-coma pattern ever since he was first admitted to the hospital almost three months ago. He's in a state of terror . . . yet his heart is calm."

"The heart's calm because he's comatose. Right?"

"Wrong. Even in a profound coma, Mr. Truman, there isn't this complete disconnect between the mind and body. When you're having a nightmare, the terror is imagined, not real, but heart function is affected just the same. The heart races during a nightmare."

For a moment, Ethan studied the violently jumping beta waves and compared them to the slow, steady heartbeat. "After fifty-six minutes of this, his brain activity returned to the long, slow delta waves?"

"That's right. Until he died the next morning."

"So if it's not two machines malfunctioning, how do you explain all of this, Doctor?"

"I don't. I can't. You asked me if there was anything unusual in the patient's file. Specifically, something . . . *uncanny*."

"Yes, but—"

"I don't have a dictionary handy, but I believe *uncanny* means something not normal, something extraordinary, something that can't be explained. I can only tell you what happened, Mr. Truman, not a damn thing about *why*."

Tongues of rain licked the windows.

With snuffle, growl, and keening petition, the wolfish wind begged entry.

Across the fabled city rolled a low protracted rumble.

Ethan and O'Brien looked toward the windows, and Ethan supposed that the physician, too, had envisioned a terrorist attack somewhere, women and babies murdered by the fascistic Islamic radicals who fed on wickedness and crawled the modern world with demon determination.

They listened to the sound slowly fade, and finally Dr. O'Brien said with relief, "Thunder."

"Thunder," Ethan agreed.

Thunder and lightning were not common to storms in southern California. This peal, in place of bomb blast, suggested a turbulent day ahead.

Beta waves, as jagged as lightning, struck repeatedly across the computer screen.

Comatose, Dunny had experienced a terrifying encounter that had occurred neither in this world nor in the land of dreams, but in some realm mysterious. He had engaged in a conversation without spoken words, as if he'd breathed in a ghost that had traveled to his lungs and thence into his arteries, by blood from heart to brain, there to haunt him in the shadowy rooms of his mind for fifty-six minutes.

CHAPTER 53

LIKE AN ARAB SHEIK IN YELLOW KAFFIYEH AND yellow cloak, brought here by the rubbing of a lamp and the magic of a genie, Corky Laputa was a bright whirl in the otherwise dismal house of the three-eyed freak.

Singing "Reunited" and then "Shake Your Groove Thing," both Peaches and Herb hits, he searched these cluttered chambers, rating them on a crud scale—cruddy, cruddier, cruddiest—as he sought what might remain of the first twenty thousand dollars that he had given Hokenberry a few weeks ago.

The beefy one might have written Corky's name in an address book, on an index card—even on a wall, considering how much these shabby walls resembled those of the grungiest public restroom. Corky didn't care about that. He hadn't given Hokenberry his real name, anyway.

Surely, with a memory about as reliable as that of a chuck steak, Hokenberry had scribbled Corky's phone number on a piece of paper somewhere in the bungalow. Corky wasn't worried about that, either. If eventually the police found it, the number would never lead them to him.

Every month or six weeks, Corky bought a new cell phone. It came with a new number and a virgin account in a false name with a phony address. He used this for all his sensitive calls related to his work in the service of chaos.

These phones were provided by a computer hacker nonpareil and anarchist-multimillionaire named Mick Sachatone. Mick sold them for six hundred bucks a pop. He guaranteed their viability for thirty days.

Usually, the phone company didn't realize that their system had been manipulated and didn't identify the bad account for two months. Then they shut off service and sought the perpetrator. By that time, Corky had thrown the phone in a Dumpster and had obtained a new one.

His purpose wasn't to save money but to guarantee his anonymity when engaged in activities that were against the law. Making a minor contribution to the eventual financial ruination of the phone company was a pleasant bonus.

Now Corky located Ned Hokenberry's trove of cash in a bedroom one degree more civilized than the hibernation cave of a bear. The floor was littered with dirty socks, magazines, empty bags of fried bacon rinds, empty paper buckets from Kentucky Fried Chicken, and sucked-clean chicken bones. The money had been stuffed in an empty box of jerky under the bed.

Of the twenty thousand, only fourteen remained. The other six thousand evidently had been spent on fast food and pork-fat snacks.

Corky took the money and left the jerky box.

In the dinette alcove off the living room, Hokenberry was still dead and no less ugly than before.

During their three previous encounters, Corky had deduced that Hokenberry was estranged from his family. Unmarried, less than ideal dating material, and not the type to have a network of friends who dropped in unannounced, the former rock-tour beef would probably not be found until the FBI came knocking, subsequent to young master Manheim's kidnapping.

Nevertheless, to guard against the accidental discovery of the body by a nosy neighbor or some such, Corky took Hokenberry's keys from a pegboard in the kitchen and locked the front door on his way out of the house. He dropped the keys into the overgrown shrubbery.

Like a growling hellhound loose in the halls of Heaven, thunder barked and grumbled through the low gray sky.

Corky's heart leaped with delight.

He looked up into the falling rain, in search of lightning, and then remembered that it would have come before the thunder. If there had been lightning, the bolt had not penetrated the clouds or had struck far away in the sprawling city.

The thunder must be an omen.

Corky didn't believe in any god or any devil. He did not believe in supernatural things of any shape or meaning. He believed only in the power of chaos.

Nonetheless, he chose to believe that the thunder should be taken as an omen, signifying that his trip this coming evening to Palazzo Rospo would unfold as planned and that he would return to his home with the sedated boy.

The universe might be a dumb machine, clattering nowhere but moving fast, with no purpose other than its own eventual cataclysmic destruction. Yet even so, it might from time to time cast off a bolt or a broken gear from which a thoughtful person could foretell its next turn of direction. The thunder was such a broken gear, and based upon the timbre and duration of it, Corky confidently predicted the success of his scheme.

If the biggest movie star in the world, living behind fortified walls and an electronic moat, with full-time security and bodyguards, could not keep his family safe, if the only son of the Face could be plucked from his Bel Air estate and spirited away, even though the actor had been explicitly warned by the delivery of six packages wrapped in black, then no family was safe *anywhere*. Neither the poor nor the rich. Neither the unknown nor the famous. Neither the godless nor the God-fearing.

That message would penetrate the public hour by hour, day by grueling day, as Channing Manheim's long and excruciating ordeal unfolded.

Corky intended first to destroy the captive boy emotionally, then mentally, and last of all physically. He would videotape this process, which he expected to take weeks. He would edit the tape, make copies on equipment that he had acquired for this project, and periodically pepper selected publications and television-news operations with evidence of Aelfric's brutalization.

Certain media would be loath to show any of the video or even still frames from it, but others would recognize the competitive advantage of acting without conscience or taste, and with noble words would justify a plunge into the grossly sensational. Thereafter, some of the squeamish would do likewise.

The boy's terror-stricken face would haunt the nation, and yet another blow in a long series would be struck at the foundations of America's order and stability. Millions of citizens would be robbed of their already shaky sense of security.

Two streets from Hokenberry's bungalow, as Corky approached his BMW, a lance of lightning pierced the clouds, thunder cracked, and a boil in the heavens burst. Rain that had drizzled suddenly fell by the ton, weight enough to press half the huff out of the wind.

If thunder alone had been an omen of his triumph, more thunder preceded by lightning was confirmation that he'd properly interpreted that first rolling peal.

The sky blazed again, and growled. Fat leaf-snapping droplets of cold rain roared through the trees and pounded, *pounded* the pavement.

For a sweet half-minute, Corky capered like Gene Kelly, singing "Shake Your Groove Thing," not caring who might see him.

Then he got in the car and drove away from there, for he had much work to do on this most important day of his life to date.

CHAPTER 54

A S ETHAN WAITED FOR MUSIC THAT WOULD wither the soul and for the hospital elevator that would bring it, his cell phone rang.

"Where are you?" Hazard Yancy asked.

"Our Lady of Angels. About to leave."

"You in the garage?"

"On my way down now."

"Upper or lower level?"

"Upper."

"What're you driving?"

"A white Expedition, like yesterday."

"Wait there. We have to talk." Hazard hung up.

Ethan rode the elevator alone and without music. Apparently the sound system was malfunctioning. Nothing but hiss-pop-crackle came from the ceiling speaker.

He had descended one floor when he thought that he detected a faint voice behind the static. Quickly it became less faint, though still too weak to convey meaning.

By the time he traveled three floors, he convinced himself that this was the eerie voice to which he had listened for half an hour on the phone the previous night. He had been so intent on understanding what it was saying that he'd fallen into something like a trance.

Drifting down from the ceiling speaker, in a fall of static as soft as snow, came his name. He heard it as if from a great distance but distinctly.

"Ethan . . . Ethan . . ."

On a foggy winter day at the beach or harbor, sea gulls in flight, high in muffling mist, sometimes called to one another with two-syllable cries that seemed part alarm and part searching signal issued in mournful hope of a reply, the most forlorn sound in the world. This call of *"Ethan, Ethan,"* as though echoing down to a ravine from a lofty peak, had that same quality of melancholy and urgency.

Listening to gulls, however, he had never imagined that he heard his name in their desolate voices. Nor had he ever thought that their plaints in the fog sounded like Hannah, as the far voice behind the speaker static sounded like her now.

She no longer called his name, but she cried out something not quite decipherable. Her tone was the same that you might use to shout a warning at a man standing on a sidewalk in complete ignorance of a terrible weight of broken cornice falling toward him from atop the building at his back.

Between the lobby and the upper level of the garage, half a floor from his destination, Ethan pressed STOP on the control panel. The cab braked, sagging slightly and rebounding on its cables.

Even if this was indeed a voice speaking to him—and to him alone—through the overhead speaker, rather than proof of mental imbalance, he couldn't allow himself to be hypnotized by it as he had been on the phone.

He thought of fogbound nights and the unwary sailors who heard the singing of the Lorelei. They turned their ships toward her voice, seeking to understand the alluring promise of her words, steered onto her rock, wrecked their vessels, and drowned.

This voice was more likely to be that of the Lorelei than that of his lost Hannah. To desire what is forever beyond reach, to seek it in disregard of reason, is the fateful rock in an endless fog.

Anyway, he hadn't brought the elevator to a halt in order to puzzle out the words of the might-be warning. Heart knocking, he pressed STOP because he'd suddenly been overcome with the conviction that when the doors slid open, the garage would not lie beyond them.

Crazily, he expected thick fog and black water. Or a precipice and a yawning abyss. The voice would be out there, beyond the water, beyond the chasm, and he would have nowhere to go but toward it.

In another elevator, Monday afternoon, ascending toward Dunny's apartment, he had been stricken by claustrophobia.

Here again, the four walls crowded closer than they had been when he'd first boarded the cab. The ceiling squeezed lower, lower. He was going to be compressed meat in a can.

He put his hands over his ears to block the ghostly voice.

As the air seemed to grow hotter, thicker, Ethan heard himself straining to breathe, gasping on each inhalation, wheezing with each exhalation, and he was reminded of Fric in an asthma attack. At the thought of the boy, his heart hammered harder than ever, and with one hand he reached toward the START button on the control panel.

As the walls continued to close upon him, they seemed to press into his mind more crazy ideas. Instead of black water and fog where the hospital garage should be, perhaps he'd step out of the elevator to find himself in that black-and-white apartment with the walls of watchful birds, with Rolf Reynerd alive and drawing a pistol from a bag of potato chips. Shot in the gut again, Ethan would receive no reprieve this time.

He hesitated, didn't push the button.

Maybe because his labored breathing had recalled Fric in an asthmatic phase, Ethan began to think that among the faint and not quite comprehensible words coming from the overhead speaker was the boy's name. *"Fric . . ."* When he held his breath and concentrated, he couldn't hear it. When he breathed, the name came again. Or did it?

In that other elevator, Monday afternoon, the passing bout of claustrophobia had been a sublimation of another dread that he had not wanted to face: the irrational and yet persistent fear that in Dunny's apartment he would find his old friend dead but animated, as cold as a corpse but lively.

He suspected that this current claustrophobia and the fear of Reynerd resurrected also masked another anxiety that he was reluctant to face, that he could not quite fish from his subconscious.

Fric? Fric was emotionally vulnerable, and no wonder, but in no physical danger. The skeleton staff at the estate still numbered ten, counting Chef Hachette and the groundskeeper, Mr. Yorn. Estate security was formidable. The real danger to Fric remained that some lunatic might get at Channing Manheim, leaving the boy fatherless.

Ethan pressed START.

The elevator moved again. In but a moment it stopped at the upper level of the parking garage.

Perhaps he would step out and find himself on a rainy street, in the path of an out-of-control PT Cruiser.

The door slid aside, revealing nothing more impossible than the concrete walls of an underground garage and ranks of vehicles huddled under fluorescent lights.

As he walked to the Expedition, his ragged breathing quickly grew normal. His racing heart not only slowed but also settled out of his throat, into his chest where it belonged.

Behind the wheel of the SUV, he pushed the master switch to engage the power locks on all the doors.

Through the windshield he could see nothing but a concrete wall mottled by water stains and car-exhaust deposits. Here and there, over time, florescences of lime had risen to the surface.

His imagination wanted to search for images in this mottling, as it sometimes hunted big game and collected menageries among the shifting shapes of clouds. Here, he saw only decomposing faces and the tumbled, tangled bodies of the cruelly murdered. He might have been sitting before a ghastly mural of the many victims in the names of whom he, as a homicide detective, had sought justice.

He tipped his head back, closed his eyes, and let the tension shiver out of him.

After a while, he considered turning on the radio to pass the time until Hazard arrived. Sheryl Crow, Barenaked Ladies, Chris Isaak, without orchestral strings and timpanis and French horns, might mellow his mood.

He was reluctant to click the switch. He suspected that instead of the usual music, news, and talk shows, he would discover, from one end of the dial to the other, only the voice that might be Hannah's, futilely trying to speak to him on every frequency.

Knuckles on glass—*rap-rap-rap*—startled him. Wearing a rolled seaman's cap and a scowl to curdle vinegar, Hazard Yancy peered through the passenger's window.

Ethan unlocked the doors.

Filling the SUV as fully as he might have filled a bumper car at a carnival, Hazard climbed into the front passenger's seat and pulled the door shut. Although he had more knees than knee space, he didn't adjust the power controls to move the seat back. He seemed nervous. "They find Dunny?"

"Who?"

"The hospital."

"No."

"Then why're you here?"

"I talked to the doctor who signed the death certificate, trying to figure it out."

"You get anywhere?"

"Right back where I started—lookin' up my own ass."

"Not a view that'll draw tourists," Hazard said. "Sam Kesselman has the flu."

Ethan needed Kesselman—the detective assigned to the ormolu-lamp murder of Rolf Reynerd's mother—to read Reynerd's unfinished screenplay and then to track down the real-life inspiration for the murderous professor depicted in its pages.

"When's he back on the job?" Ethan asked.

"His wife says he can't even keep chicken soup on his stomach. Looks like we won't see him till after Christmas."

"Anybody partners with him?"

"Right at the start, Glo Williams had a piece of it, but the case went cold fast, and he stepped out."

"Get him back in?"

"He's on the rape-and-chop of that eleven-year-old girl that's all over the news, no time for anything else."

"Man, the world gets sicker by the week."

"By the hour. Otherwise, we'd be unemployed. They call Mina Reynerd's case Vamp and the Lamp 'cause in pictures of her when she was younger, she looked like one of those vamps in the old movies, like Theda Bara or Jean Harlow. The file is strictly on Kesselman's desk, along with other active cases."

"So even after Christmas, he might not get to it first thing."

Hazard stared at the concrete wall beyond the windshield, as if stocking a menagerie of his own. Maybe he saw gazelles and kangaroos. More likely, he could not avoid seeing battered children, strangled women, the bodies of men torn by gunfire.

Memories of innocent victims. His ghost family. Always with him. They were as real to him as the badge he carried, more real than the pension that he might never live to collect.

"After Christmas isn't soon enough," Hazard said. "I had this dream."

Ethan looked at him, waited. Then: "What dream?"

Rolling his Paul Bunyan shoulders, shifting on the seat to gain legroom, looking as uncomfortable as Babe the Blue Ox in a canary cage, Hazard stared at the concrete wall while he said matter-of-factly, "You were with me in Reynerd's apartment. He shot you in the gut. Next, we're in an ambulance. You're not gonna make it.

They have these Christmas decorations in the ambulance. Tinsel, little bells. You ask me for a set of the bells. I take one set down, try to give them to you, but you're gone, you're dead."

Ethan turned his attention to the parking-garage wall once more. Among the decomposing corpses that his imagination identified in the stains and subtleties of texture, he expected to see his own face.

"I wake up," Hazard continued, still focused on the mottled concrete, "there's someone in the room with me. Standing over the bed. A darker shape in the dark. Some guy. I'm up, I'm at him, but he's not there. Now he's across the room. I go after him. He moves. He's quick. He doesn't walk, he like *glides*. My piece is in my holster, hanging on a chair. I get it. He keeps moving, quick, too quick, gliding, like he's playing with me. We circle the room. I get to a light switch, click on a lamp. He's at my closet doors, his back to me. Mirrored closet doors. He walks into the mirror. Disappears into the mirror."

"This is still the dream," Ethan suggested.

"I told you, *I wake up*, there's someone in the room with me," Hazard reminded him. "I didn't get a good look at him, his back to me, just a glimpse in the mirror, but I think it was Dunny Whistler. I open the closet door. He's not in there. Where is he—in the damn *mirror*?"

"Sometimes in a dream," Ethan said, "you wake up, but the waking up is just part of the nightmare, and you're really still dreaming."

"I search the apartment. Don't find anybody. Back in the bedroom what I *do* find are these."

Ethan heard the sweet silvery ringing of small bells.

He looked away from the concrete wall.

Hazard held up an array of three concentrically strung bells like those that had hung in the ambulance.

Their eyes met.

Ethan knew that Hazard had instantly read not the nature of his secrets but certainly the fact that he *had* secrets.

The astonishing things that had happened to Ethan in less than thirty hours, and now also to Hazard, plus the inexplicable case of dead Dunny walking and possibly orchestrating the murder of Reynerd: All this had to be connected somehow to the contents of the six black boxes and the threat against Manheim.

"What aren't you telling me," Hazard demanded.

After a long pause, Ethan said, "I have a set of bells, too."

"You get yours in a dream like I did?"

"I got mine just before I died in an ambulance late yesterday afternoon."

CHAPTER 55

FREE OF BOTH INSIPID MUSIC AND VOICES FROM Beyond, four flights of stairs led down to the lowest of the three subterranean levels of the hospital.

Ethan and Hazard followed the familiar, brightly lighted white corridor past the garden room to a set of double doors. Beyond lay the ambulance garage.

Among other vehicles belonging to the hospital, four van-type ambulances stood side by side. Empty parking stalls suggested that additional units in the fleet were at work in the rainy day.

Ethan went to the nearest ambulance. He hesitated, then opened the rear door.

Inside, red tinsel was strung at the ceiling along both the left and right sides of the compartment. Six clusters of tiny bells hung here, as well, one set at the beginning, another at the middle, and a third at the end of each garland of tinsel.

At the second ambulance, Hazard said, "Here."

Ethan joined him at the open back door.

Two lengths of red tinsel. Only five sets of bells. The missing set, in the middle of the right-hand garland of tinsel, was the one that had been given to him as he lay dying.

A cold tremble, almost a pressure, moved slowly down the center of his back, as if the fleshless tip of a skeletal finger were tracing his spine from cervical vertebrae to coccyx.

Hazard said, "One set of bells is missing, but between us we have two."

"Maybe not. Maybe we have the same set."

"What do you mean?"

Behind them, a man said, "May I help you?"

Turning, Ethan saw the paramedic who had attended to him in the racing ambulance less than twenty-four hours ago.

The discovery of the bells in his hand outside Forever Roses had already been one piece of dark magic too many. Now, to come face to face with this man, seen before only in that dream, made the death in the ambulance seem real even though he still breathed, still lived.

The shock of recognition was not mutual. The paramedic regarded Ethan with no greater interest than he might have shown toward any stranger.

Hazard flashed his department ID. "What's your name, sir?"

"Cameron Sheen."

"Mr. Sheen, we need to know what calls this particular ambulance answered yesterday afternoon."

"What time exactly?" the paramedic asked.

Hazard looked at Ethan, and Ethan found his voice. "Between five and six o'clock."

"I was crewing it then with Rick Laslow," Sheen said. "Couple minutes after five, there's a police call, an eleven-eighty, accident with major injury, corner of Westwood Boulevard and Wilshire."

That was miles from the location at which Ethan had bounced off the PT Cruiser.

"Honda tangled with a Hummer," Sheen said. "We carried the guy in the car. He looked like he'd butted heads with a Peterbilt, not just a Hummer. We took him street to surgery in personal-best time, and from what I hear, he'll come out of it good enough to jump and hump again."

Ethan named the two streets that formed the intersection half a block from Forever Roses. "You catch calls that far west?"

"Sure. If we figure we know a way to beat the gridlock, we go wherever the blood is."

"Did you answer a call to that intersection yesterday?"

The paramedic shook his head. "Not me and Rick. Maybe one of the other units. You could check the dispatcher's log."

"You look familiar to me," Ethan said. "Have we met somewhere before?"

Sheen frowned, seemed to search his memory. Then: "Not that I recall. So do you want to check the dispatcher's log?"

"No," Hazard said, "but there's one more thing." He pointed at one of the garlands of tinsel in the back of the ambulance. "The middle set of bells is missing."

Peering into the van, Sheen said, "Missing bells? Are they? I guess so. What about it?"

"We're wondering what happened to them."

Puzzlement worked Sheen's face into a squint. "You are? Those little bells? Don't recall anything happening to them during my watch. Maybe one of the guys on another shift could help you."

At a glance from Hazard, Ethan shrugged. Hazard slammed shut the ambulance door.

Sheen's puzzlement resolved into amazement. "You don't mean they send two detectives 'cause maybe someone stole a two-dollar Christmas ornament?"

Neither Ethan nor Hazard had an answer for that.

Sheen should have let it go then, but like a lot of people these days, his ignorance of the true nature of a cop's work allowed him to feel smugly superior to anyone with a badge. "What's it take to get a kitten out of a tree—a SWAT team?"

Hazard said, "The missing ornament isn't simply a matter of two dollars, is it, Detective Truman?"

"No," Ethan agreed, falling into their old rhythm, "it's the principle of the thing. And it's a hate crime."

"Definitely a felony hate crime under the California Criminal Code," Hazard deadpanned.

"For the duration of the season," Ethan said, "we're assigned to the Ornament and Manger Scene Defacement Response Team."

"That's a division," Hazard added, "of the Christmas Spirit Task Force established pursuant to the Anti-Hate Act of 2001."

A tentative smile crept across Sheen's face as he cocked his head first at Ethan, then at Hazard. "You're goofing me, right, doing *Dragnet*."

Employing the intense and disapproving stare with which he could wither everything from hard-case thugs to flower arrangements, Hazard said, "Are you a Christian hater, Mr. Sheen?"

Sheen's creeping smile froze before it fully formed. "What?"

"Do you," Ethan asked, "believe in freedom of religion or are you one of those who think the United States Constitution guarantees you freedom *from* religion?"

Blinking the smile out of his eyes, licking it off his lips, the paramedic said, "Sure, of course, freedom of religion, who doesn't believe in it?"

"If we were to obtain a warrant to search your residence right now," Hazard said, "would we find a collection of anti-Christian hate literature, Mr. Sheen?"

"What? Me? I don't hate anybody. I'm a get-along guy. What're you talking about?"

"Would we find bomb-making materials?" Ethan asked.

As Sheen's smirk had frozen and cracked apart under Hazard's cold stare, so now the color drained from his face, leaving him as gray as the unpainted concrete walls of the ambulance garage.

Backing away from Hazard and Ethan, raising his hands as if to call a time-out, Sheen said, "What is this? Are you serious? This is crazy. What—there's a two-dollar Christmas ornament missing, so I should get a lawyer?"

"If you have one," Hazard said solemnly, "maybe you'd be smart to give him a call."

Still not sure what to believe, Sheen backed away another step, two, then pivoted from them and hurried toward the dayroom in which ambulance crews waited to be dispatched.

"SWAT team, my ass," Hazard grumbled.

Ethan smiled. "You da man."

"*You* da man."

Ethan had forgotten how much easier life could be with backup, especially backup with a sense of humor.

"You should rejoin the force," Hazard said as they crossed the garage toward the doors to the garden-room corridor. "We could save the world, have some fun."

On the stairs to the upper level of the public garage, Ethan said, "Supposing all this craziness stops sooner or later—being gut shot but not, the bells, the voice on the phone, a guy walking into your closet mirror. You think it's possible just to go back to the usual cop stuff like nothing strange ever happened?"

"What am I supposed to do—become a monk?"

"Seems like this ought to . . . change things."

"I'm happy who I am," Hazard said. "I'm already as cool as cool gets. Don't you think I'm cool to the chromosomes?"

"You're walking ice."

"Not to say I don't have heat."

"Not to say," Ethan agreed.

"I've got plenty of heat."

"You're so cool, you're hot."

"Exactly. So there's no reason for me to change unless maybe I meet Jesus, and He slaps me upside the head."

They weren't in a graveyard, weren't whistling, but the tenor of their words, echoing off the crypt-cold walls of the stairwell, brought to Ethan's mind old movie images of boys masking their fear with bravado as they journeyed through a cemetery at high midnight.

CHAPTER 56

ON A GRINDSTONE OF SELF-DENIAL, WITH THE diligence of a true obsessive, Brittina Dowd had sharpened herself into a long thin blade. When she walked, her clothes seemed certain to be cut to shreds by the scissoring movement of her body.

Her hips had been honed until they were almost as fragile as bird bones. Her legs resembled those of a flamingo. Her arms had no more substance than wings stripped of their feathers. Brittina seemed to be determined to whittle herself until a brisk breeze could carry her aloft, high into the realm of wren and sparrow.

She was not a single blade, in fact, but an entire Swiss Army knife with all its cutting edges and pointed tools deployed.

Corky Laputa might have loved her if she had not also been ugly.

Although he didn't love Brittina, he made love to her. The disorder into which she had shaped her skeletal body thrilled him. This was like making love to Death.

Only twenty-six, she had assiduously prepared herself for early-onset osteoporosis, as though she yearned to be shattered in a fall, reduced to fragments as completely as a crystal vase knocked off a shelf onto a stone floor.

In their passion, Corky always expected to be punctured by one of her knees or elbows, or to hear Brittina crack apart beneath him.

"Do me," she said, "do me," and managed to make it sound less like an invitation to sex than like a request for assisted suicide.

Her bed was narrow, suitable only for a sleeper who did not toss and turn, who lay as unmoving as the average occupant of a casket, by far too narrow for the wild rutting of which they both were capable.

She had furnished the room with a single bed because she'd never had a lover and had expected to remain a virgin. Corky had romanced her as easily as he could have crushed a hummingbird in his fist.

The narrow bed stood in a room on the top floor of a narrow two-story Victorian house. The lot was deep but too narrow to qualify as a residential building site under current city codes.

Almost sixty years ago, just after the war, an eccentric dog fancier had designed and built the curious place. He lived in it with two greyhounds and two whippets.

Eventually he'd been paralyzed by a stroke. After several days passed during which their master had not fed them, the starving dogs ate him.

That had been forty years ago. The subsequent history of this residence at times had been as colorful and on occasion nearly as grisly as the life and ghastly death of its first owner.

The vibe of the house caught Brittina's attention just like the high-frequency shriek of a dog whistle might have pricked the ears of a whippet. She'd purchased it with a portion of an inheritance that she received from her paternal grandmother.

Brittina was a graduate student at the same university that had provided multigeneration employment for the Laputa family. In another eighteen months, she would earn a doctorate in American literature, which she largely despised.

Although she had not blown her entire inheritance on the house, she needed to supplement her investment income with other revenue. She had served as a graduate assistant to keep herself in chocolate-flavored Slim-Fast and ipecac.

Then, six months ago, Channing Manheim's personal assistant had approached the chairperson of the university's English department to explain that a new tutor would be required for the famous actor's son. Only academicians of the highest caliber need apply.

The chairperson consulted Corky, who was vice-chairperson of the department, and Corky recommended Ms. Dowd.

He'd known that she would be hired because, first of all, the idiot movie star would be impressed by her dramatic appearance. Cadaverous paleness, a gaunt face, and the body of an anorexic nun would be seen as proof that Brittina cared little for the pleasures of the flesh, that she enjoyed largely a life of the mind, that she was therefore a genuine intellectual.

In the entertainment business, only image mattered. Manheim would believe, therefore, that appearance equaled reality in other professions, as well.

Furthermore, Brittina Dowd was an intellectual snob who peppered her speech with academic jargon more impenetrable than the lab-speak of microbiologists. If the young woman's emaciation didn't convince the movie star of her intellectual credentials, her big words would.

The evening before Brittina went to her job interview, Corky poured on charm as thick as clotted cream, and she at once proved to be famished not only for food but also for flattery. She allowed herself to indulge her appetite for adoration, and Corky bedded her then for the first time.

Ultimately, she became Aelfric Manheim's tutor in English and literature, making regularly scheduled visits to Palazzo Rospo.

Prior to this, Rolf Reynerd and Corky had discussed, in general terms, the blow that might be struck in the name of social disorder by proving that even a celebrity of worldwide renown was vulnerable to the agents of chaos. They had not been able to settle on an ideal target until Corky's lover was hired by Channing Manheim.

From Brittina, in bed and out, Corky had learned much about the Manheim estate. Indeed, she disclosed the existence of Line 24—and, more important, told him about the security guard, Ned Hokenberry, valiant defender of Peaches and Herb, who according to Fric had been dismissed for leaving phony messages from the dead on that answering machine.

Brittina had also painted for Corky a detailed psychological portrait of Channing's son. This would be invaluable when, with Aelfric prisoner, he proceeded to destroy the boy emotionally.

In the afterglow of insect-frenzy sex, Brittina never once had been suspicious that Corky's interest in all things Manheim might be related to anything other than simple curiosity. She was an unwitting conspirator, a naive girl in love.

"Do me," Brittina insisted now, "do me," and Corky obliged.

Wind battered the narrow house and hard rain lashed its skinny flanks, and on the narrow bed, Brittina thrashed like an agitated mantis.

This time, in their dreamy postcoital cuddle, Corky had no need to ask questions related to Manheim. He had more information on that subject than he needed to know.

As occasionally was her wont, Brittina drifted into a monologue about the uselessness of literature: the antiquated nature of the written word; the coming triumph of image over language; those ideas that she called memes, which supposedly spread like viruses from mind to mind, creating new ways of thinking in society.

Corky figured that his brain would explode if she didn't shut up, after which he would *need* a new way to think.

Eventually, Brittina clattered up from their love nest with the intention of rattling off to the bathroom.

Reaching under the bed, Corky retrieved the pistol where earlier he had hidden it.

When he shot her twice in the back, he half expected Brittina to shatter into bone splinters and dust, as if she were an ancient mummy made brittle by two centuries of dehydration, but she only dropped dead in a pale, angular heap.

CHAPTER 57

DURING THE YEARS THEY'D BEEN OFFICIAL partners, Ethan and Hazard had gone by the book as much as it is ever possible to go by a book that is written largely by people who have never done the job.

On this December day, however, unofficially partners once more, they were bad boys. Being bad boys made Ethan uneasy, but it gave him the comforting feeling that at least they were taking control of the situation.

A notice on Rolf Reynerd's door warned that Apartment 2B was the site of an ongoing police investigation. The premises remained off-limits to all but authorized personnel of the police department and the district attorney's office.

They ignored the warning.

The deadbolt lock on Rolf Reynerd's apartment door was covered with a police seal. Ethan cracked it, peeled it.

Hazard had with him a Lockaid lock-release gun, an item sold exclusively to law-enforcement agencies. In ordinary circumstances, he would have requisitioned this device with the proper paperwork, specifying the exact intended use, virtually always with reference to an existing search warrant.

These were not ordinary circumstances.

Hazard had gotten his hands on one of the department's Lockaids by unconventional means. He would be walking a razor's edge between righteousness and ruin until he returned the device to the equipment locker where it belonged.

"When you're up against some mojo man who fades into mirrors," he said, "your ass is hanging over a cliff anyway."

Hazard slid the thin pick of the Lockaid into the key channel of the deadbolt, under the pin tumblers. He squeezed the trigger four times before the steel spring in the gun managed to lodge all the pins at the shear line and thereby fully disengage the lock.

Ethan followed Hazard into the apartment, closing the door behind them. He tried to step around and over the stains—Reynerd's blood—that marred the white carpet just inside the threshold.

He had spilled rivers of his own blood on this carpet. Died on it. The experience rose in memory, too vivid to have been a dream.

The black-and-white furnishings, art, and decorations proved to be as he remembered them.

On the walls, a flock of pigeons was frozen in midwhirl. Like white chalk checks on gray slate, geese flew across a somber sky, and a parliament of owls perched on a barn roof, deliberating over the fate of mice.

Hazard had been present the previous night during the first search of the apartment. He knew what had been collected as possible evidence and what had been left behind.

He went directly to that corner of the living room in which stood a black-lacquered desk with faux-ivory drawer pulls. "What we need is probably here," he said, and searched the drawers from top to bottom.

Crows on an iron fence, an eagle on a rock, a fierce-eyed heron as prehistoric as a pterodactyl: All peered into this living room from other times, other places.

Paranoid and unashamed of it, Ethan sensed that when he looked away from the large photographs, the birds therein turned their heads to watch him, all aware that he ought to be dead and that the man who had collected their images should be alive to admire them.

"Here," Hazard said, withdrawing a shoebox from one of the desk drawers. "Bank statements, canceled checks."

They sat at the stainless-steel and black-Formica dinette table to review Reynerd's financial records.

Beside the table: a window. Beyond the window: the tumultuous day, entirely in shades of gray, wind-whipped, awash, now without the thunder and lightning, yet still foreboding, dark and dire.

The light proved too dim to facilitate their work. Hazard got up and switched on the small black-and-white ceramic chandelier over the table.

Eleven bundles of checks had been bound with rubber bands, one for each month of the current year from January through November. The canceled checks from the current month would not be forwarded by the bank until mid-January.

When they finished, they would have to return everything to the shoebox and replace the box in the desk drawer exactly as Hazard found it. Sam Kesselman, the detective assigned to Mina Reynerd's murder, would no doubt review these same checks when he recovered from the flu, returned to work after Christmas, and read the dead actor's partial screenplay.

If they waited for Kesselman, however, Channing Manheim might by then be dead. And Ethan, too.

They needed to look through only those checks written in the first eight months of the year, prior to Mina Reynerd's murder.

Hazard took four months' worth of checks. He pushed four packets across the table to Ethan.

In the screenplay, an out-of-work and underappreciated actor had taken an acting class at a university, where he'd met a professor with whom he had devised a scheme to kill the biggest movie star in the world. If the fictional academic had been inspired by a murderous professor in real life, a tuition check might suggest an institution of higher learning at which the search should begin.

Soon they discovered that Rolf Reynerd had been a fiend for continuing education. His entries on the memo line of each check were meticulous and helpful. In the first eight months of the year, he'd attended a pair of three-day weekend conferences on acting, another on screenwriting, a one-day seminar on publicity and self-promotion, and two university-extension courses in American literature.

"Six possibilities," Hazard said. "I guess we've got a busy day ahead of us."

"The sooner we check them out, the better," Ethan agreed. "But Manheim doesn't return from Florida until Thursday afternoon."

"So?"

"We've got tomorrow yet."

Hazard looked past Ethan, at the window, and gazed into the storm, as though he were reading rain with the same expectation of meaning that a soothsayer might bring to the reading of sodden tea leaves.

After consideration, he said, "Maybe we shouldn't absolutely count on tomorrow. I get the feeling we're running out of time."

CHAPTER 58

THE THINLY DRESSED BONES, TUMBLED ON the floor, issued no cry of surprise, no groan, no meme.

To be sure that Brittina was dead, Corky wanted to shoot her once more, this time in the back of the head. Unfortunately, his pistol had begun to bark.

Even the highest quality sound suppressor deteriorates with use. Regardless of the material used as baffling in the barrel extension, it compacts a little with each shot, diminishing in function.

Furthermore, Corky didn't possess a suppressor of the quality employed by agents of the CIA. You could not expect materials and craftsmanship equal to those of a major firearms manufacturer when you purchased a silencer from anti-veal activists.

He had popped Hokenberry six times and Brittina twice. In just eight shots, the pistol had begun to find its voice again.

Perhaps the most recent round had not been audible outside the narrow house, but the next report would be louder. He was a man who took calculated risks, but this one didn't add up.

In the trunk of his car, in the tool kit, he kept a fresh sound suppressor, as well as a pair of night-vision goggles and a kit of hypodermic syringes with vials of sedatives and poisons. And two live hand grenades.

As always, however, he had parked a few blocks from Brittina's house, on a street different from hers. Because Corky was a tenured professor and she was a student, they had been assiduously discreet about their romantic relationship.

Going to and from the BMW to secure a replacement suppressor seemed like an unnecessary complication. Instead, he crouched beside his riddled lover and felt her throat, trying to detect a pulse in her carotid artery.

She was as dead as disco.

In the bathroom, Corky washed his genitals, hands, and face. To be in love with chaos, one did not have to be scornful of good personal hygiene.

From the medicine cabinet, he withdrew a large bottle of Scope mouthwash. With Brittina dead and quite incapable of being offended, Corky took a swig directly from the container, and gargled.

Her kisses left him with a bad taste.

As a result of Brittina's habit of fasting more than not, she had frequently been in a state of ketosis, during which her body was forced to burn what meager stores of fat it might have been jealously guarding. Among the symptoms of ketosis are nausea and vomiting, but a more pleasant symptom is sweet, fruity-smelling breath.

Corky enjoyed the fragrance of her breath, but after swapping a lot of spit, tongue to tongue, he was sometimes left with a sour aftertaste. Like all things in an imperfect world, lovemaking always comes with a price.

In this case, of course, the price had been greater for Brittina than for him.

He dressed quickly. In his stocking feet, he descended the narrow stairs to the cramped kitchen at the back of the house.

His yellow slicker and rain hat hung on a wall peg in the small screened porch off the kitchen. His black boots stood to one side of the slicker.

Rain crashed in such heavy cascades upon the porch roof that it sounded like a downpour in the jungled tropics. He half expected to see grinning crocodiles in the backyard and pythons slithering in the trees.

He slipped the pistol into one of the capacious pockets of the slicker. From another pocket he withdrew a length of flexible rubber tubing and an object that resembled a snack-size container of yogurt, though it was black with a red lid and featured no illustrations of luscious fruit.

With no reason remaining to be respectful of Brittina's clean floors, he pulled on his boots and returned to the house. The deep wet tread of his rubber soles squeaked on the vinyl tile in the kitchen.

His work was not yet completed. He had left behind evidence that would convict him of murder. Semen, hair, fingerprints—all must be eliminated.

From the day that he'd begun visiting this pinched place, months previously, he had gone without the latex gloves that he customarily wore at the scenes of capital crimes. Even though Brittina Dowd was nothing if not an eccentric, she would surely have grown suspicious of a lover who at all times wore surgical gloves.

Steeper and narrower stairs than any others in the house led down from the kitchen to a garage in which three of the four walls were underground. Gloom gathered here as luxuriously as ever it had coiled in any catacomb or dungeon.

Corky could almost hear a multitude of spiders plucking their silken harp strings.

Four small windows in the garage door would have admitted some sun on a classic California day. Now the gray storm gloom could not penetrate the dusty glass.

He switched on a bare bulb overhead, providing hardly enough light by which to drain the god of Zoroastrianism.

The god of Zoroastrianism is Ahura Mazda. Brittina's car was a Mazda, without the Ahura, but Corky enjoyed his little joke anyway.

From the trunk, he removed four hairspray-size aerosol cans with any one of which a stranded motorist could inflate a flat tire and at the same time seal the puncture in it. He set these aside and then took from the trunk a pair of empty two-gallon gasoline cans.

He had purchased these items for Brittina, in addition to road flares and a yellow pennant emblazoned with EMERGENCY in bold black letters, and had insisted that she keep them in the trunk of her Zoroastrian god at all times.

She had been touched by his concern and had said that diamonds would not have proved his love as surely as did these humble gifts. They were, in fact, part of his preparations to dispose of her body when the day arrived to kill her.

Corky would never deny that he could be brilliantly romantic when required, but greater than his flair for romance was his talent for meticulous preparation. Whether he was roasting a Thanksgiving turkey or murdering an inconvenient lover, or scheming to kidnap the son of the biggest movie star in the world, he approached the task with considerable thought and patience, taking all the time neces-sary to develop a flawless strategy as well as tactics certain to ensure success.

She had never asked why *two* fuel cans, when one would have been all that she could easily carry. He had *known* that she would not ask or even wonder, for she had been a woman of images and memes and utopian dreams, not one with an interest in math or logic.

He set the empty two-gallon cans on the floor. He fed a shorter end of rubber tubing into the fuel port of the car. A suck on the longer end was required to prime the siphon.

Much practice at this sort of thing ensured that Corky drew as lit-tle fumes into his lungs as possible and that none of Shell Oil's finest got in his mouth. The flow came quickly as he tucked the longer end into the first can.

When four gallons had been drawn and both cans filled, Corky car-ried the containers up to the ground floor. He left the trailing end of the siphon to spill a stream of gasoline on the garage floor.

He returned for the four aerosol cans. In the kitchen, he placed two of these on the lowest rack of the bottom oven. He left the other two on the lowest rack of the top oven.

On his way upstairs with one of the two-gallon cans, he switched off the thermostat on the main floor, and then the thermostat on the upper floor. This would prevent the electric starter from striking a spark in the natural-gas furnace and possibly triggering an explosion of accumulated gasoline fumes before Corky had left the house.

Leaving the cap on the can, pouring from the spout, he liberally splashed the pale naked body of Brittina Dowd. Her long hair offered tinder, but she didn't have much fat to feed the fire.

After pouring no more than a quart of fuel in the bathroom, he distributed perhaps half a gallon over the rumpled bedclothes. He didn't prime the two other small upstairs rooms because he'd never been in them and because he didn't need to saturate every corner to achieve the effect he wanted.

From the bedroom he drizzled an uninterrupted gasoline trail into the narrow upstairs hallway and down the stairs to the ground floor. At the bottom of the steps, he cast aside the empty can and picked up the full one.

He continued in a looping fashion through the living room and the dining room, to the kitchen doorway. There he set the can on the threshold. He unscrewed the cap and tossed it aside.

From a jacket pocket, he retrieved the black-and-red object that was about the size of a single-serving yogurt container: a chemical-action detonator.

The casing of the detonator was somewhat pliable. He shaped it into the hole that had been covered by the screw-on cap, plugging the two-gallon can in which approximately half a gallon of gasoline remained.

He popped a ring tab off the red cap. This initiated a chemical process that would rapidly generate heat and, in four minutes, an explosion fiery enough to ignite the remaining contents of the two-gallon can and the trail of fuel leading away from it to the bedroom on the second floor, to the corpse.

This would be a bad time for the doorbell to ring.

No chimes sounded, of course, because in addition to his fine strategy, solid tactics, and meticulous preparation, he could count on Laputa luck. His guardian angel was chaos, and he was always at the safe calm eye of its world-destroying force.

He returned to the ovens and latched both doors as required to initiate the self-cleaning cycle. On each he pressed a button marked CLEAN.

Heat would rapidly expand the pressurized contents of the cans, which would explode. Because the doors were latched, the power of the explosions couldn't easily be vented. The resultant damage to the ovens might be severe enough to cause a natural-gas leak and a larger blast.

The utter destruction of the house didn't require the oven trick to work. The four gallons of high-grade accelerant that he had poured throughout the small structure and the additional gallons pooling on the garage floor would feed the flames and obliterate every source of his DNA, from semen to hairs, and every fingerprint that he'd left behind. Nonetheless, he believed in redundancy whenever possible.

On the back porch, Corky shrugged into his voluminous yellow slicker. He jammed the droopy rain hat on his head.

He pushed through the screen door and went down the steps. At the end of the backyard, he passed through a gate into an alleyway and never glanced again at the narrow house.

He thrived in the rain.

Cataracts gushed from the sky. The racing torrents in the gutters overflowed the curbs.

This downpour would not quench the fire that he had engineered. The gasoline-fed flames would thoroughly gut the wooden structure before the walls collapsed and offered admission to the rain.

Indeed, the storm was his ally. Badly flooded intersections and snarled traffic would delay the fire engines.

He had just turned a corner and come within sight of his BMW when he heard the first explosion in the distance. The sound was low, flat, muffled, but ugly.

Soon he would have erased everyone and every clue that might have led the police to him after the assault on Palazzo Rospo.

CHAPTER 59

FROM THE MORE REMOTE ROOMS IN PALAZZO Rospo, Fric gathered earthquake lights in a picnic hamper.

The mansion and the outlying buildings had been re-engineered for seismic security and retrofitted with structural reinforcements that were supposed to ensure little or no damage even from a two-minute shaker peaking at 8.0 on the Richter scale.

Generally, 8.0 was considered to be the kiss-your-ass-good-bye number. Earthquakes that big struck only in movies.

If a humongous killer quake knocked out the city's power supply, Palazzo Rospo would be able to rely on gasoline-fueled generators in a subterranean vault that had two-foot-thick, poured-in-place, steel-reinforced walls and ceiling. Following a regional catastrophe, the mansion should remain fully lighted, the computers should continue to run, the elevators should still be operating, the refrigerators should remain cold.

In the rose garden, the carved-granite fountain of urinating cherubs should continue to sprinkle eternally.

This backup would be less useful if heretofore unknown volcanoes erupted under Los Angeles and disgorged rivers of molten lava that turned hundreds of square miles into a smoldering wasteland or if an asteroid smashed into Bel Air. But even a star as famous and rich as Ghost Dad could not protect himself from cataclysm on a planetary scale.

If the Swiss-made generators in the bunker were disabled, then Frankenstein-castle banks of twenty-year batteries, each as big as a casket standing on end, instantly came into service. These supported limited emergency lighting, all computers, the security system, and other essential equipment for as long as ninety-six hours.

Should the city's electric power fail, should the generators be wrecked, should the giant twenty-year batteries prove useless, there were many earthquake lights distributed throughout the house. Personally, Fric figured such a series of failures was likely only in the event of an invasion of extraterrestrials with magnetic-pulse weapons.

Anyway, according to Mrs. McBee, there were 214 quake lights, which meant you could safely bet your life that there were not 213 or 215.

These small but potentially bright, battery-powered flashlights were at all times plugged into electrical outlets in the baseboard, continuously charging. If the power failed, the quake lights at once switched on, providing enough pathway illumination to allow everyone to exit safely from the mansion in the darkest hours of the deepest night. Furthermore, they could be unplugged and carried as though they were ordinary flashlights.

Like the cover plate on the electrical outlet in which it was seated, the plastic casing of each flashlight matched the color of the baseboard on which it rested: beige against limestone baseboard, dark brown against mahogany, black against black marble. . . . During ordinary times, they were meant to be inconspicuous. When you lived with them day after day, you soon ceased to notice them.

No one but Mrs. McBee would be likely to realize that a dozen of those 214 were missing. Mrs. McBee wouldn't return from Santa Barbara until Thursday morning.

Nevertheless, Fric filched quake lights only from remote and little-used rooms where their disappearance was less likely to cause inquiry. He needed them for his deep and special secret hiding place.

He stowed the lights in the picnic hamper because it had a hinged lid. As long as he kept the lid closed, the contents could not be seen if he unexpectedly encountered a member of the staff.

If anyone asked what was in the hamper, he would lie and say "Sandwiches." He would tell them that he was going to camp out under a blanket tent in the billiards room, where he would pretend that he was a Blackfoot Indian living back in maybe 1880.

The whole concept of playing Blackfoot in the billiards room was monumentally stupid, of course. But most grownups believed that geeky ten-year-old boys did stupid, geeky things like that, so he would be believed, and probably pitied.

Having people pity you was better than having them think that you were as crazy as Barbra Streisand's two-headed cat.

That was one of Ghost Dad's expressions. When he thought someone didn't have both oars in the water, he said, "The guy's as crazy as Barbra Streisand's two-headed cat."

Years ago, Ghost Dad had signed a deal to make a movie directed by Barbra Streisand. Something had gone terribly wrong. Eventually, he backed out of the project.

He had never said a negative word about Ms. Streisand. But that didn't mean they were as friendly and as eager for mutual adventures as all the little animals in *The Wind in the Willows*.

In the entertainment business, everyone pretended to be friends even if maybe they hated each other's guts. They were kissy-faced, gushy-lovey, always hugging and backslapping, praising one another so convincingly that Sherlock Holmes couldn't have figured out which of them really wanted to kill which others.

According to Ghost Dad, no one in the business dared tell the truth about anyone else in the business because each of them knew that any of the others was capable of conducting a bloody vendetta of such viciousness that it would have scared the shit out of the meanest Mafioso.

Barbra Streisand didn't actually have a two-headed cat. This was just a "metaphor," as Fric's father called it, for some story element or character that she had wanted to add to her movie after Ghost Dad signed up based on a script *without* the two-headed cat.

He thought the two-headed cat was a totally crazy idea, and Ms. Streisand thought that it would win the picture a shitload of Oscars. So they agreed to disagree, kissed, hugged, swapped praise, and backed away from each other unbloodied.

This morning, in the hallway outside the kitchen, when Fric had almost told Mr. Truman about the mirror man and Moloch and all of it, he had come perilously close to being considered as crazy as Barbra Streisand's two-headed cat. He wouldn't make that mistake again.

His mother had once been committed to a booby hatch.

They would think, *Like mother, like son.*

His mother had been released after ten days.

If Fric started talking about mirror men, they would *never* let him out. Not in ten days, not in ten years.

Worse, if he were in the booby hatch, Moloch would know *exactly* where to find him. There was no place to hide in a padded cell.

Carrying the picnic hamper as if he were on an Easter-egg hunt, stealthily collecting quake lights in a back staircase, in a back hall, in the tea room, in the meditation room, Fric kept reminding himself, "Sandwiches, sandwiches," because he worried that when he finally encountered a maid or porter, he would become tongue-tied and forget what lie he had meant to tell.

By nature, he was not a good liar. In a time and place where you needed to lie merely to pass for normal, in a place and time when *he* needed to lie to survive, being a lousy liar could get him killed.

"Sandwiches, sandwiches."

He was a moronically bad liar.

And he was alone. Even with some kind of half-assed guardian an-gel, he was really *alone.*

Every time he passed a window, he was reminded also that the stormy day was melting away rapidly and that Moloch would most likely come in the night.

Short for his age, thin for his age, a bad liar, alone, *tick-tick-tick:* He had nothing going for him.

"Pandwiches," he muttered to himself. "Just some jellybutter-and-seanut pandwiches."

He was doomed.

CHAPTER 60

QUEEN PALMS, KING PALMS, ROYAL PALMS, phoenix palms shook their feathery fronds like the storm-tossed trees in *Key Largo*. Buses and cars and trucks and SUVs clogged the streets, their wipers not quite as persistent as the beating rain, side windows half fogged, horns bleating, brakes barking, jockeying for position, idling and spurting forward and idling again, the drivers exuding a palpable frustration reminiscent of the opening scene of *Falling Down*, minus the summer heat of that movie, minus Michael Douglas, although Ethan supposed that Michael Douglas might be in this mess, too, quietly going as mad as had his character. In front of a bookstore, under an awning, stood a group of spike-haired, eyebrow-pierced, nose-pierced, tongue-pierced, painted punk rockers or just plain punks, dressed in black, one of them wearing a bowler hat, which made him think of the droogs in *A Clockwork Orange*. And here came a group of teenage schoolgirls, all beautiful, enjoying their seasonal freedom, walking without umbrellas, their hair plastered to their heads, all laughing, each of them playing the part of a fey party girl, all trying to be Holly Golightly in a remake of *Breakfast at Tiffany's* shot this time three thousand miles from the original location, this time on the nation's wild coast. The storm gloom transformed midday to dusk, as if some director were shooting day-for-night. The shop lights, the neon, the cold-cathode tubes, the bright festoons of colorful and vaguely Asian lanterns that decorated streets in a politically correct nonreligious holiday spirit, the head-lights and taillights—all rippled and flared off the storefront win-dows, off the walls of the glass buildings that rose in lunatic defiance of the earthquakes to come, across the wet pavement, sparkled like sequins in scintillant quicksilver plumes of vehicle exhaust, remind-ing Ethan of atmospheric shots in *Blade Runner.*

The day was simultaneously too real and a fantasy, the dreams of Hollywood having brightened the city in a few places, darkened it in many more, changed it in every corner, until nothing seemed as solid as it ought to be.

They were in Ethan's Expedition, having left Hazard's plain-wrap department sedan at Our Lady of Angels. Since Ethan had no police authority, he couldn't arm-twist information out of anyone, but his partner couldn't both arm-twist and drive.

To check out their six leads, they would enter jurisdictions other than those strictly within the authority of the LAPD. Without prepar-ing the way through proper channels, even Hazard would not have en-tirely legitimate authority. They didn't have time for protocol.

Hazard rode shotgun, making phone calls. His voice rose from a polite and almost romantic murmur to a demanding thunder, but most often settled into an easy folksiness, while relentlessly he used his status as homicide detective to coax-pinch-push-pull-wrench co-operation from a series of higher-education bureaucrats.

Every college and university in the greater Los Angeles area had closed for the last two or three weeks of the year. Something less than a skeleton staff remained on duty to serve those students who had not gone home for the holidays.

At each institution that he phoned, he employed charm, appeals to good citizenship, threats, and persistence to get from one know-nothing to another, but always eventually to a know-something who could further their investigation.

Already they had learned that the drama professor—Dr. Jonathan Spetz-Mogg—had organized both of the weekend conferences on acting for which Rolf Reynerd had written checks. They had been granted an appointment with Spetz-Mogg at his home in Westwood, to which they were en route without benefit of emergency flashers or siren.

In the process of tracking down Dr. Gerald Fitzmartin, who had organized the three-day weekend conference on screenwriting, Hazard became so infuriated with the runaround at which all academic types excelled that he paused in the chase before frustration drove him to smash his department-issued phone to pieces against his own forehead.

"All these university cheese-eaters hate cops."

"Until they need you," Ethan said.

"Yeah, then they love us."

"They never love you, but if they need you to save their ass, then they'll *tolerate* you."

"You know that Shakespeare quote?" Hazard asked.

"There's more than one."

"About how to make the world a better place—"

"Kill all the lawyers."

"Yeah, that one," Hazard said. "Shakespeare didn't stop to think who *trains* all the lawyers."

"University cheese-eaters."

"Yeah. You want to make a better world, go to the source."

The traffic remained relentless and tight. The Expedition kissed paint with a black Mercedes SUV, spared from a bruise to the factory finish by nothing more than the lubricating lip gloss of rain.

With a start, Ethan thought that he saw Fric on the sidewalk, wandering alone among strangers. A closer look proved that the boy was younger than the Manheim heir, trailing behind his parents.

This had not been the first false Fric that he had seen and reacted to since leaving the hospital. His nerves had been rubbed raw by too much weird experience.

"What about Blonde in the Pond?" Ethan asked. "Did you get your lab report this morning?"

"Didn't check. If I've got the true goods on my city councilman, it'll just make me squirmy, having to leave him walking around full of himself, the way he is, like he's the Lord by election, which is even more infuriating when you think how many ballot boxes his thugs stuffed for him. I'll call the lab tomorrow, the day after, whenever it is we settle the situation we're in."

"Sorry about this," Ethan said.

"If you're sorry for that nose of yours, get it fixed. Anything else you're sorry for, you shouldn't be."

"Lunch and a few mamouls didn't pay you for this much trouble."

"It wasn't *you* turned my world upside down. Some guy gives me a set of dream bells out of a nightmare, then disappears into a mirror, I tend to get shook up without your help."

Hazard reached under his jacket with both hands, tugging on his cotton sweater, and Ethan said, "You bulked up since yesterday?"

"Yeah. Had me a breakfast of Kevlar."

"Never knew you to wear protection."

"I've been thinking maybe I've dodged more bullets than any man has a right to. Doesn't mean I'm not still fearless."

"Didn't say you weren't."

"I'm scared shitless, but I'm still fearless."

"That's the right psychology."

"Survivor's psychology," Hazard said.

"Anyway, what's wrong with my nose?"

"What isn't?"

The hard rain abruptly began to fall harder, and Ethan cranked the windshield-wiper speed to the highest setting.

Hazard said, "Feels like the end of the world."

CHAPTER 61

AFTER RECEIVING A FRANTIC TELEPHONE CALL from Captain Queeg von Hindenburg, Corky Laputa had to undertake an unexpected journey to the farther reaches of Malibu.

The man in Malibu currently called himself Jack Trotter. Trotter owned property, carried a valid driver's license, and paid as few taxes as possible under the name Felix Greene. Greene, alias Trotter, had once used the names Lewis Motherwell, Jason Barnes, Bobby Domino, and others.

When Jack-Felix-Lewis-Jason-Bobby had been born forty-four years ago, his proud parents had named him Norbert James Creezel. They had no doubt loved him and, being simple Iowa farm folk, could never have imagined that Norbert would grow up to be a wigged-out piece of work like Captain Queeg von Hindenburg.

Corky called him Captain Queeg because the guy exhibited the paranoia and megalomania to be found in the character of the same name in Herman Wouk's *The Caine Mutiny*. Von Hindenburg suited him in part because—like the German zeppelin that had taken thirty-six to their deaths in Lakehurst, New Jersey, in 1937—he was a gasbag and, if left to his own devices, he would one day crash and burn spectacularly.

On his way to Malibu, Corky stopped at a garage that he rented in Santa Monica. This was one of forty double-stall units accessed by an alleyway in an industrial area.

He held the lease on the garage under the name Moriarity and paid the monthly bill in cash.

A black Land Rover occupied the first stall. Corky owned this vehicle under the name Kurtz Ivory International, a nonexistent but well-documented corporation.

He parked the BMW beside the Land Rover, got out, put down the garage door, and switched on the lights.

Redolent of the crisp limy scent of cold concrete, the sweet-and-sour fragrance of old motor-oil stains, and the faint but still lingering astringency of insecticide from a termite fumigation that had been conducted a month ago, this drab space was, to Corky, the essence of magic and adventure. Here, like troubled Bruce Wayne in the Batcave, Corky became a dark knight, though with an agenda that might appeal more to the Joker than to Bruce in cape and tights.

In the war between Heaven and Earth, armies of rain marched across the corrugated-steel roof, raising such a battle roar that he could not have clearly heard himself singing if he'd chosen to break into "Shake Your Groove Thing."

After switching on an electric space heater, he took off his rain hat and yellow slicker. He hung them on a wall peg.

On the left side of the garage, toward the back, four tall metal lockers were bolted to the wall. Corky opened the first of these.

Two zippered vinyl wardrobe bags hung from a rod. On a shelf above the bags, a large Tupperware container held socks, neckties, a few items of men's inexpensive jewelry, a wristwatch, and other personal effects of a false identity. On the floor was a selection of shoes.

After pulling off his rain boots and a double layer of socks, after stripping to his underwear, Corky dressed in gray cords, a black turtleneck, black socks, and black Rockports.

The elaborate combination workbench and tool-storage cabinet at the back of the double garage featured a spacious secret drawer that Corky himself had designed. This drawer contained a selection of handguns and packets of false identification in six names.

Over the turtleneck, he strapped on a shoulder holster. He stuffed the holster with a 9-mm Glock.

He swapped his wallet for one that was filled with everything that he needed to hit the road as a different man: driver's license, social-security card, a couple of credit cards in his new name, and photographs of a wife and family that were entirely invented. The wallet was even preloaded with five hundred dollars in cash.

The packet also included a birth certificate, a passport, and a leather ID fold containing fake FBI credentials. For the task at hand, he required none of those items.

He did, however, take with him a second slim leather fold that contained fake but convincing credentials identifying him as an operative of the National Security Agency. This was who Queeg von Hindenburg believed him to be.

The NSA identification would reduce the average civilian to a swoon of cooperation, but wouldn't withstand determined verification by any authority. Corky would never dare flash it at a cop.

Because it was real, the driver's license in this false name could endure close scrutiny by any police officer who might stop Corky. In addition, it credited him with a spotless driving record.

Years ago, the state of California had lost control of many of its bureaucracies, including the Department of Motor Vehicles. Certain corrupted DMV employees sold tens of thousands of valid driver's licenses every year to men like Mick Sachatone, the multimillionaire anarchist who also regularly supplied Corky with disposable cell phones in fake account names.

Mick—and other middlemen like him—made substantial money by obtaining driver's licenses for illegal immigrants, for convicted felons who had served their time and who earnestly hoped to begin fresh criminal lives uninhibited by their arrest records, for chaos activists like Corky, and for many others.

Sufficiently IDed, with the Glock in a holster under his left arm, Corky shrugged into a stylish black leather coat tailored to conceal the bulge of the weapon. He tucked two spare magazines of ammunition into the coat pockets.

He closed the locker, closed and locked the secret drawer in the workbench, and switched off the space heater.

Behind the wheel of the Land Rover, he clicked the remote to roll up the garage door. He backed into the rain-swept alley.

He had arrived in Santa Monica as Corky Laputa. He was leaving as Robin Goodfellow, agent of the NSA.

After waiting to be sure that the garage door went all the way down, he pressed a second button on the remote, engaging an electric lock that doubly secured the premises.

The CD player in the Land Rover was loaded with the symphonies and operas of Richard Wagner, which was his preferred music when he was being Robin Goodfellow. He fired up *Götterdämmerung* and set out through the storm for Malibu, to have a serious face-to-face talk with the man who this evening would get him onto the Manheim estate undetected.

Corky loved his life.

CHAPTER 62

"S ANDWICHES," SAID FRIC.
Stupid, stupid, stupid.

After conveying the dozen quake lights to his deep and special secret place, Fric had decided to return the empty picnic hamper to the lawn-and-patio-storage room, where he had originally gotten it. He had undertaken this task for some reason that had seemed logical at the time, though he could not now recall what it had been.

Mr. Devonshire, one of the porters—the one with the English accent, the bushy eyebrows, and the weak left eye that tended to drift toward his temple—had encountered Fric in the ground-floor west hall, at the end of which lay the lawn-and-patio-storage room. By way of friendly small talk, Mr. Devonshire had said, "What've you got there, Fric?"

Sandwiches, Fric had said. Now he said again, "Sandwiches."

This was a stupid, stupid, stupid thing to say, let alone to repeat, because when Mr. Devonshire had first seen him, Fric had been swinging the hamper as he walked along the hall, swinging it in such a way that its light weight—and therefore its emptiness—must have been instantly apparent.

"What kind of sandwiches?" Mr. Devonshire asked.

"Ham," said Fric, for this was a simple response that he could not screw up in the nine thousand ways that he could probably mangle the words *peanut butter and jelly.*

"So you're having a picnic, are you?" Mr. Devonshire asked, his left eye slowly drifting out of alignment as though he expected to be able to look behind himself while simultaneously studying Fric.

When the porter had first come to work at Palazzo Rospo, Fric had thought that he possessed an evil eye and could cast curses with a glance. Mrs. McBee had corrected this childish misapprehension and had suggested that he do some research.

Fric now knew that Mr. Devonshire suffered from amblyopia. This was a little-known word. Fric liked knowing things that most people didn't.

Long ago Fric had learned to look at Mr. Devonshire's good eye when talking to him. Right now, however, he wasn't able to meet the porter's good eye because he felt so guilty for lying; consequently, he found himself gazing stupidly at the amblyopic eye.

To avoid embarrassing Mr. Devonshire and himself, he stared instead at the floor and said, "Yes, a picnic, just me, something different to do, you know, ummm, not the old routine."

"Where will you have your picnic?" Mr. Devonshire asked.

"The rose garden."

Sounding surprised, Mr. Devonshire said, "In this rain?"

Stupid, stupid, stupid.

Fric had forgotten the rain. He said, "Ummm, I mean the rose *room.*"

The rose room, as members of the staff continued to refer to it, was a small ground-floor reception parlor. Its windows presented a view of the former site of the rose garden.

A few years ago, at the urging of their feng-shui consultant, the rose garden had been moved farther from the house. Where the old rose garden had been, grass grew, and from the grass soared a massive piece of contemporary sculpture that Nominal Mom had given to

Ghost Dad on the ninth anniversary of their wedding, at which time they had been divorced for eight years.

Nominal Mom described the sculpture as "futuristic organic Zen" in style. To Fric it looked like a giant heap of road apples produced by a herd of Clydesdales.

"The rose room seems like an odd place for a picnic," said Mr. Devonshire, no doubt thinking about the Zen turd pile beyond the windows.

"Ummm, well, I feel close to my mom there," Fric said, which was so lame that it was almost clever.

Mr. Devonshire was silent for a moment, and then he said, "Are you all right, Fric?"

"Ummm, sure, I'm swell, just a little, you know, bummed out by all the rain."

After another but thankfully shorter silence, the porter said, "Well, enjoy your ham sandwiches."

"Thank you, sir. I will. I made them myself. From scratch." He was the world's worst liar. "With ham."

Mr. Devonshire walked toward the north hall, and Fric just stood there, stupidly holding the hamper as if it were *heavy*.

After the porter disappeared at the intersection of the west and north halls, Fric continued to stare after him. He was convinced that Mr. Devonshire was hiding just out of sight and that the man's eerie left eye would turn so far to one side that it would be hanging out of his head when he peeked around the corner.

The lawn-and-patio-storage room, to which Fric had been headed, was not set aside for the storage of lawns and patios. Rather, the cushions for the hundred or more outdoor chairs and sun lounges—and sometimes the furniture as well—were moved there in anticipation of bad weather. The big room also held lawn umbrellas, croquet sets, outdoor games, and such associated paraphernalia as picnic hampers.

Following his conversation with the porter, Fric could no longer simply return the hamper to the storage room. If Mr. Devonshire saw him without it anytime soon, he would be exposed as a devious liar who was actually up to some kind of no good.

Suspicious, the staff might surreptitiously watch him, even as shorthanded as they were at the moment. Without realizing it, he might reveal his deep and special secret place to a keen observer.

Now that he had committed himself to the picnic story, he must follow through. He would have to lug the hamper to the rose room and sit by the windows, gazing out at the rose garden that wasn't there anymore, pretending to eat ham sandwiches that didn't exist.

Mysterious Caller had warned him about lying.

If he wasn't ready to handle nice Mr. Devonshire, Fric wondered how he could expect to deceive and hide out from Moloch.

Finally he decided that the porter and his lazy eye were not lurking just around the corner, after all.

Certain that he appeared too grim for a picnicker, but unable to force a smile, he carried the damn hamper all the way from the south-west corner of the house to the northeast corner, to the rose room.

CHAPTER 63

JACK TROTTER, KNOWN TO THE WORLD BY MANY names, known only to Corky as Queeg von Hindenburg, didn't live in the glamorous part of Malibu. He resided far from those view hills and beaches where actors and rock stars and the fabulously wealthy founders of bankrupt dot-com companies sunned, played, and shared recipes for cannabis brownies.

Instead, he lived inland, behind the hills and beyond the sight of the sea, in one of the rustic canyons that appealed not only to those who kept horses and loved the simple life but also to troubled cranks and crackpots, weedheads with names like Boomer and Moose who farmed marijuana under lamps in barns and bunkers, ecoterrorists scheming to blow up auto dealerships in the name of endangered tree rats, and religious cultists worshiping UFOs.

A ranch fence badly in need of paint surrounded Trotter's four acres. He usually kept the gate shut to discourage visitors.

Today the gate hung wide open because he feared that Corky— known to him as Robin Goodfellow, kick-ass federal agent—would drive through that barrier, battering it off its hinges, as he'd done once before.

At the end of the graveled driveway stood the hacienda-style house of pale yellow stucco and exposed timbers. Not dilapidated enough to be called ramshackle, not nearly dirty enough to be called squalid, the place suffered instead from a sort of genteel neglect.

Trotter didn't spend much money maintaining his home because he expected to have to flee at any moment. A man with his head in the lunette of a guillotine lived with no more tension than what Jack Trotter daily endured.

A conspiracy theorist, he believed that a secret cabal ran the nation, that it intended soon to dispense with democracy and impose brutal dictatorial control. He was ever alert for early signs of the coming crackdown.

Currently Trotter believed that post-office employees would be the vanguard of the repression. They were, in his estimation, not the mere bureaucrats they appeared to be, but highly trained shock troops masquerading as innocent letter carriers.

He had prepared a series of bolt-holes, each more remote than the one before it. He hoped to escape civilization by degrees when the bloodbath began.

No doubt he would have fled after Corky's first visit had he not believed that Corky, as Robin Goodfellow, knew the location of every one of his bolt-holes and would descend on him in his hideaway with a company of cutthroat mailmen who would show no mercy.

Toward the east end of the property, away from the house, stood an ancient unpainted barn and a prefab steel building of more recent construction. Corky knew only some of what Trotter was up to in those structures, but he pretended to have full knowledge.

In the fierce heat of summer, the real threat to Trotter would be fire, not a wicked government cabal. The steep slopes behind his property, as well as half the narrow valley both up-canyon and down-canyon, bristled with wild brush that, by late August, would be as ready for burning as Brittina Dowd's house had proved to be with the application of a little gasoline.

Now, of course, the steep slopes were so supersaturated with rain that the risk was a mud slide. In this terrain, a canyon wall could descend in a tidal wave of muck with such suddenness that even a wild-eyed paranoid with every nerve fully cocked might not be able to outrun it. If he broke into a sprint at first rumble, Trotter could still wind up buried alive, but alive only briefly, sharing his grave with an ark's worth of crushed and smothered wildlife.

Corky loved southern California.

Not yet crushed and smothered, Trotter waited for his visitor on the veranda. If at all possible, he hoped to keep Corky out of the house.

On one of his previous visits, deeply into his role as a rogue government agent who used the United States Constitution as toilet paper, Corky had misbehaved. He had shown no respect for Trotter's property rights. He had been a brute.

On this twenty-second day of December, Corky didn't find himself to be mellowed out by holiday good will. He was a punk-mean elf.

Although he parked ten steps from the veranda, he didn't hurry through the downpour because Robin Goodfellow, too cool for jackboots but wearing them in spirit, was not a man who noticed the weather when he was in a foul mood.

He climbed the three steps to the veranda, drew the Glock from his shoulder holster, and pressed the muzzle to Trotter's forehead.

"Repeat what you told me on the phone."

"Damn," Trotter said nervously. "You know it's true."

"It's bullshit," Corky said.

Trotter's hair was as orange as that of the Cheshire Cat who had toyed with Alice in Wonderland. He had the pinned-wide, protuberant eyes of the Mad Hatter. His nose twitched nervously, reminiscent of the White Rabbit. His bloated face and his huge mustache recalled the famous Walrus, and he was in general as brillig, slithy, and mimsy as numerous of Lewis Carroll's characters rolled into one.

"For God's sake, Goodfellow," Trotter all but blubbered, "the storm, the *storm*! We can't do the job in this. It's impossible in weather like this."

Still pressing the Glock to Trotter's forehead, Corky said, "The storm will break by six o'clock. The wind will die completely. We'll have ideal conditions."

"Yeah, they're saying it might break, but what do they know? Do any of their predictions ever turn out right?"

"I'm not relying on the TV weathermen, you cretin. I'm relying on supersecret Defense Department satellites that not only study the planet's weather patterns but *control* them with microwave energy pulses. We will *make* the storm end when we need it to end."

This crackpot assertion played well with the paranoid Trotter, whose pinned-wide eyes stretched even wider. "Weather control," he whispered shakily. "Hurricanes, tornadoes, blizzards, droughts—an untraceable weapon as terrible as nuclear bombs."

In reality, Corky was counting on nothing more than chaos to be his ally, to bring the storm to an end when he needed calm skies.

Chaos never failed him.

"Rain or no rain, wind or no wind," he told Trotter, "you will be in Bel Air, at the rendezvous point, at seven o'clock sharp, as originally planned."

"Weather control," Trotter muttered darkly.

"Don't even think about not coming. Do you know how many eyes are on us right now—up in those hills, out in those fields?"

"Lots of eyes," Trotter guessed.

"My people are everywhere in this canyon, ready to keep you honest or blow your brains out, whichever you want."

In fact, the only eyes on them were those of the crows, hawks, sparrows, and other members of the feathered community gathered in the ancient California live oaks that sheltered the house.

Jack Trotter had fallen for these lies not because of the phony NSA credentials, not because of Corky's bravura performance as Agent

Robin Goodfellow, but because Corky had known so much about Trotter's many aliases and at least a few things about his thus far successful career as a bank robber and a distributor of Ecstasy. He believed that Corky had learned about him by means of the ruling cabal's all but omniscient intelligence-gathering apparatus.

What Corky had learned about Trotter, however, he had heard from Mick Sachatone, the hacker and multimillionaire anarchist who traded in forged documents, untraceable cell phones, and other illegal paperwork, objects, substances, and information. Mick had provided Trotter with the identities that subsequently he revealed to Corky.

Ordinarily, Mick would never disclose to one client the affairs of another. Considering the kind of people he did business with, such a lack of discretion would result, if he were lucky, in his death or, if he were unlucky, in the excision of his eyes, the extraction of his tongue, the severing of his thumbs, and castration with pliers.

Because Mick had reason to hate Trotter with an intensity nearly homicidal, he had risked sharing information with Corky. Jealous rage of operatic proportions had caused him to violate his usual standards of client confidentiality.

For his part, Trotter had earned Mick's enmity, though he seemed unaware of it. He had stolen Mick's girlfriend.

Mick's girlfriend had been a porn-movie star renowned in certain jerky circles for the inhuman flexibility of her body.

Perhaps Trotter didn't think that anyone could become profoundly emotionally attached, on evenings and weekends, to a woman who did two, six, and even ten men at a time in front of a camera, during her regular business hours.

Since the age of thirteen, however, Mick's most cherished dream had been to have a porn star for a girlfriend. He felt that Trotter had robbed him of his heart's one true desire and had thwarted his destiny.

After four months with Trotter, the woman had disappeared. Mick was of the opinion that, having tired of her, Trotter had killed her either because she had learned too much about his illegal activities or merely for sport, and had buried her deep in the canyon.

Now she was of no use to anyone, and this pointless waste of her exceptional flexibility further infuriated Mick.

Lowering the Glock from Trotter's forehead, Corky said, "Let's go inside."

"Please, let's not," Trotter pleaded.

"Need I remind you," Corky said, lying with delightful panache, "that your cooperation with me could earn you erasure from all public records, from all tax records, making you the freest man who ever lived, a man *utterly unknown to the government*?"

"I'll be there tonight. Seven o'clock sharp. Wind or no wind. I swear I will."

"I still want to go inside," Corky said. "I still feel the need to make my point with you."

A sadness came into Trotter's Mad Hatter eyes. His walruslike face drooped.

Resigned, he led Corky into the house.

The bullet holes in the walls, from the previous occasion when Corky had needed to teach Trotter a lesson, had not been repaired; however, the living-room display shelves had been filled with a new collection of Lladro porcelains—statuettes of ballerinas, princesses dancing with princes, children capering with a dog, a lovely farm maiden feeding a flock of geese gathered at her feet. . . .

That a paranoid, conspiracy-drunk, bank-robbing, drug-peddling survivalist with bolt-holes leading from here to the Canadian border should have a weak spot for fragile porcelains didn't surprise Corky. Regardless of how rough we may appear on the exterior, each of us has a human heart.

Corky himself had a weakness for old Shirley Temple movies, in which he indulged once or twice a year. Without embarrassment.

As Trotter watched, Corky emptied the 9-mm magazine, shattering one porcelain with every shot.

In the months since he had unintentionally wounded Mina Reynerd in the foot, he had become remarkably proficient with handguns. Until recently, he'd never much wanted to use a firearm in the service of chaos, for it had seemed too cold, too impersonal. But he was warming to the instrument.

He replaced the first magazine with a second and finished off the Lladro collection. The humid air was full of a chalky dust and the smell of gunfire.

"Seven o'clock," he said.

"I'll be there," said the chastened Trotter.

"Gonna take a magic carpet ride."

After replacing the second magazine with a third, Corky slipped the Glock into his shoulder holster and walked out to the veranda.

He proceeded slowly through the rain to the Land Rover, boldly turning his back to the house.

He drove down out of the Malibu canyons toward the coast.

The sky was an open beaker, pouring forth not rain but the universal solvent for which medieval alchemists had sought in vain. All around him, the hills were melting. The lowlands were dissolving. The edge of the continent deliquesced into the tumultuous sea.

CHAPTER 64

FRIC IN THE ROSE ROOM, IN A CHAIR BY THE windows, looked out at his mother's love-affirming gift of high-piled bronze road apples.

The picnic hamper stood on the floor beside his chair, the lid closed.

Although he would spend time here to support the story that he had stupidly spewed out to Mr. Devonshire, he would not actually pretend to eat nonexistent ham sandwiches, partly because if someone saw him, they would for sure think *Like mother, like son,* but largely because he didn't have any nonexistent dill pickles to go with them.

Ha, ha, ha.

At the time of the incident, almost two years ago, his mother's publicist explained to the weasels in the scandal-hungry press that Freddie Nielander had been admitted to a private hospital somewhere in Florida. She was said to be suffering from exhaustion.

With surprising frequency, supermodels were hospitalized for that reason. Apparently, being wildly glamorous twenty-four hours a day could be as physically demanding as the work of a plowhorse and as emotionally draining as tending to the terminally ill.

Nominal Mom had done one *Vanity Fair* cover too many, one

Vogue spread more than had been wise, leading to the temporary but complete loss of muscle control throughout her body. That seemed to be the official story, as far as Fric could understand it.

No one believed the official story. Newspapers, magazines, and the gossipy reporters on the TV entertainment-news shows spoke darkly of a "breakdown," an "emotional collapse." Some actually called it a "psychotic episode," which sounded like an installment of *I Love Lucy* in which Lucy and Ethel mowed down a bunch of people with submachine guns. They referred to her hospital as a "sanitarium for the richest of the rich" and as an "exclusive psychiatric clinic," and Howard Stern, the shock jock on radio, reportedly called it a "booby hatch for a broad who's got more boobies than brains."

Fric had pretended not to know what the media were saying about his mother, but secretly he had read and listened to every scrap of coverage that he could find. He'd been frightened. He'd felt useless. Reporters disagreed over which of two institutions she might be in, and Fric didn't have an address for either of them. He couldn't even send her a card.

Eventually, his father had taken him aside in the rose garden, which had already been moved away from the house, to ask if Fric had heard any strange news stories about his mother. Fric had pretended to be clueless.

His father had said, "Well, sooner or later, you'll hear things, and I want you to know none of it's true. It's the usual celebrity-bashing crapola. They'll say your mom had some nervous breakdown or something, but she didn't. The truth isn't pretty, but it's not half as ugly as you'll hear, so Ming and Dr. Rudy are going to share with you some techniques for keeping your mind at peace through all this."

Dr. Rudy was Rudolph Kroog, a psychiatrist famous in Hollywood circles for his unconventional past-life therapy. He talked to Fric for a little while, trying to determine if in a previous incarnation he might have been a boy king in Egypt during the centuries it was ruled by pharaohs, and provided a bottle of capsules with directions to take one at lunch and one at bedtime.

Remembering that boy kings had sometimes been poisoned by their advisers, which he'd learned on Saturday-morning cartoon shows, Fric had carried the capsules directly to his third-floor suite, where he flushed them down the drain. If a green, scaly monster had lived in his toilet, he killed it with an overdose that day.

As easy as Dr. Rudy had been to endure, Ming was hard. After two days of "sharing," Fric preferred to be consigned to the mercy of Mr. Hachette, the brain-diseased chef, even if he would be roasted with apples and fed to unsuspecting Bowery bums on Thanksgiving.

Eventually, everyone had left him alone.

He still didn't know whether it had been a hospital, sanitarium, or booby hatch.

His mother had been to Palazzo Rospo only once since then, but she hadn't mentioned the incident. That was the visit in which she told Fric that he was an almost perfect invisible little mouse.

Then they had gone riding on a pair of great black stallions, and Fric had been exuberant, self-assured, athletic like his father, and a superb rider.

Ha, ha, ha.

Sitting here in the rose room, gazing through the windows, he had gotten so lost in the past that he hadn't noticed when Mr. Yorn, the groundskeeper, had entered the picture. Wearing green rain togs and black wading boots, Mr. Yorn must have been checking the lawn drains or investigating a clogged downspout. Now he stared through the rose-room windows at Fric, from a distance of six feet, looking puzzled, perhaps worried.

Maybe Mr. Yorn had waved and Fric, lost in the past, had not waved back, and so Mr. Yorn had waved again, and still Fric had not waved back; and now maybe Mr. Yorn thought Fric was in a trance.

To prove that he was neither a rude little snot nor hypnotized, Fric waved, which seemed to be the right thing to do, whether Mr. Yorn had been standing there unacknowledged for ten seconds or five minutes.

Fric waved a little too vigorously, which might have been what caused the groundskeeper to step closer to the windows and say, "Are you all right, Fric?"

"Yes, sir. I'm fine. I'm just having some ham sandwiches."

Apparently the leaded glass panes and the roar of the rain filtered some of the sense out of Fric's voice, for Mr. Yorn edged closer still and spoke again: "What did you say?"

"Ham sandwiches!" Fric explained, raising his voice almost to a shout.

For a moment Mr. Yorn continued to peer in at him, as though studying a curious bug trapped in a specimen jar. Then he shook his head, causing the brim of his rain hat to flap comically, and he turned away.

Fric watched the groundskeeper walk past the bronze bowel movement. Mr. Yorn receded into the storm, dwindling across the immense lawn until he appeared to be no bigger than a garden gnome, until he was finally gone like a ghost.

Fric figured he knew exactly what Mr. Yorn was thinking: *Like mother, like son.*

Rising from the chair, stretching, shaking stiffness out of his legs, Fric accidentally kicked the picnic hamper, knocking it over.

The lid fell open, revealing something inside: a whiteness.

The hamper had been empty. No quake lights, no ham sandwiches, no anything.

Fric scoped the parlor. He saw no place in which an unsuspected companion might be hiding. The door to the hall remained closed, as he had left it.

Hesitantly, he stooped. Cautiously, he reached into the hamper.

He withdrew a folded newspaper and shakily opened it. The *Los Angeles Times.*

The headline was too bold, too black, too incredible to miss: FBI ENTERS MANHEIM KIDNAPPING.

A chill shuttled and wove in Fric.

A sudden brine moistened his palms, as if he had dipped his hands into a supernatural sea, and his fingers stuck to the paper.

He checked the date of the issue. December 24. The day after to-morrow.

On the front page, under the frightening headline, were two photo-graphs: a publicity shot of Ghost Dad, and the front gate of the estate.

Reluctant to read the report for fear that reading it would make it come true, Fric glanced at the bottom of the column and saw that the story continued on page 8. He turned to page 8 in search of the pic-ture most important to him.

And there he was.

Under his photo were these words: *Aelfric Manheim, 10, missing since Tuesday night.*

As he stared in shock at the photo, his black-and-white image morphed into that of the mirror man, Mysterious Caller, his guardian angel: the cold face, the pale gray eyes.

Fric tried to throw the *Times* down, but was unable to let go of it, not because his hands were moist with fear but because the newspa-per seemed to have acquired a static charge, and clung to him.

In the picture, Mysterious Caller became animated, as if this were not a newspaper photo but a miniature TV screen, and he spoke warn-ingly from the *Los Angeles Times:* "Moloch is coming."

Then with no recollection of having taken a step, Fric found that he had crossed the rose room to the door.

He gasped for breath, though not because of his asthma. His heart boomed louder than the thunder that earlier had knocked through the sky.

The *Times* lay on the floor by the overturned hamper.

As Fric watched, the newspaper exploded off the Persian carpet as if caught in a wild wind, although not so much as a faint draft could be felt. The several sections of the *Times* unfolded, blossomed; in seconds, they rumpled and swirled and noisily assembled themselves into a tall human figure, as if an invisible man had been standing there all the time and as if the blown newsprint had adhered to his heretofore unseen form.

This did not have the aura of a guardian angel, though surely it was. This felt . . . *menacing.*

The paper man turned from Fric and flung himself at the bay windows. When the crackling newsprint hit the glass, it ceased to be paper anymore, became a shadow, a flowing darkness, that swarmed through the beveled panes in the very way that it had pulsed through the ornaments on the Christmas tree the previous night.

The phantom faded, vanished, as though it had traveled by glass into the rain, and then had ridden on the rain to some place far away and unthinkable.

Fric was alone once more. Or seemed to be.

CHAPTER 65

DR. JONATHAN SPETZ-MOGG LIVED IN A PRICEY
Westwood neighborhood, in a fine Nantucket-style house with
cedar-shingle siding so silvered by time that not even the rain could
darken it, which suggested that the silvering might be an applied
patina.

Spetz-Mogg's British accent was eccentric enough to be captivating,
inconsistent enough to have been acquired during a long visit to
those shores rather than by birth and upbringing.

The professor welcomed Ethan and Hazard into his home, but less
graciously than obsequiously. He answered their questions not in a
spirit of thoughtful cooperation, but in a nervous, wordy gush.

He wore a roomy FUBU shirt and baggy low-rider pants with snap
pockets on the legs, looking as ridiculous as any white man trying to
dress like a homey from the hood, twice as ridiculous because he was
forty-eight. Every time he crossed his legs, which he did frequently,
the baggy pants rustled loudly enough to interrupt conversation.

Perhaps he affected sunglasses indoors more often than not. He
wore them on this occasion.

Spetz-Mogg removed the shades and put them on again nearly as
often as he recrossed his legs, though these two nervous tells were

not synchronized. He seemed unable to decide whether he had a better chance of surviving interrogation by presenting an open and guileless image or by hiding behind tinted lenses.

Although the professor clearly believed that every cop was a brutal fascist, he'd never be one to climb a barricade to shout the accusation. He wasn't incensed that two agents of the repressive police state were in his home; he was simply, quietly terrified.

In answer to every question, he vomited up a mess of information with the hope that garrulous responses would wash Ethan and Hazard out of his door before they produced brass knuckles and truncheons.

This was not the professor for whom they were searching. Spetz-Mogg might encourage others to commit crimes in the name of one ideal or another, but he was too gutless to do so himself.

Besides, he didn't have time for crime. He had written ten works of nonfiction and eight novels. In addition to teaching his classes, he organized conferences, workshops, and seminars. He wrote plays.

In Ethan's experience, industrious people, regardless of the quality of what their labor produced, rarely committed violent crimes. Only in movies did successful businessmen routinely indulge in murder and mayhem in addition to corporate responsibilities.

Criminals were likely to be failures in the workplace or just lazy. Or their material possessions had come through inheritance or by other easy means. Idleness gave them time to scheme.

Dr. Spetz-Mogg had no memory of Rolf Reynerd. On average, three hundred struggling actors attended one of his weekend conferences. Not many of them left a lasting impression.

When Ethan and Hazard rose to leave without suggesting that they torture the professor with electric wires to his genitals, Spetz-Mogg accompanied them to the door with visible relief. When he closed the door behind them, he no doubt bolted for the bathroom, his pretense of British equanimity belied by shuddering bowels.

In the Expedition, Hazard said, "I should have punched the son of a bitch on general principles."

"You're getting cranky in midcareer," Ethan said.

"What was that accent?"

"Adam Sandler playing James Bond."

"Yeah. With a twist of Schwarzenegger."

From Spetz-Mogg's house in Westwood, they wasted far too much time tracking down Dr. Gerald Fitzmartin, who had organized the screenwriting conference attended by Reynerd.

According to the university at which he taught, Fitzmartin was home for the holidays, not traveling. When Hazard called, all he got was an answering machine.

Fitzmartin lived in Pacific Palisades. They traveled surface streets, which seemed less well suited for SUVs than for gondolas.

No one answered the bell at the Fitzmartin place. Maybe he was Christmas shopping. Maybe he was too busy to come to the door because he was wrapping a hate gift in a black box for Channing Manheim.

The neighbor told a different story: Fitzmartin had been rushed to Cedars-Sinai Medical Center on Monday morning. He wasn't sure why.

When Hazard called Cedars-Sinai, he found that patient privacy was more important to the hospital than were police relations.

Under a sky as bruised as the battered body of a boxer, Ethan drove back toward the city. The wind fought with trees, and sometimes trees lost, dropping branches into the streets, hampering traffic.

The traffic matched the turbulence of the heavens. At one intersection, car had punched car, and both had gone down for the count. Five blocks farther, a truck had broadsided a paneled van.

He drove with caution that grew into an inhibiting wariness. He couldn't help thinking that if he had been run down and killed in traffic once, he might die again on another street. This time, maybe he would not get up again from death.

En route, Hazard worked the phone, tracking down the name of the professor, at yet another institution, who had organized the one-day seminar on publicity and self-promotion.

Taking neither hand off the wheel, Ethan glanced at his watch. The day was draining away faster than rain into storm culverts.

He had to be back at Palazzo Rospo before 5:00. Fric could not be left alone in the great house, especially not on this strange day.

Cedars-Sinai Medical Center was on Beverly Boulevard in a part of Los Angeles that wanted to be Beverly Hills. They arrived at 2:18.

They located Dr. Gerald Fitzmartin in the ICU, but they weren't permitted to see him. In the waiting room, the professor's son was pleased to have a distraction, though he couldn't imagine why police officers would want to talk to his father.

Professor Fitzmartin was sixty-eight years old. After a life of honest living, older men rarely turned to crime in their retirement. It interfered with gardening and with passing kidney stones.

Besides, just this morning, Fitzmartin had undergone quadruple heart-bypass surgery. If he *was* Rolf Reynerd's conspirator, he would not be killing movie stars in the immediate future.

Ethan checked his watch. 2:34. *Tick, tick, tick.*

CHAPTER 66

MICK SACHATONE, THE ANARCHIST MULTI-millionaire, didn't live in a glitzy neighborhood of multi-millionaires because he never wanted to have to explain the origins of his wealth to the tax authorities. When you make it in cash, you live without flash.

He laundered enough income to justify a spacious four-bedroom, two-story house of no architectural distinction in a clean and pleasant upper-middle-class neighborhood in Sherman Oaks.

Only a handful of Mick's most trusted customers of long standing knew his address. Mostly he transacted business on public beaches and in public parks, coffee shops, and churches.

Without stopping at the garage in Santa Monica to change from his Robin Goodfellow costume into his regular-guy clothes and yellow slicker, Corky went directly from Jack Trotter's funky digs in Malibu to Sherman Oaks. Thanks to Queeg von Hindenburg, collector of broken porcelains, Corky's schedule was screwed up. He had much yet to do on this most important but fast-vanishing day of his life.

He parked in the driveway and ran a few quick steps through the rain to the cover of the front porch.

Mick's voice came from an intercom speaker beside the bell push,

"Be right there," and Mick Sachatone himself came to the door with unusual alacrity. Sometimes, you had to wait here on the porch two or three minutes, or longer, between when Mick spoke to you via the intercom and when he greeted you in person, so routinely preoccupied was he with work or with other interests.

As usual when at home, Mick was barefoot and dressed in pajamas. Today the jammies were red, decorated with images of the cartoon character Bart Simpson. Mick bought some peejays off the rack but had others custom tailored.

Even before Mick had achieved puberty, he had been enchanted by the story of Hugh Hefner, founder of *Playboy*. Hef had discovered a way to grow up, be a success, and yet remain a big child, indulging any whim or desire to whatever degree he wished, making of his life one long party, living more days than not in pajamas.

Mick, who worked mostly at home, owned more than 150 pairs of peejays. He slept in the nude but sported pajamas during the day.

He considered himself an acolyte of Hef. A mini-Hef. Mick was forty-two going on thirteen.

"Hey, Cork, super-hip threads," Mick declared when he opened the door and saw Corky dressed as Robin Goodfellow.

This might have sounded like mockery to a stranger; but Mick's friends knew that he had long ago stopped picking up new slang in an effort to be more in the Hef groove.

"Sorry I'm late," Corky said, stepping inside.

"No sweat, my man. I'd run this pad clockless if I could."

The living room contained as little furniture as necessary. The plush sofa, plump armchairs, footstools, coffee table, end tables, and lamps had been bought as a set at a warehouse outlet. The quality was good; but everything had been chosen for comfort, not for looks.

Mick had no pretensions. In spite of his wealth, he remained a man of simple if sometimes obsessive needs.

The primary decor statement in Casa Sachatone had nothing to do with furniture or art. Except for a suite of work rooms that Mick had

added to the original structure, all but two walls in the house were
lined with shelves on which were stored a collection of thousands of
pornographic videotapes and DVDs. Shelves had even been added to
the stairwell and hallway walls.

Mick preferred videotapes to DVDs because the cassettes came in
boxes with wide, colorful spines that blazed with obscene titles and
sometimes with hard-core photographs. The effect was of one continuous erotic mosaic that flowed from end to end and top to bottom of
the residence, achieving almost psychedelic impact.

Only the work wing, this living room, and the master bedroom
contained any furniture. Other chambers, including the dining room,
were not merely lined with videocassettes but were filled with aisles
of shelves, as in a library.

Mick ate all his meals either at his computer or in bed: lots of microwave dinners, as well as home-delivery pizza and Chinese.

Of the two walls not fitted with floor-to-ceiling shelves, one was
here in the living room. This space had been reserved for four big top-
of-the-line plasma-screen TVs and associated equipment. The other
such wall was in the bedroom.

A pair of plasma screens hung side by side, and a second pair hung
side by side above the first. A DVD player and a videocassette machine served each screen; that equipment, plus eight speakers and associated amplifiers were racked in low cabinets under the screens.

Mick could run four movies simultaneously and switch, as whim
struck him, from one soundtrack to the other. Or he could—and often did—play all four soundtracks simultaneously.

Usually when you stepped into the Sachatone living room, you
were greeted by a rude symphony of sighs, grunts, groans, squeals,
squeaks, hisses, and cries of pleasure, by whispered and growled obscenities, and by a rhythmic rush of heavy breathing in one degree of
urgency or another. With eyes closed, you could almost believe that
you were in a riotously inhabited jungle, albeit a jungle in which all
the tropical species were simultaneously copulating.

This afternoon, sound accompanied none of the four porn films. Mick had muted all of them.

"Janelle was so special," Mick said tenderly, nodding toward the video wall, referring to his lost girlfriend. "One cool swingin' chick."

Although his Bart Simpson pajamas might seem frivolous, Mick dwelt in a somber memorial mood. All four screens featured classics from Janelle's extensive filmography.

Pointing to the upper-right-hand screen in the four-screen stack, Mick said, "That thing she's doing right there, no one—*no one*—ever did that in film before or since."

"I doubt anyone else could," Corky said, because the eye-popping trick in which Janelle was vigorously engaged involved her legendary flexibility, for which perhaps she alone among all humanity carried the necessary gene.

Referring to his gal's costars in the upper-right-hand video, Mick said, "Those four guys *love* her. See that? Every one of those guys just loves her. Men *loved* Janelle. She was truly groovy."

Mick's voice swelled with wistful longing. In spite of all his Hefnerian hipness, he had a sentimental streak.

"I just got back from Trotter's in Malibu," Corky revealed.

"You kill the son of a bitch yet?"

"Not yet. You know I need him for a while."

"Oh, look at that."

"She's really something."

"You'd think that would hurt."

"Maybe it did," Corky said.

"Janelle said no, it was fun."

"She do a lot of stretching exercises?"

"Her *work* was stretching exercises. You will kill him?"

"Promised you, didn't I?"

"I expected to grow old with her," Mick said.

"Really?"

"Well, *older,* anyway."

"I shot up his current collection of porcelains."

"Expensive?"

"Lladro."

"Will you torture him before you kill him?"

"Sure."

"You're a good friend, Cork. You're a pal."

"Well, we go back a long way."

"More than twenty years," Mick said.

"The world was a worse place then," Corky said, meaning from an anarchist's point of view.

"A lot has fallen apart in our time," Mick agreed. "But not as fast as we dreamed it would when we were crazy kids."

They smiled at each other.

Had they been different men, they might have hugged.

Instead, Mick said, "I'm ready to execute the Manheim package," and led Corky to the back of the house, into his work rooms.

Instead of video porn, the walls here were lined with computers, a compact printing press, lamination machines, a laser holography imprinter, and other high-tech equipment necessary for the production of the finest quality forged documents.

At his central work station, Mick had already positioned two chairs before the computer screen. He settled in the one directly in front of the keyboard.

Corky took off his leather jacket, hung it on the back of the second chair, and sat down.

Eyeing the holstered Glock, Mick said, "Is that the rod you'll use to waste Trotter?"

"Yeah."

"Can I have it after?"

"The gun?"

"I'll be discreet," Mick promised. "I'll never use it. And I'll drill out the barrel so it can't be matched to any of the rounds you kill him with. I don't want it for a gun, see, it'll just be like a sacred object to

me. Part of my private memorial wall to Janelle, on the shelves where
I keep all her films."

"All right," Corky said. "It's yours when I've done him."

"You're a champ, Cork." Indicating the computer and the data on
it, the keeper of Janelle's flame said, "This was a nut-buster job."

As a hacker of exceptional achievement, Mick customarily implied or boldly stated that for him, self-named Ultimate Master of
Digital Data and Ruler of the Virtual Universe, all came as easily as
bees to a flower; therefore, this admission that the Manheim job had
taxed his talents must mean that it had been a formidable task, indeed.

"At precisely eight-thirty this evening," Mick continued, "the telephone company's computer will shut down all twenty-four of the
lines serving the Manheim estate."

"Won't that alert Paladin Patrol, the off-site security company? One
dedicated line maintains a twenty-four-hour link between Paladin and
the estate, for alarm transmissions."

"Yeah. If the line goes dead, Paladin treats the interruption in service the same as an alarm signal. But they won't know a thing."

"It's an armed-response company," Corky worried. "Their guards
aren't Barney Fifes with pepper spray. They respond fast, with guns."

"Part of the package I've worked up for you is a breach of the
Paladin computer immediately before the Manheim phones go down.
It pulls the plug on their whole system."

"They'll have redundancy."

"I know their redundancy like I know my own crotch," Mick said
with impatience. "I'm pulling the plug on the redundancy, too."

"Impressive."

"You won't have to worry about the off-site security company. But
what about the private guards on the estate, Manheim's own boys?"

"Two on the evening shift," Corky said. "I know their routine. I've
got that covered. What about cell phones?"

"That's part of the package you're buying from me. I checked out the information you got from Ned Hokenberry, and Manheim still uses the same cell-service provider as before Hokenberry was fired."

Corky said, "Two cellular units are used by the on-duty guards. A third goes everywhere with the security chief, Ethan Truman."

Mick nodded. "They'll be shut down at eight-thirty along with the hard-wired phones. The couple that runs the estate also receive cell phones as part of their job—"

"The McBees."

"Yeah," Mick said. "And Hachette, the chef, and also William Yorn . . ."

"The groundskeeper. None of them will be there tonight," Corky noted. "It's just Truman and the kid."

"You don't want to take any chances, do you, that somebody might decide to work late or maybe come back early from vacation? If I shut them all down, there's no chance anyone on that estate can dial nine-one-one. At the same time, service will be discontinued to those members of the staff who carry personal pagers."

Previously they had talked about the Internet and ways in which it could be used to issue a call for help.

Anticipating Corky, Mick said, "Cable-direct Internet access from the Manheim estate will also be terminated at eight-thirty."

"And the on-duty guards won't know any of this has happened?"

"Not unless they try to use a phone or go on the Internet."

"There won't be a system-interrupt warning on their computers?"

"Got that covered. But like I warned you, I can't shut down the cameras, the perimeter heat sensors, or the motion detectors in the house itself. If I did any of that, they'd see their system going blind, and they'd know something was up."

Corky shrugged. "When I get in the house, I want the motion detectors operative, anyway. I might need them. As for the cameras and the perimeter heat sensors, Trotter will get me past all that."

"And then you'll kill him," Mick said.

"Not right then. Later. So what do you have left to do?"

Raising his right hand high in ceremonial fashion, Mick said, "Just this." Slowly, with a goofy sense of drama, he brought his index finger straight down to the keyboard and tapped ENTER.

The data on the computer vanished. The screen clicked to a soft, unblemished field of blue.

Corky clenched. "What went wrong?"

"Nothing. I've initiated the delivery of the package."

"How long's it take?"

Mick pointed at three words that had appeared in the center of the screen: GETTING IT ON. "When that changes, the job is done. You want a Coke or something?"

"No thanks," Corky said.

He never ate or drank anything in the Sachatone house, and he tried not to touch anything, either. You had to figure that Mick had touched everything in the place, at one time or another, and you never knew where Mick's hands had recently been. Actually, you pretty much *did* know where Mick's hands had recently been, which was the problem.

Most of Mick's friends would have avoided shaking his hand if he had offered it; but he seemed to understand their concern, if only subconsciously, and never suggested hand-to-hand contact.

Bart Simpson ran across a field of wrinkles, jumped in and out of folds of fabric, and made numerous faces as Mick got a Coke from an office refrigerator and returned to his chair at the computer.

They talked about a rare adult video, supposedly produced in Japan, which was legendary among aficionados of sleaze; the film involved two men, two women, and one hermaphrodite, all costumed as Hitler. Mick had been chasing after this item for twelve years.

The video didn't sound all that interesting to Corky, but he didn't have a chance to be bored by the conversation because in less than four minutes, the words on the computer screen changed from GETTING IT ON to the succinct SATISFACTION.

"Package delivered," Mick said.

"That's it?"

"Yeah. The seeds have been planted in the phone-company, cable-company, and security-company computers. Later today, just when you want it to happen, everything will go down."

"Without any more attention from you?"

Mick grinned. "Slick, huh?"

"Amazing," Corky said.

Mick tipped his head back to take a long swallow of Coke, and Corky drew the Glock, and when Mick lowered his head again, Corky blew him away.

CHAPTER 67

THE PROFESSOR WHO HAD ORGANIZED THE one-day seminar on publicity and self-promotion was Dr. Robert Vebbler. He preferred to be called Dr. Bob, as he was known on the motivational-speaking circuit, where he promised to turn ordinary, self-doubting men and women into doubt-free dynamos of self-interest and superhuman achievement.

Ethan and Hazard found the professor on the mostly deserted campus, in his office, preparing for a January speaking tour. The walls of the two-room space were papered with portrait posters of Dr. Bob in a size popularized by Joseph Stalin and Mao Tse-tung.

He had a shaved head, a handlebar mustache, a red-bronze tan that established his contempt for melanoma, and laser-whitened teeth brighter than irradiated piano keys. With the exception of his red snakeskin boots, everything he wore—as in the posters—was white, including his watch, which had a white band and a plain white face without any numbers or checks to indicate the hours.

Dr. Bob managed so successfully to turn the answer to every question into a mini-lecture on self-esteem and positive thinking that Ethan wanted Hazard to arrest him on charges of felony cliche and practicing philosophy without an idea.

He was just as quacky as Donald Duck, but he was no more a murderer than was that excitable mallard. He hungered to be famous, not infamous. Donald *had* on occasion attempted to kill Chip and Dale, that pair of pesky chipmunks, but Dr. Bob would instead motivate them to give up their rodent ways and become successful entrepreneurs.

He signed for Ethan and Hazard two paperback copies of his latest collection of motivational speeches and declared that he would be the first ever to pyramid a series of self-help books into a Nobel prize for literature.

By the time they escaped Dr. Bob's office, located a trash can in which to ditch the paperbacks, and returned to the Expedition, the instrument-panel clock and Ethan's watch showed a synchronized 3:41.

At five o'clock, the last of the household staff would leave for the day. Fric would be alone in Palazzo Rospo.

Ethan considered calling the guards in the security office at the back of the estate. One of them could go to the house and stay with the boy.

That would leave one man to monitor cameras and other detection systems, with no one to conduct the scheduled foot patrols. Ethan was reluctant to spread his resources thin in the current circumstances.

He continued to believe that Reynerd's unknown partner, if still determined to act, would not do so until Thursday afternoon at the earliest, when the Face returned from the location shoot in Florida. Manheim's whereabouts were public knowledge and much written about. Anyone sufficiently obsessed with the star to want to kill him would most likely know when he was expected to return to Bel Air.

Most likely . . . but not absolutely.

The element of doubt, and Hazard's intuitive sense that they didn't have until Thursday, troubled Ethan. He worried that someone would discover a way to penetrate the estate's defenses, regardless of how tightly the grounds were sealed, and lie in wait undetected until Manheim's return.

Even the most drum-tight security plan was a human enterprise, after all, and every human enterprise, due to the nature of the beast, was imperfect. A clever enough lunatic, driven by obsession and by a vicious homicidal impulse, could find a crack even in the wall of protection around a President of the United States.

From what Ethan knew of Reynerd, the man hadn't been clever, but the person who had inspired the character of the professor in the screenplay might be a higher-caliber crackpot.

"You go home," Hazard insisted as they drove off the university campus. "Drop me back at Our Lady of Angels so I can get my car, and I'll check out the last two names myself."

"That doesn't seem right."

"You're not a real cop, anyway," Hazard said. "You gave that all up for fortune and the chance to kiss celebrity ass. Remember?"

"You're only in this on account of me."

"Wrong. I'm in this because of these," Hazard said, and rang the set of three silvery bells.

The sound resonated in the fluid of Ethan's spine.

"Damn if I'm gonna have spooky shit like this in my life," said Hazard, "or guys walking into mirrors. I'm gonna explain it somehow, blow all these hoodoo thoughts out of my head, and get back to being who I was, such as I was."

The remaining two names were those of professors of American literature at yet another university. They had been put at the bottom of the list because Reynerd's partial screenplay suggested that his co-conspirator would prove to be an acting teacher or an academic associated in some other way with the entertainment business. Stuffy professors of literature, lounging about in tweed coats with leather patches on the elbows, smoking pipes and discussing participles, did not seem likely to be celebrity stalkers or murderers.

"Anyway," Hazard said, "I think maybe these two won't pan out any better than the others."

He read from notes made during phone calls that he had placed en route between Professor Fitzmartin at Cedars-Sinai and Dr. Bob.

The storm had somewhat relented. The wind that had cracked trees now merely worried them and made them shudder in expectation of a sudden resumption of the tempest.

Rain fell with a brisk measured efficiency but no longer with destructive force, as though a revolution in the heavens had turned out the ruling warriors in favor of businessmen.

"Maxwell Dalton," Hazard continued after a moment. "Evidently he's on leave or sabbatical from the university. The woman I spoke to was some holiday temp, not too clear, so I'm supposed to see Dalton's wife. And the other is Vladimir Laputa."

CHAPTER 68

CORKY REGRETTED WHAT HE HAD DONE TO Mick Sachatone's face. A good friend deserved to be executed in a more dignified manner.

Because the Glock hadn't been fitted with a sound suppressor, he had needed to make the first shot count. Maybe none of the nearest neighbors were home, and maybe if they were home, the rush of the rain would mask a single gunshot well enough to avoid piquing their interest. But a full barrage had been out of the question.

In Malibu, Corky had not wanted to suppress the fine voice of the pistol. The *bang* of each shot, punctuating the brittle chorus of the shattered porcelain figurines, had rattled Jack Trotter.

Although he had a silencer with him, the extended barrel did not permit the Glock to seat perfectly in his holster. Nor did the extra few inches allow for as smooth a draw as Corky preferred.

Besides, if poor Mick had seen the holstered Glock fitted with a sound suppressor, he might have been uneasy in spite of Corky's nonchalance.

After holstering the pistol, Corky pulled on his black leather coat and withdrew a pair of latex surgical gloves from one pocket. He needed to avoid leaving fingerprints, of course, but in this shrine to the sinful hand, he was less concerned about the evidence that he might leave behind than about what he might pick up.

Elsewhere, shelving for videos overlaid windows, making a cave of the house, but in the work rooms, the dreary face of the fading day pressed against rain-dappled glass. Corky closed the drapes.

He needed time to search the house for Mick's well-hidden cash reserves, which were most likely significant, as well as time to disconnect the computers and load them in the Land Rover to ensure that any information they contained about him would not fall into hostile hands. He would wrap the body in a tarp and haul it out of here, and then clean up the blood.

To avoid a homicide investigation that might, in spite of all his caution, lead back to him, Corky intended to make Mick disappear.

He could have instead saturated the place with gasoline and torched it to eliminate all evidence, as he had done at the narrow house of Brittina Dowd. The thousands of videocassettes would burn with intense heat, casting off great clouds of toxic smoke sufficient to foil firefighters. No clues would remain in the smoldering slag.

Yet he was loath to destroy the Sachatone archives of mindless lust, for this place was as great a monument to chaos as any that Corky had ever seen. This malignant mass sent forth vibrations with the power to spread dissolution and disorder as surely as a pile of plutonium issues deadly radiation against which, in time, no living thing can stand.

The search for Mick's cash, the dismantling of his computers, and the removal of the pajamaed corpse would have to wait, however, until Aelfric Manheim had been snatched from the cozy lap of fame and imprisoned in the room currently occupied by Stinky Cheese Man. Corky would return here in twenty-four hours.

Meanwhile, he switched off the computers and the other active machines in the work rooms. Then he went through the house, top to bottom, to be sure that no electrical appliance would be left on that might overheat and start a small blaze, bringing the fire department to these rooms before the trove of money had been located and while the corpse still waited to be discovered.

In the living room again, Corky stood for a minute, watching the four-screen erotic contortions of the incomparable Janelle, before bringing darkness to the wall of writhing flesh. He wondered if Jack Trotter had taken advantage of her astonishing flexibility to fold her into a half-size grave and save himself some digging.

With Mick now gone, both the Romeo and Juliet of porn were dead. Sad.

Corky would have preferred not to kill Mick, but poor Mick had signed his own death warrant when he'd sold out Trotter. In a fever of jealousy, sick for revenge, he had revealed to Corky the numerous fake identities that he had over the years created for Trotter. If he would betray any client, he might have one day betrayed Corky, too.

Destroying the social order is lonely work.

Corky stepped onto the front porch and locked the door with Mick's key, which he had taken from a pegboard in the kitchen.

The chill of the day had deepened.

For all the rinsing and wringing that it had undergone, the washrag sky was a dirtier gray than it had been this morning, and its light cast neither beam nor faintest shadow.

So much had happened since he had risen to face the day. But the best was yet to come.

CHAPTER 69

IN THE KITCHEN, CONFERRING WITH MR.
Hachette regarding dinner, Ethan found the chef barely communicative and stiff with anger that he flatly refused to explain. He would only say, "My statement on the matter is in the mail, Inspector Truman." He would not describe the "matter" to which he referred. "It is in the mail, my passionate statement. I reject to be lowered into a brawl like a common cook. I am *chef*, and I announce my contempt like a gentleman by modern pen, not to your face but to your back."

Hachette's English was less fractured when he wasn't angry or agitated, but you seldom had an opportunity to hear his more fluent speech.

In only ten months, Ethan had learned never to press the chef about any issue related to the kitchen. The quality of his food *did* justify his insistence on being given the latitude of a temperamental artist. His storms came and went, but they left no damage in their wake.

Responding to Mr. Hachette with a shrug, Ethan went in search of Fric.

Mrs. McBee disliked whole-house paging on the intercom. She considered it an offense against the stately atmosphere of the great house, an affront to the family, and a distraction to the staff. "We are not at work in an office building or a discount warehouse," she had explained.

Senior staff members carried personal pagers on which they could be summoned from anywhere on the sprawling estate. Squawking at them through the intercom system was seldom necessary.

If you needed to track down a junior staff member or if your position included the authority to seek out a member of the family at your discretion—which among the household staff was true only of Mrs. McBee, Mr. McBee, and Ethan—then you must proceed on the intercom one room at a time. You began with the three places where you most expected to find the wanted individual.

As five o'clock approached, only a minimal staff remained on duty to be distracted, all of them scheduled to leave within minutes. Fric was the sole member of the Manheim family in residence. The McBees were in Santa Barbara. Nevertheless, Ethan felt obliged to follow standard procedures in respect of tradition, in deference to Mrs. McBee, and in the conviction that if he paged Fric in all rooms at once, the dear lady in Santa Barbara would instantly know what had transpired and would have her brief holiday diminished by unnecessary distress.

Using the intercom feature on one of the kitchen phones, Ethan first tried Fric's rooms on the third floor. He sought the boy next in the train room—"Are you there, Fric? This is Mr. Truman"—in the theater, and then in the library. He received no reply.

Although Fric had never been sulky and certainly never rude, he might for whatever reason be choosing not to respond to the intercom even though he heard it.

Ethan elected to walk the house top to bottom, primarily to find the boy, but also to assure himself that, in general, all was as it should be.

He began on the third floor. He didn't visit every room, but at least opened doors to peer into most chambers, and repeatedly called the child's name.

The door to Fric's suite stood open. After twice announcing himself and receiving no answer, Ethan decided that, this evening, security concerns took precedence over household etiquette and family privacy. He walked Fric's rooms but found neither the boy nor anything amiss.

Returning through the east wing to the north hall, heading toward the main stairs, Ethan stopped three times to turn, to listen, halted by a crawling on the back of his neck, by a feeling that all was not as right as it appeared to be.

Quiet. Stillness.

Holding his breath, he heard only his heart.

Tuning out that inner rhythm, he could hear nothing real, only absurdities that he imagined: stealthy movement in the antique mirror above a nearby sideboard; a faint voice like that on the telephone the previous night, but fainter than before, crying out to him not from a third-floor room but from the far side of a blind turn on the highway to eternity.

The mirror revealed no reflection but his own, no blurred form, no boyhood friend.

When he began to breathe again, the distant voice that existed only in his imagination ceased to be heard even there.

He descended the main stairs to the second floor, where he found Fric in the library.

Reading a book, the boy sat in an armchair that he had moved from its intended position. The back of it was tight against the Christmas tree.

When Ethan opened the door and entered, Fric gave a start, which he tried to conceal by pretending that he had merely been adjusting his position in the armchair. Stark fear had widened his eyes and clenched his jaws for an instant, until he realized that Ethan was only Ethan.

"Hello, Fric. You okay? I paged you here on the intercom a few minutes ago."

"Didn't hear it, ummm, no, not the intercom," said the boy, lying so ineptly that had he been hooked up to a polygraph, the machine might have exploded.

"You moved the chair."

"Chair? Ummm, no, I found it like this, here like, you know, just like this."

Ethan perched on the edge of another armchair. "Is something wrong, Fric?"

"Wrong?" the boy asked, as though the meaning of that word eluded him.

"Is there something you'd like to tell me? Are you worried about something? Because you don't seem like yourself."

The kid looked away from Ethan, to the book. He closed the book and lowered it to his lap.

As a cop, Ethan had long ago learned patience.

Making eye contact again, Fric leaned forward in his chair. He seemed about to whisper conspiratorially but hesitated and straightened up. Whatever he'd been about to reveal, he let slide. He shrugged. "I don't know. Maybe I'm tense 'cause my dad's coming home Thursday."

"That's a good thing, isn't it?"

"Sure. But it's pretty tense, too."

"Why tense?"

"Well, he'll have some of his buddies with him, you know. He always does."

"You don't care for his friends?"

"They're okay. They're all golfers and sports fanatics. Dad likes to talk golf and football and stuff. It's how he unwinds. His buddies and him, they're like a club."

A club in which you're not and never will be a member, Ethan thought, surprised by a sympathy that tightened his throat.

He wanted to give the boy a hug, take him to a movie, *out* to a movie, not downstairs to the mini-Pantages here in Palazzo Rospo, but to some ordinary multiplex crawling with kids and their families, where the air was saturated with the fragrance of popcorn and with the greasiness of canola oil tricked up to smell half like butter, where you had to check the theater seat for gum and candy before sitting down, where during the funny parts of the movie, you could hear not just your own laugh but that of a *crowd*.

"And there'll be a girl with him," Fric continued. "There always is. He broke up with the last one before Florida. I don't know who the new one is. Maybe she'll be nice. Sometimes they are. But she's new, and I'll have to get to know her, which isn't easy."

They were in dangerous territory for conversation between a family member and one of the staff. In commiseration, Ethan could say nothing that revealed his true judgment of Channing Manheim as a father, or that suggested the movie star's priorities were not in proper order.

"Fric, whoever your dad's new girl is, getting to know her will be easy because she'll like you. Everyone likes you, Fric," he added, knowing that to this sweet and profoundly unassuming boy, these words would be a revelation and most likely disbelieved.

Fric sat with his mouth open, as though Ethan had just declared himself to be a monkey passing for human. A blush rose to his cheeks, and he looked down at the book in his lap, disconcerted.

Movement drew Ethan's eye from the boy to the tree behind him. The dangling ornaments stirred: angels turning, angels nodding, angels dancing.

The air in the library was as still as the books on the shelves. If there had been a low-intensity earthquake sufficient to affect the ornaments, it had been too subtle to catch Ethan's attention.

The movement of the angels subsided, as though they had been set in motion by a short-lived draft created by some passing presence.

A strange expectation overcame Ethan, a sense that a door of understanding might be about to open in his heart. He realized that he was holding his breath and that the fine hairs on the backs of his hands had risen as if to a baton of static electricity.

"Mr. Hachette," said Fric.

The angels settled and the pregnant moment passed without the manifestation of . . . anything.

"Excuse me?" Ethan asked.

"Mr. Hachette doesn't like me," Fric said, by way of refuting the suggestion that he might be more highly regarded than he thought.

Ethan smiled. "Well, I'm not sure that Mr. Hachette likes anyone terribly much. But he's a fine chef, isn't he?"

"So is Hannibal Lecter."

Although amusement at the expense of a fellow member of the senior staff was unquestionably bad form, Ethan laughed. "You may think differently, but I'm confident that if Mr. Hachette tells you it's veal he's put on the plate, it will be veal and nothing worse." He rose from the edge of the armchair. "Well, I had two reasons to come looking for you. I wanted to warn you not to open any exterior doors for the rest of the evening. As soon as I'm sure the last of the staff has left, I'm going to set the house-perimeter alarm."

Again Fric sat up straighter in his chair. Had he been a dog, he would have pricked his ears, so alert was he to the implications of this change in routine.

When Fric's father was in residence, the house-perimeter alarm would be set when the owner chose to set it. In Manheim's absence, Ethan usually activated the system when he retired for the night, between ten o'clock and midnight.

"Why so early?" Fric asked.

"I want to monitor it on the computer this evening. I think there's a problem with fluctuations in the voltage flow at some of the window and door contacts. Not anything that'll set off false alarms yet, but it needs repair."

Although Ethan was a more confident liar than Fric, the dubious expression on the boy's face most likely matched that with which he regarded Mr. Hachette's veal.

Hurrying on, Ethan said, "But I also came looking for you to see if we shouldn't have dinner together, being as it's just the two of us bachelors rattling 'round the place this evening."

Standards and Practices contained no proscriptive against senior staff dining with the boy in the absence of his parents. Most of the time, Fric did, in fact, have dinner alone, either because he enjoyed privacy at mealtimes or, more likely, because he thought he would be intruding if he asked to join others. From time to time, Mrs. McBee induced the boy to have dinner with her and Mr. McBee, but this would be a first for Ethan and Fric.

"Really?" asked Fric. "You won't be too busy monitoring the flow of voltage?"

Ethan recognized the sly jibe in that question, wanted to laugh, but pretended to believe that Fric had swallowed his lie about why he must turn the alarm on early. "No, Mr. Hachette prepared everything. All I have to do is warm it in the oven according to his notes. When would you like to eat?"

"Early's better," Fric said. "Six-thirty?"

"Six-thirty it is. And where should I set a table?"

Fric shrugged. "Where do you want?"

"If it's my choice, it has to be the dayroom," Ethan said. "The various other dining areas are strictly for family."

"Then I'll choose," the boy said. He chewed on his lower lip a moment and then said, "I'll get back to you on that."

"All right. I'll be in my quarters for a little while, then in the kitchen."

"I think we have wine this evening, don't you?" Fric asked. "A good Merlot."

"Oh, really? Should I also just pack my bags, arrange for a taxi, write myself a letter of dismissal in your father's name, and be ready to leave as soon as you've passed out drunk?"

"He doesn't need to know," Fric said. "And if he knew, he'd just figure it was typical Hollywood-kid stuff, better booze than cocaine. He'd make me talk to Dr. Rudy to see maybe does the problem come from when I was the son of an emperor back in ancient Rome, when maybe I was traumatized by watching the stupid lions eat stupid people in the stupid Colosseum."

This cheeky rap would have seemed funnier to Ethan if he hadn't believed that the Face might, in fact, have reacted to his son's drinking in pretty much that fashion.

"Maybe your father would never find out. But you're forgetting about She Who Cannot Be Deceived."

Fric whispered, "McBee."

Ethan nodded. "McBee."

Fric said, "I'll have Pepsi."

"With or without ice?"

"Without."

"Good lad."

CHAPTER 70

ALTHOUGH FRIGHTENED, BITTER, AND STRUG-gling against despair, Rachel Dalton remained a lovely woman, with lustrous chestnut hair and blue eyes mysterious in their depths.

She was also, in Hazard's experience, uncommonly considerate. Having agreed by phone to an interview, she had prepared coffee by the time he arrived. She served it in the living room with a plate of miniature muffins and butter cookies.

In the line of duty, homicide detectives were rarely offered refreshments, never with damask napkins. Especially not from the wives of missing men for whom the police had done embarrassingly little.

Maxwell Dalton, as it turned out, had vanished three months earlier. Rachel had reported him missing when he had been four hours late from an afternoon class at the university.

The police, of course, had not been interested in an adult who was missing only four hours, nor had they been intrigued when he'd not shown up in a day, two days, or three.

"Apparently," Rachel told Hazard, "we're living in a time when a shocking number of husbands—and wives—go off on drug binges or just suddenly decide to spend a week in Puerto Vallarta with some tart they met at Starbucks ten minutes ago, or walk out on their lives altogether without warning. When I tried to explain Maxwell, they couldn't believe in him—a husband so reliable. They were sure he would turn up in time, with bloodshot eyes, a sheepish look, and a venereal disease."

Eventually, when Maxwell Dalton had been gone long enough for even contemporary authorities to consider the length of his absence unusual, the police had allowed the official filing of a missing-persons report. This had led to little or no activity in search of the man, which had frustrated Rachel, for she had wrongly assumed that a missing-persons case triggered an investigation only a degree less vigorous than a homicide.

"Not when it's an adult," Hazard said, "and not when there are no indications of violence. If they had found his abandoned car . . ."

His car had not been found, however, nor his discarded wallet stripped of cash, nor any item that might have indicated foul play. He had vanished with no more trace than any ship that had sailed into but not out of the Bermuda Triangle.

Hazard said, "I'm sure you've been asked already, but did your husband have any enemies?"

"He's a good man," Rachel said, as he expected she would. Then she added what he had not expected, "And like all good people in a dark world, of course he has enemies."

"Who?"

"A gang of thugs at that sewer they call a university. Oh, I shouldn't be so harsh. Many good people work there. Unfortunately, the English Department is in the hands of scoundrels and lunatics."

"You think someone in the department might . . ."

"Not likely," Rachel admitted. "They're all talk, those people, and meaningless talk at that." She offered more coffee, and when he declined, she said, "What was the name of the man whose death you're investigating?"

He had told her only enough to get through her door; and he did not intend to elaborate now. He hadn't even mentioned that already he had chased down and shot Reynerd's killer. "Rolf Reynerd. He was shot in West Hollywood yesterday."

"Do you think his case might be related to my husband's? I mean, by more than the fact that he took Max's class in literature?"

"It's possible," he said. "But unlikely. I wouldn't . . ."

Oddly enough, a sad smile rendered her more lovely. "I won't, Detective," she said, responding to what he had been hesitant to say. "I won't get my hopes up. But damn if I'll let them fade, either."

As Hazard rose to leave, the doorbell rang. The caller proved to be an older black woman with white hair and the most elegant hands he had ever seen, slender and long-fingered and as supple as those of a young girl. The piano teacher, come to give a lesson to the Daltons' ten-year-old daughter.

Drawn by the music of her teacher's voice, Emily, the girl, came downstairs in time to be introduced to Hazard before he left. She had her mother's loveliness but not yet as much steel in her spine as her mother did, for her lower lip trembled and her eyes clouded when she said, "You're going to find my father, aren't you?"

"We're going to try hard," Hazard assured her, speaking for the department, hoping that what he said would not prove to be a lie.

After he crossed the threshold and stepped onto the front porch, he turned to Rachel Dalton, in the doorway. "The next name on my list is a colleague of your husband's, from the English Department. Maybe you know him. Vladimir Laputa."

As sadness did not diminish Rachel's loveliness, neither did anger. "Among all those hyenas, he's the worst. Max despised . . . despises him. Six weeks ago, Mr. Laputa paid me a visit, to express his sympathy and concern that there'd been no news of Max. I swear . . . the weasel was feeling me out to see if I'd grown lonely in my bed."

"Good Lord," Hazard said.

"Ruthlessness, Detective Yancy, is no less a quality of the average university academic than of the average member of a street gang. It's just expressed differently. The day of the genteel scholar in his ivory tower, interested only in art and truth, is long gone."

"Recently I've begun to suspect as much," he told her, though he would never reveal that, for want of a better candidate, her husband had risen to the top of his list of suspects in the matter of the threat to Channing Manheim.

He found it difficult to believe that a woman like Rachel and a girl like Emily could love a man who was not exactly—and all—that he appeared to be.

Nevertheless, Maxwell Dalton's disappearance might, in fact, mean that he *had* started a new life, a demented one that included making threats against celebrities either with the intent to do harm or in the naive hope that intimidation could serve extortion.

Even setting aside bells out of dreams and men into mirrors, Hazard Yancy had seen stranger things in his career than a once-honest professor, a man of reason, gone bad, made mad by envy, by greed.

The Daltons lived in a good neighborhood, but Laputa lived in a better one, less than fifteen minutes from their door.

The early winter twilight had crept in behind the storm while Hazard had been having coffee with Rachel Dalton. Dusk drained all light from the day as he drove to Professor Laputa's place, until the low clouds were no longer gray and backlit, but sour yellow and underlit by the rising radiance of the city.

He parked across the street from the home of the reputed worst of all academic hyenas, switched off the headlights and windshield wipers, but left the engine running to keep the heater in action. Local kids wouldn't be building snow forts; but with the coming of night, the air had grown wintry by southern-California standards.

He'd been unable to reach the professor by phone. Now, although the Laputa house was dark, he tried again.

As he let the number ring, Hazard noticed a pedestrian turn the corner at the end of the block, on the far side of the street, coming in the direction of the Laputa residence.

Something was wrong about the guy. He had neither an umbrella nor a raincoat. The downpour had diminished to a steady, business-like drenching, but it was not weather in which anyone went for a stroll. And that was another thing: The guy didn't hurry.

Attitude, however, was what really cranked up the Hazard Yancy suspicion machine. If the guy had been a sponge, he'd have been so saturated with attitude that he couldn't have made room for one drop of rain.

He swaggered under the streetlamps, not like genuine tough guys sometimes swaggered, but as movie stars swaggered when they thought they were getting the tough-guy thing just right. His gray pants, black turtleneck, and black leather coat were soaked, but he seemed to *defy* the rain.

Theatrical. In this weather no other pedestrians were in sight, and at the moment no traffic moved on this quiet residential street, yet the guy appeared to be performing without an audience, for his own amusement.

Tired of listening to Laputa's phone ring, Hazard pressed END on his cell keypad.

The pedestrian appeared to be talking to himself, although from across the street Hazard could not be certain of this.

When he rolled down his window and cocked his head to listen, he was defeated by the drumming of the rain. He caught a few snatches of the voice and thought the guy might be singing, though he couldn't recognize either tune or lyrics.

To Hazard's surprise, the swaggering man left the sidewalk and fol-lowed the driveway at the Laputa house. He must have been carrying a remote control, because the segmented garage door rolled up to ad-mit him, and then at once closed.

Hazard put up the car window. He watched the house.

After two minutes, a single soft light appeared toward the back of the residence, in what might have been the kitchen. Perhaps half a minute later, another light came on upstairs.

Whether or not the lover of rain was Vladimir Laputa, he knew his way around the professor's house.

CHAPTER 71

FROM THE ENTRANCE ROTUNDA, AT A WINDOW beside the front door, Ethan watched as Mr. Hachette's car dwindled along the driveway, into the tintack rain and the riddled darkness. The chef had been the last member of the day staff to leave.

Set flush in one wall of the rotunda, tucked discretely near a corner, a dark display screen brightened when Ethan lightly pressed one finger to it. This was a Crestron touch-control unit by which he could access all the computerized features of the house: the heating and air-conditioning, the music system, the gas heating for swimming pools and spas, both the in-house and landscape lighting, the phone system, and much more.

Crestron panels were positioned throughout the mansion, but the same features could also be controlled from any computer work station, such as the one in Ethan's study.

After Ethan activated the screen with a touch, three columns of icons were presented for his consideration. He tapped the one that represented the exterior surveillance cameras.

Because eighty-six outdoor cameras were positioned across the estate, he was next presented with eighty-six designating numbers. For the most part, to obtain quickly a view of any specific portion of the grounds, you had to have memorized the numbers—at least those that, in your particular staff position, you were most likely to use frequently.

He touched 03, and the Crestron screen at once filled with a view of the main gate as seen from outside the estate wall. This was the same camera that had captured Rolf Reynerd delivering the package that contained the doll's eye in the apple.

The gate rolled open. Mr. Hachette's car drove off the grounds, onto the public street, turned right, and disappeared from the frame.

As the front gate rolled shut, Ethan touched the screen and exited the exterior-camera menu. He pressed the icon for the house alarm system.

Not all staff members were authorized to activate and deactivate the alarm; consequently, the screen requested Ethan's password. He entered it, was granted access, and set the house-perimeter alarm.

All public areas of the mansion—virtually everything except bedrooms, bathrooms, and staff quarters—featured motion detectors that would register the passage of anyone moving along a hallway or through a room. They were activated 24/7, but were actually linked to the alarm only when it was in the "nobody-home mode," when the house was entirely deserted, a rare occurrence.

With Fric and Ethan in residence, if the motion detectors had been linked to the alarm, the breach siren would have gone off every time that they passed through a monitored space or so much as made a gesture with one hand.

All he needed was the assurance that the siren would sound if a door or window were opened. This precaution, along with the team of guards monitoring the additional layers of detection on the grounds beyond the house, ensured that no one could set upon him or Fric by surprise.

Nevertheless, he didn't want Fric to sleep alone on the third floor. Not tonight, not tomorrow night, not anytime soon.

Either they would make arrangements for the kid to camp out on the ground floor or Ethan would spend the night in the living room of Fric's third-floor suite. He intended to discuss the matter with the boy after dinner.

Meanwhile, for the first time since returning home, he went to his apartment, to his study, to the desk where he had left the three silvery bells. They were gone.

In the deepest garage at Our Lady of Angels, when he had found only a single set of bells missing from the ambulance, he'd suspected that the set currently in Hazard's possession was the same one that he had found in his hand outside Forever Roses.

The phantom that he had seen in the bathroom mirror at Dunny's apartment, the phantom that had vanished into a mirror in Hazard's bedroom, had somehow come here during the night, as Ethan slept, had taken the bells, and had transferred them to Hazard, for reasons that were mysterious if not forever beyond understanding. And the phantom, more likely than not, was Dunny Whistler, dead but risen.

Ethan marveled that he could stand here, entertaining such bizarre thoughts, and still be sane. At least he believed himself to be sane. He might be wrong about that.

Although the bells were gone, the items from the black boxes remained on display. He sat at the desk and studied the six parts of the riddle, hoping for enlightenment.

Ladybugs, snails, a jar containing ten foreskins, the cookie jar full of Scrabble tiles—OWE, WOE—a book about guide dogs, the eye in the apple . . .

On better days, in a better mood, he'd been unable to make sense of these messages. He hoped that in his current state of wound-tight tension and mental exhaustion, his intellectual fences might fall away, allowing him suddenly to see everything from a new perspective and to understand what before had seemed indecipherable.

No luck.

He phoned the guards in the security office at the back of the estate, in the groundskeeper's building. On duty from four until midnight, they were already aware that he had set the house-perimeter alarm earlier than usual, because that action had registered on their displays.

Without giving them a reason, he asked that they be especially alert this evening. "And pass that request along to the guys on the graveyard shift when they get here."

He phoned Carl Shorter, the chief road warrior who managed the squad of bodyguards protecting the Face in Florida. Shorter had nothing disturbing to report.

"I'll call you tomorrow," Ethan said. "We'll need to go over new arrangements I'm going to make for your L.A. arrival on Thursday. More security at the airport and all the way here to home base, new procedures, a new route, just in case anyone has tumbled to our usual routine."

"Is your fan still clean?" Shorter asked.

"No shit's hit it yet," Ethan assured him.

"Then what's up?"

"I told you about the weird gifts in the black boxes. We've got an issue related to those, that's all. It's containable."

After signing off with Carl Shorter, Ethan went to the bathroom to shave and freshen up for dinner. He pulled off his sweater, put on a clean shirt.

A few minutes later, standing at the desk in the study, he took one more look at the enigmatic six items.

An indicator light on the phone caught his attention: Line 24, first fluttering and then burning steadily.

CHAPTER 72

OWNED BY KURTZ IVORY INTERNATIONAL, serving as the principal vehicle for Robin Goodfellow, the Land Rover must never be seen at Corky's home. It might too easily link him to criminal activities committed by his fascistic alter ego.

He parked around the corner and walked home in the rain, singing bits of *Das Rheingold* by Richard Wagner, admittedly not well but with feeling.

In the garage, he stripped naked and left his sodden clothes on the concrete floor. He took the wallet, National Security Agency ID fold, and the Glock into the house with him, because he was not yet done being Robin Goodfellow for the day.

He toweled dry in the master bedroom. He slipped into a pair of thermal underwear.

From the walk-in closet, he retrieved a black Hard Corps Gore-Tex/Thermolite storm suit made for skiers. Waterproof, warm, allowing a full range of easy movement, this would be the perfect costume for the assault on Palazzo Rospo.

Hazard could have phoned Vladimir Laputa or whoever had recently entered the professor's house through the garage, but after brooding for a minute about the wisest approach, he decided to appear at the doorstep unannounced. Something might be gained by the surprise—or lack of it—with which the swaggering man would react to the sight of Hazard and his badge.

He switched off the engine, got out of the car, and came face to face with Dunny Whistler.

As pale as a sun-bleached skull, features drawn from his days in deathlike coma, Dunny stood in the rain yet remained untouched by it, drier than bone, than moon sand, than salt. "Don't go in there."

Hazard startled and embarrassed himself by doing the next best thing to a feets-don't-fail-me-now routine. He tried to back up but had nowhere to go because the car was immediately behind him, yet he couldn't stop his shoes from slipping against the wet pavement, as his feet tried to propel him backward *through* the sedan.

"If *you* die," Dunny said, "I can't bring you back. I'm not *your* guardian."

As solid as flesh one instant, liquid the next, Dunny collapsed without a splash into the puddle in which he stood, as though he had been an apparition formed of water, shimmering to the wet pavement in vertical rillets, vanishing in an instant, even more fluidly than he had slipped away into a mirror.

The waterproof storm suit featured a foldaway hood, anatomically shaped knees, and more pockets than a kleptomaniac's custom-tailored overcoat, all with zippers. Two layers of socks, black ski boots, and leather-and-nylon gloves—almost as flexible as surgical gloves but less likely to arouse suspicion—completed the ensemble.

Pleased by his reflection in a full-length mirror, Corky went down the hall to the back guest room, to learn if Stinky Cheese Man was dead and to give him a scare if he wasn't.

He took with him the 9-mm pistol and a fresh sound suppressor.

At the door to the dark room, the stench of the incapacitated captive could be detected even in the hallway. Past the threshold, what had been a mere stink became a miasma that even Corky, an ardent suitor of chaos, found less than charming.

He switched on the lamp and went to the bed.

As stubborn as he was stinky, the cheese man still held on to life, although he believed his wife and daughter had been tortured, raped, and murdered.

"What kind of selfish bastard are you?" Corky asked, his voice thick with contempt.

Weak, having for so long received all liquid by intravenous drip, kept perilously close to mortal dehydration, Maxwell Dalton could not have replied except in a fragile voice so full of rasp and squeak as to be comical. He answered, therefore, only with his hate-filled stare.

Corky pressed the muzzle of the weapon against Dalton's cracked lips.

Instead of turning his head away, the lover of Dickens and Twain and Dickinson boldly opened his mouth and bit the barrel, though this act had the flair of Hemingway. His eyes were fiery with defiance.

Behind the wheel of the sedan, parked across the street from the Laputa house, trying to get a grip on himself, Hazard thought of his Granny Rose, his dad's mother, who believed in mojo though she didn't practice it, believed in poltergeists though none had ever dared to trash her well-kept home, believed in ghosts though she'd never seen one, who could recite the details of a thousand famous hauntings that had involved spirits benign, malign, and Elvis. Now eighty years old, Granny Rose—Hoodoo Rose, as Hazard's mom called her with affection—was respected and much loved, but she remained a figure of amusement in the family because of her conviction that the world was not merely what science and the five senses said it was.

In spite of what he had just seen in the street, Hazard couldn't get his mind entirely around the idea that Granny Rose might have a better grasp of reality than anyone he knew.

He had never been a man who harbored much doubt about what to do next, either in daily life or in a moment of high peril, but sitting in the car, in the rain, in the dark, shivering, he needed time just to realize that he should turn on the engine, the heater. Whether or not he should ring the bell at the Laputa house, however, seemed to be the most difficult decision of his life.

If you die, I can't bring you back, Dunny had said, with the emphasis on *you.*

A cop couldn't back off just because he feared dying. Might as well turn in the badge, get a job in phone sales, learn a craft to fill up the empty hours.

I'm not your guardian, Dunny had said, with the emphasis on *your,* which was a warning, of course, but which also had implications that made Hazard dizzy.

He wanted to pay a visit to Granny Rose and lie with his head on her lap, let her soothe his brow with cool compresses. Maybe she had homemade lemondrop cookies. She could brew hot chocolate for him.

Across the street, through the screen of rain, the Laputa house didn't look the same as it had when he'd first seen it. Then it had been a handsome Victorian on a large lot, warm and welcoming, the kind of home that protected families in which all the kids became doctors and lawyers and astronauts, and everyone loved one another forever. Now he looked at it and figured that in one of the bedrooms there had to be a young girl strapped to a levitating bed, vomiting violently, cursing Jesus, and speaking in the voices of demons.

As a cop, he must never allow fear to inhibit him, but also as a friend, he couldn't walk away from this and leave Ethan with no one to guard his back.

Information. In Hazard's experience, doubt came from having too little information to make an intelligent decision. He needed someone to chase down the answers to a couple questions.

The problem was that officially he had no reason to be pursuing these leads. If this cheese-eater were related to any active case, it was Mina Reynerd's murder, which was on Kesselman's desk, not on Hazard's. He couldn't seek information through the usual department channels.

He phoned Laura Moonves in the Detective Support Division. She had dated Ethan, she still cared for him, and she had helped him track down Rolf Reynerd from the plates on the Honda that had been filmed by one of the estate's video cameras.

Hazard worried that she would have left for the day, but she took his call, and with relief he said, "You're still there."

"Am I? I thought I'd left. I thought I was halfway home, already stopped for a bucket of takeout fried chicken, double slaw. No, son of a bitch, here I still am, but what does it matter, since I don't have a social life."

"I tell him he's an idiot for letting you slip away."

"I tell him he's an idiot, too," she said.

"Everyone tells him he's an idiot."

"Yeah? So maybe we all ought to get together and come up with a new strategy, because this telling-him-he's-an-idiot thing isn't working. I like him *so much*, Hazard."

"He's still getting over Hannah."

"Five years, man."

"When he lost her, he lost more than her. He lost his sense of purpose. He couldn't anymore see a bigger meaning to things. He needs to see it again, 'cause that's him."

"The world's full of sexy, smart, successful guys who wouldn't recognize a bigger meaning to life if God punched them in the face wearing a ring that left His initials in their foreheads."

"That would be your pissed-off Old Testament version of God."

"Why do I have to fall for a guy who needs meaning?"

"Maybe because you need it, too." That thought silenced Laura, and into the silence, Hazard said, "Remember that guy you helped him track down yesterday morning—Rolf Reynerd?"

"Famous wolf," she said. "Rolf means 'famous wolf.' "

"Rolf means *dead*. Don't you watch the news?"

"I'm not a masochist, am I?"

"So check the homicide overnights. But not now. Right now I need you to do something for me, for Ethan, but off the record."

"What do you need?"

Hazard glanced at the house. The place still radiated that dual atmosphere: as if the Brady Bunch had built their home over the gate to Hell.

"Vladimir Laputa," Hazard said. He spelled it for Laura. "Let me know as quick as you can, does anyone with that name have a rap sheet, even just a DUI, failure to pay parking tickets, anything."

Instead of pulling the trigger, Corky withdrew the barrel from Dalton's mouth, bearing down to scrape the steel across the teeth, which were loose from malnutrition.

"One shot would be too easy for you," Corky said. "When I'm ready to finish you, it'll be slow . . . and memorable."

He put the pistol aside, told Dalton some delicious lies about disposing of the bodies of Rachel and Emily, and eventually selected a fresh infusion bag from the nearby refrigerator.

"I'll be bringing someone back with me this evening," Corky said as he worked. "An audience for your final suffering."

In the wasted face, surrounded by a raccoon mask of livid skin, glistening in sunken sockets, the eyes rolled to follow Corky during his caregiving, no longer radiant jellies spiced with hatred, but once more flavored with fear, the haunted eyes of a man who at last believed in the power of chaos and understood its majesty.

"He's a ten-year-old boy, my new project. You'll be surprised at his identity when I introduce you."

After replacing the infusion bag, he went to the drug cabinet, from which he withdrew a packaged hypodermic syringe and two small bottles of drugs.

"I'll strap him in a chair next to your bed. And if he can't watch what I've got planned for you, I'll tape his eyes open."

Laura Moonves could find no rap sheet for Vladimir Laputa, not even a history of unpaid parking tickets. But when, after less than fifteen minutes, she called Hazard back, she had interesting news.

Robbery/Homicide had an open case under the name Laputa. The investigation wasn't currently active, due to a lack of evidence and leads.

Four years ago, a woman named Justine Laputa, age sixty-eight, had been murdered in her home. The crime-scene address proved to be the residence that Hazard now had under surveillance.

Watching the house as he spoke with Laura, Hazard said, "How did she die?"

"The entire file isn't on computer-network access, just the open-case extract. According to that, she was bludgeoned to death with a fireplace poker."

Mina Reynerd had been shot in the foot, but the actual cause of her death had been bludgeoning with a marble-and-bronze lamp.

A fireplace poker. A heavy lamp. In both cases, the killer had resorted to a blunt instrument near at hand. This might not be proof enough of one modus operandi, one killer, but it was a start.

"Justine's murder was savage, unusually violent," Laura said. "The medical examiner estimates the killer delivered between forty and fifty blows with the poker."

Mina Reynerd's death, by lamp, had been likewise brutal.

"Who were the detectives on the case?" Hazard asked.

"Walt Sunderland, for one."

"I know him."

"I got lucky," Laura said, "caught him on his cell phone five minutes ago. Told him I couldn't right now explain why I needed to know, then asked if he'd had a suspect in that case. Didn't hesitate. Said Justine's son inherited everything. Walt says he was a smug creep."

"The son's name is Vladimir," Hazard guessed.

"Vladimir Ilyich Laputa. Teaches at the same university that his mother retired from."

"So why isn't he in some hard-time joint, trading romance for cigarettes?"

"Walt says Vladimir had an alibi so six-ways airtight that an astronaut could go to the moon and back in it."

Nothing in this world was perfect. A designer alibi with triple-stitched seams always cocked the trigger of a cop's suspicion because it looked *made*, not found.

The house waited in the rain, as though alive, alert, its few lighted windows like irregularly positioned eyes.

In the syringe, Corky blended a paralytic cocktail of drugs to keep his captive quiescent, immobile, but alert.

"By dawn you'll be as dead as Rachel and Emily, and then this will be the boy's room, his bed."

He didn't administer either a sedative or a hallucinogenic. When he returned well before midnight, he didn't want Dalton to be fuzzy-minded or lost in illusions. The vile man must be clearheaded to experience every subtle nuance of his long-planned death.

"I've learned so much from this adventure of ours."

Corky introduced the hypodermic needle into the drug port on the IV drip line.

"It's given me so many good ideas, better ideas."

With his thumb, he slowly depressed the plunger, feeding the contents of the syringe into the saline solution that seeped into Dalton's vein.

"The boy's experiences in this room will be only somewhat like yours, but more colorful, more shocking."

Having administered the full dosage, he withdrew the needle from the port and discarded it in the trash can.

"After all, the whole world will be watching the videos I send out. My little movies must have tremendous entertainment value if I'm to keep so many millions of people enthralled."

Already, Stinky Cheese Man's wobbly teeth had begun to chatter. For some reason, this brew of paralytic drugs gave him spasmodic chills.

"I'm sure the boy will be thrilled when, in his first starring role, he fascinates the masses in greater numbers than his father ever has."

The storm lost its strength, became a windless drizzle. Fog plumed through the street, like cold breath come down out of the hidden moon.

Alerted now to the nature of the individual with whom he was dealing, Hazard sat in the car, mulling over how best to approach Vladimir Laputa.

His cell phone rang. When he answered it, he recognized the voice that he had heard a short time ago, in the street, issuing from the apparition.

Dunny Whistler said, "I'm Ethan's guardian, not yours, not Aelfric's. But if I save him—if I *can*—there'll be no point to it if either you or the boy dies."

Usually able to draw upon a rich account of words, Hazard found himself bankrupt in this case. He had never talked to a ghost before. He didn't want to start.

"He'll blame himself for the loss of either of you," Whistler continued. "And then the shadow on his heart will become a darkness deep within it. Don't go in that house."

Hazard found a voice not too much thinner and shakier than the one he usually could rely upon: "Are you dead or alive?"

"I'm dead *and* alive. Don't go in that house. The Kevlar vest won't matter. You'll be head shot. Two bullets in the brain. And I have no authority to resurrect you."

Dunny hung up.

Corky in the kitchen, stylishly outfitted to storm the castle of Hollywood's reigning king, glanced at the wall clock and saw that he had less than an hour until his rendezvous with Jack Trotter in Bel Air.

Murder and mayhem sharpened the appetite. On his feet, roaming back and forth from refrigerator to pantry, he made a makeshift meal of cheese, dried fruit, half a doughnut, a spoonful of butterscotch pudding, a taste of this, a bite of that.

Such a chaotic dinner was well suited to a man who had brought so much disorder into the world in one day, and who still had much work to do before lying down to sleep.

The Glock, with sound suppressor attached, lay on the kitchen table. It would just fit in the deepest pocket of his storm suit.

In other pockets, he had spare magazines, far more ammunition than he ought to need, considering that he didn't expect to have to kill anyone else today except Ethan Truman.

If Hazard had been nothing more than a man who wanted to live, he would have driven away without crossing the street to ring that doorbell.

He was, however, also a good cop and Ethan's friend. He believed that police work was not just a job, that it was a calling, and that friendship required commitment exactly when commitment was hardest to give.

He opened the door. He got out of the car.

CHAPTER 73

U PON RECEIVING THE CALL, DUNNY AT ONCE responds to it not by automobile this time but by highways of fog and water, and by the *idea* of San Francisco.

In a Los Angeles park, he pulls about him a cloak of earthbound cloud, and hundreds of miles to the north, he arrives through the soft folds of another fog, having traded the footpath in the park for the planking of a wharf.

Because he is dead but has not yet moved on from this world to the next, he inhabits his own corpse, a strange condition. After he died in a coma, his spirit had resided briefly in a place that had felt like a doctor's waiting room with neither tattered magazines nor hope. Then he was readmitted to the world, to his familiar mortal shell. He is no mere ghost, nor is he a traditional guardian angel. He is one of the walking dead, but his flesh is now capable of whatever amazing feat his spirit demands of it.

In this more northern and colder city, no rain falls. Water laps at the pilings of the wharf, an unpleasant chuckling that suggests mockery, conspiracy, and inhuman hunger.

Perhaps the thing about being dead that most surprises him is the persistence of fear. He would have thought that with death came freedom from anxiety.

He trembles at the sounds of the water beneath the wharf, at the *ponk* of his footsteps on the dock planking wet with condensation, at the briny semen scent of the fertile sea, at the frosty rectangles, fluorescent in the mist, that are the large windows of the bay-view restaurant where Typhon waits. For most of his life, he had perceived no meaning in anything; now dead, he sees meaning in every detail of the physical world, and too much of it has a dark significance.

One finger of the wharf leads past the restaurant windows, and at a prime table sits Typhon, in the city on business but currently alone, beautifully dressed as always, regal in demeanor without appearing pretentious. Through the pane of glass, their eyes meet.

For a moment, Typhon regards him somberly, even severely, as though with displeasure certain to have consequences that Dunny does not wish to consider. Then his plump face dimples, and his winning smile appears. He makes a gun of thumb and forefinger, pointing it at Dunny as if to say, *Gotcha.*

By way of fog and glass and the candlelight on the table, Dunny could in a wink travel from the wharf to the chair opposite Typhon. With so many people in the restaurant, however, that unconventional entrance would be the essence of indiscretion.

He walks around the building to the front door and follows the maitre d' through the busy restaurant to Typhon's table.

Typhon graciously rises to greet Dunny, offers a hand to be shaken, and says, "Dear boy, I'm sorry to have summoned you at such a critical moment on this night of all nights."

After he and Typhon settle into their chairs and after Dunny politely turns aside the maitre d's solicitation of a drink order, he decides that disingenuousness will not play any better here, and perhaps far worse, than it had the previous night at the hotel bar in Beverly Hills. Typhon had explicitly required integrity, honesty, and directness in their relationship.

"Sir, before you say anything, I must tell you that I know I've stretched my authority to the snapping point again," Dunny says, "by approaching Hazard Yancy."

"Not by approaching him, Dunny. By the *directness* with which you approached him." Typhon pauses to sip his martini.

Dunny starts to explain himself, but the white-haired mensch begs his patience with a raised hand. Blue eyes twinkling merrily, he takes another sip of his martini, and savors it.

When he speaks, Typhon first addresses a matter of deportment: "Son, your voice is raised just a tad too loud, and there's an anxiety in it that's likely to make you an object of interest among those of our fellow diners who are too curious for their own good."

The clink of flatware and china, the almost-crystal ring of wine-glasses lightly knocked together to the accompaniment of toasts, the graceful music of a piano caressed rather than pounded, and the murmur of many conversations do not swell to the pitch that had so conveniently masked Dunny's and Typhon's exchanges in the hotel bar.

"Sorry," Dunny says.

"It's admirable that you wish to ensure not only Mr. Truman's physical survival but also his emotional and psychological well-being. This is within your authority. But in the interest of his client, a guardian such as you must act by indirection. Encourage, inspire, terrify, cajole, advise—"

"—and influence events by every means that is sly, slippery, and seductive," Dunny finishes.

"Precisely. You have pushed the limits by the way you've handled Aelfric. Pushed against them but haven't yet exceeded them."

Typhon's manner is that of a concerned teacher who finds it necessary to provide remedial instruction to a problem student. He seems neither wrathful nor riled, for which Dunny is grateful.

"But by bluntly telling Mr. Yancy not to go into that house," Typhon continues, "by informing him that he would be shot twice in the head, you have interfered with what was his most likely destiny at that point in time."

"Yes, sir."

"Yancy may now survive not because of his actions and choices, not because of his unfettered exercise of free will, but because you revealed to him the immediate future." Typhon sighs. He shakes his head. He looks sad, as though his next words sorrow him a little: "This is not good, dear boy. This is not good for you."

Only a moment ago, Dunny had been grateful for his mentor's lack of anger. Now he's made apprehensive by Typhon's quiet dismay and expression of regret, for they suggest that a judgment has already been reached.

Typhon says, "There were many tricks with which you could have turned Mr. Yancy away from that house by indirection."

The older man's cheerful nature cannot be long suppressed. He breaks into a smile again. His blue eyes twinkle with such merriment that, with a fake beard to match his white hair, and with a suit less elegant, he might board a sleigh two nights hence and harry wingless reindeer into flight.

Leaning conspiratorially across the table, Typhon says, "Son, any of a thousand bits of spooky business would have sent him running from that house, to his Granny Rose or to a bar. You didn't need to be so direct. And if you continue in this fashion, you will certainly fail your friend, Ethan, and in fact may yourself be the cause of his death and the death of the boy."

They stare at each other.

Dunny is hesitant to ask if he will be allowed to remain on the case, for fear that he already knows the answer.

After Typhon tastes his martini again, he says, "My, but you are a firecracker, Dunny. You're headstrong, impetuous, frustrating—but you're also a hoot. You tickle me. You do."

Uncertain how to interpret those statements, Dunny waits, still and silent.

"I don't mean to be rude," Typhon says, "but my dinner guests will shortly be arriving. Your lean and hungry look—to quote the Bard—

and your rough edges might alarm them. They are a wary group, and skittish. One politician and two of his handlers."

Dunny dares to ask, "May I continue to protect Ethan?"

"After your repeated breaches, I'd be justified in removing you now. There must be standards for guardian angels, don't you think? Something more than good intentions. The position ought to require greater ethics than those of United States senators and cardsharps."

Typhon rises from his chair, and Dunny gets quickly to his feet, as well.

"Nevertheless, dear boy, I'm inclined to cut you some slack this one last time."

Dunny accepts his mentor's offered handshake. "Thank you, sir."

"But understand that you're on a minute-by-minute reprieve. If you can't operate within the terms of agreement, then your authority and powers will be at once revoked, and you will instantly be sent home for eternity."

"I'll abide by our deal."

"And when you're sent home, Ethan will be fending for himself."

"I'll walk the line."

Putting one hand on Dunny's shoulder, squeezing affectionately, like a father counseling a son, Typhon says, "Dear boy, you've walked a crooked line so long that keeping to a straight one isn't easy. But now, minute by minute, you must watch your step."

By foot, Dunny leaves the restaurant and follows the wharf into mists reverberant with the low, hollow notes of boat horns. Traveling by fog, by the moonlight above the fog, and by the *idea* of Palazzo Rospo in Bel Air, he departs and makes his journey and arrives all at the same time.

CHAPTER 74

TWO BULLETS IN THE BRAIN.
Wearing his Kevlar chest protector and conscious of what an easy target his lionesque head would make, Hazard closed the car door and crossed the street.

The house of the mother-killer seemed to attract the incoming fog, which moved not in a monolithic bank but in curious eddies and lithe plumes: one quick-footed vaporous slinkiness after another, tail following tail of Angora mist, as though here were a thousand cats drawn home by the scent of tuna fresh from the can.

The aura of the house so entranced Hazard that he had crossed the street and followed the private walkway while remaining oblivious of the rain. Only when he reached the foot of the front-porch steps did he realize that he had approached with such deliberation that he had gotten wet to the skin.

Ascending the porch steps, he felt something in his hand—and discovered the cell phone on which he had spoken to Dunny Whistler.

I'm dead and *alive*, Dunny had said, and Hazard at the moment was of much that same sentiment.

At the top of the steps, instead of proceeding straight to the door and ringing the bell, he paused, realizing that he had neglected to do a

standard bit of follow-up to Dunny's call that he would have done
had he received a menacing message from anyone else who should
not have had his mobile number. He pressed *69.

The call was answered on the second ring, but the person at the far
end of the line said nothing.

"Somebody there?" Hazard asked.

A hard voice came back at him: "Oh, somebody here. Somebody
here, sure enough, you hook nigger."

Gang talk: *hook* meaning phony, imitation.

"I be here, got lit up by you, punched twice, and still taste pencil."

Pencil meaning lead, meaning bullets.

Hazard had never heard this voice before, but he knew to whom it
might belong. He could not speak.

"When you come across after me, you wannabe ofay, better get
ready for a million nightmares of eastlies. You know eastly, man?"

"Yeah. An ugly person," Hazard said, surprised that he had spoken,
sensing at once that responding was a bad idea, that it was an *invitation*.

"Worse than ugly, man. Extreme butt-ugly. This crib ain't got
nothin' *but* eastlies. I be here when you come across, ofay. I be first in
line."

Hazard wanted to press END, clip the phone to his belt, but grim
fascination held it to his ear.

He was standing ten feet from Vladimir Laputa's front door. This
wasn't a wise place to engage in a phone chat with one of the restless
dead.

"Ofay, you know that four-five I shoulda capped you with last
night?"

In his mind's eye, Hazard saw Calvin Roosevelt, alias Hector X, on
the lawn outside Reynerd's apartment house, both hands around a
.45, squeezing off a shot, the muzzle spitting fire in the rain.

"Check this out, queerboy. You get here, I have me somethin' bigger than my four-five I'll shove up your ass, and then all the eastlies can jam you, too. Gonna see you soon."

Hazard pressed END, and at once the phone rang in his hand. No need to answer it, no *way* to answer it, knowing who it would be.

He was wet. Cold. Scared.

The phone continued to ring.

He needed either to think hard about this or to think about it never again, and he couldn't make up his mind which way to go while he stood here, on the mother-killer's porch.

He shoved the ringing phone into a jacket pocket, turned his back to the door, and descended the steps, into the rain once more.

CHAPTER 75

THE GENTLY CIRCULATING WATER IN THE POOL stirred the light that rose through it, causing shimmering auroras and shadows to quiver ceaselessly across the limestone walls and barrel-vaulted ceiling.

Fric brought a linen tablecloth to one of the poolside tables and arranged place settings of good china and silverware.

He almost added candles, but figured that two guys wouldn't have dinner by candlelight. Maybe by the glow of a firepit or Polynesian party torches, maybe beside a campfire in a forest full of prowling wolves, but not by candlelight.

With a dimming switch, he adjusted the sconces on the limestone columns until they produced a soft golden glow.

In good weather, Fric enjoyed eating by the outdoor pool, when he was the sole member of the family in residence and when Ghost Dad's girlfriends weren't lying around in bikini bottoms, thickly slathered in number-fifty sunblock, like plucked ducks in a marinade.

The indoor pool didn't measure up to the one outdoors: only eighty feet long and fifty-two feet wide, not quite large enough if you wanted to hold powerboat races. The room was warm in winter, however, and a double shitload of palm trees in huge pots gave it a pleasant tropical feeling.

Three walls of the pool room featured big windows framing the parklike grounds. The windows in the third wall were shared with the conservatory, offering a view into its jungly realms.

A poolside dinner appealed to Fric because in the adjacent conservatory he had carefully prepared his deep and special secret place. Given the slightest reason to believe that Moloch was coming, he could bolt for cover and be out of sight as quick as a rabbit.

Weirdly, he suspected that Mr. Truman, too, expected Moloch. The voltage-flow-testing story was crap. Something must be up.

He hoped that Mr. Truman wouldn't page him by intercom, as he had earlier paged him in the library. Not even under duress would Fric press the RESPOND button, because he was afraid that like *69, it might connect him with that place from which something had tried to squirm through the handset cord and into his ear.

Finishing the table preparation sooner than expected, he checked his wristwatch. Mr. Truman would not arrive with the food for perhaps ten minutes.

The rain-soaked, fog-swaddled grounds beyond the windows were revealed by many landscape lights, but the theme was enchantment and romance, which meant that shadows ruled. If Moloch had scaled the estate wall without being detected by the security system, he might be out there, shrouded in the murk, watching.

Fric considered hurrying to the kitchen under the pretense of lending a hand with dinner, but he didn't want to appear to be needy, nerdy, geeky.

If he actually might run away and join the Marine Corps someday, instead of hiding out in Goose Crotch, Montana, he ought to start thinking like a Marine and behaving like one, sooner rather than later. A Marine wouldn't be spooked by the darkness beyond a window. A Marine would sneer at that darkness and boldly piss on it. He'd open the window first, of course, so as not to mess up the glass.

Fric wasn't up to that level of Marine confidence just yet. Instead, he sat at the table, wishing the minutes would speed past.

He withdrew the photograph from a back pocket, unfolded it, and stared at the pretty lady with the special smile, distracting himself from the watching night. His make-believe mom.

As yet he had not done as Mysterious Caller had suggested, had not asked anyone if they knew who this woman might be.

For one thing, he hadn't been able to concoct a convincing story to explain either the origin of her photo or why he was so interested in knowing her identity. He was a lousy liar.

Besides, the longer he didn't ask anyone about her, the longer she would be his, and his alone. As soon as he found out who she was, she could no longer be his make-believe mom.

Something rapped against a window.

Fric sprang from the chair, dropping the photo.

The face at the window was hooded and hideous, but the hood was rain gear, and the face belonged to one of the security guards, Mr. Roma. Because he had a long upper lip and a small nose, Mr. Roma could pull his lip over his nose, and it would stay that way, so his face looked deformed and his teeth appeared to be huge. Held at his chin and aimed upward, the beam of a flashlight enhanced this effect.

"Ooga-ooga," said Mr. Roma, because without the use of his upper lip, he couldn't pronounce the *b* in *booga*.

When Fric went to the window, Mr. Roma allowed his face to pop back into shape. The guard said, "How you doin', Fric?"

"I'm fine now," Fric replied, raising his voice to be heard through the glass. "For a second there, I thought you were Ming."

"Ming's in Florida with your dad."

"He came back early," Fric said. "He's out there walking in the rain somewhere."

Mr. Roma's smile froze.

"He wanted me to walk with him," Fric said, "so he could teach me all about how rain washes the planet's spirit or something."

The frozen smile cracked, crumbled. Mr. Roma lowered the light from his face and turned his back to Fric, sweeping the night with the beam.

"You'll probably run into him," Fric said.

Realizing that the flashlight pinpointed his position, Mr. Roma switched it off. "See you, Fric," he said, and dashed away into the foggy gloom.

Although Fric was a lousy liar and had not sounded convincing even to himself, Mr. Roma didn't dare call his bluff if there was a one in a thousand chance that Ming, in a talkative mood and in full guru mode, might be in the vicinity.

CHAPTER 76

I N THE CAR, OUT OF THE RAIN, SHIVERING IN the warm blast from the heater, still sought by the dead Hector X, Hazard listened to the ring, ring, ring until he wanted to roll down the window and throw the cell phone into the street.

The ringing stopped just as he noticed activity at the Laputa residence. A man came out of the house, paused to lock the front door, and descended the porch steps.

Even in the rain and steadily clotting fog, Hazard recognized the guy who had earlier entered the house by way of the garage. All but certainly, this was Vladimir Laputa.

At the junction of private walkway and public sidewalk, Laputa turned right and retraced the route by which he had arrived. He still swaggered, but he didn't seem to be either talking to himself or singing.

He had changed into an entirely black outfit that appeared to be weatherproof, as if he would soon be driving north to Mammoth or to some other ski resort in the Sierras.

Like a premonition of snow, white masses of fog drifted around him, nearly obscuring him, before he turned right at the corner and moved out of sight.

Having already released the hand brake and put the car in gear, Hazard switched on the headlights and drove to the corner, where traffic splashed past on the cross street. He looked to the right and saw Laputa walking northward. When the professor was almost out of sight, Hazard turned the corner and followed him.

Whenever he drew within half a block of Laputa, he pulled to the curb and waited, letting his quarry proceed toward the limits of fog-diminished visibility. Then he drove after him again.

In these fits and starts, Hazard tracked the professor two and a half blocks. There, never having glanced back, Laputa got into a black Land Rover.

Remaining too far behind to read the license plate, letting other traffic intervene from time to time to mask his continuous presence, Hazard shadowed the Land Rover along a direct route to the Beverly Center, at Beverly Boulevard and La Cienega. Although somewhat oddly dressed for a trip to the mall, Laputa apparently intended to go shopping.

Conducting on-the-roll surveillance in a parking garage was a lot trickier than doing the same thing on public streets. Hazard followed the Land Rover up ramp after ramp, floor by floor, past ranks of parked vehicles, until Laputa found an empty space.

Near the end of that aisle, a slot waited for Hazard's sedan. He parked, switched off the engine, got out, and watched his man over the roofs of the parked cars.

He expected the professor to follow the signs to the nearest mall entrance. Instead, Laputa returned on foot to the ramp up which he had just driven.

Although other shoppers were walking through the garage, and although numerous vehicles roamed in search of parking spaces and exit routes, Hazard hung back from his quarry as far as he dared. He worried that the professor would spot him, and would know him at once for what he was.

Laputa descended one long ramp, then another. Two floors below the level on which he'd left the Land Rover, he walked up to a parked Acura coupe, which chirruped as he unlocked the doors with a remote.

Frozen by surprise, Hazard halted as the professor got into the driver's seat.

The guy had not come here to go shopping. He was picking up new wheels.

The Land Rover or the Acura almost certainly was a Kleenex car, meant to be used in the commission of a crime, and then tossed away. Maybe both vehicles were Kleenex.

Hazard considered making an arrest on the basis of suspicious behavior.

No. He couldn't risk it. Not with a respectable university professor. Not with Blonde in the Pond about to break wide open and a powerful city councilman about to become his mortal enemy. He was already the subject of an OIS investigation for shooting Hector X. In these circumstances, every mistake he made would be woven into the rope with which they would hang him.

He had no legitimate reason to be following Laputa. The murder of Mina Reynerd wasn't his case. All day he had been using his city-paid time and his police authority to help a friend in a personal matter. He had put his pecker in a vise and had tightened the handle himself; now he couldn't make a sudden move against the professor without big-time grief.

In the Acura, unaware that he was under surveillance, Laputa pulled shut the driver's door. He started the engine. He seemed to be fiddling with the radio.

Hazard sprinted back the way that he'd come, up two ramps, to the department sedan.

By the time he drove pell-mell down to the garage exit, hoping to fall in behind the Acura, Laputa had gone.

CHAPTER 77

YOU KNOW THAT CHOCOLATE POP CALLED Yoo-hoo?" Fric asked.

"I've had it a few times," Mr. Truman said.

"It's cool stuff. Did you know you can keep Yoo-hoo just about forever and it won't go sour?"

"I wasn't aware of that."

"They use a special steam-sterilization process," Fric revealed. "As long as it's unopened, it's as sterile as like, say, a bottle of contact-lens solution."

"I've never drunk any contact-lens solution," said Mr. Truman.

"Did you know that civet is used in a lot of perfumes?"

"I don't even know what civet is."

Fric brightened at this admission. "Well, it's a thick yellow secretion that's squeezed from the anal glands of civet cats."

"They sound like remarkably cooperative cats."

"They aren't really members of the cat family. They're mammals in Asia and Africa. They produce more civet when they're agitated."

"Under the circumstances, they must be agitated all the time."

"Civet stinks terrible," Fric said, "in full strength. But when you dilute it with the right stuff, then it smells really good. Did you know when you sneeze, all bodily functions stop for an instant?"

"Even the heart?"

"Even the brain. It's like a temporary little death."

"That's it then—no more pepper on my salads."

"A sneeze puts humongous stress on the body," Fric explained, "especially on the eyes."

"We always do sneeze with our eyes shut, don't we?"

"Yeah. If you sneezed violently enough with your eyes open, you could pop one out of the socket."

"Fric, I never realized you were such an encyclopedia of unusual facts."

Smiling, pleased with himself, Fric said, "I like knowing things other people don't."

Dinner had progressed immeasurably better than Fric had feared that it might. The chicken breasts in lemon-butter sauce, the rice with wild mushrooms, and the asparagus spears were delicious, and neither he nor Mr. Truman had yet died of food poisoning, though Mr. Hachette might be saving murder for dessert.

At first, conversation had been stiff because they started with the subejct of films, which inevitably led to Manheim movies. They weren't comfortable talking about Ghost Dad. Even if they said only nice things, they seemed to be gossiping behind his back.

Fric asked what it was like to be a homicide detective, and sought especially to hear about the most grotesque murders, hideously mangled bodies, and bugshit-crazy killers that Mr. Truman had ever encountered. Mr. Truman said much of that stuff wasn't suitable for table talk and that some of it wasn't fit for the ears of a ten-year-old kid. He did tell cop stories, however, most of them funny; a few were gross, although not so gross that you wanted to puke up your lemon-butter chicken, but gross enough to make this by far the best dinner chat that Fric had ever experienced.

When Mr. Truman noted that Mr. Hachette had prepared a coconut-cherry cake for dessert, Fric tapped his knowledge about the island nation of Tuvalu, exporter of coconuts, to make a contribution to their conversation.

Tuvalu led him to lots of other things he knew about, like the biggest pair of shoes ever made. They were size forty-two, cobbled for a Florida giant by the name of Harley Davidson, who had nothing to do with the motorcycle company. Size forty-two shoes are twenty-two inches long! Mr. Truman was properly amazed.

Giant shoes led eventually to Yoo-hoo, civet, and sneezing, and as they were finishing dessert—as yet showing no signs of arsenic ingestion—Fric said, "Did you know my mother was in a booby hatch?"

"Oh, don't pay attention to ugly stuff like that, Fric. It's an unfair exaggeration."

"Well, my mother didn't sue anyone who said that stuff."

"In this country, celebrities can't sue for slander or libel just because people tell lies about them. They have to prove the lies were told with malice. Which is hard. Your mom just didn't want to spend years in a courtroom. You understand?"

"I guess so. But you know what people might think."

"I'm not sure I follow you. What might people think?"

"Like mother, like son."

Mr. Truman appeared to be amused. "Fric, no one who knows you could believe you've ever been in a booby hatch or ever will be."

Pushing aside his empty cake plate, Fric said, "Well, say like someday I see a flying saucer. I mean, *really* see one, and a bunch of big greasy extraterrestrials. You know?"

"Big and greasy," Mr. Truman said, nodding and attentive.

"So then if I tell anyone, the first thing they'll think is *Oh, yeah, his mother was in a booby hatch.*"

"Well, whether or not they remembered those stories about your mom, some people in this world wouldn't believe you if you had one of those big greasy extraterrestrials on a leash."

"I wish I did," Fric murmured.

"They wouldn't believe me, either, if I had one on a leash."

"But you were a *cop*."

"Lots of people are unable to see all kinds of truths right in front of their eyes. You can't worry about them for a minute. They're hopeless."

"Hopeless," Fric agreed, but he was thinking less about other people than about his own circumstances.

"If you came to me or Mrs. McBee, however, we'd drop anything we were doing to run and see those big greasy freaks because we know you can be taken at your word."

This statement immensely heartened Fric, and he sat up straight in his chair. Into his mind crowded all the things about which he wanted to tell Mr. Truman—Mysterious Caller stepping out of a mirror and flying through the attic rafters, spirits trying to come through the telephone cord and into your ear when you pressed *69, guardian angels with strange rules, child-eating Moloch, the *Los Angeles Times* with the story of his kidnapping—but he hesitated too long, trying to put all this stuff in order, so it wouldn't gush out of him in one hysterical torrent.

Mr. Truman spoke first: "Fric, until I can troubleshoot it and figure out what needs to be repaired, this voltage-flow problem in the alarm system has me concerned."

The security chief's words might as well have been the three-pronged hook on a fisherman's well-cast fly, so firmly did they snare Fric's full attention. The phony voltage-flow story again.

"Nothing's going to happen, but I'm a worrier. Your dad pays me to worry, after all. So until this is fixed, I'd rather you didn't sleep alone on the third floor."

An edgy quality in Mr. Truman's eyes suggested that he himself had seen big greasy ETs, or expected to see them shortly.

"I'd like to set up camp for the night in the living room of your suite," he continued. "Or you could come down to my apartment, sleep in my bed, and I'd move to the sofa in my study. What do you think of that?"

"Or I could sleep on your sofa, and you wouldn't have to give up your bed."

"That's thoughtful of you, Fric. But I've already changed the sheets on my bed in case that was the option you chose. Now if it turns out I changed them for no reason and used up an unscheduled set of linens, I'll have to answer to Mrs. McBee. Don't put me in that position, I beg of you."

Fric knew that Mr. Truman wanted the sofa for one reason and one only: He intended to be stationed between the entrance door to his apartment and the bedroom in which Fric would be sleeping, not because Fric might fall down a set of stairs while sleepwalking, but because maybe some thugs would break down the apartment door and try to get to Fric, in which case they'd have to go through Mr. Truman.

Something was going on, for sure.

"All right," Fric said, worried but also pleasantly excited. "I'll come to your place, and you can have the sofa. This'll be great. I've never stayed overnight away from home."

"Well, you're not exactly going to be away from home."

"No, sir, but I've never been in your apartment," Fric said. "Not even before you came here. It's unknown territory, like the dark side of the moon—you know?—so this is like a totally real sleepover."

While he should have been brooding about how to avoid being kidnapped and killed, Fric instead found himself thinking that if they stayed up late, maybe they could make s'mores and sit on the floor by candlelight and tell ghost stories. He knew that this was a stupid idea, everything from the stupid s'mores to the stupid ghost stories, but the thought delighted him, anyway.

Consulting his wristwatch, Mr. Truman said, "It's almost eight o'clock." He got to his feet and began transferring dishes from the table to the stainless-steel cart on which he'd brought them. "I'll haul these to the kitchen, then we'll get you set up at my place."

"I'd like to go up to the library and get a book," Fric said, though he actually wanted to pee in the potted palm.

Even in the security chief's apartment, with a former cop standing armed guard, Fric wasn't too keen on the idea of using the bathroom, where there would be mirrors. You were seriously vulnerable when you were peeing.

Mr. Truman hesitated, glancing toward the windows, at the night, the rain, the fog.

"I always fall asleep reading," Fric pressed.

"All right. But don't take too long, okay? And once you've got the book you want, come straight to my apartment."

"Yes, sir." He headed toward the exit from the pool room, but halted after two steps. "Maybe later we can tell ghost stories."

Frowning as if Fric had suggested that they blow up the west wing, maybe even turning just a little pale, Mr. Truman said, "Ghost stories? Why would you say that?"

"Well, ummm, because that's, you know, what people do, like, at sleepovers. At least that's what I've heard." *Stupid.* But he couldn't stop talking. "They sit on the floor, ummm, by candlelight, you know, and they tell real scary stories, and then they, ummm, like sometimes they make s'mores." *Stupid, stupid.* "Or you can make, ummm, popcorn instead, and you can tell secrets." *Stupid, stupid, stupid.*

Mr. Truman's frown phased into a smile. "Are you telling me that after all we ate for dinner, you could chow down on s'mores, too?"

"Not right now, sir, no, but maybe in an hour."

"And you have some deep dark secrets to reveal, do you?"

"Ummm, I've got some stuff, yeah, some experiences I've had."

"Experiences. Do they involve big greasy extraterrestrials?"

"No, sir. Nothing that simple."

"Then when I take these dishes to the kitchen, I'll pick up the ingredients for a pile of s'mores. You've got me curious."

Relieved in one sense, needing relief in a different sense, Fric went to the library to deal another blow to the dying palm tree.

CHAPTER 78

I N HIS DEPARTMENT SEDAN, HAZARD FELT AS
adrift as any sailor's ghost on an abandoned and rotting ship,
chained to his floating haunt by nothing more than the stubborn
habit of living. Disoriented, with no purpose that made sense.

In the rain and mist, the streets seemed like the shipping lanes of a
strange spook-ridden sea, and it was easy to imagine—and almost
possible to believe—that many of the seemingly diaphanous vehicles
gliding past him in the veiled night were piloted by spirits that had
given up the flesh but not the city.

He had phoned in the license number on the Land Rover and had
learned that it was registered to Kurtz Ivory International, whatever
that might be. According to DMV records, the only vehicle registered
to Vladimir Laputa was a 2002 BMW, not an Acura like the one that
had been salted in the parking garage.

Having obtained that information, Hazard didn't know what he
could do next. He didn't like being at a loss for action.

Every time he tried to puzzle out his next move, however, into his
memory came the image of Dunny Whistler sorcerously transformed
from flesh into a cascade of water, in an instant becoming one with

the puddle in which he had stood, performing a splashless vanishment.

In the wake of that sight, in the cold continuing echo of the conversation with the dead Hector X, logical reasoning failed Hazard. He found his thoughts spiraling again and again through the same disturbing chambers, down into a nautilus shell of dread.

Although he had missed lunch, he wasn't hungry. Although he had no appetite, he stopped at a drive-in fast-food palace for a king's plate of cheeseburgers and French fries.

The king's plate proved to be a bag, of course, and the chalice of coffee was a Styrofoam cup full of a bitter swill that had been brewed with tree bark. Probably hemlock.

He remained too agitated to sit in the restaurant parking lot to have dinner. He drove while he ate.

He needed to keep moving. Like a shark, he felt that he would die if ever he stopped.

Eventually he returned to the tony neighborhood in which the professor lived. He parked across the street from the house.

Sitting there, he heard in his mind the warning voice of Dunny—*Two bullets in the brain*—and he knew beyond doubt that he would have suffered precisely that end if he had rung Laputa's doorbell.

For now the hyena, as Rachel Dalton had called him, was out on an Acura adventure. Without its resident demon, the house was just a house, not a killing ground.

Hazard phoned Robbery/Homicide and obtained Sam Kesselman's home telephone number.

In possession of the number, he considered what he was about to do. He knew that with this move he might be handing his enemies all the weapons they would need to destroy him.

His Granny Rose had once told him that woven throughout the very fabric of the world is an invisible web of evil, and that across this vast construction, deadly spiders quiver to the same secret seductive music, and do the same dark work, each in its own way. If you don't resist this sticky web when you feel it plucking at you, as often it does, then you will become one of the twisted eight-legged souls that dance upon it. And if the poisonous spiders are not crushed at every opportunity, there will sooner than later be spiders uncountable, but no humanity at all.

Hazard keyed in the number.

Sam Kesselman himself answered, first with a cough and a sneeze and a curse, but then in a voice so cracked and rough that he sounded like the product of a genetic-engineering lab working on human-frog crossbreeds.

"Man, you sound bad. You seen a doctor?"

"Yeah. Flu's a virus. Antibiotics don't work. Doctor gave me some cough medicine. Said get lots of rest, drink lots of fluid. Been drinkin' ten beers a day, but I think I'm gonna die anyway."

"Go to twelve."

Kesselman knew about Rolf Reynerd's murder by Hector X, and he knew that Hazard had in turn shot the shooter. "How are you with the OIS team?"

"I'll come through with a clean report. Sounds like they're ready to give it to me now. Listen, Sam, there's a connection with the murder of Reynerd's mother, and that's your case."

"You're gonna tell me Reynerd was involved with it."

"You've smelled something wrong with him all along, huh?"

"His alibi was just *too* airtight."

"There's a lot of that going around."

Hazard told Kesselman about the partial screenplay, but he edited the story line. He recounted the part about the swap of a killing for a killing, as in Hitchcock's *Strangers on a Train,* but not the part about the scheme to murder a movie star.

"So you think . . . Reynerd had . . . a kill buddy," Kesselman said between explosive coughs.

"I know he did. I'm pretty sure it's this guy named Vladimir Laputa.

I know Vamp and the Lamp is your case, Sam, but I'd like to develop this further, nail this Laputa if I can."

Maybe Kesselman really did need to hack up a Guinness-record weight of phlegm, or maybe all the throat clearing was a delaying tactic to give him time to think. Finally he said, "Why? I mean, you have your own caseload."

"Well, I think this one is on both our desks as of last night." He hadn't directly lied to Kesselman yet. Now he started: "Because I think Laputa didn't just murder Mina Reynerd, he also hired the hit man, Hector X, who dropped Rolf."

"Then even though the file's on my desk, it's de facto your case, too. The way I feel now, I'm gonna have to stay at all times less than twenty steps from a bathroom until at least next week, so you might as well go for it."

"Thanks, Sam. Just one more thing. If you're ever asked about you and me and this, could I have stopped by your house instead of phoning you, and could we have had this conversation earlier today, like twelve hours ago?"

Kesselman was silent. Then he said, "What kind of hellacious destruction are you bringing down on us?"

"When I'm done," Hazard said, "they'll kick your ass out of the department, strip away your pension, and clean a public toilet with your reputation, but they'll probably let you go on being a Jew."

Kesselman laughed, and the laugh turned into a cough, but when the coughing finally ended, he finished the laugh. "As long as we wind up in the same gutter, at least it'll be entertaining."

After he concluded the call, Hazard sat in the car for a while, staring at the Laputa house, thinking through his approach. He was committed to bold action, but he didn't want to act rashly.

Getting into the place was the easy—even if not legal—part. He still had the Lockaid lock-release gun that he had used to spring the deadbolt at Reynerd's apartment.

Conducting a search without leaving evidence that he had been there, then getting out again, all as smooth as an apparition first manifesting and then fading back to the spirit world: *that* was the hard part.

Throughout his career, he'd largely gone by the book, no matter how incoherent the text sometimes might be. Now he had to convince himself that the justification for rogue action was overwhelming.

From a jacket pocket, he removed the set of silvery bells. He turned them over and over in his hand.

At ten minutes past eight o'clock, he got out of the car.

CHAPTER 79

FOLLOWING A BRIEF STOP IN THE KITCHEN, Ethan returned to his apartment, intending to put away the six items that had come in the black gift boxes. If Fric saw them, he would inevitably ask questions that couldn't be answered without making him worry unnecessarily about his father's safety.

In the study, the computer screen glowed. Ethan had not switched it on since coming home.

He quickly searched the apartment but found no intruder. Someone must have been here, however. Perhaps someone who had come and gone by mirrors.

Returning to the desk, taking a closer look at the screen, Ethan saw that a message had been left for him: HAVE YOU CHECKED YOUR NETWORK E-MAIL?

Network e-mail—netmail for short—originated from computers on the estate, those in Channing Manheim's offices on the studio lot, and those in the hands of the security detail on location with the actor in Florida. Netmail was sorted into a different box from the one containing e-mail sent by all other correspondents.

Ethan had just three messages in the netmail box. The first was from Archie Devonshire, one of the porters.

MR. TRUMAN, AS YOU KNOW, I AM NOT ONE WHO FINDS IT INCUMBENT UPON HIMSELF TO MONITOR AELFRIC AND TATTLE ON HIS BEHAVIOR. IN ANY EVENT, HE'S AS WELL BEHAVED AS ANY CHILD CAN BE AND USUALLY ALL BUT INVISIBLE. THIS AFTERNOON, HOWEVER, HE WAS ENGAGED IN SOME CURIOUS BITS OF BUSINESS THAT I MIGHT HAVE DISCUSSED WITH MRS. MCBEE HAD SHE BEEN IN-HOUSE. YOUR VISITING FRIEND, MR. WHISTLER, BROUGHT TO MY ATTENTION THAT AELFRIC—

Ethan read the startling revelation without fully comprehending it, and had to back up to read it again.

YOUR VISITING FRIEND, MR. WHISTLER, BROUGHT TO MY ATTENTION—

The ghost or walking dead man, whichever he might be, if either, had ceased to perform his mysterious work at the edges of perception, and had boldly walked the halls of the mansion, talking to staff.

—BROUGHT TO MY ATTENTION THAT AELFRIC WAS UNPLUGGING QUAKE LIGHTS FROM ODD PLACES IN THE HOUSE, GATHERING THEM IN A PICNIC HAMPER. MRS. MCBEE WOULD SURELY DISAPPROVE OF THIS BECAUSE OF THE RISK THAT, IN A NIGHT EMERGENCY, SOME MEMBER OF STAFF OR FAMILY MIGHT FIND HIS ESCAPE FROM THE HOUSE HINDERED OR ENTIRELY THWARTED BY THE ABSENCE OF THE VERY QUAKE LIGHT CRUCIAL TO HIS EXIT.

Up in Santa Barbara, Mrs. McBee was no doubt uneasily aware that *something* had changed.

Archie Devonshire's netmail continued:

LATER, WHEN I ENCOUNTERED AELFRIC WITH THE HAMPER, HE TOLD ME IT CONTAINED HAM SANDWICHES, WHICH HE CLAIMED TO HAVE MADE HIMSELF, AND THAT HE INTENDED TO HAVE A PICNIC IN THE ROSE ROOM. LATER I FOUND THE HAMPER EMPTY IN THAT VERY ROOM, WITH NO EVIDENCE OF BREADCRUMBS OR SANDWICH WRAPPINGS. THIS SEEMS ALL VERY ODD TO ME, AS AELFRIC IS GENERALLY A TRUTHFUL BOY. MR. YORN HAS LIKEWISE HAD AN UNUSUAL ENCOUNTER AND INTENDS TO WRITE YOU ABOUT THAT SEPARATELY. YOURS IN SERVICE TO THE FAMILY, A. F. DEVONSHIRE.

The netmail from William Yorn, the groundskeeper, proved to be in a tone different from Devonshire's.

FRIC IS MAKING HIMSELF A HIDEY-HOLE IN THE CONSERVATORY, STOCKED WITH FOOD, DRINK, AND QUAKE LIGHTS. YOUR FRIEND WHISTLER BROUGHT IT TO MY ATTENTION. IT'S NONE OF MY BUSINESS. OR WHISTLER'S. BOYS PLAY AT ROBINSON CRUSOE. THAT'S NORMAL. FRANKLY, YOUR FRIEND WHISTLER SCRAPES MY NERVES. IF HE TELLS YOU I WAS ABRUPT WITH HIM, PLEASE UNDERSTAND I MEANT TO BE. LATER, I SAW FRIC AT THE ROSE-ROOM WINDOWS. HE SEEMED TO BE IN A TRANCE. THEN HE SHOUTED SOMETHING AT ME ABOUT HAM SANDWICHES. LATER, IN RAIN GEAR, HE WENT OUT TO THE LITTLE WOODS PAST THE ROSE GARDEN. HAD BINOCULARS. SAID HE WAS BIRD WATCHING. IN THE RAIN. HE WAS OUT THERE TEN MINUTES. HE HAS A RIGHT TO BE ECCENTRIC. HELL, IF I WAS IN HIS SHOES, I'D BE FULL CRAZY. I'M WRITING YOU ABOUT THIS ONLY BECAUSE ARCHIE DEVONSHIRE INSISTED. ARCHIE GETS ON MY NERVES, TOO. I'M GLAD I WORK OUTSIDE. YORN.

The thought of Duncan Whistler, dead or alive, prowling Palazzo Rospo, secretly watching Fric, brought a chill to the nape of Ethan's neck.

He suspected that the mind of a detective was inadequate to solve this increasingly Byzantine puzzle. Deductive and inductive reasoning are poor tools for dealing with things that go bump in the night.

CHAPTER 80

BEFORE COMMITTING AN ILLEGAL ENTRY, Hazard rang the doorbell. When no one responded, he rang it again.

Darkness in the Laputa house didn't mean that the place was deserted.

Rather than slinking around to the back of the residence, where his furtive behavior might catch the attention of a neighbor, Hazard entered boldly by the front. With the Lockaid, he popped both locks.

Pushing the door inward, he called out, "Anyone home or is it just us chickens?"

This was prudence, not comedy. Even when silence greeted his question, he crossed the threshold cautiously.

Immediately upon entering, however, he located the wall switch and flicked on the foyer-ceiling fixture. In spite of the rain and fog, some passing motorist or pedestrian might have seen him enter. The unhesitating use of lights would establish his legitimacy in suspicious minds.

Besides, if Laputa came home unexpectedly, he would be alarmed to see one lamp lit that had not been on when he'd left, or the beam of an inquiring flashlight in the darkness, but he would be disarmed to find the house blazing with light. The success of an operation like this depended upon boldness and quickness.

Hazard closed the door but didn't lock it. He wanted easy exit in the event of an unexpected confrontation.

The ground floor most likely did not contain the incriminating evidence that he sought. Murderers tended to keep mementos of their crimes, gruesome and otherwise, in their bedrooms.

The second-favorite repository for their treasures was the basement, often in concealed or locked rooms where they were able to visit their collections without fear of discovery. There, in an atmosphere of calculated dementia, they could dreamily relive the bloody past without fear of discovery.

In respect of land prone to earthquakes and mud slides, houses in southern California seldom had basements. This one, as well, had been built on a slab, with no door that opened to a lower darkness.

Hazard toured the ground floor, not bothering to search cabinets and drawers. If he found nothing upstairs, he would take a second pass at these rooms, probing them with greater care.

Right now he cared only about establishing that no one lurked in any of these chambers. He left lights on everywhere behind him. Darkness was not his friend.

In the kitchen, he unlocked the back door and left it standing ajar, providing himself with a second unobstructed exit.

Tentacles of fog wove through the open door, drawn by the warmth but dissipating in it.

Everything in the house appeared to have been scoured, scrubbed, vacuumed, polished, and buffed to a degree that approached obsession. Collections of decorative items—Lalique glass, ceramic boxes, small bronze figures—were arranged not with an artful eye but with a rigid sense of order reminiscent of a chess set. Every book on every shelf stood precisely half an inch from the edge.

The house seemed to be a refuge against the messiness of the world beyond its walls. However, in spite of conveniences aplenty, in spite of comfortable furnishings, in spite of cleanness and order, the place was not welcoming, with none of the warmth of hearth and home. Instead, entirely apart from the tension that Hazard felt due to being here illegally, an air of edgy expectation was endemic to the place, and a desperation not quite nameable.

The only clutter on the ground floor lay on the dining-room table. Five sets of charts or blueprints, rolled and fastened with rubber bands. A long-handled magnifying glass. A yellow, lined tablet. Rolling Writer pens—one red, one black. Although these items had not been put away, they had been arranged neatly side by side.

Satisfied that the lower rooms held no nasty surprises, Hazard climbed to the upper floor. He was confident that his activities thus far would have drawn an inquiry if anyone were home, so he proceeded without stealth, switching on the lights in the upper hall.

The master bedroom was near the head of the stairs. This, too, proved antiseptically clean and almost eerily well organized.

If Laputa had killed his mother and Mina Reynerd, and if he had kept tokens of remembrance, not of the women but of the violence, he would most likely have chosen pieces of their jewelry, bracelets or lockets, or rings. Probably the best that could be hoped for were bloodstained articles of clothing or locks of their hair.

Often, a man of Laputa's position in the community, a man with a prestigious job and many material possessions, if driven to commit a murder or two, might keep no memento. Motivated not by psychopathic frenzy but rather by financial gain or jealousy, their type had no burning psychological need to relive their crimes repeatedly in vivid detail with the aid of souvenirs.

Hazard had a hunch that Laputa would prove an exception to that pattern. The uncommon savagery with which Justine Laputa and Mina Reynerd had been beaten suggested that within the upstanding citizen resided something worse than a mere hyena, a Mr. Hyde who relived his brutal crimes with pleasure if not glee.

The contents of the walk-in closet were organized with military precision. Several boxes on the shelves above the hanging clothes were of interest to him. He studied the position of each before he moved it, hoping to be able to return all the boxes to exactly the position in which he'd found them.

As he worked, he listened to the house. He checked his watch too often.

He felt that he was not alone. Maybe this was because the back wall of the closet featured a full-length mirror, repeatedly catching his attention with reflections of his movements. Maybe not.

CHAPTER 81

I N THE RAIN AND FOG, THE RUINS OF THIS HOUSE recalled for Corky the final scene in du Maurier's *Rebecca*: the great mansion known as Manderley ablaze in the night, the inky sky "shot with crimson, like a splash of blood," and ashes on the wind.

No fire had touched these ruins high in Bel Air, nor was there currently either a wind or blown ashes, but the scene excited Corky nonetheless. In this rubble, he saw a symbol of greater chaos to come in the years ahead.

Once this had been a fine estate, where grand parties had been thrown for the rich and famous. The house, in the style of a French chateau, had been designed with graceful proportions, executed with elegant details, and had stood as a monument to stability and to the refined taste distilled from centuries of civilization.

These days, among the new princes and princesses of Hollywood, classic French architecture was passé, as in fact was history itself. Because the past was not fashionable, nor even comprehensible, the current owner of this property had decreed that the existing house must come down, to be replaced by a swooping-sprawling-glassy-shining residence more in tune with contemporary sensibilities, more hip.

In this community, after all, the value is in the land, not in what stands on it. Any real-estate professional will confirm this.

The house had first been stripped of all valuable architectural details. The limestone architrave at the front entrance, the carved window pediments, and numerous limestone columns had been salvaged.

Then the wrecking crew had been brought in. Half of their work had been completed. They were artists of destruction.

Minutes before seven o'clock, Corky had arrived on foot at the estate, having parked the four-year-old Acura several blocks away. He had purchased the Acura cheap, under a false identity, for the sole purpose of using it in this operation. Later, he had one more use for it, then would abandon it with the keys in the ignition.

At the entrance drive to the three-acre property, a two-panel construction gate with a steel-pipe frame and chain-link infill barred the way. A chain had been wound between the two panels and secured by a heavy padlock with a virtually indestructible case and a thick, titanium-steel shackle highly resistant to a bolt cutter.

Corky ignored the padlock and cut the chain.

Shortly thereafter, at the open gate, posing as NSA agent Robin Goodfellow, wearing a small backpack that he had taken from the trunk of the Acura, he had greeted Jack Trotter and his two-man prep crew, who arrived in a thirty-eight-foot truck. Corky directed them along the curved driveway, where they parked close to the house.

"This is madness," Trotter had declared as he climbed out of the truck.

"Not at all," Corky disagreed. "The wind has died completely."

"It's still raining."

"Not furiously. And a little rain provides some covering noise, just what we need."

In full Queeg von Hindenburg mode, Trotter wore pessimism with the grim authority of Nostradamus in his darkest mood. His bloated face sagged like a deflating balloon, and his protuberant eyes were wild with visions of doom. "We're screwed in this fog."

"It's not that thick yet. Just enough to give us extra cover. It's perfect. The trip is short, the target easily identifiable even in a medium fog."

"We'll be seen before we're half ready to go."

"This property's on a knoll. No houses have a view down on it. We're surrounded by trees, can't be seen from the street."

Trotter insisted on disaster: "We're damn sure to be seen by someone between here and there."

"Maybe," Corky acknowledged. "But what will they make of what they've seen between palisades of fog?"

"Palisades?"

"I have an interest in literature, the beauty of the language," Corky said. "Anyway, your entire mission time is probably seven or eight minutes. You'll be back here, out of here, on the road before anyone can figure where your staging area was. Besides, I've got agents all over these hills, and they won't let cops get near you."

"And when I split from Malibu, I disappear from all government records. Me and all the names I've used."

"That's the deal. But you'd better get your ass in gear. The clock is ticking."

Grimacing like a man in an advertisement for a diarrhea remedy, Trotter looked Corky up and down, then said, "What the hell do you call that getup you're wearing?"

"Weatherproof," Corky said.

Now, more than an hour later, Trotter and his two-man crew had nearly completed preparations.

During that time, Corky had entertained himself by studying the ruins of the half-demolished chateau from numerous angles.

He had not, of course, worked with Trotter and his men. As Robin Goodfellow, he was a highly trained human weapon, a valued government agent. Robin had signed up to pursue truth, justice, and adventure, but had never agreed to perform menial labor of any kind. James Bond does not dust furniture or do windows.

Without his assistance, however, the blimp had been fully inflated.

CHAPTER 82

THE THIRD NETMAIL WAS FROM MR. HACHETTE. INSPECTOR TRUMAN: I MYSELF BITTERLY EXPRESS HEREWITH EXTREME DISPLEASURE AT BEING EXPECTED TO CREATE THE MOST SUPERIOR OF HAUTE CUISINE THAT I AM CAPABLE ON A MOMENT'S NOTICE FOR THE BOTTOMLESS STOMACH OF A GUEST WHOSE PRESENCE IN THE HOUSE ISN'T REVEALED UNTIL HE APPEARS IN MY KITCHEN, SURPRISING ME LIKE A WEEVIL IN THE FLOUR SUPPLY. MR. WHISTLER'S MAGNIFICENT TASTE IN FOOD AND HIS PRAISE FOR MY UNIQUE COQUILLES ST. JACQUES, AS FOR EVERY REFINED DISH OF MY DIFFICULT PREPARATION, IS PLEASING BUT DOES NOT GLUE TOGETHER MY SHATTERED NERVES, WHICH I WARN YOU ARE DEVASTATED AND FRAYED. IF THIS IS DONE TO ME AGAIN, BY YOU, I MUST RESIGN WITH CONSEQUENCES OF UNSPEAKABLE EXTREMITY. I AM ALSO DISPLEASED TO ANNOUNCE THAT THE BOY CLAIMS TO HAVE MADE HAM SANDWICHES IN MY KITCHEN WITHOUT PERMISSION, AND THAT I AM SHARPLY INVENTORYING THE PANTRY AT THIS TIME TO LEARN THE EXTENT OF HIS DESTRUCTION. HOPING THAT THESE OUTRAGES MUST NEVER BE REPEATED, I REMAIN, CHEF HACHETTE.

Dead Dunny had moved right in. And with an appetite.

This was crazy. Ethan wanted to laugh, but he couldn't work up as much as a smile. His mouth had gone dry. His palms were damp.

He went back to Yorn's message: FRIC IS MAKING HIMSELF A

HIDEY-HOLE IN THE CONSERVATORY . . . YOUR FRIEND WHISTLER BROUGHT IT
TO MY ATTENTION . . . BOYS PLAY AT ROBINSON CRUSOE . . . WHISTLER
SCRAPES MY NERVES. . . .

During Hannah's battle with cancer, Ethan had felt helpless as
never before. He had always been able to take care of the people who
mattered to him, to do everything for them that needed to be done.
But he couldn't save Hannah, she who had been the dearest to him.

Once more, he felt control slipping out of his hands. With a state-
of-the-art security system, on-site guards, and well-conceived security protocols, with full diligence, he could not keep Dunny off the
estate, out of the house. Man or ghost, or a force to which no easy label applied, Dunny somehow had a connection with Reynerd and
probably with the professor about whom Reynerd had written in his
screenplay. Dunny must be part of the threat, and he mocked Ethan
by his every intrusion, proving that no one here was safe.

If Ethan failed Channing Manheim, if someone got at the star in
spite of all precautions, he would be failing not only his boss but also
the special boy who'd be left fatherless. Fric would be remanded to
the mercy of his self-absorbed mother, set further adrift than ever,
consigned to a deeper loneliness than the one he already endured.

Ethan had gotten up from the computer without realizing it. He
stood in a state of agitation, overwhelmed by the need to move, to do
something, but unable to understand what must be done.

At the phone, he pressed INTERCOM and the number for the library.
"Fric, are you there?" He waited. "Fric, you hear me?"

The boy's voice came wrapped in a curious caution: "Who's that?"

"Nobody here but us broken-down old former cops. Have you
found a book?"

"Not yet."

"Don't take too long."

"Gimme a couple minutes," Fric said.

As Ethan released the intercom button, a light flashed on the telephone, then burned steadily: Line 24.

He studied the items arranged on the desk between the computer and the telephone. Ladybugs, snails, foreskins . . .

His attention drifted back to the phone. The indicator lamp. Line 24.

The half-heard voice issuing from the far side of the moon, to which he'd listened for half an hour on this phone the previous night, had been resonating in his heart ever since. And the faint voice that he'd thought he heard coming from the musicless speaker in the hospital elevator just this morning.

Cookie jar full of Scrabble tiles, the book *Paws for Reflection,* the stitched apple with the eye at its core . . .

In the elevator, he had pressed STOP, not merely to listen longer to the voice but because he'd had the feeling that when he reached the hospital garage, no garage would be there. Only lapping black water. Or an abyss.

At the time, he had sensed that this absurd phobic response must be the sublimation of a more realistic fear he was reluctant to face. Now he was on the verge of grasping the true terror.

Suddenly he knew that reality as he perceived it was like the colored-glass image presented by the angled mirrors at the end of a kaleidoscope. The pattern of reality that he'd always seen was about to change before his eyes, about to shift into one far more dazzling, and fearsome.

Ladybugs, snails, foreskins . . .

Line 24, engaged.

The faraway voice echoed in his memory, like the cries of sea gulls, melancholy in a mist: *Ethan, Ethan . . .*

Phone calls from the dead.

Ladybugs, snails, foreskins . . .

The indicator lamp: a tiny version of the dome light high atop Our Lady of Angels Hospital, the last line on the phone board, last line, last chance, last hope.

Ethan caught the scent of roses. There were no roses in the apartment.

In his mind's eye: Broadway roses on her grave, red-gold blooms against wet grass.

The fragrance of roses grew stronger, intense. The scent was real, not imagined, stronger here than in Forever Roses.

The skin crawling on the back of his neck, across his scalp, was the result less of ordinary fear than of humbling awe. A cool quiver in the pit of his stomach.

He had no key to the forbidden room behind the blue door, where calls on Line 24 were recorded. Suddenly he was in a mood that made keys unimportant.

With an intuitive sense of urgency that he could not explain but that he trusted, Ethan ran from the apartment to the back stairs and all the way to the third floor.

CHAPTER 83

TETHERED BY TWO FAINTLY THRUMMING ROPES to the sturdy limbs of a pair of old coral trees and by a taut nose line to the truck, the blimp appeared to be straining like a hooked fish, reeled here to the shallows of the air, but desperate to soar again into the depths of the sky.

Gray and whalelike, perhaps thirty feet in length and ten or twelve feet in diameter, the airship was a minnow compared to the Goodyear blimp. Yet to Corky it looked huge.

The leviathan loomed impressively, underlit by two Coleman lanterns that provided work light. Tinsel-silver rain streamed from its round flanks. The craft was more striking than its dimensions would suggest, perhaps because here in Bel Air in the first decade of the new millennium, a blimp was both out of place and out of time.

In addition to being a survivalist, a conspiracy-theory fanatic, and a nut case of several dangerous varieties, Jack Trotter was also a hot-air balloon enthusiast. He found inner peace only in the air, traveling with the wind. As long as he remained aloft, the agents of evil could not seize him and cast him down into a dank cell with no light other than the red glow of rats' eyes.

He owned a traditional rig—the colorfully striped envelope, the inflation fan, the propane-fueled burner, the basket for pilot and passengers—which he sometimes took up alone, the sole balloonist on a sweet spring morning or on a golden summer evening. He also joined rallies of celestial navigators, when twenty or thirty or more bright balloons launched in rough synchronization and drifted in a school through the heavens.

A hot-air balloon was all but entirely at the mercy of the wind. The pilot could neither plan a pinpoint destination nor provide an estimated time of arrival to the minute or even to the quarter hour.

The assault on Palazzo Rospo required a highly maneuverable craft that could travel at cross purposes to at least a light wind. As well, it must be able to ascend without the ungodly roar of a propane burner, which always set dogs barking within a quarter-mile radius. Furthermore, it must be able to descend as smoothly as a dove glides from cloud to bower, if more slowly than a dove, and must also be able to hover like a hummingbird.

Trotter enjoyed the astonishment and excitement with which fellow sky sailors regarded his custom-made craft on those occasions when he left his hot-air balloon at home and brought the little blimp instead. Not garrulous by nature, lacking many social graces, Trotter nonetheless could expect to be the hit of the rally in his miniature airship.

Corky suspected that in his perpetually fevered mind, Trotter also regarded the blimp as a last-ditch escape vehicle in the event that an abruptly declared dictatorship tried for any reason to seal off highway traffic in and out of major metropolitan areas like Los Angeles and surrounding communities. He probably envisioned himself foiling the totalitarians on a night of a crescent moon, with enough light to navigate but not enough to be easily seen, sailing high above roadblocks and concentration camps, north into farm country and toward the Sierra foothills, where he could eventually set down and proceed on foot, overland, to one of his well-prepared bolt-holes.

After drawing Corky away from the ruins of the chateau, Trotter said, "We'll be out of here in less than five minutes."

The two-man prep crew was conducting final checks of the airship systems and gear.

They were rent-a-thugs involved in Ecstasy distribution with Trotter. After he delivered Corky to Palazzo Rospo and returned to the chateau in the blimp, when these men had snared the nose line and anchored him by three tethers, Trotter would kill them.

"I haven't heard you charging the batteries," Corky said.

"They were fully charged before we came here."

"Airborne, we can't use the engine, not for a minute."

"I know, I know. Man, haven't you busted my ass about it enough already? We won't need the engine for this short a trip, with the air this calm."

The blimp's twin can-mounted propeller fans, slung from the back of the gondola, were usually driven by a riding-lawnmower engine. The turning blades produced an acceptably soft sound, but the engine racket made stealthy travel impossible.

"With little or no headwind," Trotter said, "I can run two hours on batteries, maybe longer. But I hate this rain."

"It's just a light drizzle now."

"Lightning," Trotter said. "The thought of lightning makes my bowels loose, and it ought to do the same to yours."

"It's inflated with helium, isn't it?" Corky asked, indicating three discarded cylinders of compressed gas, each the size of a hospital oxygen tank. "The Hindenburg was hydrogen. I thought helium didn't explode."

"I'm not worried about an explosion. *I'm worried about being struck by lightning!* Even if lightning doesn't rupture the bag and set it afire, it could fry us in the gondola."

"The storm's winding down. No lightning," Corky observed.

"There was lightning earlier today."

"Only a little. I told you, Trotter, we in government *control* the storm. When we want lightning, it strikes where we need it, and when we *don't* want lightning, not one bolt leaves the quiver."

In addition to being inflated with nonflammable helium instead of hydrogen, the blimp was different from a zeppelin in that it had no rigid internal structure. The skin of the *Hindenburg*—a vessel as long as the Eiffel Tower is tall, nearly as long as four Boeing 747s standing nose to tail—had been stretched around an elaborate steel frame that contained sixteen giant gas cells, great cotton sacks made airtight by a coating of plastic, as well as an entire luxury hotel. Trotter's blimp, any blimp, was just a flat bag when deflated.

With no missing strawberries to obsess about and with no roller bearings to manipulate obsessively in one hand, a la Bogart in *The Caine Mutiny*, Captain Queeg von Hindenburg studied the slowly seething fog overhead, squinting to catch a glimpse of the clouds above the fog. He looked worried. He looked angry. With his orange hair pasted to his head by rain, his protuberant eyes, and his walrus mustache, he looked like a cartoon. "I don't like this at all," he muttered.

CHAPTER 84

O N THE THIRD FLOOR, AT THE NORTH END OF
the west wing, across the hall from the thirty-five-hundred-
square-foot suite that included the Face's bedroom, Ethan arrived at
the blue door. No other door in the house resembled it.

Ming du Lac had seen the appropriate shade of blue in a dream.
According to Mrs. McBee, the interior decorator had then gone through
forty-six custom blends of paint until the spiritual adviser had been satisfied that reality had been matched to dream.

As it turned out, the necessary blue was precisely the same as that
on any box of Ronzoni pasta.

Merely dedicating a telephone line to calls from the dead and
hooking up an answering machine to service it was not sufficient to
satisfy Ming's and Manheim's vision of a serious investigation of the
phenomenon. A space apart had been required for the equipment,
which grew in complexity from a simple answering machine. And
they decreed that the ambience of this chamber must be serene, beginning with the color of the door.

A sacred place, Ming called it. Sacrosanct, Channing Manheim
had instructed.

The simple lockset—no deadbolt—featured a keyhole in the knob. If he wasn't able to loid the latch, he'd kick his way into the room.

A credit card, slipped between door and jamb, forced the spring latch out of the striker plate, and the blue barrier opened to reveal a sixteen-by-fourteen-foot room in which the windows had been covered with wallboard. The ceiling and the walls had been padded and then upholstered in white silk. The carpet was white, as well. The inside of the door was not blue but white.

In the center of this space stood two white chairs and a long white table. On the table and under part of it was what Fric might have called a shitload of high-tech equipment supporting a computer with tremendous processing capacity. All the equipment had white molded-plastic casings; the logos had been painted over with white nail polish. Even the connecting cables were white.

You could go snowblind in this room if the lights were turned too bright. The concealed cold-cathode tubes in the coves near the ceiling came on automatically when someone entered, and they were set at a comfortable level that caused the silk walls to shimmer radiantly like fields of snow on a winter twilight.

Ethan had been in this room once previously, during his first day of orientation, when he'd been new to the job.

The computer and supporting equipment operated twenty-four hours a day, seven days a week.

Ethan sat in one of the white chairs.

On the white answering machine, the indicator light had gone dark. Line 24 was no longer in use.

The blue screen, a different shade from the door, provided the only vibrant color in the room. The icons were white.

He had never used this computer before. The software that organized the incoming calls was, however, the same used for the rest of the mansion's telephone system.

Fortunately, the letters, numbers, and symbols on the keyboard had not been painted white and thus obliterated. Even the gray-shaded keys were in the state intended by the manufacturer. By comparison to the surroundings, the keyboard was a riot of color.

Ethan called forth data exactly as he would have done for Lines 1 through 23, using the computer in his study. He wanted to know how many calls Line 24 had received in the past forty-eight hours.

He had been told that five or six messages were received each week on Line 24. Most were wrong numbers or cold-call sales pitches.

The list of Monday and Tuesday calls appeared with the latest count at the head of the column: fifty-six. Ten weeks' worth had been received in two days.

He'd been aware that Line 24 was carrying higher than usual traffic, but he hadn't realized that it was being hit more than once per hour, on average.

The temperature in this talk-to-the-dead zone was with great effort maintained always at sixty-eight degrees, a figure from Ming's original dream. This evening, the air felt colder than sixty-eight.

Scrolling through the phone log, Ethan saw that every one of the fifty-six entries lacked an incoming-caller number. This meant that none of them were from sales operations, which were now required by law to forego Caller ID blocking.

Maybe some were wrong-number calls made by people who did have Caller ID blocking. Maybe. But he would have bet everything he owned against that proposition. These calls had come from a place where the phone company couldn't offer service.

At the bottom of the log, he highlighted the most recent entry, the call received while he had been downstairs in his study, trying to make sense of ladybugs, snails, and foreskins.

Boxed options appeared in the upper right corner of the screen. He could receive a printout of the call transcript; he could read the transcript on the screen; or he could listen to the call.

He chose to listen.

If the call was like the one to which he'd bent his ear for nearly thirty minutes the previous night, an open line full of hiss and pop woven through with a faint voice half-imagined and not at all understood, he would hear something better from this equipment. The computerized audio analyzer filtered out static, identified patterned sounds that fit the profile of speech, clarified and enhanced that speech, and finally eliminated gaps in order to condense the call to its essence before storing it.

Caller 56 still sounded as though she cried out from a great distance, across an abyss. Her fragile voice made him lean forward in his chair, afraid that he would lose it. Nevertheless, because of the computer enhancement, he could hear every word spoken, though the message puzzled him.

The voice was Hannah's.

CHAPTER 85

I N HIS MIND'S EAR, CORKY LAPUTA LISTENED TO Richard Wagner's *Die Walküre*, particularly to the music meant to portray the flight of the Valkyries.

Through the drizzle and fog, through the windless Bel Air, the mad Queeg's miniblimp sailed as smoothly as one dream melting into another.

The swish and sizzle of the rain entirely masked what noise the battery-powered propellers made, so that it seemed as though Corky and his sour-faced pilot journeyed in utter silence, without sough or bated billow. Neither the sun nor the moon could claim a quieter ascent and transit of the sky.

Suspended under the airship, the open gondola was similar to a rowboat, but with rounded stern and prow. The two bench-style seats were capable of accommodating four.

Facing forward, Trotter sat at the yoke on the bench nearer the stern. He was immediately in front of the engine, the helium feed, and the other controls.

At first Corky faced Trotter, looking back the way they had come. Then he turned to look forward, frequently leaning out to one side or the other to spot landmarks through the misty murk.

Treetops slid by only a few feet below them. Casting no faintest shadow in the absence of the moon and stars, they progressed with such stealth and with such minimal disturbance to the air that birds in the highest branches, sheltering from the rain, were not once frightened into flight.

This wealthy community had been built in a forest of oak and ficus and evergreen, of metrosideros and podocarpus and California pepper. More accurately, a forest had been imported to dress these hills, glens, and canyons, which long ago had been only semiarid pastures of wild grass and bleak ravines cluttered with scrub.

To pass all but invisibly above unsuspecting Bel Air, they were required to stay at the lowest prudent altitude. In these hills, most streets were serpentine and quite narrow, flanked and often overhung by huge trees, providing motorists with tightly circumscribed views of the sky. As long as the blimp seldom crossed above streets and thereby took full advantage of the forests that would screen it from all eyes except those directly below, it might slip all the way to Palazzo Rospo and back again without being noticed, for few if any residents would be afoot on their properties—and in a position to look up—in this weather.

A direct route as the blimp flies, from the ruined chateau on the knoll to Palazzo Rospo, downslope, measured less than half a mile. In windless conditions like these, running on batteries, the airship could make a top speed of fifteen miles per hour. To disturb the fog as little as possible and thus shroud themselves in its welcome veils, they were making just ten miles per hour, which would get them from door to door in approximately three minutes.

Through the Internet, Corky had accessed not only maps and city-planning charts but also a trove of aerial photography produced by the state of California, offering a bird's view of these exclusive and secluded enclaves. A majority of the homes in this community were true estates, particularly in that portion over which they now flew; and Corky had memorized the roof lines and the salient features of each palatial structure that lay along their route.

Trotter had done his homework, too. He consulted landmarks less often than Corky, however, for he relied more on compass readings.

The only light associated with the airship was the soft glow of the compass, the altimeter, and the few other gauges on the control panel. They were swivel-mounted on a stanchion, allowing Trotter to position them as needed. The combined radiance of these instruments was insufficient to paint the faintest glimmer on the curve of the helium bag immediately overhead.

Indeed, more light rose from the great houses over which they glided than from the craft controls. Gold and silver reflections of this rising incandescence glimmered briefly across the belly of the blimp, as if luminous lichen encrusted it.

Past chimneys they sailed, skimming wet rooftops with but a few feet to spare. They were close enough for Corky to discern individual roofing tiles and shingles even in the night and fog.

Some impatient child at a bedroom window, eager for Christmas, sky gazing, dreaming of a reindeer-drawn sleigh, might see Trotter's folly sailing through the rain and think that Santa Claus had come two nights early and by unconventional transport.

And here, now, after so much planning: the Manheim estate.

Undetected, they crossed approximately forty feet above the monitored wall.

They crossed over the motion detectors that were alert for intruders at ground level.

They crossed scores of sentinel cameras, not one of which was aimed at the sky.

Corky did not wish to be deposited at the house. Instead, he must lower himself with great care from the gondola to the roof of the groundskeeper's building at the back of the property.

To this point, Trotter had not done a great deal of piloting, for the line of travel had been straight and true. Now he needed to maneuver the airship to the target building, align it just-so with a particular portion of the roof, and hover with as little lateral and stern-to-bow drift as possible.

The four fins at the back of the blimp each featured a rudder. These were operated by electrical switches that were signaled through low-voltage cable, by controls on the yoke.

Trotter could lose altitude by bleeding helium from the vessel. If he needed to gain altitude, he would do so by feeding more helium into the gas bag overhead or, more quickly, by dumping water from the ballast tanks along both sides of the gondola.

Gracefully, almost majestically, the airship adjusted course for the groundskeeper's building and arrived there as soundlessly as the stars turn through the sky from dusk to dawn. With a grace equal to a series of perfectly executed ballet steps, with a delicate touch equal to that required to construct a house of cards, Jack Trotter brought the blimp lower and positioned it as required.

According to the wristwatch favored by discerning anarchists—a reliable Rolex—transit time had been three minutes, twenty seconds.

8:33. Service to all Manheim phones, hard-wired and cellular, had been discontinued three minutes ago.

CHAPTER 86

"FRIC WAS BORN . . . ON A WEDNESDAY."
In the white room behind the blue door, Ethan sat enraptured by the voice of his dead wife.

"Fric was born . . . on a Wednesday."

This was exquisite music to him, pure and thrilling. The effect of a much-loved hymn on a religious heart or of a national anthem on one deeply patriotic could not have elicited a fraction of the strong emotion that this voice wrenched from Ethan.

"Hannah?" he whispered, though a recording could not reply to him. "Hannah?"

The tears that blurred his vision were largely tears of joy, pressed from him not because he had missed her so desperately these past five years but because this curious message delivered in her voice meant that somewhere the essence of Hannah survived, that the hateful cancer had won a battle but not a war. His loss was no less crushing than ever it had been, but now he knew that it was not a loss eternal.

She had repeated the same six words twice. He played Call 56 three times before he could shift the focus of his attention from the miraculous sound of her voice to the content of the message.

"Fric was born . . . on a Wednesday."

Although Hannah clearly judged this information to be important, Ethan couldn't see why the day of Fric's birth had relevance to the current situation.

Working from bottom to top of the log, he accessed Call 55. As before, he chose the audio option over a printout of the transcript.

Hannah again. This time she spoke but one word, twenty or thirty times. His name. *"Ethan . . . Ethan . . . Ethan . . ."*

The poignant yearning in her voice matched that in Ethan's heart. Listening, he could barely hold fast to what little of his composure he had not already lost.

By phone, by elevator speaker, perhaps by other means, she had struggled to reach him, but she had not been able to make herself heard. Ironically, behind that Ronzoni door, in this ridiculous white room, with the aid of all this elaborate equipment, she had broken through.

God worked in strange ways, indeed, when He worked through the likes of Ming du Lac.

Ethan had come here with a sense of urgency that had briefly abated but that now overtook him once more.

Backward to Call 54. Hannah yet again.

"Monday's child is fair of face. . . ."

Ethan's breath caught in his throat. He slid to the edge of the chair.

"Tuesday's child is full of grace. . . ."

He knew this. A children's rhyme. He mouthed the words of the third line along with her.

"Wednesday's child is full of woe. . . ."

The Cookie Kitten was filled with Scrabble tiles that spelled WOE ninety times.

A kitten was a young cat. A kitten was a *child*. Like Fric.

Why ninety? Maybe it didn't matter. Ninety of each letter, two hundred and seventy tiles in total, were the number needed to fill the jar. Wednesday's child is *full* of woe.

Call 53. Hannah.

Even with the static filtered out and the speech enhanced, her message could not be understood, as if on this occasion, the river between life and death had widened until the far shore lay at the other side of an ocean.

Call 52. Also unclear.

Call 51. Hannah with another nursery rhyme.

"Ladybug, ladybug, fly away home. . . ."

As he shot to his feet, Ethan knocked over his chair.

"Your house is on fire, and your children will burn."

Channing Manheim would not arrive home until the afternoon of December 24. The operative theory had been that the Face wouldn't be in danger until that time, at the earliest.

Maybe the Face himself had never been in danger. Maybe the target had always been Fric.

Twenty-two ladybugs in a small glass jar. Why not twenty-three or twenty-four? Unlike the cookie jar, the beetle container had been less than half full. So why not fifty ladybugs packed to the lid?

This was Tuesday, December 22.

CHAPTER 87

AS CORKY SLID FROM THE CENTER OF HIS BENCH toward the port side of the gondola, Trotter said, "Easy, easy."

The sudden shift of Corky's 170 pounds could cause the mini-blimp to wallow, perhaps even bobble, which was a risk they couldn't take this close to the roof.

While Corky moved slowly, balancing breast-down on the gunwale, one leg in and one leg out of the gondola, Trotter employed his own body as a counterweight, shifting starboard on his bench, and he used the controls to fine-tune the attitude of the vessel.

The blimp wallowed but not dangerously.

At a signal from Trotter, Corky slid the rest of the way out of the gondola, though he did not at once drop free of it. First he hung by both hands from the gunwale, while the pilot compensated for this further shift of weight.

As the airship steadied, Corky lowered his left hand from the gunwale to a ballast-tank bracket, then his right. The metal was cold and wet, but with his leather-and-nylon gloves, he got a firm grip.

Peering down, he saw that his dangling feet were still eighteen or twenty inches from the roof.

He dared not drop that far. Though he would most likely keep his balance, he would land with too much noise, alerting the two guards who were in the security office that occupied half the second floor of the groundskeeper's building.

Evidently, Trotter recognized the problem. He vented a whisper of helium, and the vessel sank until Corky felt the roof under him.

Straddling the ridge line, one foot on the south slope of the roof, one foot on the north slope, he let go of the ballast-tank bracket. He had touched down almost as softly as Peter Pan.

Freed of his weight, the blimp at once soared ten feet, fifteen. The tail began to rise, which wasn't good, but with an adjustment of the rudders, Trotter raised the nose and recovered even as he brought the vessel around for the return trip to the knoll, which he would be making alone.

With the boy in his control, Corky would leave Palazzo Rospo in style, using one of the automobiles in Manheim's first-rate collection.

Back at the ruined chateau, once the three tethering lines were well anchored to truck and trees, Trotter would shoot the two men who served as ground crew. Although the abandonment of the airship would be a wound to his heart, he would leave it behind and walk to a car that earlier today he'd parked two blocks away.

Immediately upon returning to his canyon home in Malibu, he would switch vehicles and hit the road, leaving behind forever his life as Jack Trotter. Perhaps he would never realize that he'd been duped into believing that a genuine NSA agent had made a deal with him to erase him from every government record and to allow him to live hereafter as a ghost in the machinery of America; because he intended to live like a ghost anyway, he might actually escape all official notice entirely by his own efforts.

Authorities investigating the kidnapping of Aelfric Manheim would probably stall out when they traced the blimp back to Trotter in Malibu. They would have no way of discovering what new identity he had assumed, what his new appearance might be, or where he had gone.

If someday, against all odds, they caught up with Trotter, he would have no collaborator's name to give them except that of Robin Goodfellow, secret agent extraordinaire.

Still straddling the ridge line, Corky took two cautious steps forward. His boots had been made for true winter conditions, for snow and treacherous ice. Mere rain-slicked slate tiles should be easily negotiated.

Nevertheless, a slip now would be disastrous even if he avoided or survived a fall. With the estate guards in rooms directly under him, the rain would do little to mask any sounds he made, and silence remained essential.

The vent pipe that he sought stood where the blueprints had shown it, less than eighteen inches down the south slope from the peak of the roof.

Feeling like a gremlin engaged in naughty work, Corky would have liked to murmur a suitable gremlin song or to entertain himself with other antics. He recognized that on this occasion, however, he must as never before restrain his natural exuberance.

Uphill to the east, Captain Queeg von Hindenburg and his Jules Vernesian contraption tunneled through the thickening fog, which closed in his wake, granting him concealment as completely as the sea had conspired to hide Nemo and the *Nautilus*.

Corky sat on the ridge line, facing the pipe. This vent, which penetrated the roof to a height of one foot, led through the attic and to the bathroom in the security office.

Reaching over his shoulder, Corky unzipped the top compartment on the backpack. He fished out a ten-gallon plastic trash bag and a roll of all-weather tape.

A peaked and flared metal cap had been mounted on four-inch legs to the top of the pipe itself. This prevented rain and windblown debris from getting into the vent, while allowing air to be cycled out of the room below.

Corky pulled the trash bag over the flared cap and with one hand snugged it as tight as possible around the pipe.

If the bathroom exhaust fan had been in operation, it would have pumped the trash bag full of air, and he would have been forced to delay this critical phase of the mission until the fan was switched off. The limp plastic did not swell into a balloon.

With the all-weather tape, he quietly fixed the mouth of the bag to the pipe shaft, creating a relatively airtight seal.

Reaching over his shoulder once more, he withdrew a hairspray-size can from the backpack. This was not an ordinary spray can, but a "weaponized aerosol-dispersal unit (ADU) with a super-accelerant feature," which had been designed by one of his university colleagues working under a generous grant from the Chinese military.

The ADU would release its entire highly pressurized contents in six seconds. The molecules of the active ingredients were bonded to a gas that boasted such a highly efficient expansion factor that both floors of the groundskeeper's building would be contaminated in fifty to seventy seconds.

The ADU had been designed to contain anything from a sedative to a deadly nerve toxin that killed upon first inhalation.

Corky had been unable to get his hands on a unit containing the nerve toxin. He'd had to be satisfied with the sedative gas.

Sedating the two guards suited him well enough. Although deeply committed to societal collapse and its rebirth, he was not a man who killed indiscriminately. Lately, of course, more murder than usual had been required to advance his noble cause. But he liked to think of himself as one who could exercise restraint as easily as he could, in a pinch, let loose the beast within.

With one finger, he poked a hole in the plastic sack, widened it, and slipped the upper half of the aerosol can into the bag. Using the all-weather tape, he created a seal where can and trash bag met.

Holding the exposed end of the can in his left hand, he felt through the plastic with his right hand until, between thumb and forefinger, he was able to get a firm grip on the ring-pull, which functioned much like that on a grenade. He plucked out the ring and let it slide down the inside of the bag.

The ten-second delay between activation and dispersal of the contents allowed the can to be thrown through an open door or window. Corky held fast to it and waited.

When the contents erupted out of the revolutionary nozzle, the can vibrated in his left hand and instantly turned so icy cold that he could feel the radical temperature change through his glove. If he had been holding it barehanded, his skin would have frozen to the aluminum.

Whoosh! The trash bag inflated as abruptly as an automobile air bag in a head-on collision. Corky thought it might pop in his face, bathing him in sedative gas.

The vent offered a route for expansion, however, so instead of stretching the plastic to the bursting point, the gas traveled down the pipe, past the stilled exhaust fan that would have blown it out if activated, into the security-office bathroom, and from there into the entire building.

Closed doors would not inhibit dispersal. The sleep-inducing vapors would rush between door and threshold, between door and jamb, through any tiniest crack and crevice, through heating vents and plumbing chases.

Prior to the scheduled nine o'clock foot patrol of the grounds, both guards were in the office below Corky. The sedative was so fast-acting that in ten seconds from the time the ADU emptied, the two men would have collapsed unconscious.

He waited more than half a minute before departing the ridge line for the north slope of slate. The roof was not steeply pitched, and he descended it with ease.

At the front of the building, which was as large as an upscale suburban house, a loggia was covered by a sturdy redwood trellis entwined for decades by a trumpet vine. He jumped from the roof onto the trellis.

From the trellis, he leaped to the lawn, allowed his knees to buckle as would a parachutist, fell, rolled, and sprang to his feet.

He felt like Vin Diesel.

After shrugging out of his backpack, he withdrew from it a gas mask. He tossed the pack aside and put on the mask.

The central entrance to the groundskeeper's building was not locked. He stepped into a service foyer.

Just like the blueprints.

To his right: a door into a gardening-supplies storeroom large enough also to garage the three riding lawnmowers as well as the two electric carts with which Yorn and his day crew moved fertilizer and other materials around the immense grounds.

To his left: a door to Yorn's spacious office, another door to the bathroom used by gardeners.

Directly ahead were stairs to the second floor.

Upstairs, Corky found the two evening-shift guards unconscious in the main monitoring room. One sprawled on the floor, and the other slumped in a chair in front of a bank of video monitors.

They would be profoundly unconscious for between sixty to eighty minutes. That was plenty of time for Corky to do his job and be gone.

He pulled up a chair in front of a computer. Neither the power supply nor the estate-specific networking arrangements had been affected by the careful severance of outgoing and incoming phone service.

In his gas mask, his breathing sounded like that of Darth Vader.

At the start of the shift, as always, one of the guards had earlier accessed the security system with a personal password. To Corky, the elaborate status display on the screen revealed, among many other things, that the house-perimeter alarm had been activated, making it impossible to enter Palazzo Rospo by window or door without triggering sirens.

According to Ned Hokenberry, the three-eyed freak—now the

two-eyed freak, now the *dead* two-eyed freak—the perimeter alarm usually wasn't engaged until eleven o'clock or even midnight. This evening they had closed up early.

Corky wondered why.

Perhaps they had been spooked by certain black boxes and the contents thereof.

Delighted to have made them uneasy and yet still have slipped this far past their defenses, Corky began to sing the Grinch's theme from *The Grinch Who Stole Christmas.* The gas mask lent the tune a wonderfully spooky, even savage quality.

Mick Sachatone, poor dead Mick in his Bart Simpson pajamas, had hacked the Manheim security system by linking to it via the computer of the off-site armed-response company that maintained a 24/7 line to this room. He'd given Corky some rudimentary instruction in its operation.

First, Corky checked the status of the two panic rooms in the mansion. Neither was in use.

Using the computer, he put the two panic rooms in siege mode, engaging their locks by remote. They could no longer be opened using their hidden on-site lock releases. No one could take refuge in them.

The house-perimeter alarm could be armed or disarmed simply by selecting from a YES-NO option. Currently the YES was lit on the screen. Corky used the mouse to click the NO.

Now, with a door key, he could enter Palazzo Rospo as though it were his own sweet home. Keys dangled from the belt of each sleeping guard. He unclipped one set, jingled them, and smiled.

When he picked up a phone, he heard no dial tone. He tried one of the guard's cell phones. It didn't function. Reliable Mick.

Leaving the guards to their dreams, Corky descended the stairs and returned to the loggia under the trellis and the trumpet vine. He stripped off the gas mask and threw it away.

Through a screen of trees and darkling rain, the great house could be seen perhaps two hundred yards to the north. With only Ethan

Truman and the boy in residence, not many windows were lighted, yet the mansion nonetheless reminded Corky of an enormous luxury liner making way on a night sea. And he was the iceberg.

He unzipped the deepest pocket on his storm suit and withdrew the Glock that previously he had fitted with a sound suppressor.

CHAPTER 88

*L*ADYBUG, LADYBUG, FLY AWAY HOME.... YOUR *house is on fire, and your children will burn. ..."*

After listening to Call 51, Ethan had no doubt that some of the first fifty recordings also contained messages of value to him, but he did not think he dared take time to review them, and he *knew* that he didn't need to hear them in order to solve the riddle.

Twenty-two ladybugs. The twenty-second of December.

Today. And only a little more than three hours remained until the calender turned to December 23. If something terrible were going to happen, it would occur soon.

His pistol was in his apartment.

By now Fric must be waiting there, as well.

He fled the white room, leaving the blue door open behind him.

No need to panic. The perimeter alarm would shriek at the first breach of door or window. Between wails of the siren, a voice module would announce, in a clear computerized voice, the room in which the break-in had occurred.

Besides, the men in the security office would know the moment anyone crossed the estate wall, long before an intruder could reach the house. At the first evidence that the property had been violated, they would call 911 and the private armed-response security firm.

Nevertheless, with no time for the elevator, first to the back stairs in a sprint, then down six flights, down and around he went in a thunder, slamming through the door at the bottom of the stairs, into the ground-floor west wing.

He threw open the door to his apartment, called to Fric, and got no answer.

Evidently the boy was still in the library. Not good. He had gotten through ten years of life alone more often than not, but he wouldn't make it through this night by himself.

Ethan hurried to the desk in the study. He had left the pistol in the top right-hand drawer.

Pulling open the drawer, he expected to find that the gun had been taken. But there it was. A beautiful thing.

As Ethan slipped into the shoulder holster, he surveyed the items on top of the desk, between the computer and the telephone.

Nursery rhymes.

Your house is on fire, and your children will burn. . . .

Wednesday's child is full of woe. . . .

Nursery rhymes.

Foreskins circumcised from ten men. Ten because Fric was ten years old. What are foreskins? Rags of tissue. Scraps. *Snips.*

And snails are *snails.*

The book of dog stories, *Paws for Reflection,* a collection of puppy-dog *tales.* Different spelling, same word to the ear. *Tails.*

What are little boys made of?

Snips and snails, and puppy dogs' tails.

That's what little boys are made of.

The note that had come with the apple lay on the desk: THE EYE IN THE APPLE? THE WATCHFUL WORM? THE WORM OF ORIGINAL SIN? DO WORDS HAVE ANY PURPOSE OTHER THAN CONFUSION?

In this case, confusion was their sole purpose. The sixth object had been the easiest to interpret, so the professor, whoever the hell he was, had confused the issue with distracting—and mocking—words.

The eye in the apple is blue, the same color as the famous eyes of Channing Manheim. Not the eye in the apple. *The apple of his eye.*

Not that good Fric was ever the apple of his father's eye. He was the *blind spot* in his father's eye, too often overlooked, never seen in the fullness of his character. In this instance, the sender of the black boxes had made an incorrect assumption. The Face himself was the apple of his own eye, and there could be no other.

If you knew the true relationship between this father and this son, you might be forgiven for not making the connection between the doll's eye nestled in the black-sutured apple and the wonderful boy. Yet Ethan cursed himself for missing the clue.

He pressed INTERCOM on the telephone keypad and then the line number for the security office at the back of the estate. "Pete? Ken? We might have a situation brewing."

No one answered.

"Pete? Ken? Are you there?"

Nothing.

Ethan snatched up the handset. No dial tone.

CHAPTER 89

THE HYENA SLEPT IN A CLEAN DEN, UNSOILED by mementos of his killings. No articles of clothing stained with the victims' blood that he could press to his face to savor the scent of death. No items of women's jewelry that he could fondle. No Polaroid photos of Justine Laputa or Mina Reynerd after he tested their mortality with a fireplace poker and a bronze-encrusted marble lamp. Nothing.

After a quick but meticulous search of the walk-in closet, the bureau drawers, the nightstands, and every place else in the bedroom where Laputa might have hidden the kind of pornography that appealed not to prurient interest but to an obsession with violence, Hazard turned up no evidence of either a crime or psychopathy.

As before, the most notable thing about the Laputa house was the scrupulous cleanliness, which rivaled that in any hermetically sealed and frequently sanitized biochemical-weapons lab, and the fetishistic alignment and geometry of every object large and small. Not only the items on open display but also the contents of drawers were placed as though with the aid of micrometer, protractor, and straightedge. The socks and sweaters appeared to have been folded and stowed away by a precision-programmed robot.

Again, Hazard sensed that, for Vladimir Laputa, this house was a desperate refuge from the messiness of the world beyond its walls.

He retreated from the bedroom, into the upstairs hall, where he stood for a moment, listening intently, hearing only the tepid tattoo of the diminishing rain on the roof. He glanced at his watch, wondering how much time, if any, he had to pore through the other second-floor chambers.

Instinct seldom failed Hazard, but it told him nothing now. The professor might return at any moment or not for hours, days.

He tried the first door past the master bedroom, on that same side of the hall, snapped on the light.

Judging by appearances, this was a storeroom. Plain cardboard cartons emblazoned only with red stenciled numbers were stacked three high, in well-ordered rows.

A quiver of interest drew Hazard a few steps past the threshold. Then he realized that the boxes were sealed with precisely applied strips of strapping tape. If he tore open a few, he would not be able to restore them to the degree necessary to conceal the fact of his unauthorized explorations.

Approaching the last room on that side of the hall, he detected an unpleasant odor. By the time he reached the open door, the malodor had become a stench.

Central to the stink, Hazard recognized the smell of corrupted flesh, of which he'd had more than a little experience in his career with Robbery/Homicide. He suspected that here he would find at least one of Laputa's mementos that would make him wish he had not stopped earlier for cheeseburgers and fries.

The glow from the hall sconces spilled only a short distance into the room. Hazard couldn't see much.

When he stepped across the threshold and flipped up the wall switch, a nightstand lamp came on. For a moment he thought the man in the bed, less than half concealed by a sheet, must be a corpse.

Then the bloodshot eyes, which were fixed on him in pitiful appeal, blinked.

Hazard had never before seen firsthand a living human being in such wretched condition as this. Here was what the starved slave laborers in concentration camps looked like when, at last worked to death, they were tumbled into raw graves.

In spite of the IV rack and catheter-fed urine jar, Hazard knew at once that in this situation Professor Laputa was not a caregiver tending to a family member. The man in the bed had been afforded none of the tenderness due a patient but all the brutality that could be rained upon a prisoner by a demented jailer.

Both windows had been boarded over and sealed with caulking to keep out daylight and to hold in all sound.

On the floor in one corner were tumbled chains and handcuffs and ankle shackles. Surely these bonds were from the early days of the imprisonment, when the man in the bed had been strong enough to require restraints.

Hazard had been speaking aloud for a while before he quite heard himself. He had been reduced to the childhood prayers that Granny Rose had taught him long ago.

Here was evil as pure as he had ever seen it, forever beyond the understanding of a simple sinner like himself. This way a wicked thing had come and gone, and would come again, a demon on sabbatical from Hell.

The uncommon neatness and order elsewhere in the house didn't represent Laputa's need for a refuge from the disorder of the world outside. It was instead a desperate denial of just how apocalyptic was the chaos that churned within him.

By the time that Hazard reached the side of the bed, each breath he drew further sickened him. Weeks' worth of dried sweats, rancid body oils, and festering bedsores raised a nauseating stench.

Nevertheless, Hazard gently took hold of the nearer of the

stranger's fragile hands. The man had insufficient strength to lift his arm, and he could barely squeeze his rescuer's hand in return.

"It's all right now. I'm a cop."

The stranger regarded him as though he might be a mirage.

Although instinct had failed Hazard a minute ago in the hall, it served him well now. He was surprised, but then at once not, to hear himself say, "Professor Dalton? Maxwell Dalton?"

The widening of the withered man's rheumy eyes confirmed his identification.

When the prisoner strove to speak, his voice proved to be so thin, so dry, so cracked and reedy, that Hazard had to bend close to puzzle meaning from the words: "*Laputa . . . killed my wife . . . daughter.*"

"Rachel? Emily?" Hazard asked.

Dalton squeezed his eyes shut in grief, bit his lower lip, and nodded shakily.

"I don't know what he told you, but they're not dead," Hazard assured him.

Dalton's eyes opened as snap-quick as camera shutters.

"I saw them only today, at your home," Hazard continued. "Only a few hours ago. They're sick with worry about you, but they've not been harmed."

For a moment the prisoner appeared reluctant to believe this news, as though convinced that it must be yet another cruelty with which he would be tormented. Then he discerned truth in Hazard's forthright stare. His bony hand tightened slightly on his rescuer's, and from somewhere his desiccated body found the moisture to flood his eyes with tears.

As moved as he was nauseated, Hazard examined the dangling infusion bag, the drip line, the cannula inserted in Dalton's vein. He wanted to strip all this away, for surely none of it was doing the man good. But he was afraid of inadvertently harming Dalton. This had best be left to the paramedics.

Originally, Hazard had entered the house with the intention of conducting an illegal and clandestine search, after which he would have closed up and gone away to ponder what evidence he found, having left said evidence behind with no slightest proof of his visit. That plan no longer worked. He had to make a 911 call, and quickly.

Judges existed, however, and not merely a few, who would set Vladimir Laputa free because Dalton had been found during an illegal search, made without warrant or due cause. Furthermore, with Blonde in the Pond still ahead of him, Hazard could afford no censures or disciplinary actions on his Ten Card.

"I'll get you out of here," he promised the prisoner. "But I need a couple minutes."

Dalton nodded.

"I'll be right back."

Reluctantly the withered man let go of his hand.

At the threshold, about to leave the room, Hazard halted, retreated from the doorway, and drew his handgun. When he ventured into the upstairs hall, he went with caution.

He remained wary all the way down the stairs, through the ground floor, and into the kitchen. He closed the back door that earlier he had left open as an escape route. He locked it.

Adjacent to the kitchen was a small laundry room. The door at the end of the laundry opened into the garage.

No cars stood in the garage. A sodden pile of clothes lay on the concrete floor: the outfit that Laputa had been wearing when he had come home swaggering like a tough guy.

Here also were good tools in drawers and racked on a pegboard. They were as clean and as obsessively ordered as the Lalique-crystal collection in the living room.

Hazard selected a claw hammer and raced back upstairs, glad that he had turned on so many lights when he'd first come into the house.

He was relieved to see that the prisoner was still alive. Dalton appeared to be on the trembling edge of expiration, as if he might slip away at any moment.

Hazard put his gun on the floor and used the claw hammer to pry nails from one of the thick sheets of particle board with which Laputa had sealed off the windows. They were three-inch spikes and pulled loose reluctantly, with bark and screech. He tore the board away from the window and stood it aside, against the wall.

The pleated drape had been captured between board and window. Although wrinkled and dusty, it was just the thing with which to wipe his fingerprints off the hammer before he dropped it on the floor.

This was a back bedroom only in the sense that it was farthest from the stairs. Like the master bedroom, it faced the front of the house. Through the window, he could see his sedan parked across the street.

Returning to the bed, Hazard said, "I came in here on a hunch, without a warrant, and now I've got to clean up the situation to save my ass and to be sure we nail Laputa. You understand?"

"Yes," Dalton rasped.

"So what you're gonna say happened is, he was so sure of your total disability, of your inability to even make a sound anyone could hear outside, that the bastard took that board off this evening just to torment you with the sight of freedom. Can you sell that?"

On an arid whisper of breath, brittle words scraped and grated from Dalton's throat. "Laputa said . . . he'll kill me . . . tonight."

"All right. Okay. Then it makes a little sense that he might do this."

From the nightstand, Hazard snatched up an aerosol can of pine-scented disinfectant. The container felt half full, heavy enough.

"Next," he told Dalton, "you have to tell them that you reached way down inside yourself, to your deepest reserves of strength, and somehow you found the will, the energy, the *anger* necessary to pull this can off the nightstand and to pitch it at that window."

"Can do," Dalton promised shakily, though he looked as if he could do nothing more than blink his eyes.

"The can smashed through the window and rolled down the porch roof as I was coming up the front walk. I heard you feebly calling for help, so I forced entry."

The story sucked. The first officers on the scene would know that it was bogus, but in light of Dalton's ordeal, this would be a flavor of bogus that they could swallow.

By the time Laputa found himself in a courtroom, Dalton would have largely recovered, and the jury would not know just how horribly weak he had been on the night of his rescue. Time could give this shabby story enough luster to make it look attractive.

Shifting his eyes from the open doorway to Hazard, Dalton said anxiously, "Hurry," as if he feared Laputa's imminent return.

Hazard threw the can of disinfectant at the window. The glass shattered with a satisfying crash.

CHAPTER 90

HAVING FURTHER SEARED THE ROOTS OF THE potted palm with his mighty Manheim urine, which he could probably have bottled and sold to his father's craziest fans, Fric shopped the library shelves for a book, mindful that Mr. Truman had said not to dawdle.

In case they didn't make s'mores and sit on the floor telling scary stories, he took the trouble of finding a book that he might actually enjoy reading. He figured that he would be awake most of this long night, and not because he was excited about Christmas Eve coming in just two days. If he didn't have a book to pass the time, he would go as crazy as Barbra Streisand's two-headed cat.

He had just found a novel that looked good when he heard noise overhead: a shimmering, bright music much like the soft ringing of a hundred tiny wind chimes all agitated at once.

When he looked up at the stained-glass dome, he saw hundreds of pieces of glass break out of the leading and fall toward him.

No. Not glass. The stained-glass mosaic remained in place across the entire arc of the thirty-foot dome. Shards of color and shadow fell out of the glass without breaking it, fell *through* it from the night above or maybe from somewhere immeasurably stranger than the night.

The shards fell slowly, not to the demand of gravity, and as they drifted down they changed color. As they changed color, they tumbled upon one another and fused together. As they fused together, they acquired greater dimension and a form.

The gathered shards became Mysterious Caller, whom Fric had most recently seen pictured in the *Los Angeles Times* in the rose room this afternoon, whom he had last encountered life-size in the memorabilia maze the previous night. As the guardian angel had on that occasion glided without benefit of wings from rafters to attic floor, so now he descended with soundless grace to the carpet only a few feet from Fric.

"You have this knack for entrances," Fric said, but his shaky voice belied his cocky Hollywood-kid attitude.

"Moloch is here," the guardian declared in a tone of voice so dire that it would have made Fric's heart clench and then punch his ribs even if the message had been a fraction as terrifying as this. "Run to your deep and special place, Fric. Run *now*."

Pointing to the stained-glass dome, Fric said, "Why don't you just take me up there, out of here, where you came from, where I'll be safe?"

"I told you, boy, you must make your own choices, exercise your free will, and save yourself."

"But I—"

"Besides, you can't go to the places I go or travel by the means I do, not until you're dead." The guardian stepped closer, leaned forward, thrusting his pallid face within an inch of Fric's. "Do you want to *die horribly* just to be able to travel more conveniently?"

Fric's hammering heart knocked all the words out of his throat before he could speak them, and as he struggled to sputter through his silence, he was lifted off his feet and held high by his weird guardian.

"Moloch is in the house. Hide, boy, for God's sake, *hide*."

With that, Mysterious Caller threw Fric as though he were only a bundle of rags, but threw him with a magical knack that prevented him from crashing hard into furniture. Instead, he tumbled in slow motion across the library, over the club chairs and tables, past the islands of bookshelves.

As he rotated on a curious axis, head over heels, Fric saw the photograph of the pretty lady, his make-believe mom, which had slipped out of his pocket and now drifted lazily beside him through the air, in his sphere of influence. Like an astronaut reaching for a floating tube of food in the gravity-free environment of a space shuttle high in orbit, he grasped for the picture but could not quite close his hand on it.

Abruptly he hit the floor on both feet, near the Christmas tree that was hung with angels, hit the floor running, whether he wanted to run or not, as if his legs were spellcast to churn him out of here.

Past the tree, at the open door to the library, he turned to look back.

The guardian had vanished.

The photograph was nowhere to be seen.

Moloch is in the house.

Fric fled the library, sprinting for the conservatory by the shortest route.

CHAPTER 91

AT ONE OF THE BRONZE-AND-BEVELED-GLASS French doors that looked out on the half-acre of patio, the fountains, and the swimming pool, Corky Laputa used the security guard's keys to let himself into the grand drawing room.

With the fine brocade drapes, he toweled himself as dry as he could. When he began moving through the house along limestone-floored hallways, he must not leave a betraying trail that Truman might find before he found Truman.

He switched on the lights.

He had no fear of being noticed. Only three of them were afoot in a house larger than some shopping centers. They were not likely to blunder into one another by accident.

A magnificently decorated Christmas tree graced the room. He was tempted to poke around until he found the string-light switch, to see this spruce beauty in its full twinkling glory. But chaos could at times be a tough taskmaster, and he had to remain focused on the plot that had brought him here by blimp and bluster.

Crossing the enormous room, he squinched his feet back and forth in the antique Persian carpets with each step, thoroughly drying his boots.

Two widely separated sets of double doors led to the north hall. Beside one of these exits, a Crestron touch-control unit was mounted flush in the wall.

He touched the dead gray screen. The panel at once came to life, presenting him with three columns of icons.

Mick Sachatone had given Corky basic instructions in its use. Mick hadn't made him an absolute master of the system, but he knew enough to get by.

He fingered the icon for the interior motion detectors, and a list of ninety-six locations appeared. Per Ned Hokenberry, no motion detectors had been installed in bedrooms and bathrooms, or in any rooms of Channing Manheim's third-floor suite.

At the bottom of the list was the word SCAN, which he pressed. This gave him the option of scanning for movement on the third floor, the second floor, the ground floor, the first subterranean level, and the second subterranean level.

Later he would use this feature to search for the boy. First, he needed to locate Ethan Truman and kill him.

He might have been able to snare the boy and spirit him out of the house under the security chief's nose. He'd feel more comfortable dealing with Aelfric, however, if he knew the ex-cop was dead meat.

Any floor of the mansion was too large to fit entirely on the Crestron screen in a scale easy to read. Consequently, the eastern half of the ground level appeared first.

A single blip of light blinked, indicating Corky's position in the grand drawing room. He wasn't moving, but the motion detectors were in fact motion *and* heat detectors. Even in his insulated storm suit, he produced a sufficient heat signature to register with the sensitive sensors.

He took two sideways steps to his right.

On the screen, the Corky blip moved a tiny bit to the right, in synch with him.

When he stepped back in front of the touch-control panel, his blip moved, as well.

The complex floor plan of the western half of the ground level appeared on the screen, also with only a single lonely blip blinking in all those chambers and hallways: Ethan Truman, no doubt, in the living room of his apartment.

This was where Corky had hoped and expected to find the man.

He exited the motion-detector display, went to the nearest set of double doors, and stepped quietly into the north hall.

Ahead of him lay the entrance rotunda and another spectacular Christmas tree. The residents and staff were rich with the Christmas spirit in Palazzo Rospo.

Corky wondered what exquisite holiday cookies people of this wealth enjoyed. Once he had killed Truman and secured the boy, maybe he would dare to take a few minutes to investigate the stock of baked goods in the kitchen. He might pack a tin of homemade treats to enjoy later at home.

He turned right and followed the north hall past the tea room, the intimate dining room, the grand dining room, toward the kitchen and ultimately toward the west hall where Truman waited to be killed in his apartment.

CHAPTER 92

ON THE DESK IN ETHAN'S STUDY, THE TELE-phone produced no dial tone, and when he tried to use his cell phone, he discovered that he had no service.

Land lines might on rare occasion experience disruption after a two-day downpour. Not cell phones.

In the bedroom, when he tried the telephone on his nightstand, he heard only a dead line. No surprise.

From the nightstand drawer, he extracted a second magazine of ammunition for his pistol.

He had prepared this spare on the evening of his first day in Palazzo Rospo, ten months ago. At the time, he'd seemed to be taking an unnecessary precaution. An extended shootout requiring more than ten rounds, within these well-protected walls, had been a possibility so slim as to be beyond calculation.

Dropping the magazine in a pants pocket, Ethan hurried back into his study.

The apple of his eye.

Fric. Fric must still be on the second floor, in the library, selecting a book to get him through the night.

Okay. The thing to do was go to the library. Hustle the boy into the nearest panic room. Tuck him away safely in that comfy, armored, self-contained vault. Then chase this situation to its source, find out what the hell was happening.

He stepped out of his apartment, turned left in the west hall, and ran to the back stairs that earlier he had taken to the third floor and the white room.

Goofing, having more fun than the law allowed, proceeding at times with exaggerated stealth, in a crouch like a commando slipping through an enemy fortress, at other times strutting like Vin Diesel when he knows the script specifies that all bullets will miss him, Corky followed the north hall past the breakfast room, the butler's pantry, the kitchen.

He wished that it would have been practical to wear his yellow slicker and his droopy yellow hat. He would have enormously enjoyed seeing Truman's amazed expression when confronted by a banana-bright assassin spitting death.

In the west hall, the door to the security chief's apartment stood open.

At the sight of this, Corky at once grew more serious. With caution he approached the apartment. He stood with his back to the hallway wall, beside the open door, listening.

When he crossed the threshold, he went in low and fast, holding the Glock in two hands, sweeping left to right, right to left.

The study was deserted.

Quickly but prudently, he searched the rest of the apartment and found no sign of his quarry.

Returning to the front room, he noticed the contents of the six black boxes on the desk. Evidently, Truman was still trying to solve the riddle. Amusing.

Lines of text on the computer screen drew his attention. Truman appeared to have stepped out in the middle of reading e-mail.

Indulging the curiosity that was such a fundamental part of him and that had served him remarkably well over the years, Corky spotted YORN at the end of the e-mail. William Yorn, the groundskeeper.

He read the message from the top: FRIC IS MAKING HIMSELF A HIDEY-HOLE IN THE CONSERVATORY. . . . Much of Yorn's complaint meant nothing to Corky, but the stuff about the hidey-hole definitely interested him.

With his two targets roving beyond Corky's ken, he needed to get to another Crestron panel, and fast. One was inlaid in the bedroom wall here in the security chief's apartment, but Truman might return at any moment, while Corky was distracted in the other room.

He saw something on the floor, near the sofa. A cell phone. As if it had been not dropped but flung aside.

Cautiously he returned to the west hall. He followed it to the door of the McBees' apartment.

The blueprints had specified a Crestron panel in their living room. Happily, they were in Santa Barbara.

According to Ned Hokenberry, in order to facilitate cleaning and other household services, the live-in staff seldom locked the doors to their private quarters other than when they were in residence.

Good old dead Hokenberry, the freak, proved to be as reliable as the blueprints. Corky entered the McBee apartment and closed the door behind him.

Next to the front door, the Crestron panel brightened at his touch. He didn't bother with a lamp.

A quick motion-detector scan through the ground floor showed no blip except Corky's, here in the McBee living room.

On the second floor, someone turned out of the west hall into the long north wing, proceeding in the direction of the library. Perhaps Truman. Perhaps the young Manheim. Whichever, he appeared to be hurrying.

No movement or detectable body heat on the third floor.

He surveyed the two subterranean levels. Nothing.

The figure on the second floor had reached the library. The blip had to be Ethan Truman. He must have gone up there by the back stairs in the west wing.

Where was the boy? Undetected. Not moving. Not producing any heat within range of the sensors.

The kid could be in his bedroom or a bathroom. No sensors in those areas.

Or he might be hunkered in his hidey-hole in the conservatory.

This hidey-hole business was odd. Judging by Yorn's message, the staff thought it was peculiar, too.

Truman running to the library. The kid missing. The cell phone flung aside on the floor of Truman's apartment.

Corky Laputa believed in meticulous planning and on the faithful execution of the plan. He was also a friend of chaos.

He recognized the hand of chaos in this moment. He suspected that Truman knew the property had been breached.

Ditching the plan for the time being, his heart thrilling to this unexpected development, Corky trusted chaos and sprinted for the conservatory.

Leaving Maxwell Dalton alone with assurances that he would return in a minute, Hazard Yancy hurried downstairs while the window-breaking can of pine-scented disinfectant was still bouncing from the porch roof to the lawn.

Tall sidelights flanked the front door, but neither was wide enough to accommodate a man, especially not one as large as Hazard. Furthermore, the relationship of the sidelights to the door lock made it impossible for him to claim to have reached inside and disengaged the deadbolt after smashing either pane.

Having holstered his handgun, opening the door, Hazard suddenly expected to be confronted by Laputa. Or Hector X. Only the night came face to face with him, cold and wet.

He stepped onto the front porch. As far as he could see, the sound of shattering glass hadn't brought curious neighbors outside.

Someone might be watching at a window. He'd taken bigger risks.

On the porch were several potted plants. He picked a small one.

After waiting for a car to splash past in the street, he threw the ten-pound terra-cotta pot, with plant, through one of the living-room windows. The consequent crash-clink-clatter of exploding and falling glass ought to have attracted attention in the most mind-your-own-damn-business neighborhood.

He drew his gun and used the butt to smash out a few stubborn shards still bristling from the sash. Then he climbed inside through the window, thrusting aside the drapes, knocking over a pedestal and a vase, blundering as though he had never been in the Laputa house before.

He had his story now. In answer to the cry for help that had come through the broken bedroom window, he had rung the bell, pounded on the door. When he received no response, he broke a window, went upstairs, and found Maxwell Dalton.

This concoction had the texture not of smooth sweet truth but of a cow pie; however, it was *his* cow pie, and he was going to serve it with enthusiasm.

After returning to the front porch by the more conventional route of the door, in consideration of Dalton's perilous condition, Hazard used his cell phone to call 911. He gave the dispatcher his badge number and explained the situation. "I need paramedics and some jakes here sooner than soon." As an afterthought he said, "Jakes are uniformed officers."

"I know," she said.

"I'm sorry," he said.

"That's all right," she said.

"I need a CSU—"

"I know," she said.

"I'm sorry," he said.

"Are you new, Detective?"

"I'm forty-one," he said, immediately realizing that his reply qualified for a stupidity commendation.

"I mean new to Robbery/Homicide," she said.

"No, ma'am. I've been washed so many times I shouldn't have any color left."

This was, however, his first case involving a ghost, or whatever the hell Dunny Whistler might be when he could shape your dreams and disappear into a mirror. This was also his first involving a phone call from a dead hit man, and his first involving a perp who starved and tortured a victim while keeping him alive on an IV drip.

Some days you thought you had seen everything. This wasn't one of them.

Having concluded the 911 call, he darted across the street in the rain, to his department sedan. He stowed the Lockaid lock-release gun under the driver's seat.

By the time he returned to the front porch, he heard approaching sirens.

Coming through the library door, Ethan saw the creased and tattered photograph on the floor. Hannah. The same picture that had once stood on the desk in Dunny's apartment, that had been torn out of the silver frame.

The disappearance of the string of little bells from Ethan's desk suggested that Dunny had been in Palazzo Rospo. The e-mails from Devonshire, Yorn, and Hachette had supported what the missing bells suggested. As far as Ethan was concerned, this photo qualified as hard proof.

Dead, stone-solid-perfect dead, according to Dr. O'Brien at Our Lady of Angels, Dunny remained at large in the world, but with powers that defied reason and that *defined* a supernatural entity.

He had been in Palazzo Rospo.

He was here now.

Ethan wouldn't have believed in a walking dead man if he hadn't been shot point-blank in the gut, hadn't died and been resurrected, if he hadn't been trashed by a PT Cruiser and a truck, hadn't been on his feet again an instant after his second death. He himself wasn't a ghost, but after the events of the past two days, he could believe in a ghost, all right, and in lots of things to which previously he had given no credence.

Maybe Dunny wasn't a ghost, either. He might be something else for which Ethan had no name.

Whatever Dunny proved to be, he was no longer merely a man. His motives, therefore, couldn't be identified either by the process of deduction or by the intuition on which a cop relied.

Nevertheless, Ethan sensed now that his childhood friend, so long estranged, wasn't the source of the threat to Fric, that Dunny's role in these bizarre events was more benign than not. A man who had loved Hannah, who had kept her picture five years after her death, must have within him at least the potential for good and surely could not harbor the purity of evil required to harm a blameless child.

Folding the photo away into a pocket, Ethan called out, "Fric! Fric, where are you?"

When he received no answer, he hurried through the library, along the canyons of books, from Aesop and Conrad Aiken to Alexandre Dumas, from Gustave Flaubert to Victor Hugo, from Somerset Maugham to Shakespeare, all the way to Emile Zola, afraid of finding the boy dead and of not finding him at all.

No Fric.

The reading nook farthest from the library entrance included not only armchairs but also a worktable with a telephone and a computer.

Although the outgoing lines were no longer working, the in-house intercom was a function of the system separate from phone service. Only a power failure could disable it.

Ethan pressed the button labeled INTERCOM, then pressed HOUSE, and broke one of Mrs. McBee's cardinal rules by paging the boy from the third floor to the lower garage. His summons issued from the speaker in every phone in the mansion: "Fric? Where are you, Fric? Wherever you are, speak to me."

He waited. Five seconds was an excruciatingly long time. Ten equaled eternity.

"Fric? Talk to me, Fric!"

Beside the telephone, the computer switched on. Ethan hadn't touched it.

The ghost operating the computer accessed the house-control program. Instead of presenting him with the usual three columns of icons, the screen immediately revealed the floor plan of the ground level of the mansion, the eastern half.

Before him, unbidden, was the motion-detector display. A blip, signifying movement and body heat, blinked in the conservatory.

Seventy-four feet in diameter, forty-eight feet from floor to ceiling, the conservatory was a jungle with windows, tall panels of leaded glass, salvaged from a palace in France that had been mostly destroyed in World War One.

Here Mr. Yorn and his men maintained and continually refreshed a collection of exotic palm trees, tulip trees, frangipanis, mimosas, many species of ferns, spaths, smithianthas, orchids, and a shitload of other plants that Fric was not able to identify. Narrow pathways of decomposed granite wound through the curbed planters.

A few steps after you entered the green maze, the illusion of tropical wilderness was complete. You could pretend to be lost in Africa, on the trail of the rare albino gorilla or in search of the lost diamond mines of King Solomon.

Fric called it Giungla Rospo, which was Italian for "Toad Jungle," and felt that it had all the cool stuff of a real tropical forest but none of the bad. No humongous insects, no snakes, no monkeys in the trees, shrieking and throwing their crap at your head.

At the center of its carefully orchestrated wildness, Giungla Rospo offered a gazebo built of bamboo and bubinga wood. There you could have dinner or get puking drunk if you were old enough, or just pretend to be Tarzan before the nuisance of Jane.

Fourteen feet in diameter, raised five feet above the floor of the conservatory, reached by eight wooden steps, the gazebo held a round table and four chairs. A secret panel in the floor, when slid aside, revealed the door to a small refrigerator stocked with Coke, beer, and bottles of natural spring water, though not so natural that it came with dysentery, typhoid fever, cholera, or ravenous parasites that would eat you alive from the inside out.

Another secret panel, when slid aside, provided access to the five-foot-high space under the gazebo. This allowed the refrigerator to be serviced if it broke down, and made it possible for the guys with the monthly pest-control service to get under the gazebo and ensure that no nasty spiders or disease-bearing mice would establish nests in this cozy dark refuge.

Dark it was. During the day, no hint of sunshine penetrated to the subgazebo den, which meant at night the quake lights would not be seen from outside if the conservatory lamps were all extinguished.

Bringing doughnuts, other noiseless foods, foil-wrapped moist towelettes, and Rubbermaid chamber pots, Fric earlier in the day had claimed this as his deep and special secret place. With Moloch in the house, he now sat powwow-style, legs crossed, in this bubinga bunker, which his guardian angel apparently believed would save him from that eater of children.

He had been in his hideaway less than two minutes, listening to his heart mimic runaway horses, when he heard something other than the stampede in his chest. Footsteps. Ascending to the gazebo.

More likely than not, it was Mr. Truman, looking for him. Mr. Truman. Not Moloch. Not a child-eating beast with baby bones in its teeth. Just Mr. Truman.

On a tour, the footsteps circled the platform, first moving toward the concealed panel, then away. But then toward it again.

Fric held his breath.

The footsteps halted. The tongue-and-groove planks creaked overhead as the man above shifted his weight.

Fric silently poured out the staleness in his lungs, silently eased fresh air in, and held this breath, as well.

The creaking stopped and was followed by subtle sounds: a faint brushing, a soft scrape, a click.

Now would be a bad time for an asthma attack.

Fric almost screamed out loud at himself for being so stupid as to think such a stupid thought at a dangerous time like this. Stupid, stupid, stupid.

Only in movies did the asthmatic kid or the diabetic kid, or the epileptic kid, suffer a seizure at the worst of all possible moments. Only in movies, not in real life. This was real life or at least something that passed for it.

Did he feel an itchiness between his shoulders? Spreading to the back of his neck? A real itch would be a sign of an impending asthma attack. An imaginary itch would be a sign that he was a totally lame, lily-livered, hopelessly feeble geek.

Directly above him, the secret panel slid open.

He found himself face to face with Moloch, who was evidently smarter than Fric's guardian angel: a freckle-faced guy with jackal eyes and a big grin. No splinters of baby bones in his teeth.

Brandishing the six-inch blade that he had requisitioned from Mr. Hachette's cutlery drawer, Fric warned, "I've got a knife."

"And I've got this," said Moloch, producing a tiny aerosol can the size of a pepper-spray container. He blasted Fric in the face with a cold stream of stuff that tasted like nutmeg and that smelled like undiluted civet probably smelled.

CHAPTER 93

AT NIGHT, THE CONSERVATORY WAS MAGI-cally illuminated: every golden nimbus, starry twinkle, and silken scarf of faux moonlight as enchanting as the finest Hollywood wizards of stage lighting could design. After sunset, with the flip of a switch, a mere pocket jungle became this tropical Shangri-la.

Entering, pistol in a two-hand grip, Ethan didn't call out to Fric. The blip he'd seen on the motion-sensor display in the library might not have been the boy.

He was unable to imagine how the estate grounds and then the house could have been penetrated without setting off numerous alarms. But the idea of an intruder getting into Palazzo Rospo astonished him far less than other things he'd witnessed lately.

The loose pebbles in the decomposed-granite pathways crunched under him, making a stealthy search impossible. He stepped carefully to minimize noise. The tiny, shifting bits of stone provided unstable footing.

He didn't like the shadows, either. Shadows, shadows everywhere in layered complexity, calculated for dramatic effect, unnatural and therefore double deceiving.

Nearing the center of the jungle, Ethan heard a strange sound, *thhhup*, and then again, *thhhup*, and heard greenery click-rustle-snap, but he didn't realize that he was being shot at until the bole of a palm tree took a bullet inches in front of his face, spraying him with flecks of its green tissue.

He dropped fast and flat. He rolled off the path and crawled through ferns and pittosporum, through mimulus drenched with red-purple flowers, into sheltering gloom where he was grateful for all shadows, natural and not.

The jakes arrived before the ambulance, and after Hazard briefed them and told them where to send the paramedics, he went upstairs to look after Maxwell Dalton.

The withered man, more hideously emaciated on third sight than he had appeared to be on first and second, rolled his sunken eyes and grimaced, greatly agitated, struggling to cough up barbed words from his no doubt cracked and bleeding throat.

"Easy, easy now," Hazard said. "Calm down. Everything's going to be all right now. You're safe now, Professor."

The hooked edges of the words pained Dalton as he spat them out, but he insisted on saying, "He's . . . coming . . . back."

"Good," Hazard said, grateful to hear the ambulance siren rising in the night beyond the broken window. "We know just what to do with the sick son of a bitch when he shows up."

Greatly distressed, Dalton managed to roll his head side to side and produce an anguished mewling.

Thinking Dalton might be worried about his wife and daughter, Hazard revealed that he had just sent a pair of uniformed officers to their house not only to inform Rachel that her husband had been found alive but also to give her and Emily protection until Laputa could be located and arrested.

In a hiss-and-hack voice, Dalton said, "Coming back with," and winced in pain as his throat seized up.

"Don't stress yourself," Hazard advised. "You're pretty fragile right now."

At the end of the block, the shrieking ambulance turned the corner. The rainy night licked away and swallowed the last shrill note of the siren as the brakes barked on the blacktop in front of the house.

"Bringing back . . . a boy," Dalton said.

"A boy?" Hazard asked. "You mean Laputa?"

Dalton managed a nod.

"He told you?"

Another nod.

"Said he was bringing a boy back here tonight?"

"Yes."

As he heard the paramedics thundering up the steps, Hazard leaned closer to the withered man and said, "What boy?"

Crouching among mimulus and Mauna Loa spaths and ferns, Ethan heard a second burst of fire, three or four shots, from a weapon fitted with a sound suppressor, and after half a minute of silence, a third burst.

None of these rounds seemed to come near him. The gunman must have lost track of him. Or maybe the guy had never known where Ethan was, had fired blindly through the jungle, and had come close with the first spray of bullets solely by chance.

Gunman—singular. Guy—one.

Common sense argued that an assault against this estate required teamwork, that one man couldn't jump the wall, deceive the electronic security measures, disable the guards, and breach the house. That was Bruce Willis on the big screen. That was Tom Cruise in makeup. That was Channing Manheim playing a role from the dark side. That wasn't anyone real.

If a coordinated team of kidnappers had gotten inside Palazzo Rospo, however, there would be more than one gunman squeezing off short bursts of suppressing fire. They would have chopped at Ethan with one, two, three fully automatic carbines. Uzis or worse. By now he would be down, dead, and dancing in paradise.

When silence persisted after the third brief volley, he rose from cover and eased warily through the ferns, between the palms, to the edge of the pathway.

In any jungle movie, stillness like this always signaled the wilderness-savvy characters that villainy in one form or another had stepped into the natural world, silencing cricket and crocodile alike.

Green-juice smell of crushed vegetation rising from underfoot.

Muffled voice of a heating-system fan purring in the walls.

A gnat, a midge, hovering in the air before him, hovering.

Taste of blood in his mouth, the discovery that he'd pinched tongue with teeth when he dropped to the ground, the throb just now arising in the bite.

A flutter of foliage spun him around, and he brought the pistol toward the sound.

Not foliage. Wings. Through the jungle, high above the pathway, flew a flock of brightly colored parrots, blue and red and yellow and the iridescent green of certain strange sunsets.

No birds made their home in the conservatory. Neither a flock of parrots nor a single sparrow.

Plummeting in front of Ethan but then swooping high again, the colorful birds passed without one screech or squawk, and became white doves on the rise.

This was the phantom in the steam-clouded mirror. This was the impossible set of bells in his hand outside the flower shop. This was the heavy fragrance of Broadway roses in his study when no roses had been there, the precious voice of his lost wife speaking of ladybugs in the white room. This was the hand of some supernatural force held out to him and eager to lead.

After spiraling high in a frenzied flapping, down again came the swarming doves, feathering the air, toward him, past him, with a *thrum* that both exhilarated and frightened him, that plucked notes of wonder from his heart but also struck hard the jungle-drum terror of the primitive within.

They flew. He ran. They led. He followed.

"Wait," Hazard told the paramedics as they came quickly to the bed in spite of the vile stink, as they stood wide-eyed and gaping in spite of all the horrors that they had seen day after day in the conduct of their vital work.

"Boy," Dalton croaked.

"What boy?" Hazard asked, having taken the withered man's hand once more, holding it in both of his.

"Ten," said Dalton.

"Ten boys?"

"Ten . . . years."

"A ten-year-old boy," Hazard said, failing to understand why Dalton thought Laputa meant to return here with a boy, not sure that he was correctly interpreting what the wracked man meant to tell him.

Dalton strained to speak in spite of throat pain that threatened to convulse him: "Said . . . famous."

"Famous?"

"Said . . . famous *boy*."

And Hazard *knew*.

In the elevator, Moloch dropped Fric, and Fric tumbled in a loose heap on the floor, not sure what had happened to him. No mere pepper in that pepper spray. He could see but could not turn his eyes with the usual quickness, could blink but only slowly. He was able to move his arms and legs, but as though straining against the pressure of deep water, like a weary swimmer being pulled down by a relentless undertow. He couldn't strike a blow in self-defense, couldn't even fully close his hand into a fist.

As they descended toward the garage, Moloch grinned at Fric and brandished the little aerosol can at him. "Short-acting semiparalytic inhalant developed by a colleague with the help of a generous grant from the Iranian secret police. I wanted you docile but *alert*."

Fric heard himself breathing. Not an asthmatic wheeze.

"That gazebo didn't appear on the architectural plans," said Moloch. "But the moment I saw it, I *knew*. I'm still in touch with the child in me, the wild spirit that we are when we're born, and I *knew*."

Fric didn't hear the sound of healthy breathing, either. Clear but shallow, a faint whistle in his throat.

With scary face-twitching spasms of glee that would have caused Fric's bladder to empty in a rush if he had not such a short time ago relieved himself on the potted palm, Moloch said, "I wanted you alert to experience all the terror of being snatched out of your posh digs, knowing that your big-shot daddy can't swoop down in cape and tights or on a flying motorcycle like you once thought he could. Not all the muscled movie stars in the world, certainly not all the supermodels, not even all the beefed-up bodyguards in Bel Air can save your pampered ass."

Fric knew then that he was going to die. No chance to sneak off to Goose Crotch, Montana. No hope of someday leading a real life. But maybe at last some peace.

As the shepherd to the sheep, as the hound to the posse, as the scout to the cavalry, the doves showed Ethan the way, bird by bird, out of the conservatory, into the east hall, past the indoor pool, to the north hall and then westward toward the rotunda.

Such a sight: thirty or forty luminous-white birds flowing along the corridor, a feathered river in this canyon of sumptuous decor, as might a party of freed spirits soar toward Valhalla.

Into the entry rotunda they flew, and circled there as if caught in the whirlpool currents of a forming cyclone, until Ethan caught up with them, whereupon the many birds swarmed closer to one another, closer, until they knitted together in one turbulent entity. They flowed down from the three-story heights to the floor, changing color as they came, changing form again, becoming that friend of childhood who had lost his way.

Standing but ten feet from Ethan, the apparition that was Dunny Whistler said, "If you die this time, I can't bring you back. I am at the limits of my authority. He's taking Fric down to the garage. He's almost out of here."

Before Ethan could speak, dead Dunny was not Dunny anymore, but doves again, exploding in a glory of radiant wings, knifing straight at the enormous Christmas tree. They fled not into the needled boughs but into the silvery and scarlet shine of the ornaments, no longer birds but only the shadows of birds, darkening across the glimmering curves, then gone.

By a fistful of his shirt, semiparalytic Fric was dragged across the garage floor, facing away from his captor, watching the elevator alcove recede into the distance.

Moloch had snared car keys from the pegboard, where every set hung under a label citing the make, model, and year. The kidnapper seemed to know his way around as well as if he had lived in Palazzo Rospo.

Also receding from Fric was his medicinal inhaler, his precious asthma drug. The device had come unclipped from his belt. He tried to grab the inhaler when first it rattled loose, but his limbs were jelly.

Moloch might be insane or just evil. But Fric couldn't imagine what the Iranian secret police had against him.

In his ten years, he had known fear. In fact it had been nearly a constant. The fear familiar to him for so long, however, had been of the quiet variety, a nagging rather than threatening force, more like the persistent pecking of small birds than like the rending ferocity of a pterodactyl. Worry that his father's absences would grow ever longer, until they stretched into years, like those of his mother. A gnawing concern that he would forever be the geek that he was now, that he would never figure out what to do with life or with himself, that he would grow old and still be more than anything else the son of Channing Manheim, the Face. During every second of the journey between the conservatory and the garage, however, a great dark terror thrashed its leathery wings in the cage of his heart, swooped through the hollows of body and soul, shivered flesh and blood, and bone.

For his getaway, Moloch could have chosen from the collection any of the older classic cars worth hundreds of thousands of dollars. Instead he selected a more recent model, a favorite of Fric's: the cherry-red 1951 Buick Super 8, with chromed fins and fender wings.

He heaved Fric into the front passenger's seat, slammed the door, hurried around the Buick, and got in behind the wheel. The engine started at once because every vehicle in the collection was maintained in perfect condition.

Guardian angels apparently could not be relied on in a pinch. Mysterious Caller had never seemed much like an angel, anyway: too spooky looking, his style too ominous, and such sorrow in his eyes.

As Moloch backed out of the parking stall, Fric wondered what had happened to Mr. Truman. He must be dead. When he focused on the thought of Mr. Truman dead, Fric discovered that the semiparalytic inhalant didn't prevent him from crying.

Entering the upper garage by way of the stairs, Ethan heard the growl of an engine, smelled exhaust fumes.

The Buick was poised for flight at the foot of the exit ramp, where the garage door had almost finished rolling up and out of its way.

A man behind the wheel. One man. No accomplices in the back-seat. No gunmen elsewhere in the garage.

The passenger's side of the car was nearest to Ethan as he ran toward it. Against the side window at the front, Fric's tousled head was tipped against the glass. He couldn't see the boy's face, but the head seemed to loll, as if Fric were unconscious.

Ethan almost reached the Buick before the rising door provided clearance. Then the car jumped toward the door and the ramp beyond at such acceleration that a man on foot couldn't catch it.

Stepping from a run into an isosceles shooting stance, squarely facing the target, right leg quartering back for balance, left knee flexed, both hands on the weapon, Ethan risked three quick shots, aiming low in fear of hitting Fric with a ricochet, targeting the rear tire on the passenger's side.

The fender skirt shielded almost half the wheel, giving him a narrow window in which to place the shot. One round pocked metal, one went wide, but one popped the tire.

The car sagged back and to one side. Kept going. Still too fast to be chased down. The *slap-slap-slap* of loose rubber marked its ascent along the lower half of the ramp.

The quartzite paving provided good traction, dry or wet, but the Buick's rear tires spun briefly, churning up a spray of dirty water and blue smoke, maybe because of the cant to the right.

As Ethan closed the gap once more, the Buick found its footing, lunged forward, upward. Spin-shredded rubber flapped louder than before, and the exposed wheel rim bit at the quartzite with a sound like a stone saw cutting cobbles.

When Ethan reached the top of the ramp, he saw the car following the driveway along the side of the mansion. Heading toward the front. Forty feet away. Making speed in spite of being crippled. Nothing to stop it from grinding all the way to the distant gate, which opened automatically from the inside when sensors buried in the pavement of the exit lane detected traffic.

Ethan gave chase. He couldn't catch the car. No hope.

He pursued anyway because he could do nothing else. Too late to go back, get keys, another car. By the time he was driving out of the garage, the Buick would have cleared the main gate and vanished. He ran, ran, splashing through cold puddles, ran, pumping his arms and trying to compensate for the weight, the bulk, of the pistol in his right hand, because running well was a matter of balance, ran, ran, because if Fric were killed, then Ethan Truman would be a dead man, too, dead inside, and would spend the rest of his time in this world looking for a grave, a walking corpse as sure as Dunny Whistler ever had been.

CHAPTER 94

CORKY LAPUTA, PLEASED TO BE PROVING THAT Robin Goodfellow was as daring and as formidable as any *real* agent of the NSA, had always intended to leave the estate in one of the actor's expensive classic cars. The complication of a blown tire would not force a change of plan; it qualified as a mere annoyance.

The ride was rough, the steering wheel pulled stubbornly in his hands, but as a connoisseur of chaos and a master of disorder, he met this challenge with the delight familiar to any child who had fought to control a vehicle in the bumper-car pavilion at a carnival. Every twitch and wobble gave him a thrill.

He needed only to nurse the Buick out of the gate and three blocks to the street on which he had parked the Acura. From there, the drive home would be quick. Within half an hour, the pampered boy would be introduced to Stinky Cheese Man, would understand the horror that he was about to inherit, and would begin his long ordeal as well as his own career as a media star.

If anything went wrong en route, if for the first time chaos failed to serve Corky, he would kill the boy rather than surrender him to anyone. He wouldn't even use young Manheim as a trade for his own survival. Cowardice had no place in the valiant lives of those who would usher in the collapse of society and raise a new world from the rubble.

"Anyone stops me," he promised the kid, "I'll blow your brains out—*pop, pop, pop*—and make you the biggest object of worldwide mourning since Princess Di."

He made the corner of the house. At some distance to the left lay the reflection pond at the center of the turnaround in front of the mansion. He was still traveling on the tributary driveway, which would join the main drive in fifty or sixty yards.

Just beyond the reach of the headlights, something so strange occurred that Corky cried out in surprise, and when the twin beams revealed the true nature of the obstacle ahead, terror seized him. He jammed his foot down on the brakes so hard that he put the car into a spin.

Moloch said that he would blow Fric's brains out, but Fric had more immediate worries because the itching between his shoulders was real this time, not imaginary, and it quickly spread to the back of his neck.

He had expected to suffer an attack the moment that he'd been spritzed in the face, but perhaps the drug that Moloch administered had, as a side effect, delayed the asthmatic response. Now here it came, and with a vengeance.

Fric began to wheeze. His chest tightened, and he couldn't get enough breath.

He didn't have his inhaler.

As bad, maybe worse: He remained semiparalyzed, unable to claw himself up from a slack-limbed slump into a full sitting position. He had to be more upright to use the muscles of his chest walls and of his neck to squeeze out every trapped breath.

Worse still: The feeble effort he made to sit upright instead caused him to slide farther down. In fact he seemed about to slip off the seat.

His legs buckled and twisted upon themselves, folding into the knee space in front of the dashboard, and his butt hung off the edge of the seat. From the waist to his neck, he was lying flat on the seat, his head tipped up against the back of it.

He felt his airways narrowing.

He wheezed, sucked, snorked for breath, drew in little, squeezed out less. That familiar hard-boiled egg settled in his windpipe, that stone, that blocking wad.

He could not breathe on his back.

He could not breathe. He could not breathe.

Moloch stomped the brakes. The car fishtailed, then spun.

On the driveway, running toward Corky as he sped toward them, were Roman Castevet, whom he'd killed and stored under a sheet in the cold locker at the morgue, and Ned Hokenberry come back to retrieve the locket that contained his third eye, and anorexic Brittina Dowd as naked and bony as he had left her on the floor of her bedroom but not burnt, and Mick Sachatone in Bart Simpson pajamas.

He should have known them for mirages, should have boldly run them down, but never had he seen the like of this, nor dreamed that such a thing was possible. They were not transparent but appeared to be as solid as a fireplace poker or a bronze-and-marble lamp.

Tramping the brake pedal, he jammed too hard, and perhaps pulled the wheel without intention. The Buick whipped around so sharply that the pistol on his lap was flung to the floor at his feet and his head rapped the side window hard enough to crack it.

At the end of the 360-degree pivot, his four victims had not vanished during the rotation, but loomed *right there*, and all flung themselves at the car, shocking from Corky a scream that sounded too girlish for Robin Goodfellow. One, two, three, four, the angry dead burst against the windshield, against the cracked side window, eager to be at him, but *burst*, not real after all, merely figures of rain and shadow, plumes of cast-up water that splashed into shapeless sprays, flowed away, were gone.

A full turn didn't drain the Buick's momentum, and they spun another ninety degrees, colliding with one of the trees that lined the driveway, thereby brought to an abrupt stop as the passenger's door sprung open and the windshield dissolved.

Laughing in the face of chaos, Corky reached down past the steering wheel, feeling for the Glock on the floor between his feet. He touched the handgrip of the gun, grasped it, brought the weapon up to shoot the boy.

The driver's door opened with a shrill protest of buckled metal, and Ethan Truman reached in for Corky, so instead of shooting the boy, he shot the man.

Arriving at the Buick in the moment that it crashed to a stop, Ethan slammed his pistol down on the roof and left it there because he didn't want to shoot into the car, not with Fric in the line of fire. Heedless of the risk, he yanked open the tweaked door and reached inside. The driver thrust a handgun at him—*thhhup*—and he not only saw the muzzle flash but also *smelled* it.

He felt no consequence in the instant of the shot, too focused on the struggle for the gun to be able to assess whether he'd been hit or not. He swore he felt the second shot part his hair, and then he had the pistol.

At once flinging the weapon away into the dark, he would have dragged the driver out of the Buick, but the bastard came without coaxing, barreling into him. They both went down harder than gravity required, Ethan on the bottom, rapping the back of his head against the quartzite cobblestones.

On impact, when the door flew open, Fric found himself sliding off the seat, out of the Buick, onto the puddled pavement. Flat on his back, the worst of all positions when he couldn't breathe.

Rain falling in his eyes blurred his vision, but he worried less about the blurring than about a crimson tint that seeped across the night, making rubies of the raindrops.

His thoughts clouded to match his vision—too little oxygen to the brain—but he was clearheaded enough to realize that the effect of the crap he had inhaled might be wearing off. He tried to move, and could, but not with any grace or control, rather like a hooked fish flopping on a shore.

On his side, he had more ability to clench and relax his neck, chest, and abdominal muscles, which he must do in order to force out the stale air condensed like syrup in his lungs. More ability, but not enough. If paper were a sound, it would not be as thin as his wheeze had become, nor a human hair as thin, nor a film of dust.

He needed to sit up. He couldn't.

He needed his inhaler. Gone.

Although the world was crimson to him, he knew that he must look blue to the world, for this was one of the really bad attacks, worse than any he'd known before, an occasion for the emergency room, for the doctors and nurses with their talk of Manheim movies.

No breath. No breath. Thirty-five thousand dollars to refurnish his rooms, but no breath.

Funny thoughts crowded his head. Not funny ha-ha. Funny scary. Red thoughts. So dark red at the edges that the red was really black.

Currently not in a mood to teach the deconstructionist theory of literature, but in a mood to deconstruct anything in his way, with a wolfish fury howling in his skull, Corky *needed* to gouge eyes, to chew at the face below him, to tear with teeth, to claw and rip.

Cracking his jaws for the first bite, he realized that Truman had

been stunned when he rapped his head on the pavement, that his resistance was not as strong as expected. In his savage frenzy, Corky
dimly realized, too, that if he succumbed to the animalistic urge to
finish this by tooth and nail, something would snap in him, some last
organizing restraint, and he would be found hours hence, still bent to
the savaged body of his victim, his snout and jowls in the fleshy ruins, searching for grisly morsels as a pig for truffles.

As Robin Goodfellow, who had not actually received training to be
a lethal weapon but who had read his share of spy novels, he knew
that a sharp blow with the heel of his hand to an enemy's nose would
shatter nasal bones and drive the wicked splinters into the brain,
bringing instant death, and so he did this, and cried with delight as
Truman's blood answered the blow with a bright spray.

He rolled off the useless cop, rose, turned toward the Buick, and
went looking for the boy. Corky leaned down at the driver's door to
peer inside, but Fric had apparently gotten out through the sprung
door on the passenger's side.

The semiparalytic inhalant would not yet have worn off entirely.
The brat couldn't have crawled far.

Straightening up from the driver's door, Corky saw a handgun on
the roof of the Buick, in front of his eyes.

Rain gleaming like diamond inlays on the checking of the grip.

Truman's weapon.

Find the boy. Shoot him but only in the leg. To keep him from going anywhere. Then hustle back to the garage for another set of keys,
another getaway car.

Corky could still salvage the plan, for he was the son of chaos as
surely as Fric was the son of the biggest movie star in the world, and
chaos would not fail its child as the actor had failed his.

He rounded the car and saw the boy on his side, kicking at the sodden ground, hitching forward like a crippled crab.

Corky went after him.

Although Fric proceeded by the strangest form of locomotion that

Corky had ever seen, making a thin whistling sound that suggested the stripped-gear-popped-spring protest of a broken windup toy, the kid had gotten off the driveway, onto the grass. He seemed to be trying to reach a stone garden bench that appeared to be an antique.

Approaching, Corky raised the pistol.

William Yorn, diligent groundskeeper, monitored every tree and shrub for disease and treated his green wards at the first sign of mold or blight, or pestilence. Occasionally, however, a plant could not be saved, and a replacement was then ordered from a tree broker.

Large trees were replaced with the same specimen in the largest available box size. The new beauty was either delivered by truck and then swung into place by a rented crane or flown to the site by a big logging-industry helicopter with dual sets of rotors and positioned from the air.

Smaller specimens were planted with strategies and tactics less military in nature, and in the case of the smallest of the new trees, a lot of hand labor proved sufficient to get the job done. In some instances, a tree would be small enough to require staking to guide its growth for a year or two and to give it resistance to the wind.

While some in positions equivalent to his still used tall wooden stakes to prop these slender new trees, Mr. Yorn preferred one-inch and two-inch steel poles, in eight- and ten-foot lengths, for they would not rot, provided sturdier support, and could be reused.

After wrenching an eight-foot pole from the ground and tearing the stretchy plastic ties securing it to the tree, Ethan staggered after the crazy son of a bitch in the storm suit, swung the steel at his head as hard as he knew how, and clubbed him to the ground.

Toppling, the kidnapper reflexively fired the pistol. The bullet ricocheted off the granite garden bench and shrieked into the rain and darkness.

The thug collapsed, rolled onto his back. He should have been dead or unconscious, but he looked only dazed, confused. He still held the gun.

Ethan dropped on his assailant with both knees, driving the breath out of him, with luck breaking a few of his ribs and crushing his spleen to paste. He clawed at the gloved hand that held the gun, seized possession of the weapon, fumbled it, and with dismay saw it clatter out of easy reach.

Although his skull must be ringing like the bells of Notre Dame, the creep flailed at Ethan and snared a fistful of his hair, twisted it painfully, tried to pull his face down toward bared and snapping teeth.

Fearing the teeth, Ethan nevertheless clamped his right hand on the man's throat to pin him, and then punched, left knuckles to right eye, and punched again, but still his hair was twined in those iron fingers and being drawn out by the roots. He felt a thick jewelry chain around the maniac's throat and thought to twist it, twisted and punched, twisted and punched, until his left hand ached and the taut chain, having scored the fingers of his right hand, finally broke like cheap string.

The teeth stopped snapping. The eyes fixed on something beyond Ethan, beyond the night itself. Limp fingers released twisted locks of hair.

Gasping, rising from the dead man, Ethan looked at the chain in his hand. A locket. A glass sphere in which floated a watchful eye.

Moloch seemed to be dead, but he had seemed to be dead before. Fric watched the fight from an art-film angle and through a crimson haze, wondering why the director of photography had chosen to shoot an action scene with a distorting lens *and* a red filter.

All this he wondered and worried about not with full attention but dreamily, as if he were asleep and having two nightmares at the same time, one involving two men in mortal combat and the other about suffocation. He was back in the old suffacatorium, wheezing like a geezer of a coal miner with black-lung disease, like in that movie Ghost Dad had been wise to turn down, and the mother of the original owner of Palazzo Rospo was trying to smother him with a fur coat.

Mr. Truman lifted him and carried him to the garden bench. Mr. Truman understood that during an attack Fric needed to be sitting up to better use his neck, chest, and abdominal muscles to force air out of his lungs. Mr. Truman knew the drill.

Mr. Truman propped him on the bench. Held him upright. Checked Fric's belt for the medicinal inhaler.

Mr. Truman spewed out a string of vulgar and obscene words, all of which Fric had heard before in his years among the entertainment world's elite, but he'd never heard them from Mr. Truman until now.

More red everywhere and more of it darkening to black, and so little air getting through the mink, the sable, the fox, whatever fur it might be.

Breathing through his mouth because his nose had clogged with wacked cartilage and clotting blood, Ethan didn't know if he had enough wind left to carry the boy back to the house at a run, all the way to Mrs. McBee's office where spare inhalers were stored.

A bullet had nicked his left ear, too, and though the wound was superficial, blood followed the folds of the ear, into the resonant depths, half deafening him but also oozing down his eustachian tube and into his throat, causing him to cough in fits.

After a hesitation, realizing that Fric was experiencing worse than an asthma attack, that this was something life-threatening, he scooped the boy off the bench, into his arms, turned toward the house—and confronted Dunny.

"Sit down with him," Dunny said.

"Get out of my way, for God's sake!"

"It'll be all right. Just sit down, Ethan."

"He's bad, I've never seen him this bad." Ethan heard in the hoarseness of his voice an emotion deeper and better than fear and anger: the raw and wrenching love for another human being that he'd not been sure he still had the capacity to feel. "There's no strength in him to fight this time, he's so weak."

"That's the paralytic spray, but the effect is wearing off."

"Spray? What're you talking about?"

With one hand and with a gentle force greater than mere mortal strength, Dunny Whistler pressed Ethan backward with the boy in his arms, and guided him down onto the wet garden bench.

Standing over them, a pale and somewhat haggard man in a fine suit, Dunny appeared to be nothing special, yet he walked through mirrors, transformed himself into parrots that flew themselves into doves, vanished into the ornaments of a Christmas tree.

Ethan realized that his old friend's suit remained dry in the rain, as did Dunny himself. The drizzle appeared to strike him but with no effect. No matter how intently Ethan stared, he could not see what happened to any drop that met Dunny's suit and face, could not puzzle out the secret to the trick.

When Dunny placed one hand on Fric's head, the trapped breath exploded from the suffering boy's lungs. Fric shuddered in Ethan's arms, tipped his head back, and *breathed,* sucked cold air without inhibition, exhaled a pale plume of air with no asthmatic wheeze.

Gazing up at Dunny—coma-thinned, waxy-looking Dunny— Ethan felt no less bewilderment than when, after being killed in traffic, he had found himself alive outside the door of Forever Roses. "What? How?"

"Do you believe in angels, Ethan?"

"Angels?"

"The last night of my life," Dunny said, "as I lay dying in the coma, I received a visitation. This spirit who calls himself Typhon."

Ethan thought of Dr. O'Brien at Our Lady of Angels, earlier this same day. The DVD recording of Dunny's brain waves. The inexplicable beta waves of a conscious, alert, and agitated person spiking across the screen when Dunny had been in a deep coma.

"In the hours before my death," Dunny continued, "Typhon came to me to reveal the fate of my best friend. That's you, Ethan. In spite of the lost years between us and all the ways I went wrong, that's still you. My friend . . . and Hannah's husband. Typhon showed me when and where and how you would be murdered by Rolf Reynerd, in that black-and-white room with all the birds, and I was so afraid for you . . . and grieved for you."

At several points, the EEG had recorded a wildly spiking beta tracery that according to Dr. O'Brien represented the brain waves of a terrified individual. Subsets of beta had indicated conversation.

Dunny said, "I was made an offer . . . was given the chance to . . . to be the guardian you needed these past two days. With the power granted to me for this short mission, I could among other things fold back time."

When a guy stands before you, saying he can turn back time, and you at once believe him, and you also accept with rapidly diminishing amazement that he remains dry in the rain, you have changed forever—and probably for the better, even though you feel as if the earth itself has been pulled out from under you, as if you have fallen into a rabbit hole deeper and stranger than Alice ever dreamed.

"I decided to let you experience your death in Reynerd's apartment, your scheduled destiny, then take you back to the moment before it happened. I figured to scare the shit out of you and give you the extra edge you were going to need to get through the rest of what was coming—and to get this boy through it."

Dunny smiled at Fric, and arched an eyebrow as though to suggest that he knew there was something the boy would want to say.

Still weak of body but once more quick of mind, Fric said to Ethan, "You're probably surprised angels can say 'shit.' I was, too. But then, you know, it's in the dictionary."

Ethan remembered a moment in the library with Fric, earlier this evening, when he had told the troubled boy that everyone liked him. Disbelieving, disconcerted, Fric in his enduring humility had been at a loss for words.

On the library Christmas tree behind Fric, the angel ornaments had turned, nodded, and danced in the absence of a draft. A strange expectation had overcome Ethan, a sense that a door of understanding might be about to open in his heart. It had not opened then, but now it had been flung wide.

Dunny sees his friend holding the boy in his lap, in his arms, and he sees the boy holding as tightly as he is able to Ethan, but he sees far more than their wonder at his supernatural presence and more than their relief to be alive. He sees a surrogate father and the son whom he will unofficially adopt, sees two lives raised from despair by the complete commitment of each to the other, sees the years ahead of them, filled with the joy that is born of selfless love but marked also by the anguishes of life that in the end only love can heal. And Dunny knows that what he has done here is the best and cleanest thing that he has ever done or, ironically, ever will.

"The PT Cruiser, the truck," Ethan wonders.

"You died a second time," Dunny says, "because destiny struggles to reassert the pattern that was meant to be. Your death in Reynerd's apartment came by your own free will, because of choices you made. In setting time back, I thwarted your self-made destiny. You don't need to fully understand. You can't. Just know that now . . . destiny won't reassert that pattern. By your choices and by your acts, you've now made another destiny for yourself."

"The bells from the ambulance," Ethan asks, "all the games with them . . . ?"

Dunny smiles at Fric. "What are the rules? How must we angels work?"

"By indirection," the boy says. "Encourage, inspire, terrify, cajole, advise. You influence events by every means that is sly, slippery, and seductive."

"See, there's a thing you now know that most other people don't," Dunny says. "More important perhaps than knowing that civet is squeezed from the anal glands of cats into perfume bottles."

The boy has a smile to make his model mother's fade from memory, and he has an inner light that shines without the help of spiritual advisers.

"Those people that . . . that rose up out of the driveway and threw themselves at the car," Ethan says with lingering bewilderment.

"Images of Moloch's victims, which I conjured out of water and sent running at his car to frighten him," Dunny explains.

"Damn, I missed that!" Fric says.

"Furthermore, we guardian angels don't pull our white robes around us and just harp-strum ourselves from here to there the way movies would have you believe. How do we travel, Fric?"

The boy starts well but falters: "You travel by mirrors, by mist, by smoke, by doorways . . ."

"Doorways in water, by stairways made of shadows, on roads of moonlight," Dunny prompts.

Fric picks up the thread of memory: "By wish and hope and simple expectation."

"Would you like one last exhibition of an angel flying in this way that angels *really* fly?"

"Cool," the boy says.

"Wait," Ethan says.

"There is no waiting," Dunny says, for now he receives the call and must answer. "I'm done here forever."

"My friend," Ethan says.

Grateful for those two words, grateful beyond expression, Dunny transforms his body by the power granted in his contract, becoming hundreds of luminous golden butterflies that rise gracefully into the rain and one by one, with flutter of wings, fold themselves into the night, away from the sight of mortal eyes.

CHAPTER 95

WHEN DUNNY MATERIALIZES ON THE THIRD floor of the great house, in answer to the call, Typhon steps through the double doors from Channing Manheim's private suite, into the north hall, shaking his head in amazement. "Dear boy, have you taken a tour of these rooms?"

"No, sir."

"Even I myself have not enjoyed quite such luxury. But then again, with all my traveling, I stay mostly in hotels, and even the finest of them offer no suites comparable to this."

Sirens arise in the night outside.

"Mr. Hazard Yancy," Typhon says, "has sent the cavalry a tad too late, but I'm sure they'll be welcome."

Together they walk to the main elevator, which opens as they approach.

With his usual grace, Typhon indicates that Dunny should enter ahead of him.

As the doors close behind them and they begin to descend, Typhon says, "Splendid work. Magnificent, really. I believe you achieved all you hoped and much more."

"Much more," Dunny admits, for between them he is required to speak only the truth.

Merry eyes twinkling, Typhon says, "You must acknowledge that I honored all the terms to which we agreed, and in fact I interpreted them with considerable elasticity."

"I'm deeply grateful, sir, for the opportunity you gave me."

Typhon pats Dunny's shoulder affectionately. "For a few years there, dear boy, we thought we'd lost you."

"Not even close."

"Oh, much closer than you think," Typhon assures him. "You were almost a goner. I'm so glad it worked out this way."

Typhon pats his shoulder one more time, and Dunny's body drops to the floor of the elevator, while still his spirit stands here in suit and tie, the very image of the corpse at its feet, but far less solid in appearance than the lifeless flesh.

After a moment, the body vanishes.

"Where?" Dunny wonders.

With a pleasant chuckle of delight, Typhon says, "There's going to be some shocked and confounded people in the garden room back at Our Lady of Angels. The naked cadaver they lost is suddenly found well-dressed, with folding money in its pockets."

They have reached the ground floor. The garages wait below.

With that note of sweet concern that is so characteristic of him, Typhon asks, "Dear boy, are you afraid?"

"Yes."

Afraid but not terrified. At this moment, in his immortal heart, Dunny has no room for terror.

Minutes ago, looking at Ethan and the boy on the stone bench, aware of the love between them and of the future they would share as father and son in everything but name, Dunny had been pierced by a regret sharper than any he had known before. The night that Hannah died, a sorrow flooded through him, almost swept him away, sorrow not only for her, not only at the loss of her, but sorrow for the mess he had made of his life. Sorrow had changed him but had not changed him enough, for it brought him no further than to the point of regret.

This anguish that now comes upon him on the way from ground floor to garage is not, in fact, merely a keener regret, but is instead remorse so powerful that he feels sharply bitten and torn by guilt, which is the mother of remorse, feels a terrible gnawing in the bones of his spirit. He trembles, shakes, shakes violently with the first true realization of the hideous impact that his misled life has had on others.

Faces rise in memory, the faces of men he has broken, of women he has treated with unspeakable cruelty, of children who have found their way to a life of drugs and crime and ruin along the path that he has led them, and though these are faces painfully familiar, he sees them as if for the first time because he sees in each face now, as never he had seen before, an individual with hopes and dreams and the potential for good. In his life, all these people had been but the means with which he satisfied his desires and needs, not people at all to him, but merely sources of pleasure and tools to be used.

What had seemed to him to be a fundamental transformation of the heart following the death of Hannah had been more sentimental self-pity than meaningful change. He had known sorrow, yes, and a degree of regret, but he had not known this fierce remorse and the wracking humility that comes with it.

"Dear boy, I understand what you're going through," Typhon says as they pass the upper garage. He means the terror that he believes now consumes Dunny, but for Dunny terror is the least of it.

Mere remorse is an inadequate description, as well, for this is such devastating remorse, such a grinding anguish, that he knows no word for it. As the faces plague him, faces from a life squandered, Dunny asks forgiveness of them, one by one, *begs* forgiveness with a profound humility that is also new to him, cries out to them though he is dead and cannot make amends, though many of them died before him and cannot hear how desperately he wishes he could undo the past.

The elevator has passed the lower of the two garages, and still they descend. They are not in the elevator any longer, merely in the *idea* of an elevator, and a strange one. The walls are mottled with mold, filth. The air reeks. The floor looks like . . . compacted bones.

Dunny is aware that changes are occurring in Typhon's face, that the sweet androgynous features and the merry eyes are giving way to something that better reflects the spirit within the grandfatherly form that he has heretofore assumed. Dunny is aware of this only from the corner of his eye, for he dares not look directly. Dares not.

Floor after floor they descend, though the numbers on the panel above the door run only from one to five.

"I am developing quite an appetite," Typhon informs him. "As far as I am able to recall—and I've got a fine memory—I've never been as famished as this. I'm positively ravenous."

Dunny refuses to think about what this might mean, and in fact he is beyond caring. "I have earned whatever comes," he says, as the faces from his life still haunt his memory, faces in legions.

"Soon," Typhon says.

Dunny stands in spirit bowed, looking at the floor from which his body had disappeared, ready to accept whatever suffering comes if it will mean an end to this unbearable anguish, this gnawing remorse.

"As terrible as this will be," Typhon says, "perhaps it would have been as bad for you if you had rejected my offer and chosen to wait a thousand years in purgatory before moving . . . up. You weren't ready to go directly to the light. The sweet deal I gave you has spared you from so much *tedious* waiting."

The elevator slows, stops. A *ping* signifies arrival, as if they are going nowhere more exotic than to work in an office building.

When the doors slide open, someone enters, but Dunny will not look up at this new arrival. There is room in him for terror now, but still he is not dominated by it.

At the sight of the person who has entered the elevator, Typhon curses explosively, with a rage inhuman, voice still recognizable but with none of its former humor or charm. He thrusts himself in front of Dunny and says with bitter condemnation, "We have a bargain. You sold your soul to me, boy, and I gave you more than you asked for."

By the exertion of his greater will, by the awesome power at his command, Typhon makes Dunny look at him.

This face.

Oh, this *face*. This face of ten thousand nightmares distilled. This face that the mind of no mortal ever could imagine. Had Dunny been alive, the sight of this face would have killed him, and here it withered his spirit.

"You asked to save Truman, and you did," Typhon reminds him in a voice that by the word grows more guttural and more saturated with hatred. "Guardian angel, you told him. *Dark* angel was nearer the truth. Truman is all you asked, but I gave you the brat and Yancy, too. You're like those Hollywood pooh-bahs in that hotel bar, like the politician and her handlers that I snared in San Francisco. You all think you're clever enough to slip out of the deals you make with me when the time comes to fulfill the terms, but all pay in the end. *Bargains are not broken here!*"

"Leave," says the new arrival.

Dunny has chosen not to look at this person. If there are worse sights than what Typhon has here become—and surely there will be an infinite progression of far worse sights—he will not look at them by choice but only as he is forced to look, as Typhon forced him.

More insistently this time: *"Leave."*

Typhon steps out of the elevator, and as Dunny starts to follow him, going to the fate that he has earned and accepted, the doors slide shut, barring his exit, and he is alone with the new arrival.

The elevator begins to move once more, and Dunny trembles at the realization that there may be even deeper realms than the abyss into which Typhon has gone.

"I understand what you're going through," the new arrival says, echoing the statement Typhon had made earlier as they had descended out of Palazzo Rospo to places stranger still.

When she'd spoken the single word, *leave,* he had not recognized her voice. Now he does. He knows this must be a trick, a torment, and he will not look up.

She says, "You're right that the word *remorse* can't describe the anguish that's come over you, that tears so painfully at your spirit. Neither can *sorrow* or *regret* or *grief*. But you're wrong to think you don't know the word, Dunny. You learned it once, and you still know it, although until now it's been an emotion beyond your experience."

He loves that voice so much that he can't forever avert his gaze from she who speaks with it. Steeling himself for the discovery that the gentle voice issues from a face as hideous as Typhon's, he raises his eyes and finds that Hannah looks as beautiful as she did in life.

This surprise is followed by an astonishment: He has misjudged the motion of the elevator. They are not going down to a darkness even deeper than the darkness visible. They are ascending.

The walls are no longer encrusted with mold and filth. The air no longer reeks.

With wonder, not yet daring to hope, Dunny says, "How can this be?"

"Words are the world, Dunny. They have meaning, and by virtue of the fact that they have meaning, they have power. When you open your heart to sorrow," Hannah says, "when after sorrow you learn regret, and when after regret you achieve remorse, then beyond remorse lies contrition, which is the word that describes your anguish now. This is a word of awesome power, Dunny. With this word sincerely in your heart, no hour is too late, no darkness eternal, no stupid bargain binding on a man as changed as you."

She smiles. Her smile is radiant.

The Face.

Her face is lovely, but within it, he sees another Face, as within Typhon had been another, though this visage is not poured from a distillery of nightmares. Impossibly, this Face—*the* Face—within her face is yet more beautiful than hers, the source of her radiance, so profoundly beautiful that he would be stunned breathless if he were not a spirit who had given up breathing when his body had been shorn from him.

The Face of infinite and beautiful complexity is also the Face of a mercy that—even now, in his ascendant state—he can't fully comprehend but for which he is inexpressibly grateful.

And yet another amazement: He realizes from Hannah's expression that she recognizes within his countenance the same shining awesome Face that he sees within hers, that in her eyes, he is as radiant as she to him.

"Life is a long road, Dunny, even when it's cut short. A long road and often hard. But that's behind you." She grinned. "Get ready for the next and better ride. Man, you ain't seen nothin' yet."

Ping!

CHAPTER 96

ETHAN AND FRIC STOOD SIDE BY SIDE AT A
window in the second-floor drawing room, which was known as
the green room for reasons obvious to all but the color-blind.

Ming du Lac believed that no great house of this size could be a
place of spiritual harmony without one room furnished and decorated entirely in shades of green. Their feng-shui consultant agreed
with this green decree, perhaps because his own philosophy included
such a notion, but more likely because he knew better than to cross
Ming.

All the shades of green that had been applied herein to walls, upholstery, carpet, and wood finishes were seen by Ming in dreams. You
had to wonder what he'd been eating before bed.

Mrs. McBee called this room "the horrid moss pit," though not
within Ming's hearing.

Beyond the window, the sprawling estate presented better shades
of green, and above it all hung a glorious blue sky rinsed clean of even
the memory of rain.

From where they stood, they could see the front gate, and the mob
of media in the public street beyond. Sunlight flared off cars, news

vans, and larger network-television trucks with satellite-uplink dishes on their roofs.

"Gonna be a circus," Fric said.

"Gonna be a carnival," Ethan agreed.

"Gonna be a freak show."

"Gonna be a zoo."

"Gonna be Halloween on Christmas Eve," Fric said, "if you look at how they'll use us on the TV news."

"Then don't look," Ethan suggested. "To hell with the TV news. Anyway, it'll all blow over soon enough."

"Fat chance," said Fric. "It'll go on for weeks, big story about the little prince of Hollywood and the nut case who almost got me."

"So you see yourself as the little prince of Hollywood?"

Fric grimaced with disgust. "That's what they'll call me. I can hear it now. I won't be able to go out in public until I'm fifty, and even then they'll pinch my cheeks and tell me how worried they were about me."

"I don't know," Ethan said. "I think you're overestimating how interesting you are to the general population."

Fric dared to look hopeful. "You think so?"

"Yeah. I mean, you aren't one of those Hollywood kids who wants to go into the family business."

"I'd rather eat worms."

"You don't take bit parts in your dad's movies. You don't sing or dance. You don't do imitations, do you?"

"No."

"Do you juggle or keep a dozen plates spinning at the top of a dozen bamboo poles all at the same time?"

"Not all at the same time, no," said Fric.

"Magic tricks?"

"No."

"Ventriloquism?"

"Not me."

"See, I'm bored with you already. You know what I think's got them all excited about this story, that's really the focus of it?"

"What?" Fric asked.

"The blimp."

"The blimp," Fric agreed, "is totally cool."

"No offense, but a kid your age, with your lack of experience . . . I'm sorry, but you just can't compete with a blimp in Bel Air."

Out at the north end of the property, the gates began to open.

"Here comes the gang," Fric said as the first black limousine glided in from the street. "You think he'll stop out there and give the reporters face time?"

"I've asked him not to," Ethan said. "We don't have anywhere near enough manpower to police a media mob like that, and they don't like being policed."

"He'll stop," Fric predicted. "Bet you a million bucks to a pile of cow flop. What limousine is he in?"

"Number five out of seven."

The second limo cruised through the gate.

"He'll have a new girlfriend," Fric worried.

"You'll do fine with her."

"Maybe."

"You've got the perfect ice breaker."

"What's that?"

"The blimp."

Fric brightened. "Yeah."

The third limousine appeared.

"Just remember what we agreed. We're not going to tell anyone about . . . the stranger parts of it all."

"I sure won't," Fric said. "I don't want to be booby-hatched."

The fourth limousine entered, but the fifth paused outside the gates. From this distance, without binoculars, Ethan could not see that Channing Manheim had in fact gotten out of the limo to meet the cameras and charm the press, but he was nevertheless morally certain that he owed Fric a pile of cow flop.

"Doesn't seem like Christmas Eve," Fric said quietly.

"It will," Ethan promised.

Christmas morning, in his study, Ethan listened yet again to all fifty-six messages that had been recorded on Line 24.

Before Manheim and Ming du Lac had returned to Palazzo Rospo, Ethan had loaded the enhanced recordings onto a CD. Then he erased them from the computer in the white room and removed them from the phone logs. Only he would ever know that they had been received.

These messages were his, and his alone, one heart speaking to another across eternity.

In some of them, Hannah solved every element of the maniac's riddles. In others, she only repeated Ethan's name, sometimes with yearning, sometimes with gentle affection.

He played Call 31 more times than he could remember. In that one, she reminded him that she loved him, and when he listened to her, five years seemed no time at all, and even cancer had no power, or the grave.

He was opening a box of cookies left by Mrs. McBee when his phone rang.

Fric always set the alarm clock early on Christmas morning, not because he was eager to discover what had been left under the tree for him but because he wanted to open the stupid gifts and be done with it.

He *knew* what the fancy wrappings concealed: everything on the list that he had been required to give to Mrs. McBee on the fifth of December. He had never been denied the things for which he'd asked, and each time that he asked for less, he had been required to amend his list until it was at least as long as the list from the previous year. Downstairs, under the drawing-room tree would be a shitload of fabulous stuff, and no surprises.

On this Christmas morning, however, he woke to a sight that he had never seen before. While he had slept, someone had crept into his room and left a gift on his nightstand, beside the clock.

A small box wrapped in white with a white bow.

The card was bigger than the box. No one had signed it, but the sender had written these words: *This be magic. If there be no blink, you will have great adventures. If there be no tear shed, you will have a long and happy life. If there be no sleeping of it, you will grow up to be the man you want to be.*

This was such an amazing note, so mysterious and so rich in possibilities, that Fric read it several times, puzzling over its meaning.

He hesitated to open the white box, for he did not believe that anything it contained could equal the promise of this note.

When at last he peeled away the glossy paper, lifted the lid, and folded aside the tissue paper, he found that—*oh!*—the contents were the equal of the note.

On a new gold chain hung a glass pendant, a sphere, and in the sphere floated an eye! He had seen nothing like this in his life and knew that he never would again. A souvenir from the lost continent of Atlantis, perhaps, the jewelry of a sorcerer, or the protective amulet worn by knights of the Round Table fighting for justice under the protection of Merlin.

If there be no blink, you will have great adventures.

No blink, no blink ever, for this eye had no lid.

If there be no tear shed, you will have a long and happy life.

No tear, no tear from now until time immemorial, for this eye could not cry.

If there be no sleeping of it, you will grow up to be the man you want to be.

No sleep, no shortest nap, for this eye was always open wide with magical meaning, and needed no rest.

Fric examined the pendant by sunlight, by lamplight, by the glow of a penlight in his otherwise dark closet.

He studied the orb under a powerful magnifying glass and then by indirection through an arrangement of mirrors.

He put it in the shirt pocket of his pajamas and knew that it was not blinded.

He held it in his closed right hand and felt its wise gaze on the pads of his cupped fingers, and knew that if he kept his heart pure and dedicated his mind to the defense of what is good, just as knights were supposed to do, then one day this eye would show him the future if he wished to see it and would guide him in the path of Camelot.

After Fric had thought of a thousand things that he might say and had rejected nine hundred ninety-nine of them, he returned the pendant to the box and, while meeting its patch-eyed-pirate gaze, placed his phone call.

He grinned, hearing in his mind the first nine notes of the *Dragnet* theme song.

When the call was answered, Fric said, "Merry Christmas, Mr. Truman."

"Merry Christmas, Fric."

With only those words, they hung up by mutual unspoken consent, for at this moment in time, no more needed to be said.

NOTE

In Chapter 32, Mr. Typhon counsels Dunny Whistler that he should take inspiration from Saint Duncan, for whom he was named. No Saint Duncan has ever been canonized. We can only speculate on Mr. Typhon's motives for this seemingly minor deception.

—DK